THE LOST MAGE

BEN ALDERSON

To Winston, who makes sure I take breaks from these dark worlds.

Please be aware this novel contains scenes or themes of toxic relationships, murder, loss of family members, death, abuse, manipulation, anger, grief/grieving, depression and blood/gore.

I

THE FALSE SON

I LOATHED MAGIC. IT WAS TO BLAME FOR THE WAY OF THE world. Whereas everyone else praised its memory, I was never more thankful for something disappearing—burned away from our history when the source of the southern mages was destroyed.

I stared at the painting of the Mage Oak; a tree bathed in black flame.

The end of the South's ties to magic. For such a devastating day it earned itself the largest of the paintings in this room.

There were countless reasons as to why the library was my favorite room within the Gathrax estate. The manor was a maze of brick and mortar; ballrooms adorned with elaborate chandeliers, dining halls larger than the humble homes in the town only a stone's throw away from the boundary of the estate. Out of them all, the library warmed my very soul. A place of comfort and escape, it pleased every sense from the moment I walked among the rows of full, towering shelves until I would leave.

My nose twitched as the scent of ancient novels struck

me. Dust and age blended into a pleasant smell; a breath of nostalgia. I had spent as much time within this overwhelming room as I had within my apartment at the rear of the estate. Before the age of six, when Master Gathrax made all the children work, I would shadow Mother from dawn till night. If I wasn't helping Mother dust the counters, I was watching her from my perch on the cushioned windowsill as she told me stories from each of the books she touched.

The air carried stories the many books held within their sun-stained pages. Stories of dragons and dryads, phoenix kings who dwelled on thrones of fire, and the nymphs that once resided within the waterways of this world. They were stories I knew better than the lines on my palm. Many were historic imaginings of Aldian's history, full of accurate accounts. Others exaggerated and false. Made up to reflect the world in the way the author deemed necessary.

Light cut through the red-stained windows that towered along the eastern wall of the room, washing across the uncountable number of tomes. The late afternoon Gathrax glow, usually golden and warm, now only added to the ominous reminder of the color that ruled around me.

Red.

"Maximus, the festival starts in just shy of an hour. Get a move on if you want to make it on time," Dame said, passing over a dust cloth and a vial full of a thick, brown oil.

I couldn't remember a time without Dame. Her long white hair pinned up in a neat bun, the same apron wrapped around her aged frame. Most of the staff feared her, but not me. I could see past her creased eyes and lined mouth to the quiet kindness that lurked behind her stone-cold expression. An expression only gained by her age.

"I'll be finished in no time," I told her, moving for the large oak doors that shut the library away from the rest of the grand estate. "Even sooner if you leave me to it."

Dame clicked her tongue across her teeth. "You will have a pink neck if you are late meeting your parents."

I raised a hand and rubbed the phantom ache at Dame's threat.

She just rolled her shallow eyes at me and moved for the door on slow limbs.

"If you see *them*, tell them not to wait," I said. Especially Mother. She deserved to enjoy as much of the festival as any other. It would be the only day she would finish up early looking after the two demonic heirs to the Gathrax estate—second in line, anyway.

"If I see her, I shall," Dame replied, brushing her liver-spotted hand down her apron. "Get the job done and I will see you at the Green. And, Maximus, try not to lose yourself in those bloody books. I don't know how many excuses I can conjure for you if Julian comes asking again."

I pushed the threat of Julian, Gathrax's first in line of succession, to the back of my mind. It had been a few weeks since he last caught me with a book. Drowning in the words of a fictional retelling of the *War of the Wood*, I had not heard him come in.

It wasn't that we, the servants to this monstrous estate, were not allowed to read. But for Julian—a man-child who thrived off conflict—any little step out of line would only encourage him to let out one of his royal hissy fits.

I shrugged. "Can you blame me for wishing for adventure?"

"How about you restrict yourself to dreaming in the fringes of sleep, dear boy?" Dame slipped between the oaken doors, only turning to finish her jibe before leaving me alone. "For punishment leaves no scars during a dream. I cannot say the same for the hand of the Gathrax heir."

What Dame said was true. But I hadn't the heart to tell her that Julian's slap never left a lingering mark. And I would know.

I raised a hand to my heart, the corner of my mouth turning into a smirk. "Promise."

Even as she closed the doors, it was impossible to ignore the sigh which echoed in the barren hall beyond.

The sky darkened beyond the windows, giving the library a sense of quiet. With each breath the day slipped into dusk, and the red glow dimmed from bright amber to blood ruby.

I slipped around the room, dabbing the brown cloth in the vial of diluted oil and rubbing it across the oak shelves until they glistened. The deeper I got into the library, the more I lost myself in whispers and stories.

There was a sense of identity to this place, and it warmed me better than any burning fire. So many histories of those who came before me. That was something I would never have—history. I lived the life of a ghost. My existence would leave no mark on the map of this world. I was only a nameless servant, moving from room to room, and completing the same tasks day to day. Unlike the many whose stories sat around me, I would never have a life worth writing about.

For ghosts were beings of shadow, not parchment and quill.

The thought used to bother me. But now, with age, it didn't. Never had I heard Mother complain about her duties. Even after busy days minding the twins when she came home with arms black and blue. Nor Father as he worked tirelessly on the estate's endless grounds. Or when, during the winter months, he would come home and sleep before raising a morsel of food to his mouth.

No. Now I pushed on, realizing how selfish that childhood wish had been.

It'd been a week since my last foray within the library, and the layers of dust were impressive. I pulled up the stool that nestled in one corner and climbed onto it. Holding back a sneeze, I cleared as much as I could reach and watched it fall to the dark cedar floor like a sprinkling of fresh snow.

"Pompous prat," I muttered, running the now filthy cloth along the top of a golden frame. The painting was of a round man, cheeks as red as the jacket he wore, which was bursting at the seams. Some forgotten relative of the long Gathrax family tree.

My arms ached by the time I reached for the last portrait.

A familiar shiver coursed up my spine as I took in the depiction mere inches from my face. My legs wobbled slightly as I reached to clean the glass that protected it. I would usually not dwell on the picture. Instead, I'd give in to the strange fear that it provoked in me and hurried along. But today, I did not take my eyes off it.

The End of Red.

Most of the image was painted with dull, earth tone colors, save for the angry splashes of crimson that cut across the man slain amongst a circle of his enemies. Mage Gathrax, the last mage to fall in the War of the Wood, his wand snapped at his side, and blood pooled beneath him. The masked army of the North was no more than a smear of shadows amongst the spindle-like trees that crowned the depiction.

"Pull yourself together," I whispered, shaking off the tension in my shoulders. Turning to step down from the stool, I lost my footing. As I gripped the wall for balance, the vial of oil fell to the floor.

The smash of glass echoed across the room.

Annoyance burned through me as I knelt to the carpet, hands fumbling over the wet puddle and broken glass.

"Look what you have done now." Out of the darkness, the deep voice rumbled. "Clumsy, clumsy."

Julian. His voice was unforgettable. I nicked my finger on a broken piece of glass, my sharp intake of breath a response to the pain and sudden panic.

Even the characters in the books around me would have heard my swallow as I patted down my tunic and turned to face him.

"I'm sorry, I didn't hear you come in." I kept my gaze lowered to my feet.

"And what exactly are you apologizing for this time… *Maximus?*" My name sounded alien on his tongue. He dragged it out, hissing as it came to an end.

I looked up at him, my gaze stabbing into his own —unwavering.

He was leaned up against the shelf, taut arms folded across his chest. His jacket was the shade of a ripened blood orange, the shirt beneath it white and full like the feathers of a proud bird. He was taller than me, only by a few inches, but I knew just how those few inches could make such a difference. Like his father, his hair was the color of autumn leaves, another sign of his powerful heritage. That, and the same sharp nose his great-grandfather, Mage Gathrax, had. The very same whose picture towered behind me.

"Can I help you with anything, Julian?" I asked. "I am in a hurry tonight, and as much as I enjoy our… surprise encounters, I have a job to finish."

If anyone else had listened in, they might have thought I laced my words with some ounce of respect.

"I have been encouraging Father to award me the privilege of teaching manners to those who we allow to reside among us. I think you may be my first student." Julian's grin cut wider across his face, his thin lips almost disappearing into his pale skin.

I was rooted to the spot, my finger throbbing as a bead of blood dripped down my hand.

As if he could smell it, Julian's gaze locked onto my hand.

"You are hurt." He strode forward, hand reaching for my own. "Here, let me take a look." His touch was ice. I closed my eyes as his nails scratched ever so slightly against my warm skin. A wave of lavender and mint cascaded over me.

He smelled of wealth. Of power.

I did not pull away from him as he raised my finger to his lips and pressed it there. A kiss. Like a mother would do to a child.

Horror froze my legs. My breath hitched in my throat. His misplaced concern was wrong.

"Better?" he questioned.

"Th-thank you," I said, voice shaking. Julian's grip tightened on my hand as he felt my attempt to tug away from him.

"Riddle me this. Do you believe I am kind like my father?" Julian leaned in, hot breath offensive.

"I think you can be," I lied, unsure as to what test this was.

"Ah," he breathed, his flame-colored hair falling over his wide eyes. "Maximus, I wanted to find you this night. To apologize for my behavior with you the last time we saw each other. You see, it has been hard not to think of you these days."

"I—" I took a step back, glass crunching beneath my boot. "I really should go."

A shadow crossed over Julian's angular face. His sharp brow furrowed and his smile straightened. Before my eyes, his calm demeanor melted.

"Please, Julian," I said, knowing what came next.

"Please, Julian!" he mocked, voice forced high and eyes rolling into his hairline. "Father gifted me something, and I would like very much to show you what it is. Be very still, Maximus—very still, indeed."

He pulled something from the leather belt at his reedy waist. The blade caught the fading light. "Beautiful, isn't *she*? You see, the handle was crafted straight from the antlers of a fully grown stag. One I took down myself during last year's Hunt."

I watched my distorted reflection in the blade as Julian turned it around before my eyes. The metal seemed to mute my colors, all except the forest green of my wide eyes. My mouth dried with each turn of the blade.

"Give me your arm," Julian purred.

Even if I wanted to, I couldn't will my body to move.

He sounded bored as he spoke again. "Please, do not make me ask again."

Julian flashed his teeth and grunted as he lunged for me. He pulled my dirtied work-shirt up as he exposed the skin of my forearm. I could see the blue and purple veins beneath the surface as if my skin were glass, the constellation of freckles hiding among the hairs on my arm.

Julian snaked the blade with drama, pressing the tip into my wrist until the skin beneath the point turned white.

"Scream if you want." He grinned. "No one will come to find you. And when they do, they will think it was your *own* clumsy nature that caused *my* mark." His eyes flicked to the broken vial that lay by our feet.

"Get off me." Anger sparked deep within, a rush of emotion warming my once frozen body, allowing me to pull back from him. "Do not touch me again."

Julian's taunting laugh echoed back at me. Squinting an eye, he lifted the blade and looked down the edge at me. "I own you. Do you know what that means?"

I moved away from him, and he stalked me until my back pressed against the shelf behind me.

"It means that I get to do what I like when I like, *how* I like."

I felt the shift in the air as he lunged forward. Without thinking, I pulled my arm back. The sound of the slap silenced the room. Julian gasped as he turned away from me, his hand pressed against his cheek.

It took three heavy breaths for the realization to catch up to me.

Through tear-filled eyes, Julian glared at me, spit lining his slack mouth. Before his scream made it past his lips, I shot forward, pushing against his narrow chest with both hands until he went sprawling backward.

The clink of a dagger fell into the shadows of the room.

Then I ran.

2

"I WILL GUT YOU! MAXIMUS, RUN, RUN AS FAST AS YOU CAN. Oh, I do love the *Hunt*."

Julian's taunting cry chorused with the crunching of twigs and leaves beneath my boots.

My breath fogged before me as I ran through the connecting gardens of the estate and into the woods at the far end. Each breath of cold autumn air burned my lungs. *Just keep running*. The muscles in my legs screamed, and my arms felt weak as jelly. But regardless of my discomfort, I kept up my pace.

Deep in the corner of my mind where the panic didn't reach, I was thankful for the years of tireless work the Gathrax family put upon me. Without it, my physique would hinder my chance of escape. That, as well as my long legs that carried me ahead and my small frame which helped me fly over rocks and ditches I leaped over.

"You vile rat," Julian panted after me. "I'm going… to carve my name… into you."

He must have got up quickly after I left the library as

his voice grew closer. The dull thud of his chase only an earshot away.

His threats came out in rushed, breathless attempts. He was unfit. A life of easy treatment had not had the same positive effects on his body.

There, up ahead, the line of tall trees signaled the beginning of the wood. I would lose him in there. Among the impenetrable darkness. The evening had arrived, but even beneath the midday sun, the wood was always cloaked in shadow.

Branches clawed at my arms and exposed face as I passed the guarding line of trees. I risked a glance over my shoulder, the wood swallowing the little light the night offered up. I couldn't see him, but the sound of his heavy thud was close by.

Panic seized my body and mind.

Fuck. Fuck. Fuck. This time was different. I had hit back. *Fuck.* And now I ran with no idea of where I would find myself.

Beatrice. I could go to her. If I turned sharp to my left and followed the line of outer trees it would circle me back round to the outskirts of Gathrax town. *She would help me*, I thought. But then, in my mind's eye, I saw what would happen to her when Julian found me.

No. The word was sharp ice in my mind. *You did this. Keep running.*

The whizzing of a small rock shot past my head. The projectile leaving a kiss of wind across my cheek.

My chest tightened as I inhaled the nightly air. A sharp stabbing materialized in my side. I felt my own body trying to slow me down.

You did this.

As I faced the dark wood, I scolded myself. What did I expect? That I'd just run and run, and Julian would simply forget this by the time tomorrow's sun peered its face over the mountains? No. Julian would *never* drop this. Not till he got what he wished. That was how Julian's family brought him up. Never stopping till they achieved what they wanted, no matter what that would be. Selfish, arrogant and proud. If he wanted something, he took it. That truth fueled my fear. I pushed as much force and power into my legs just to keep ahead, but his singsong voice grew closer which each footfall.

"Maximus." My name sounded grotesque as Julian sang out behind me. "My Maximus. Run little… rabbit. Run."

Even among his breathy, weak shout, his intention was still as clear as day.

My skin crawled as he shouted the nursery rhyme at me. A song I'd not heard for years. Mother used to sing it to me. But her intent was different.

Julian urged me to keep running, his humorous tone made it clear he enjoyed the chase.

"Run… run. Rabbit run."

A cold chill spiked through my body, a forewarning of the next mistake.

My foot smashed into something firm. My ankle cried out in pain as I lost my footing for a moment.

Julian must have heard my shriek as his laugh echoed back.

It was too dark in the deep belly of the wood, away from the light of the Gathrax estate. Not even the many stars could penetrate the thick foliage of oak and cedar.

Pain laced up my leg. A jarring slice of agony with each footfall. But it was nothing compared to what would be if Julian got to me. So I continued running.

The farther we ran into the belly of the wood, the colder it became. My legs sliced through the layering of mist that clung to the bottom of trunks and slithered across the overgrown ground. Looking behind me, I saw nothing but the dark. But *his* heavy, deep breathing seemed to fill the darkness around me.

My invisible assailant. He was close.

My face slammed into the ground before my arms could stop my fall. Agony ripped through my neck. Around I rolled, leaves and dirt getting into my open mouth and eyes as I twisted across the wood's carpet. I stopped only when my back slammed into the base of a tree. Breath was snatched from my body beneath the final impact. The dark world spun.

The heaviness was upon me. Julian. He weighed down on me, pinning my arms to my side and straddling my waist. Fingers dug into my forearms. Nails cut crescent moons into my skin.

"Get off me." I gathered spit in my mouth. With a great force I spat, the glob of spittle splattering onto his cheek.

Julian grinned wildly as my spit dribbled down his face. "Is this the respect you show me, your master?"

In the dark, I barely made out his red-flushed face. Yet the minimal light seemed to illuminate his gaze. His eyes burned with malicious intent. Hot pokers, I felt the stare burrow into me.

"You're not my master," I said, half growling and half weeping with panic. "Your father is, not you!"

"Oh, you are right, Maximus. I am not my father. *I* am much worse."

Julian giggled. The high trill sent a crazy dose of icy fear across my damp skin.

"Please…" I found myself begging. To whom I was not sure. Julian would show no mercy.

I wished for the wood to fight back as it did in the

stories I had left behind in the library. Ancient beings that would swallow the souls of the mundane who found themselves lost in the city of trees.

"There are many things I would like to do to—with you; I just need to decide where to start," Julian whispered, flashing the dagger before me again. I longed to scream, but this far into the wood no one would hear me. Perhaps phantoms watched on, waiting to greet me.

His gaze traced up and down my body, looking for his mark. Then, before my eyes blinked and blocked out the horror, Julian swiped his blade at my chest, teeth flashing with glee.

I waited for the pain. But only warmth responded. I tried to look down, neck aching as I stared in wonder at my chest. At what bloomed there. With a strong push, Julian smacked me back down. My head cracked against something as I was forced to the ground.

The pain became a friend in this wood. It coddled my body. From my chest to my legs, to my ankle and head.

"Give up, Maximus." Julian sounded bored now. This was too easy for him. He did not shout. He did not need to. "I expect more from you. Yet I admit this was not how I saw this evening going. But you see, you have left me no choice."

I thought of my parents. In the Green waiting for me. But, like the settling calm of a storm, I knew that they would not find me. Not now.

One last time I tried to plead with the madman atop me. "Let me go, Julian. You do not want to do this."

"Do what?" he asked, voice lifting at the question.

"I swear I will not say a word," I muttered, lips trembling.

Julian sighed, his chin wet from his uncontrolled dribbling.

"Obedience suits you, Maximus." Then the cold tip of his blade pressed into my neck. I felt my skin bow beneath its force.

"Do not move or it will end with you drowning in your gore."

I obeyed. *For now.*

Julian's bright eyes glanced toward my stomach where my shirt had ridden up during our tussle. His tongue trailed his lower lip, eyes unblinking.

"This is the perfect place," he said, finger tickling around my navel. "No one will see the mark I leave you. A special place, our secret. Just for you and I."

He was going to let me live. The thought jarred through me.

Julian's spare hand reached awkwardly for my tunic. The chill of night brushed across my exposed stomach as he lifted it up.

I moved my fingers across the bed of the wood. Searching for something; anything to use against him. Over twigs and dried leaves, across stones and the familiar edge of pinecones. Anything.

Julian hummed as he removed the dagger from my neck. A light tune that was misplaced as he held me in his trap.

I was his rabbit, he was my fox.

My heart stopped as my middle finger brushed over something. Julian was too busy wiping my blood from his blade to see me drag my own weapon into my hand and ready myself. I couldn't see it, but my touch told me it was nothing more than a twig of sorts. There was no time to look for another. This would have to do.

Not once had I dropped my stare from Julian. First in fear. Now in scheming.

"I do hope you scream," Julian said. "It will sound beautiful so deep in the woods."

Julian trailed the tip of the dagger down my stomach and rested it inches above my belly button.

"Wait…" I spluttered. "That will—"

"Kill you? I know. Unless you are blessed with luck."

I made my move. Putting as much force beneath my back, I jerked myself upward. Julian didn't have enough time to make a sound as I lifted the stick with as much might as I could summon.

A bright and scalding warmth spread down my arm. As if a star exploded within my bones. The sensation lit me from the inside. A bolt of striking light lit up the short space between us.

Julian's face melted into shock. Then he was gone, dragged into the dark beyond beneath a conjured force. Air pushed my chestnut hair from my face and snatched the breath from my lungs. I closed my eyes against the surprising force, face cringing.

Then it disappeared. Gone. The tidal wave of darkness crashed over the scene once again.

Silence.

I sat still for a moment, my heart pounding in my ears.

Peace. Welcome peace. Yet it only blessed me for a moment.

I yelled out in sudden pain, dropping the stick into the dark. My hand spasmed. The feeling was pure, fiery, agony. The pain stole my breath. Hand clenched into a fist, I brought it to my chest, hissing. The skin seemed to sizzle as the smell of burnt flesh infiltrated my nose.

The world seemed to tilt as lightning enveloped my mind.

Then it was gone. Peace once again. All but the throbbing that made the skin of my palm dance.

I pried my hand open and held it close to my eyes. There. I could see the mark which caused me pain.

Impossible.

My thoughts moved slowly. My mind a bog of mud as I tried to make sense of things.

The mark on my hand was as clear as the waning moon in the sky above. Three silvered circles, each within another and two sharp marks cutting an X through them. This mark I had seen many times before. Almost every day since I could remember.

This is not real.

I stood up. The world tilted at the sudden movement. Shaking breaths racked my chest as the smell of my burnt skin had me on the edge of vomiting across my boots.

The stick. Discarded next to my feet.

My knees ached as I bent down to pick it up. My actions no longer my own.

Then I remembered.

"Ju... Julian?"

Thoughts passed through my mind in quick, frantic succession. Should I run before Julian gets up? Do I return to the estate or find my parents at the festival? All these questions battered my mind as I stood in the cold forest. Stick gripped tight in my searing hand.

"Shit, shit, shit." I turned around in circles, panicked.

The urge to just run without stopping was overwhelming. Then my mind caught up with my body, and I stopped dead in my tracks. If I helped Julian and threatened him back, he might not mention this? Maybe there an agreement we could both come to.

Giving in to the anxiety of possibilities, I moved in the direction Julian had landed. I waded through the darker patch of wood, but I couldn't see him. No sign of his ruby-toned jacket. His lanky, sinister frame.

Maybe he had already run to tell his family? My body stopped at the thought. Even if I left the Gathrax Estate, the other three estates of the south would hand me back the moment I passed through their borders. Anything for the right price.

I stumbled, forcing myself forward. Lost in a maze of towering trees and night. It was better knowing he was unconscious or hurt than figuring out he was on his way back to me.

If Julian doesn't kill me, my family sure will.

"Julian?" I called out again into the dark, hoping to hear his wretched voice. But there was no response.

I step farther into the shadow's waiting embrace, the only noise, besides my raspy breathing, is the slow drip of water.

Drip. Drip. Drip.

This was a living hell. The repetitive noise got into my mind and threatened and taunted me.

It got louder and louder as I stepped forward.

Drip. Drip. Drip.

Something splashed onto the crown of my head. I shot up my hand to feel for it among my curly hair, only to find that my fingers came back wet and warm. I looked up, searching for the source when another splash hit the side of my face, close enough to my mouth that the taste leaked inside of it. Copper burst across my tongue. My stomach knotted in disgust.

Then I saw him. In the pale light from the rising moon, I caught a glimpse of his body.

Julian dangled above, a large branch protruding from his stomach.

The single beam of moonlight reflected off the crimson droplets as they fell in quick succession into a puddle of its own making, on the ground beside me.

I stumbled back, losing my footing until I scrambled across the uneven ground. The twig still tight in my hand; I wouldn't let go. Couldn't. The feeling strange to me.

It took a moment for my gaze to focus and my heart to fix its irregular beat. Then I screamed. I yelled until my voice went hoarse and tears trailed down my face.

Julian Gathrax, dead, by my hand.

His head was bent at an awkward angle, his mouth wide open. His arms and legs just dangled in the air, the branch through his stomach the only thing keeping him up in the tree.

I attempted to scream again but instead spewed the little contents of my stomach down myself. I gagged until nothing but forced air came out. Head drenched in sweat, sick covering my clothes, I looked up a final time at Julian's body.

I did this. I had killed him. In a strange, detached moment it was another realization that frightened me the most.

Peering back at my palm, I studied the mark in the new light. As clear as morning bells I knew what it meant.

I, Maximus Wodlin, was mage marked.

3

I LEFT JULIAN'S FRESH CORPSE LODGED IN THE TREE. Hanging like a puppet on a string. Lifeless. Limp. His body a mere shell.

I feared that if I touched him, the forest spirits would feel threatened. For Julian now belonged to them.

With haste, I sprinted back to the estate. Muscles burning in my legs. The need to create as much distance between the body and myself boiled through my very veins. *No one will know.* I would rather die than admit that it was my doing. Die. That's what would happen if they found out. Dead, just like Julian. Punished.

Horror flooded me. True, riling fear that blinded my vision.

His taunting song an echo in my whirling mind.

Run little rabbit, run.

Time was broken. Reality slipped through my fingers. My murderous fingers shook.

The world stayed eerily quiet as I left the embrace of the wood. Owls refused to cry out their evening song. Nobody was left at the estate; they were out enjoying the evening's festivities at the Green in the center of town. Quiet. Deathly silent.

On my legs moved, closer and closer to the towering walls of the estate. I blurred back through the very same gardens I had not long left. This time only the haunting voice of my victim followed me.

It was impossible to focus on one thought for more than a short moment before another, more overwhelming one, took precedence.

My feet slowed as yet another truth barreled through my mind.

I looked down at my fisted hands. There. The stick gripped firmly as if my hand had a mind of its own. The rough bark pinched into my scarred palm.

It had been years since the era of wands and magic. The South had deprived itself of all magic the moment the last mage succumbed to his death.

I blinked. The painting from the library burned in my mind.

Although the four main families still ruled in the shadow of their ancestors, the only known living mage was far beyond the Forest of Galloway, hundreds of miles north.

Not anymore, an inner voice taunted.

Peeling back my stiffened fingers, I studied the mark on my palm. Puckered, angry, red. The same as a fresh burn.

I stood still, breathing labored. The estate's rear loomed ahead of me. Windows alight with forgotten candles—a face of stone watching me, grinning and all-knowing.

My parents. *I need to find them.* The thought was hot coals. Enough to urge me on.

I dodged the pools of light that slipped from the windows, staying in the shadows as I circled toward home. Home. No more than a cramped dwelling in the far eastern corners of the estate. A place out of sight from the Gathrax family—yet close enough for their benefit.

A place all the staff lived.

I pushed my anxiety into the pit of my stomach. No one would be here to see me. Not covered in my own sick and gore.

The moment I closed the door behind me I found myself falling to the ground. Back trailing down the oak door until I slumped in a heap.

I did not know how long I sat like that. Sobs racked my chest, body trembling with intense emotion. But never once did I drop the stick. *Wand.* No. That stayed firmly gripped in my hand.

I kept my eyes open, barely allowing myself to blink. My eyes stung at the attempt. Every time I gave in to the darkness, I saw his face.

In a trance, I changed into a fresh set of clothes. Without more than a thought, I had thrown the bloodied garments into the dwindling hearth in our living quarters. Only leaving once I was satisfied all remnants of evidence was nothing more than ash.

"You're as pale as piss," Beatrice called from the shadowed doorway of the blacksmith's.

I had come to find her. My friend. Predictable as ever, I guessed that she would not be at the festivities. For the few years I had known her she had never partaken in them.

Embers cast a glow across her face—highlighting the genuine concern that furrowed her thick brows.

"Evening," I said, hands clasped behind my back. The

wand was hidden from her view. I forced a smile, cheeks aching in protest.

"Not like you to be late for the festival." She laughed, turning her attention back to the anvil before her. "Has Master Gathrax been overworking you on a night like this? Even he should respect the old Gods and give you some relief."

"One would be so lucky." I almost choked at the mention of my master, the urge to admit what I had done to my old friend was hard to bury. "Yet here you stand with greased hands and smudges across your cheeks. Does *your* master not let you join in the festivities?"

Her uncle. Not by blood, she had told me years ago, but by choice. A man too old to raise the hammer upon his creations so he'd drafted young Beatrice into helping. A woman built for this work. Broad shoulders and a strong waist to hold them.

"You know as well as I that mine urges me to join in. But do you *really* think I am going to be spending my only evening off surrounded by painful sonnets and off-beat dances? I leave the flamboyancy to you, Maximus."

I kept my distance from Beatrice, hoping the shadows around me would hide the true emotions I fought to bury within.

"Aren't you a kind one!" My voice cracked as I spoke. Enough to garner her full attention.

"Seriously, what is up?" she asked, reaching a hand into the sheet of black hair. Straight as a blade and thick as Galloway Forest, it needed muscle to tame. And she had an abundance of it; plenty to spare. The weathered tie that was wrapped around her wrist came loose with a single tug of her teeth, only to then be knotted around her hair to keep it up and off her shoulders.

"Nothing," I lied through a toothy smile. I urged to

give her the wand. To spill my crimes to her in hopes that she could help.

But the subtle voice inside me kept my lips closed.

"You look like you've had a fight with the dryads themselves. Don't think I have ever seen you so unkept before. Whatever will the boys think when they see you?"

Her comment caught me off guard and my expression reflected that. With a thick, calloused finger, she pointed to my curls. My fingers found the root of her concern. A single leaf which had entrapped itself within my hair. *Shit.*

"Yes, something like that," I muttered, trying to look everywhere but her inquisitive glare.

"Well, the costume suits you," Beatrice said, turning to the anvil and picking up the hulking hammer that rested atop it. Her reminder was a wave of relief. My shoulders sagged and I let loose a shuddered breath. It was not uncommon for those who dwelled within the borders of the Gathrax Estate to smudge their skin with leaves and bark this evening. It was the patrons way of respecting the forgotten spirits of the forest. The *dryads*.

"I thought I'd join in for once, looked like a lot of fun last year."

"You never did turn down the opportunity to show off your, well, whatever it is you show off."

I grinned, looking toward the distant clatter of music and noise. The Green was only a short walk away.

"Well, you pull off the I-live-in-the-forest-and-don't-wash look pretty well." Beatrice smudged a hand over her brow, leaving a streak of grease across it. "Some of us want to get a head start before tomorrow. If I can get a few more pieces finished I might have a better chance at surviving the coming winter."

"Smart," I replied meekly, my gaze wandering in the

direction of the estate as if Julian was going to walk out and tell everyone what I had done.

"Rumor is, the Gathrax Estate will not be giving out as much coin as—who *are* you waiting for?" Beatrice followed my gaze to where it was pinned. "Wait, have you left a lover in there? Is *that* why you look so disheveled?"

"No." My throat croaked the response. "And you are not one to be commenting on my outfit. You are covered in soot and grime."

"Why don't I believe you?" A single brow raised above her amber eyes.

"You never believe anyone." I avoided her gaze before she found a reason to read me further. "I should go. I promised Father I would meet him earlier and I am already—"

"Go," she interrupted, "and try and look less, I don't know, worried. Enjoy yourself. Dryad knows you deserve it."

My lips parted. Words almost spouted out to tell her. But silence.

"See you at the Hunt," she called as I turned to leave. I couldn't muster up a reply. Head down, I pushed on. Beatrice's gaze burned into the back of my head until I was far enough out of view.

The Hunt, an annual affair hosted by the heir of the estate. By Julian.

My breathing faltered once again as his cunning face passed through my mind.

Murderer. The word brushed across the gentle evening wind. *Murderer*.

4

WITH EACH STEP TOWARD THE GREEN, THE LOUDER THE music became. It reached every tree and leaf. Shaking the very air, it urged the clouds above to shift with urgency. Through the thin soles of my boots, I felt the vibrations of drums.

The cobbled street was covered in trodden mud and muck. Hundreds of townsfolk would have walked this very path hours before. Each adorned in clothes of green and earthen tones. A gaggle of painted faces with skin covered in foliage, they would dance around the blazing bonfire. From early evening till morning.

All in memory of the dryads.

With each shuddered breath the scent of smoke and charred wood fogged my lungs. The smell brought a sense of nostalgia to coat my panic for just a moment of relief.

Old chairs and tables helped the fire burn. But it was not the only thing to be thrown into the crimson flames this evening.

Each family would also create a wand as an offering. Each carved from fallen sticks collected from the mundane trees speckled at our borders. Anything they could salvage from the forest bed. Then, toward the end of the festival after the final dance, they would take turns throwing their creations into the waiting flames.

This year, so would I.

It was all that occupied my mind as I trudged closer. The wand in my hand engulfed in flames.

A trickle of cold realization dribbled down my neck. It was not the growing heat from the bonfire that caused me to sweat.

It was the internal war that raged within. The desperate urge to rid myself of the weapon of murder and the strange, protective sickness that gripped my insides at the thought.

A fleeting memory surfaced through the haze.

"Why do our masters not throw an offering into the fire?" I had asked, small hand engulfed in Mother's. Her touch as soft as fresh snow.

"In their eyes, they have sacrificed enough."

It was a reply that stayed with me every year as I watched the Gathrax family observing the festivities from their seats on the erected podium.

I never understood. The Gathrax family were wealthy beyond belief; careless and driven by mad privilege. Just like Mage Gathrax who founded the estate. Now his family lived within the mage's shadow, draining taxes to keep their control afloat.

The very funds that were handed to us once a month in the brown pay packet.

Blood money. I took it anyway. I spent it and lived from it. By the time the end of a month came around, I was drooling for the next payment.

Flashes of the red and orange light bathed over my skin, flickering in my peripheral.

Glancing down the quiet street, the flames of the festival were visible through a thick line of tall pencil pines that edged the open green. The sweet scent of popping corn greeted me.

These sensations would normally conjure excitement. Now, I only dreaded being under the watchful gaze of my employers. Under the father and mother of the boy I had just murdered.

But I must. To get to my parents and tell them. To leave with them.

I couldn't leave without them.

Lifting the wand before me, I studied it under the orange glow. Still the same. I did not know what I expected to see every time I glanced at it. Perhaps a sign that it truly was nothing but useless.

I must rid myself of it. The thought was as intense as the sudden tickling on my palm.

This will be my sacrifice tonight.

No one will know. No one will know.

I walked the remainder of the way and slipped through the wall of guarding pine trees. The warmth of the bonfire tingled across my skin.

Swaying bodies moved like a rush of a river. Arms waving and reaching. Cries and screams of delight, chorus with the popping of wood in the bonfire only yards ahead.

The Dance of the Dryads had already began. I was late. Very late. The festival was in full swing.

I tried to pass the many swaying green bodies who moved clockwise around the bonfire. Some wore masks, imitating the dreaded army of the North. Others were covered in painted symbols, emerald leaves, and cherry blossom. Dryads.

I recognized many beneath the paint. Gill the cook from the Gathrax Estate and her daughter Mary. Many of the staff from the estate laughed with joy during their evening of reprieve.

Countless bodies free of work and stress for this night.

Off to the side, waiting to join the dance when the drum signaled, were others dressed in darker colors. Dragons, creatures that haunted the stories of our past. Monsters that helped strip the power from the four mages of the South. Beasts of wind and ice.

These customs were pathetic yet terrifying. Smashed plates lined wooden masks to resemble teeth. Ice blue eyes were painted in a rush. Ripped, muddied sheets draped over outstretched arms like wings.

The watching crowd booed and jeered at the dragon dancers.

Like cats of the night, they prowled, waiting for their cue to join the dance.

I knew as little of the winged creatures as I did the dryads that we worshiped. But I couldn't deny the elegance of them. It had been years since the dragons and mountain wyrms last flew through southern skies, but their memory was as fresh as the blood they had spilled in their wake. Once haunting the skies above, they now only filled children's stories and their parent's nightmares.

Behind the crowd, sitting in a line, were the Gathrax family. Four out of five. One missing. One dead.

I killed him.

You did. A voice haunted in the depths of my mind.

The heat of the fire intensified, and my skin shivered with stress. I felt all eight eyes on me as I fumbled through the crowd. Did they know? Could they sense it?

The Gathrax family were dressed in their estate color. Red.

Master Gathrax was robed in a blood-orange colored suit with gold rope stitching and round coral buttons. His

31

wife, Remi Gathrax, was sat beside him with her hands in her lap. Her dress was large and hideous, surrounding her like raised dough. Blood red, the shoulder sleeves were so large they dwarfed her thin, pointed face. Her expression pinched with misery, even with the large ruby that hung around her neck and the many golden rings imprisoning her fingers. Even from afar, her eyes shifted across the crowd. Looking, searching. Julian's name whispered across her painted lips.

I slipped into the shadows of the podium quickly, catching a glimpse of the Gathrax twins. The two girls were nine years younger than Julian. Now the oldest children in the Gathrax family.

I killed him. I killed him.

No one spared me a glance as I passed through busy crowds, holding offerings of different sizes and designs. I pulled my offering free from my sleeve and held it. No one would suspect a thing. Soon, once the Dance of the Dryads was over, it would no longer be with me. The fire could claim it.

Away from the probing gaze of the Gathrax family, I searched for my parents. They would be close. Being their keeper, Mother never left the sight of the twins. And Father would never leave Mother's side.

I didn't blame him. We had all seen them pinch and hurt her countless times. Both girls as twisted and vile as the other. Each only adding to my desire to protect my family, to one day escape from this place and live free from the control of the four estates. A dream that was now forced upon me.

Find them. Discard the wand. Leave before daylight.

That was the only plan I had for now. The gaps would have to be filled in as we went.

"Maximus," a deep voice growled behind me. "Where

in this *world* and the next have you been?"

The owner of the voice gripped the top of my arm and spun me around. Father. He had found me first.

His expression was thunderous and as red as Master Gathrax's suit. I melted into his hold, a shudder of a sigh bursting out my mouth.

"Your mother has been out of her mind; you know not to worry her when she is with the little *demons*." His voice was muffled as I pressed my ear into his chest. "She has enough on her plate."

Demons, a nickname my father always used when referring to the twins. It was not their appearance, both sweet with heart-shaped faces, ocean blue eyes, and fire-red hair in tight curls. His nickname for them was birthed after their true personalities began to show around their second birthday.

I pulled back from his grasp and glanced into his flushed face. "I... I was caught up."

Could he sense the lie? His face gave no indication. No raised brow or screwed mouth.

I couldn't admit to him what I had done. Not yet. We needed to find Mother first.

"You are never late to the festival," he whispered, pulling me out the way of a dancing couple.

I took a deep inhale, breathing in his apple grove scent. "I need to find Mother. Where is she?"

Scanning the bustling crowds, it was near impossible to make anything out. Bodies moved around us. A sea of flesh and distraction. I could not spy her natural chestnut braids and large, wide eyes. My eyes. Green as grass and leaves.

Father tugged at my arm, moving us toward the podium where *they* sat.

"The twins demanded a toffee apple," he replied, voice dull. "Let's hope they hurt their teeth on them."

The last part he muttered beneath the noise of the crowds.

Father was a towering man. His height was unmatched by anyone else that worked and dwelled on the estate. His height was the only comparable thing to me. His gaze was a stormy sky. Skin sun-kissed no matter the season. But that was about all I got from my father. I had brown hair, a gift from my mother, as well as the cluster of freckles that bridged my nose. Dad was pure honey. From his light hair to his golden-hued gaze.

Someone scowled as I bumped into their shoulder.

Waving an apology, I hardly listened to Father until the mention of a single name.

"…with Julian missing she has been forced to entertain the twins more than usual."

"Is… missing?" My throat dried. I looked everywhere but at him.

"I don't know, nor do I care to find out. That spoilt *shit* will be floundering off doing his own thing."

I forced a laugh only to hide the sickness that clamped across my stomach. "Maybe I should go and get Mother, I need to talk to—"

"Oh no, you don't. The dance is almost up, and I see you have an offering. At least you remembered that much. She will not be free until after so let's *murder* some time and go together."

My breath hitched as I peered at the wand in my hand.

Father made a move for it. My body jerked, snatching my arm away from his.

"Son, what has got into you tonight?" Father truly looked at me. Studied me from boot to curl. "Something has happened, Maximus. Tell me."

And I nearly did tell him. My mouth parted to allow the truth of my crime to pass out of my lips. Unblinking, I would not allow myself to ignore the horror that would burn in his eyes.

The crowd erupted in cheers. Heavy beats of the drum called for the end of the dance. The moment lost.

Father turned sharp, mimicking the crowd's attention. I followed his gaze, mine resting upon the face of our employer.

Master Gathrax had stood from his seat and clapped, slowly. All eyes were on him. The dancing had stopped. Singly silenced.

Over his narrow shoulders laid a river of hair. Thin and dull, the ginger strands gave way to make gaps across his head. His scalp white and visible in places. He ran a finger over his beard, salted with silver and pepper, surveying the crowd. Looking, searching. Much like his wife that still sat poised beside him.

For Julian.

I moved instinctively, standing behind my father. Enough to keep watch but not to be seen.

Master Gathrax was a thin man, his waist cinched and narrow. For a man with his wealth, it would be expected that a belly of comfort would protrude from beneath his shirt. But not for Master Gathrax.

The crowd watched on, tension thick in the air as he raised a hand. A silent signal.

But it was the movement behind him that stole my attention. Mother. Her round, calm face unreadable of emotion as she pandered to the twins. I could not hear her from this distance but I watched her lips move as she spoke to them.

"You are shaking," my dad muttered over his shoulder.

"Mother, she is there," I replied, keeping my face forward. I took a step as the crowd around us surged to life. Like a wave they captured Father and I, dragging us in the opposite direction to where I had seen her. Father laughed as I looked frantically for a way out of the crowd. But it soon became clear as to the direction we were driven toward. A line of people began to form around the bonfire.

Urgency burned through me. I pushed and shoved at the people around me. Fighting to break away from the line, to get to Mother. But in the bustle, I lost sight of her.

Dad tripped on the back of my feet. His hiss blended in with that of the bonfire that raged ahead. "Calm down, son." A firm hand was now planted on my shoulder. "We will get her once this is done."

I wanted to refuse, but my tongue had swelled to what felt like the size of a pomegranate. Words failed me as another wave of icy realization flooded over me.

The fire crackled as offerings were thrown into the wild flames.

It is time.

An overwhelming urge to turn and walk away built within me. The anxiety swelled in my throat and caused rivulets of sweat to run down my temples. It was becoming harder and harder to ignore.

I cannot do this.

My legs and arms were turning to stone from the inside out. Even my own body wanted me to stop.

I wanted to rid myself of the wand and whatever presence lingered within it. But in the same breath I couldn't.

Lost to my thoughts as the crowd moved on. Carvings and offerings were thrown in the fire. The crowd's cheers lifting with each throw. On it went. My feet moved without my control, stopping when I stood before the flames.

I squinted against the heat and cringed from the reaching hands of flames that called out for me. Could it sense what I held? Did it know what it was?

"You're causing a scene, son."

Someone else said something. A muttering of annoyance as I held up the line behind me.

"Throw the damn thing in…"

I raised it before me, looking at its smooth surface and pointed tip.

You are a murderer. I sent my awareness toward it. *You killed Julian.*

No, no. That was all you. A voice picked up across my thoughts.

Time was unmeasurable as I stood there.

In a blink, the weight of the wand was yanked from my fist. I hardly had time to register as Father took it, cocked his arm back, and threw *my* wand. It left his hand and sailed into the bonfire.

My entire body creased with agony. Despair split my face in a breathless cry.

I watched the place in which it had disappeared. Father tugged at me to move. He was saying something. But all I could focus on was the flames.

Then it changed. The color morphed before my eyes. Father's grip faltered. The new, raw instinct within me took over.

I dove forward, outstretched arm reaching straight into the blackened fire.

Thunder clapped in the night above.

My name. A scream across the panicked crowds. Somewhere in the depths of my mind, I registered who it belonged to.

Mother.

A cold sensation crawled up my arm as the fire engulfed it, yet my mind shut off from the pain.

Then, as the wand blindly found my hand, the world exploded in light, engulfing the festival and everyone within it.

5

"WAKE UP, CHILD." A VOICE CALLED BEYOND THE VEIL OF darkness. Soft. It coaxed me from the shackles of my dreamscape. "Maximus."

My name was beautiful. A ballad as the voice called it. Then a touch. Gentle upon my skin.

In a single gasp, I opened my eyes and crashed face-first through the barrier of dark. Like a newborn taking its first breath, I gulped in a lungful of air as I bolted up in the bed.

Mother was sitting before me, lips parted and eyes wet. I blinked, eyes straining against the sudden brightness. It haloed around her frame. She embraced me in a hug, pressing my face into her wild hair as she smothered me with her love. "I have been so worried."

Words failed me as I tried to respond. My mouth was dry, and my arms numb. I stared endlessly at her. The bright light exposed every mark upon her. Every pore, every line of age.

The look she gave me... it raked talons down my spine.

Her familiar chestnut curls were not tangled in her

usual braids, but down across her shoulders like dark, wild waves of water. Her cheeks were flushed red, long lashes clumped together.

I moved, grimacing in discomfort.

Mother raised her hands and hushed. "Be still, you need to relax."

I wanted to reach out and touch her, maybe if I did she would smile like normal when she woke me in the morning.

"Let your mind catch up with itself, my boy."

And it did.

Flashes of memory chilled my very bones.

"The bonfire… what happened?" I croaked, trying to grasp the difference between dream and reality. I half expected Julian to be standing in the room with us from the intensity of my dream.

"Lots, my boy," Mother whispered, looking down for a moment. "You have been asleep for a long while."

She moved, reaching for something beside me. I strained my neck in time to see the cup which she lifted to my lips.

"Drink first. You will need your energy."

I did not drop her gaze as I gulped the fresh, welcoming water. It gushed into me, waking my senses with a spark. I hardly wasted a drop, besides the one that dribbled down my chin.

The tension in my head eased.

"Where's Father?"

"Occupied, as I will soon be. We will not have long together, you have to listen carefully to me, my boy—"

Noise from beyond her stole my attention. I peered over her shoulder, finally making sense of the room around me.

This was not our dwellings. Not the usually exposed stone walls and cluttered floors.

No.

Julian's room imprisoned me. The bed. So comfortable with its down feather pillows and the thick blanket. Unwanted comfort.

I tried to swing my legs from the bed and failed. A clink of metal sounded by my feet.

"What is going on…" I shook entirely. Voice and body. Mother reached for me, a single tear escaping from her swollen eyes.

I kicked by the blanket, exposing the truth around my ankles. Chains. Locked and sealed. I had knocked the tankard of water from Mother's hand, which now seeped into the red carpet beneath her feet. Red. Gathrax red. The same carpet I had brushed and washed over and over. Julian's carpet.

"Calm down, Maximus." I cringed against her calm, yet commanding tone. "There is no good struggling against this. You need to listen to me… please."

Her tone cracked, revealing her plea.

I stilled, chest heaving. No matter how many times I tried to breathe it did not seem enough.

"Maximus," Mother whispered, slapping my full name at me again. "The wheels of motion are turning and gone is the time for action. Soon you will be faced with a choice. One I have done my absolute best to shield you from. It was only a matter of time before this happened…" She was talking to the ghost over my shoulder now. Her gaze was lost in thought. "We were fools to believe we would keep you safe from this."

"From what?" My voice came out in a harsh croak.

"I only have a moment with you before *they* come."

My stare darted to the large oaken doors beyond her

and the grand walls covered in blood-red patched wallpaper. A hearth burned beneath the brick feature wall beside one of many varnished oak pieces of furniture that filled the room. A room I had not long been in, sweeping the floors and polishing the sides until they reflected like mirrors.

Mother lifted my hand, damp palm and shaking fingers. She turned it, palm upward, and pried my fingers away to reveal the mark beneath. "You must not act out. They already see you as a threat. You are going to need your wits about you. I do not know what they have planned for you, my boy, but you must be prepared for anything."

Her gentle touch traced the scar across my palm. The angry mark had healed since I last looked upon. The silver interloping circles shone no more than an ancient scar.

"I'm… I'm sorry." The apology hung between us.

She shook her head, pinching her doe-like eyes closed. "You are mage-marked, my boy. I wish we had more time. Time to tell you full truths. Master Gathrax and his consort have been occupied within the town. Bless Dame for sparing me a moment with you. But he will return. For you."

The smell of the bonfire clogged my nose and lingered on my skin. Even Mother smelt like ash and burnt wood.

"I killed him."

Even I registered the lack of emotion as I finally admitted my crime.

Mother raised a finger and pressed it to my lips. "Master Gathrax has yet to link Julian's absence with you."

"I killed him, Mother, I did it," I said again, waiting for her slap. Waiting for the hate that would surely gleam in those beautiful eyes. My eyes.

"That does not matter now…" she whispered.

"But I killed him… Master Gathrax will do the same to me."

She sighed, long and heavy. "He will not kill you, Maximus. I regret to admit this but your presence has solidified the Gathrax families' power whether they have registered that yet or not. This is not your fault, but mine. I should never have…" She trailed off with what she was about to admit.

"I don't understand," I pleaded, her words only confusing me more. "Tell me what you must."

"The *amplifier*. How long have you been hiding it? If only you told me, my boy, I would have sent you North long before you were ever found out."

Amplifier?

"They may not kill you, but you *will* receive punishment." Deep-set lines burrowed across her forehead. "Promise me, you will play along. Do as they say until you are no longer on southern soil."

There was noise beyond the door to Julian's room. We both turned toward it. Rushed, Mother turned to me and took my face in her hands. Placing a warm kiss on my head, she leaned in. "Promise me."

"I will, but—"

"I love you."

The door flew open, smashing against the bedroom wall. The bed shook beneath the impact. Mother jumped from her perch. Back turned to me. Hands raised.

Master Gathrax. The sunlight hardly reached him as he seethed in the shadows of the hallway beyond. His demeanor was a statue of disdain. Shoulders curved, back hunched. His hands in balled fists at his side.

Then he sprang forward. Long steps, he reached Mother, knocking his fist into the side of her face.

I cried out, but he didn't stop. As he brought his hand

down on her, time after time, I pulled at my chains and pleaded for him to stop. Mother made no noise as she cowered on the floor, taking his beatings in silence. My heart synchronized with his attacks.

Bang. Bang. Bang.

Two men followed in after Master Gathrax, taking a hold of my mother where she lay splayed on the floor.

Disheveled, Master Gathrax wiped his wet mouth with the back of his shaking hand. His gaunt eyes unblinking as he glared down at the woman beneath him.

"Remove her," Master Gathrax seethed. "And find out which fool let her within this room. They shall share equal punishment."

The men reached for Mother, lifting her from the floor without an ounce of compassion. Her head lolled to the side, revealing the track of blood that traced down her nose and mouth.

I did not take my eyes from her as they pulled her into the shadows of the hallway beyond. Willing for her to open her eyes and look at me. But she did not.

A stare itched at my skin. Master Gathrax stood watching with his calculated gaze.

I swallowed my fear and looked back at him.

Master Gathrax's face held no emotion. Gone was his anger and lack of control. He raked a hand through his hair, laying the wispy ropes and brushing out any sign of the moment that had just passed.

He straightened up, shoulders rolling back as far as they would allow. Calmly he closed the doors. Shutting us in together.

"That is much better." He spoke with his back turned to me. "I think it better that we have this conversation without any more uninvited guests."

When he turned to face me, a wide grin sliced across his face.

He stalked to the bed, a bejeweled finger trailing the sheets until he came to the spot Mother had not long left. Her mark still indented on the bed.

"Let us first deal with the more pressing matter at hand. Tell me where my son is." Spit linked on his thin lips, his overlapping teeth blinking between them.

"Tell me, *mage*, where is Julian."

I swallowed, blades slicing down my throat.

His hand shot out and gripped my wrist. Long, thin fingers, a vise-like grip as they pinched my skin. He was cold. The many rings that adorned his hand the only sign of warmth upon his touch.

"Speak fast, boy. Each moment I am kept in this room is another away from me stopping the men that have just removed your dear mother. They will only stop once I give the command to."

As he said it, a scream registered far within the estate.

"In the wood," I spat.

He smiled down at me. "Good."

His lack of response sparked fear within me.

"My most trusted advisors had warned me of your presence. However, I would have hoped for more of a spy from the North. They sent you…" He laughed then. A high chirp. "A boy mage. Pathetic."

"I am not a spy." I tried to keep my voice calm and steady as I replied. "I am not a mage."

"You think me stupid?" His smile vanished. Lips white as his mouth pursed. "You think me a fool. Enough. These games will stop now."

"No," I said quickly. "I found it, the wand. I swear."

I tried to scream at him through my unwavering gaze.

To tell him I spoke the truth, no matter how unbelievable it sounded to me as I said it aloud. I *willed* him to believe me.

"Interesting. It has been over sixty years since the Eye of the Forest was destroyed. You expect me to believe you just found it?" He leaned in close until his face was inches from mine. A wave of stale breath fogged over me. Spirits. Not long drunk. "Entertain me further, boy. Where did you find it? The Heart Oaks burned years ago. I know you did not simply pluck it from its branches. So please, tell me more as to where you found it."

"I don't know." It took everything in my power not to blink. I did not want Master Gathrax to miss a single slither of honesty my gaze provided.

Master Gathrax reached into his long sleeve and produced the wand. My breath faltered.

It was unmarked, not a single burn. No blacked wood or broken frame. It looked like it never had been thrown into the fire.

"It has been many years since my bloodline has touched Heart Oak. My father, Mage Gathrax, being the last ever to grace this smooth wood and its magic affinity. And now, a lowborn like you just stumbles across one in my wood. My land. Forgive me, but I do not believe such accusations."

I watched as he twisted the wand in his fingers, looking at it with keen, lustful eyes. I wanted nothing more than to look away, but the territorial burning in the pit of my stomach bubbled. I bit down on my lip to stop myself from shouting.

Give it to me.

"It would have been simple if I could just take it. But you have linked yourself with its power already. This is no good to me than simple kindling." He looked back at me then. "Except we saw what happened when you threw it into the flames. Foolish boy."

My cheeks were wet. How long I had been crying was lost to me. "I do not want it."

A lie.

"You have it. I am sorry… I did not mean to do this. Any of this. I am not a mage."

I said it again. Hoping that voicing it aloud would make it true.

"This mark speaks otherwise. You have linked to it. It belongs to you…" His dark eyes flickered with terror. "But you belong to me."

He leaned in now. His words dipping to a low whisper.

"This is what will happen. From this morning onwards, you are now my son; you will help restore my family's name to its highest peak. For the first time since the War of the Wood, the Gathrax name has the chance to repay those North with the very destruction they had gifted us. We will finally get our revenge. It will be my name that is put in the history books, and you shall be my guarantor."

"I…"

"And in time, with your cooperation, you will come to benefit from the change in tide."

Master Gathrax slipped the wand back into his sleeve, and for a brief moment, I saw the holder that was wrapped around his forearm. I had only seen them in glass cases that filled the many empty rooms of this estate. Like sheaths for swords, a quiver for arrows, this kept the wand of a mage close.

"Let us discuss the matter of *Julian*." Master Gathrax's tone deepened. "I see the death notch on the wand. I know you have killed with it and the only missing person in this estate is Julian. Everyone else is accounted for. It does not take a scholar to link two and two. I have searched miles of the forest since sunrise and found no sign of him. Which means you shall take me to him."

He knew.

"I didn't mean to—"

"That *child* would have made a mockery of my estate. His behavior granted him an early death. His mother may not recognize that yet, but I do. He was nothing but a spoiled child. A problem, one now solved."

The lack of anger on his face scared me the most. How could a father not want to kill the person who murdered his own flesh and blood?

Master Gathrax laughed, slow and cold.

"I have a new heir to the Gathrax Estate. Riddle me this, for what is better than a son?"

His face was creased with pleasure. "A mage." He laughed again, throwing his head back. The lump in his throat protruded uncomfortably as he cackled.

"I will not," I stammered, unsure where it came from. The manic laughter stopped in a beat and I felt the pressure of Master Gathrax's hand on my head. It was not a harsh touch, but the same I would have felt when my father used to stroke my hair to sleep.

"Now, I do not want to hear that again. The old Julian spoke like that excessively. What is it you want, boy, power? Riches? I could give you anything. Ah, I know…" He smiled, small eyes wide and unblinking. "Tell me what you want and it shall be yours."

"My family."

Mother's screams echoed in my mind. Father's location was a mystery to me. All I wanted was for them to be safe. That was all I ever wanted.

"Do as I say and your family will be treated like royalty. I am certain that is a deal you could abide by, I trust I am correct?"

He latched onto my weakness, tethering his strings to the fear of my family getting hurt.

"Yes."

The single word signed the treaty between us.

"Good," Master Gathrax breathed. His hand moved slowly, back and forth across my head. His rings caught in my curls, tugging at my scalp.

"Welcome to the family, my son."

6

Five members of the estate's staff flooded into the room where I lay chained to the bed. Not a single one glanced my way. Their hands were clasped together before them; their eyes glued to the floor. A single line stood at the end of the bed. One was ancient. Wrinkles carved out in her skin. Back hunched over her round frame. Three girls stood around her. Heads bowed, eyes trained to the floor.

Then a boy. No. A man. His eyes trained to mine. Wide, dark eyes like jewels across his angular, face. There was something in his stare. The way his plump lips perched and jaw clenched that screamed his emotion.

Pity.

"I will return shortly, my *son*. I have matters to attend," Master Gathrax said, stealing my attention back to him. "I trust you will behave whilst I am absent."

Matters to attend. My parents. I wanted to cry after him as he closed the bedroom door behind him. To remind him of our deal, not to hurt my parents.

But words failed me.

As I had failed myself.

Silence in the bedroom. A long pause that I thought would be never-ending. I waited, longing for one of the servants to look at me.

I sank my teeth into my tongue, stopping myself from shouting out in distress. I was a ghost in their presence. Even when the youngest of the three girls looked up she seemed to stare straight through me.

I thought I recognized one girl, but even in my seven years of working for the family, I had never seen the others.

The eldest maid, a woman with black hair gathered in a braid that hung limply down her spine, walked toward me first. Her gaze was occupied while she fiddled with the brass key that hung by a chain on her worn belt.

Her hands, cold yet tough, reached for my ankle to hold me still. A slip of a cry escaped past my cracked lips as she inserted the key into the hulking padlock. She turned it and the metal imprisonment broke free from my skin. With a hollow click, the tension around my ankle vanished.

My skin beneath had reddened. The maid noticed, relaxing her grip on me with one hand and with the other she ran her fingers gently across my wound. She was nothing but gentle; a motherly touch.

"Millie, get a damp cloth and some scotch."

One of the girls moved with haste, dashing beneath the arched doorway into Julian's bathing chamber. She returned with both hands full in moments. All the servants seemed to be busy around the room. All but the man. He stood still. Eyes burning two holes in my forehead.

The light beyond the room shone across his deep, brown skin. Silver strands stood out against the black, tight curls that crowned his head.

Handsome.

"This will heal, in time," the older maid said, brushing a gentle hand across my ankle. I dropped the boy's gaze for only a moment.

"Poor lad," she said with a shake of her head. "Poor, poor lad."

Her hand reached for my cheek this time. She cupped it, her fingers shaking.

"Help me get him into the bath, he'll need a good scrub... and more."

Another word was not needed to be said. I heard their feet scuffle across the floorboards, then their hands were on me. Within moments they guided me out of the bed and lead me into the bathing chamber on the side of Julian's room. I leaned on them for support, my legs wanting nothing more but to give in.

The weakness that gripped me was alien. Not the same as if I had run for miles or worked tirelessly for a day straight. No. This feeling. In the very pit of my stomach was a longing ache. It drained the power from my body. A tugging for something.

For the wand.

The golden clawed tub sat beneath a sash window. Its surface still shone from when I'd last scrubbed it. Steam seeped from the water which filled it. I felt its warmth from where I stood at the doorway of the bathing room.

"Undress," the eldest maid said.

The sudden weight of many eyes upon me grew heavy. Mouth agape, I stared at the crowd. Warmth flooded my cheeks, pinching them red. Then I looked to the boy again. His eyes were familiar. But I was unable to place where I had seen them.

"It is nothing we have not seen before," the old maid cooed, tugging at my dirtied shirt.

Suddenly, beneath his stare, I was aware of the stench that coddled me.

I turned my back to him. Them. Pulled the clothes from my body and discarded them in a heap on the floor. Covering what little modesty I had left, I took small steps toward the tub which waited for me.

As my feet passed through the water I felt nothing for a moment. Then the sudden heat itched at my skin. Forgetting about my exposed body, I bolted up, slipping on the overly cleaned metal surface.

"Simion." His name. And as if it was the call needed to wake him from a trance, he sprang forward.

"New blood," the old maid said. "Always needing extra guidance. We do not have time to be standing around. Get to work."

And they all did.

Steam seeped off my very skin as I slipped back beneath the water, hoping the clouds of bubbles would keep my pride intact.

I allowed myself a moment as the warmth hugged my body, morphing from discomfort to pleasure. The water in our dwellings was never this hot. Always on the verge of cold and lukewarm. But this. This must be what the waters of kings felt like.

The boy, Simion, strode forward. Everything about his movements was confident. He kept my attention on him until he was out of view behind me.

Then hands. Warm, gentle hands dipped into the water behind me. Frozen, I did not resist. Did not say anything as he pulled the soaked sponge from the shallows of the tub and began to rub it across my shoulders and back. But soon still as they pull soaked sponges from the depths of the tub and proceed to rub them across my exposed body, a shiver ran across me.

I sank deeper into the water in hopes no one would notice the bumps that spread across my skin.

It did not stop until my skin stung with delight.

The girls filled jugs of water and tipped it above my head until it cascaded over my face. My hair clung to my neck and covered my eyes. I didn't care to unblock my vision from the brown strands.

Once they had finished working on me, I was acutely aware of the scent that seeped from my skin.

Lavender and mint.

Julian's scent.

Only I seemed to notice when Simion slipped from the room. I watched the door, waiting for his haunting stare to return.

But he did not.

Sat in the cushioned chair, I watched clumps of brown curls fall around me like snow. Every now and then I would wince against the sudden snip of the blades that nipped close to my ears. The hair littered the checkered stone floor until one maid took a long broom and swept it up. I kept my eyes pinned to the floor, unable to watch the shake of the young maid's hand as she cut my hair.

Pained nicked at the tip of my left ear. My hand shot up, fingertips wet with a blossom of blood. I held it tight to cease the throbbing; when I brought my hand back to my lap, my fingertips were red.

"Forgive me, Julian," the young maid murmured.

I wanted to scream my name at her. Maximus, Maximus, over and over again.

But I did not. Master Gathrax''s warning to behave still chimed like bells in my mind.

They had called me Julian at every given moment. A taunt.

Each had hardly spoken, but when they did that wretched name would be thrown at me.

The prodding of the girls did not stop until dusk settled beyond the window. Light drained from the rooms, only replaced by the amber glow of the fire from the hearth and many candles that lined the room. I stood before the gilded mirror where it rested up against the wall. Unable to tear my eyes away from the vision before me.

"It is the best we can do," the eldest maid said from where she stood behind me. Her thick, doughy arms folded over her chest as she studied me.

If this was the best they could do, then they had truly outdone themselves.

It was not my reflection that looked back at me. But a different one. My eyes were the same. Green and bright. But my hair. My clothes. It was all that was needed to make me look the part.

They had cut it short. A length I had not had in years. And the color. The thick slathering of cream they had rubbed into my scalp and made my eyes water had done this. Changed the color from deep brown to pale yellow.

I raised a hand to touch it, the unfamiliar brush of cold air tickling across my neck. But the clothes that encased me made it difficult to move. The material was thick and stiff.

The jacket, although slightly too big for my frame, made my shoulders square and wide. My posture looked stronger. An illusion draped in finery. The shirt beneath scratched at my skin, the buttons deep obsidian against the material.

And the trousers. They hugged my legs. Deep crimson with two stripes of white down the seams.

"You have not said a word."

I looked at the maid's reflection. "What would you have me say?"

I felt sick. Deep in the pits of my very being as I stared at the boy they made me.

She shrugged, shadows beneath her eyes from the long day of working me into this lie. "Julian…"

I didn't let her speak as the bubble of anger burst out of my mouth. I turned on my heel to face her.

"I am not Julian Gathrax!" I shouted, control of my emotions slipping away from me. My entire body buzzed with the need to scream. The tension inside vied for release.

My shoulders heaved with each, deep shuddering breath. I fisted my hands to still the shaking as I waited for her to snap back at me. Instead she said nothing. Only dipping her head as she took a step back.

"Yes, yes you are."

Master Gathrax slipped into the room unannounced. His light frame able to shift across the cobbled floors without sound. He pushed off from the wall where he waited and prowled toward me.

"What is your name?"

A trick. A test. The warmth of the fire barely reached me as I was pinned beneath his stare.

"Need I remind you about our deal?"

I shook my head.

The hearth danced shadows across his gaunt face. "It shall do. For now at least."

His hungry eyes searched every inch of my body, looking for a detail that was out of place, a thread that might reveal the truth to those who look upon me.

"My parents?"

He waved a hand at me. The tugging in my gut eased in his presence. His closeness to me. I looked at his sleeve, sensing what lay beneath in the leather holder strapped around his forearm.

"Later. But for now, you will rest. Tomorrow at dawn I will come for you. Only when you take me to the body will I consider showing you to your parents."

"Are they OK?" My voice shook.

He clicked his tongue over his crooked teeth and hissed a breath. "Of course. But remind me again... What is your name?"

Long after he left, locking me in the bedroom once again, did my answer repeat over and over. Even when sleep claimed me as the promise of dawn glittered beyond the room did it finally cease.

Julian Gathrax.

7

A frost had settled over the world. For as far as I could see, it was white. It clung to every tree, shrub, and blade of grass. Crunching beneath my heavy steps as I lead the party of three toward the wood.

The polished, leathered boots did nothing to protect me from the wet ground. Each step meant more moisture leaked inside the poor design, freezing my toes and making the woolen socks I wore soggy. Only when we passed through the dark barrier of the wood did I finally have a reprieve from the wet ground. It seemed even the winter chill was frightened to enter the Wood.

I walked, steps heavy, as the weight of what Master Gathrax revealed as he woke me this morning played over in my memory.

He had disposed of them. A term he used. The five servants who had tended to me the day before. Each life taken. To prevent the threat of what they had seen and done from escaping into the estate.

"*I will do anything to hold up this illusion boy, anything.*"

And he meant that. His words had buried deep in my

mind. From his actions it was clear that he meant what he said. He truly would do anything.

And out of those lives, one name seemed to linger. Simion. The boy with eyes full of mystery.

I added the death to my list. My fault. *Your fault.*

So on I trod, moving over thick roots and around clusters of cedar, maple, and oak in search for the boy I had killed first.

It was dark when it happened. Returning now felt different. I scanned the tree line, not knowing where to turn to look for him.

"Problem?" A prod in my back followed the question.

Master Gathrax's eyes burned holes into the back of my head, his huddle of two trusted advisors followed suit. Each man was old. Weathered. The pin of folded red cloth stabbed across their chest to show their allegiance to the ruling family.

I should have admitted before we left that I had no clue where I left him. It was so dark that night. The days between dragging into a millennium. But to admit that meant talking. And silence was preferable for me right now.

I led the hunting party by foot. Master Gathrax not messing his boots where he sat atop his midnight horse. Only I and his two advisors walked. Me ahead. One of them on each side. My instruction was simple enough to follow. Guide them to the body of Julian. That way they can deal with it discreetly.

Then I, Maximus Wodlin, will take Julian's place.

On we trod. Deeper into the wood. Only the humming from my master atop his horse. A deep yet cheery tune that he repeated on and on. Only breaking to question if we were close to finding the body. "I would appreciate it if this is all resolved before lunch."

I kept my head down.

"I trust the birds have been released?" This question was not for me.

"They have, my Sire. During the night," a short, stubby out of breath man replied. "It would be easier for the messages not to be intercepted by the North. Nightfall is our best option for discretion."

"Good job, Xander," Master Gathrax replied, speaking down to the man in all manners. "Remind me, how long until we are to receive a response?"

I had not seen Xander before. The round man's name being the only thing I recognized from the gossips across the estate. Docile and quiet, but it was said he had reaching hands. Unwanted hands.

"I expect our sibling counties will need a day to mull over the news before responding. This is not a simple invitation."

"Let them take all the time they need," hissed the second man. Silas. This man I knew. Tall as a weed. Pale lips were always wet. His hands are pinned carefully behind his back but his eyes always reaching. Touching. "Once their replies reach us the first of the counties will follow within days. We will need time to prepare. There is much to do."

All eyes were on me after Silas's comment.

"And what of our people? I trust you have worked on them thoroughly?" Master Gathrax Said.

"Of course, Sire," Silas said. "Once word spread of the passing of the boy and the announcement of your coming display, all thoughts no longer dwell on the incident. Our people are fickle. Give them something new to chew on, and they soon forget about their discarded scraps."

Me. The scraps.

"Our people, Silas?" Master Gathrax's voice was sweet. Divinely light and questioning.

The horse stopped for a moment. I heard the tightening of the reins as its signal.

I risked a glance. Silas looked at the ground as he replied. "Your people, my Sire. Forgive my slip. It has been a long day."

I paused as their breaths fogged past their perched lips.

"Forgiven," Master Gathrax said. "Let us proceed forward."

My feet were rooted to the spot.

"Are you waiting for something, boy?" Another poke in my back from his cane and I was walking once again. All conversation behind me ceased.

The wood was a never-ending maze. A sense of confusion baffled me as we surrounded ourselves deep within the towers of bark and leaves. I tried to keep my emotion neutral, unsure what punishment awaited me if Master Gathrax caught wind that I was leading them astray.

A fresh bed of leaves covered the floor, destroying all signs of struggle and footprints, leaving me blind in the hunt for the body. On and on we went. The heavy breathing from Xander as he struggled to keep up blended with the humming that Master Gathrax picked up once again.

"Do you smell something?"

The question called behind me. But I could not register who said it. Not when the strong smell invaded my nose. Iron. Intense, stinging iron. My nose wrinkled as it attacked my nose.

"We are here." Master Gathrax clicked with a tongue to signal the horse to stop. A thud sounded as he jumped from its saddle, and then a few steps he was behind me.

He squeezed a hand on my shoulder. "Well done, my boy, you already have *his* sense of tracking conquered."

"Silas, Xander, I trust this is kept among us."

Their complicit silence was enough to please their master.

"Let us see just what mess you have left in your wake, mage."

His grip did not falter from my shoulder as he pushed. Urging me on.

The smell intensified as we prowled further on. Then we found him. The two advisors crying out with a collective gasp. Master Gathrax silent as he peered upward to the body of his son.

Daylight hid nothing from us. Its rays highlighted every inch of horror that hung from the tree.

Julian was blue. His skin was so pale it was almost see-through. Bulging stare a mix of yellow and red. The red jacket he wore did nothing to hide the branch that kept him aloft. Stabbed right through his stomach. The bark stained ruby. Julian's neck was at the most awkward of angles. Although his chin rested on his chest, his face was angled to exactly where I stood.

Horror riled through me, rooting me to the spot.

Do not look away.

I wished nothing more than to turn away. But my own body would not allow me the reprieve.

But a hand once again gripped upon my shoulder, keeping me in place.

In my mind, there was nothing but screaming and shrieking as I could not tear my eyes off the dead boy. And he, in turn, had his open, lifeless eyes pinned on me.

"Take him down." Master Gathrax waved a dismissive hand at the body. "Remove him now and bury him here. Dig the hole thrice as deep and ensure it is covered completely. I do not want his body being dug up until the very earth has absorbed every bone."

He turned to face me. I half expected tears. Some glimmer of sadness.

But he was expressionless.

Unlike his advisors.

Xander's skin had turned a pale green. His thick, stubby hand covering his wide mouth. Silas stood quiet. His eyes were unblinking but the rest of his face calm. He looked to his master instead of the body that hung behind me.

"Do I need to ask again?"

I took a step back as the men moved into action. They first hacked at the branch with long swords they unsheathed from their sides. Iron clashed against wood in a steady rhythm.

Do not look away.

Once the wood had broken enough, they were able to pull Julian from his impalement. I gagged at the wet noise his open stomach made as it slid over the bark. Once he was almost free, the men let Julian's corpse fall to the ground in a dull thud.

A discarded puppet, Julian laid in a heap as the men dug his earthly grave.

Master Gathrax did not command me to quiet as I wept. The intense guilt washed over me, drowning me in a wave of unignorable intensity. I cried until I had no more tears left. Only the sodden damp at the collar of my shirt a sign that I had cried at all.

Do not look away.

Only when my sobs lessened did he address me.

"Dry your face," he said, passing me the embroidered handkerchief from his breast pocket. "This weakness you have will be buried alongside the body today."

"I do not deserve kindness," I spluttered, not taking it from his hand.

My fists clenched, nails cutting crescent moons into my palm. Defiance. Hot as amber coals crashed over my sadness.

"You are very right, mage, you do not deserve anything. But, to maintain our little illusion, you will accept whatever I offer you with graciousness." He thrust the handkerchief at me again. "So, take it."

I dropped his gaze, looking to my boots as I took the offering from him. Unable to watch on as the two men dug at the tough ground. All I focused on was the small splattering of mud and dirt that hit our boots as they worked at the grave.

8

"I ADMIT I AM NOT SURPRISED WITH THE SUDDEN RESPONSE from our sister estate." Master Gathrax chewed on his lip as he conversed with his closest confidant. "Mistress Calzmir would delight in knowing she was the first to accept our invitation."

The letter held firm in his hands from where he sat at the head of the table. The parchment was indented from the blue ribbon that had not long held it rolled up.

"Gossiping wench," Silas joked, his tongue wetting his lips as he raised the fork to his mouth. The hulk of braised pork barely held on.

"And let her spread the word. It will save you and your *mice* a job, Silas."

It was one of his *mice* that had delivered the letter to the dining room. A young boy. Hooded in a cloak with the familiar red ribbon pinned to his chest.

"And we shall welcome them with open arms… and cold tea. They do not have the power in this situation, Master Gathrax, only you hold the mage boy. They are empty-handed," Silas explained, speaking about me as if I did not sit between them. "You have done as well as a job as you can to make him look the part. Now it is only keeping him in line long enough to not shatter our chances. Even if *they* do contest to him being a true Gathrax, the collateral will keep his actions in line."

He spoke of my parents. His sneering gaze shot my way as he did. My lips shivered at the want to snarl, but I had to look away. I had to play the part just as Mother asked.

"Enough of this talk. It has been a long day and I would like to end it as I do most nights."

"A man your age should spend fewer hours with bought company and be with your beloved. She will catch wind soon enough and I am afraid I cannot lie to such an esteemed lady."

Master Gathrax tapped his cane on the floor, silencing his friend. "Now you will lie for me just as I do for you, Silas. Do not let me remind you why."

Silas raised both hands in defeat. "I jest, good Sire. Do as you deem fit."

"I shall."

There was something unspoken left between them both.

"Back to the matters at hand. Romar is the farthest estate. It may take a few days for the news to reach them of the mage boy, then another two for them to arrive by carriage." Master Gathrax played with the food before him. His plates were as untouched as mine. "The boy must display his power, it is the only way to show the truth of what he is. The more who hear news of the mage boy, the higher the risk a bird carries it to the North. They will lay claim to him."

"My mice have been instructed to shoot down any

unwanted bird that passes over our skies. We will keep the North in the dark for now."

"And what if they already know?"

"Then we prepare for a visit from the mountain wyrms."

Mountain wyrms, a southern term for dragons.

"Let them find out." Silas raised his glass in cheers. "It has been many years since we were a threat to the North. It is about high time that they begin to fear us."

I looked at Master Gathrax's face as it slowly slipped into a grin.

"Tread carefully, boy, the next days and how they turn out is down to you." His stare cut through me. I tried to keep my face straight as he stood from the table, prowling toward me until he stood behind my shoulder. Silas licked his lips in anticipation. And something more. His eyes glinted with something more sinister. *Lust.*

"Silas will return every morning over the coming days. You will listen to him, learn from him. I trust you do not need a reminder as to the consequences if I hear otherwise?"

His threat burned defiance through me. I choked on it. "I want to see my parents," I spat.

If I did not wear the gloves I would have seen pale knuckles as I gripped onto the knife and fork. His threat a shadow over the room.

"You are in no position to make requests, boy." Master Gathrax leaned in close to my ear and whispered. The warmth of his breath having me cringe away.

"It is no request," I said, jaw taut. "I simply wish to see them. To ensure you hold up your end of the deal."

There was silence. Then a laugh. Master Gathrax slapped a hand on my shoulder and squeezed.

"You already sound much like him."

Silas joined in, his chuckle low and breathy. "Indeed he does."

I tensed my shoulder, hoping he felt the tension.

"So be it. I will allow you to see them."

My mind spun. I did not imagine this to be his answer. Even Silas spluttered through a mouthful of roasted potato at Master Gathrax's reply.

"When?" That was all I managed to ask. The spark of defiance melting like the last of winter's snow.

"I will let good old Silas decide when after his initial visits. Behave. Learn. Prepare for the arrival of our sister and brother estates. Once he is satisfied, then I will be too."

I stilled, looking to the snake of a man that watched me with unwavering eyes, crow's feet pinching at the corners, his tongue slipping from his lips enough for me to dread his plans.

Footsteps, and Master Gathrax was no longer behind me but beside me. A hand extended to me.

"Do we have an agreement, mage?"

I look to his hand. Nails manicured and fingers decorated with wealth. And I took it. Seeing my parent's faces in the darkness as I blinked.

Master Gathrax smiled, looking down his nose at me and whispered. "Obedience suits you, *Julian*."

The name vibrated in the dull air of the dining room., lingering long after I was escorted back to the bedroom, the door locked behind me.

───

Night painted over the sky beyond the window, bringing with it a cold that not even the hearth could battle away.

The fire had dwindled to weak embers long ago, leaving me to the hungry chill which seeped through the bricks into the room. I sat on the bed, woolen sheet wrapped around my shoulders as my teeth chattered together. But I did not call for a maid. Even when I heard the rustling of feet beyond the door. Waiting for an order.

I stayed silent.

At first, when I was left within the ominous room amongst the dancing shadows and ghost-like memories of Julian's existence, I wished for no one to return for me. Only when my stomach spasmed with hunger did I wish for company. Someone to bring me food or water. Someone to bring news of my parents and their whereabouts.

Dame. She would help, I know she would.

If I could only get a message to her. But the threat of Master Gathrax finding out coiled fear through me.

Being the only child of two working parents, all I remembered was being left to fend for myself whilst they spent their days at the estate. From sunrise to sundown. When I was of age to finally take a job within the estate it was like the weight of the world was lifted from my shoulders. No longer did I dread waking to an empty room and falling asleep in one as well. I suppose it was those years that made me fear loneliness and the way it mutilated my inner mind.

I tried to keep myself occupied by counting window-panes and stone slabs. *One, two, three, four*. On and on I counted until my eyes grew heavy and numbers failed me. I had to keep my mind off the deeds that went on beyond the bolted door of this room. Once I grew tired of that, I moved onto scanning the room, mapping in my mind every detail there was to see.

How many doors in or out. The window. How far it

opened. The countless items of fashion and accessories that were stuffed into the cabinets and drawers that lined the walls of the room.

At night it was different here. As it was within the rest of the estate. Barren and eerie. But as the opal moon's light graced the sky and illuminated everything before me I saw things I'd missed during daylight. Imperfections hidden in light became clear in the dark. Scratches on the bedposts. Strange stains on the rugs and stone floor. How the room held no warmth once the fire died. And the strange paintings of the Gathrax ancestors whose expressions changed as evening rested upon their faces.

Giving up, I curled into myself. Swallowed by the cloudy quilt that filled the bed. The pangs of hunger only an added agony alongside the pain and worry that had embedded itself deep within me.

But for my parents, I *would* do this. For them.

I repeated it over and over in my mind.

For them. For them.

It was all that kept me quiet. From screaming and tearing through Julian's belongings in anger.

I would be a pawn for Master Gathrax and his plan. I would cooperate.

But for how long? The question echoed through me as I closed my eyes. *Until I had learned all I needed to. Until I knew they were safe.*

Then what will you do? The voice asked again.

I did not have the answer.

At least not yet.

9

"Max."

The name tickled against my ears. My name. Called by a voice of honey and silk. A gentle voice that coaxed me from the dreamscape.

"Wake up, Max."

I scrunched my eyes, expecting the morning light to blind me.

The voice hushes, a warming sound that dulls any urgency from being awoken. "Quiet now, your guard sleeps beyond the door. Do not wake him."

I cracked my eyes open to the face, haloed in darkness.

And I go still. My body was frozen as I looked upon the hooded figure before me.

I cannot move as the kiss of a bone cup is brought to my lips, a strong hand guiding my neck upward. "This will help."

My arms are still weak with sleep, sloppy and awkward as I try and pull away. But the grip, although gentle, is powerful. Holding me in place as the cooling liquid slips down my parched throat.

In a breath I am alert. Mind as sharp as a blade.

Exhaustion disappeared in a heartbeat.

"Who are you?" I asked the figure, their shape familiar. So familiar that fear seemed to escape my grasp. A feeling that should be natural as the stranger's weight sits at the edge of the bed.

I sit up, eyes taking a moment to adjust to the darkness.

"Beatrice?" I questioned.

A thrum of hope lit through me.

"Beatri—"

Her hand clamped across my mouth, stifling the shout. Rough skin brushed across my lips.

"Quiet!" she hissed, eyes wide. We sit in silence for a moment, waiting for a sound beyond the door. "Max, you've got to listen to me. I do not have a lot of time."

A breeze dusts across my exposed chest where the sheets had slipped. The window across the room open to the night.

"How did you get here?" I whispered, gripping hard onto her hand. I feared this to be a dream. An illusion. But her touch was real. Warm and real.

"It does not matter now." She shook her head.

The room was on the third floor. Far too high for her to climb up the straight walls of the estate.

"The door is locked," I said, a statement more than a question.

"I know." Her response was matter of fact. She stood up, shifting the weight from the bed. "It has been near impossible to get to you. I am sorry I did not come sooner."

My brows furrowed. "You are not making sense, Bea."

The days of frustration poured out of me. I had to bite down on my lip to stop myself from shouting at her.

"Do you think I care if I am making sense to you or

not?" she snapped, stifling my response. "All of this has gone wrong, Maximus. You should have told me when you saw me before the festival. I could have helped then. We would have been long gone by now."

"Why?" I asked, breathless.

She held a hand to her head, sighing away her sudden bout of annoyance. "Because that was my task, Max. To find you. The lost mage. To take you back home."

"I do not understand."

My voice was a spear of ice as I replied.

"Max, the next time I come for you we are leaving. Getting you far away from here before your prolonged absence causes a war."

A war?

"The North has been waiting for you to show yourself. I should have known. Should have guessed it was you. This god-awful place dulled my senses as Simion said it would."

That name.

"I know him," I muttered. "They... they killed him. And the other maids that did this."

I lifted a hand, pulling at the short strand of fake, sun-kissed hair.

"My brother is not that easy to dispose of." She side-eyed me as she paced the carpet. "Trust me."

Brother. It all came flooding back to me at that moment. Why his dark eyes had been so familiar. The very same as the girl before me.

Questions roared through me as I watched her from my perch. The girl I had believed to know well. Now a stranger as she unraveled her truth in a confusing string of statements.

Yet I asked one that sprung to my lips before I could think.

"Who are you?"

She stopped, back to me. Even in the dark, I saw her take a heavy breath.

"An agent from the North. Sent to retrieve the mage who was taken from us years ago." She turned away, not before I caught the faint sadness in her eyes. "Next time I come for you, Max, we are leaving this place. Together."

I spring from the bed as she takes steps toward the window.

"Take me now!" I called out, loud enough for panic to slice across her storm-stricken face.

There was noise from beyond the door. The clink of keys as the right one is looked for.

"Shit," Beatrice muttered under her breath. Climbing onto the windowsill, knees beneath, her posture feline. "Leave the window unlatched, Max. I will come back."

I wanted to call for her to stop.

Take me with you. Take me.

She glanced to the door then back to me. A finger is pressed to her lips and she shushed me to quiet. Then, in a blink, she was gone. Thrown back into the night.

I spluttered a gasp, feet slapping against the floor as I ran for the window. Only to see nothingness beyond. Straining my neck, I looked to the ground, expecting to see a body. But the ground is clear. Beatrice no longer in sight.

Then I heard it. A low, slither with a chorus of creaks. The vines moved like snakes across the stone wall. Living, brushing fingers of thorns and roots as they settled. If I blinked I would have ignored it as an illusion conjured by tiredness.

"Julian," a voice sounds from the doorway, now open. A girl. Young, with messy hair and eyes shadowed with tiredness. "Are you alright?"

It takes a moment to recognize that she was speaking directly to me.

My true name still ringing in my ears as Beatrice had spoken it.

"Fine, just cold," I said, swallowing the roaring emotion within. With all my effort I hid the shaking of my hands as I reach for the window and close it. No longer hearing the brush of vine across the stone wall.

The girl stands there, watching. Waiting. Her eyes flicked back to the window and then at me. "Can I get you anything?"

"Leave me," I called to her, voice spiked with authority as I clambered back into the bed. I did not miss the sudden fear that coated her expression before she bowed her head and looked down. Fear caused by me. No, the boy she thinks I am.

She stepped out, whispering her apologies before she closes the door. Locking me within once again.

1 0

"WRONG." SILAS'S HAND SLAPPED AGAINST THE WOODEN table, inches from where my gloved hand lay. "Try again."

This had been our routine over the past two days. From dawn until dusk, my days full of grilling and questioning from the day's lessons. Even Silas had grown tired of my company—his demeanor cracking to reveal the true poison within the beastly man that lay beneath his wretched skin.

"You truly do not want to see your dear mother, do you. Your father."

I ground my teeth, hissing my response. "I do."

"Then get it right. Again."

From the beginning, we started our dance. His question followed by my answer.

"Who was the last mage to fall in the War of the Wood?"

"Mage Gathrax, grandfather to Master Gathrax."

When we had first started this game of cat and mouse he would grin at my correct answers. But now, the fifth time of asking, his face was void of expression.

"Why did the war begin?"

"Jealously of the Mad Queen."

He ran a tongue across his thin lip as he sauntered around the table. Hands folded behind his crooked back.

"And pray tell, what was the wench jealous of?"

I paused for a moment. Imagining the age of the woman who had lived longer than any known in Aldian's history. The Mad Queen of the North. Echoes of her reign still reached us in the South. Whispers across the trees that would filter into people's homes.

"The combined power of the four mages of the South. Mage Gathrax the Red. Mage Calzmir the Blue. Mage Makan the Gray and Mage Zendina the White."

A nod of Silas's head and we were onto the next. "Before the War of the Wood, how did the family of the ruling mage pass down their heritage. Passing on their gifts to their successors?"

A blink and I saw the tree behind my eyes. Tall and proud. A drawing of the Heart Oak rested on the page of the open journal before me. "Heart Oak, in the belly of the wood. They would take wood from the tree. Letting it choose the child with the strongest bloodline to become the next mage."

My palm tingled. The story. One that I knew well, everyone in Aldian knew it. However, I sat here, back aching in the hard, stiff chair with the mage mark on my palm.

Evidence that had me second-guessing the information taught to me during these lessons.

"Go on…" Silas urged on, finger twirling in the air before him.

"She burned it. Destroyed the Heart Oak with fire and ice."

He tsked, passing behind me like a ghost. "But Heart

Oak does not simply burn by mundane flames do they, boy?"

I shook my head, expecting his reaching hand to brush over my neck as it had done so many times these past days. "No," I said, back stiff. "With a blaze that burned black."

"Dark power, boy, a power that we have come to fear. To live day by day waiting for her to come again. To squash us where we sit powerlessly. But you. You will change that for us all." Silas's hungry eyes met mine. "With your help, you'll restore the power of *this* great family. This time it will not be wasted."

This time?

I would not. Not with the promise of Beatrice's return. It was a surprise that Silas did not comment on the rings beneath my eyes these past two days. I had hardly slept. From the anticipation of her return or the freezing temperature of the room as I had left the window unlatched all night. Just as she had requested.

But Beatrice had not returned.

She will. I promised myself. My mind had made up stories of where she could be. What she could be doing. But with each worry, another took its place.

"Tell me about a mage's power. Of what they can do."

I wanted to reach for the journal before me. The golden, embossed name of Darrian, the last Gathrax Mage, scrawled on its worn spine. It held the answers. The very source of Silas's knowledge. Its crinkled pages and bent edges left from Silas's many read throughs.

"Their magic came from the dryads, which reflected the earthen abilities that they could conjure."

To my left, sketches of the spirits of the forest were laid out across the polished wood of the table. Different depictions of them. The humanoid beings were created from bark, leaves, and mud. Glowing emerald eyes, wide as moons. Every picture was different, yet all similar in their own way. Pointed teeth of twigs and stones. Moss-like hair and fingers of sticks and twigs. Magical beasts but so human. Even the drawings reflected how mundane their stare had been.

"And..." Silas urged on, dragging me from my thoughts of the woodland sprites.

"They were able to think and do. Imagine a force of power and create it. Heal crops from the brink of ruin. Complete feats of pure wonder."

Silas sighed, gaze lost for a moment. "Do you feel it?"

"I do not understand."

He strode to me. I flinched from his touch, but he struck forward to make contact. A shiver of disgust burned through me. "Darrian described it as an unfulfilled hunger when his first wand broke. A burning ache in his stomach at the separation as he trudged to the Heart Oak to receive a new wand. Do you sense something similar while Master Gathrax withholds your wand?"

We had read the story today. Studying the time when the Mage's wand snapped during a vengeful argument with his brother, resulting in his death. The very wand he had broken in the tussle stabbed through his neck.

I had felt the pulling. An ache that eating did not calm. It was a constant since the night in the wood. Sometimes a sharp pain stabbed across my stomach, and other times the feeling was nothing more than a dull shiver.

"I do," I told him.

Something knowing passed over his dark eyes. "Soon you will be reunited. Tomorrow in fact."

I wanted to question him further, but he interrupted.

"Master Gathrax has asked for our lesson to finish earlier than normal tonight. To allow you some extra rest before the Hunt tomorrow. A gift for your cooperation during our lessons."

His touch lingered on my chest long after he removed his hand.

"Does this mean I can see them?" Longing coated my voice.

Silas looked to me, his face a picture of forced confusion. "Who?"

"My parents," I barked.

"Ah, of course. Yes." He rolled his eyes into his bulging skull and smirked. "Of course you will see them. And very soon indeed."

My hands shook, my breathing shallow. "When?"

"Patience, mage, although I enjoy seeing you beg, I urge you to have patience. For all good things come to those who wait."

11

The *prey* stood in the clearing of the wood before us. Shivering.

Over the days passed I had unearthed horrors I could never believe. Horrors I never knew people were capable of. The Hunt, an annual affair I was aware of. I used to long for the day when the entire Gathrax family would leave the estate at dawn, returning only for supper at the end of the day. I expected them to hunt game. Pheasant and deer that braved the dark wood beyond the estate. But not this.

Not people.

Three of them, each hooded with their hands tied behind their backs. In a line they stood, heads bowed. Clothes ripped and stained with filth. Even the fresh air of the day could not coat the stench that clung to them. I held my breath against the smell.

Neither flinched nor showed signs of fear as our convoy closed in on them. Master Gathrax rode on his grand midnight stallion, armored in silver plates and gold-dyed reins. Whereas I was not given a horse. I followed by foot the entire journey into the first layer of the wood. That was not the only difference between myself and those partaking in the Hunt. I was the only one without a weapon.

Master Gathrax had a bow strapped to the side of his mount. Silas and Xander walked in line with me, both also adorned with a quiver and arrows. They were not permitted to ride alongside their leader. No one was.

"Three this year, Master Gathrax, oh how you do spoil us," Silas sang, the group around him riled up by his praise. "I know this year is one for great celebrations, but this... This is fantastic."

Xander echoed Silas's praise. "Appreciations, Master."

He tipped a chin at his two closest confidants and pulled on the reins. We all stopped as he did. His eyes surveyed the crowd. A gaggle of Gathrax elite. Other members of rich, established families who benefited beneath the red banner of the Gathrax estate. Women and men. Names of whom I had been forced to memorize at breakfast.

"This year's Hunt marks the special events that have occurred among my family these days. As you have each heard of my son Julian, and his mage-ship, we celebrate the truth of the once-great power of the Gathrax bloodline returning."

The crowd murmured in pride and celebration. Eyes full of wonder looked to me as they listened on to the greatest lie ever told.

I kept my chin raised. My shoulders back. The promise of seeing my parents today if I behaved. If I played the part well. Hoping my faked confidence would trick the watching crowd long enough for them to see past my dyed hair and elaborate clothing.

But as Xander had cooed to Master Gathrax this

morning. "Even if they did not believe the boy was Julian. If they questioned his change in appearance. They would never question you. Not for fear of what may happen to them."

As we had all met beyond the estate in the rolling green lawns, Master Gathrax had declared his grand lie to his closest followers. I expected those to question me as I was presented. I might have looked similar to the murdered Julian, but my body language spoke volumes of my truth. My shoulders were not held back likes his had been, nor my chin held high with privilege and pride. He had informed them all before we rode into the wood of the wand, and my power.

I watched as faces had reddened with a mixture of excitement and disbelief as he explained they were all the first to know. The towns and Gathrax's people would be educated on me later. Today was solely for his closest followers to celebrate.

Respect and awe gleamed in the eyes of those who dared to hold my gaze. It made me sick. I tried to hold each of their stares. Unwavering in hopes to sell this illusion to them.

There was only one soul among the large crowd that oozed pure, boiling hate for me. Radiating off her. Her very red eyes hollow and dark.

Mistress Gathrax.

It was the first time I had seen her since the festival. As she searched the crowds for her son. Yet now she looked upon him. The false pretender.

She stayed at the back of the convoy, handmaids fussing over the twins. Each time I looked behind me she tried to murder me with her gaze. Her eyes glistening with the tears that pooled there. Not wet with sadness. But with hateful anger.

I did not blame her. Unlike her husband, she did not find it easy to simply replace Julian. I was not a twisted pawn for her gain. No, I was the boy who killed her first-born. The twins were a different story. They were around seven years of age and cared more about making those handmaids around them miserable than to pay me any attention.

A job Mother would be doing.

I will see her soon.

At that thought, I swallowed the lump of anxiety and relaxed my face. Smiling out to the crowd as Master Gathrax still addressed them.

"My son, are you ready?" Master Gathrax's climbed from his mount with the help of Xander who fussed over him. "Did I not tell you it would be a special one? Just for you. All for you." He waved his hand toward the three concealed figures ahead of us.

No.

Master Gathrax laughed, turning to the crowd with arms wide. "He is so thankful words have escaped him."

The crowd echoed his amusement. Hands pressed to bellies and cheeks flushed as they faked their chuckles in return.

They were too focused to hear the whispered threat he spat at me.

"Say something, mage."

He'd turned his back on his followers. His mouth hardly moving as he spoke.

"Where is the deer I was promised?" I forced the question out. Edging my words with whiny compliant, just as the old Julian would have done. The only action missing to solidify my bratty comment was a stamp of my foot on the ground.

"Deer." Silas jumped to Master Gathrax's aid. "Have

not returned to these parts of the wood since you drove them all out last year. So, as you see, we have something much better."

"Precisely." Master Gathrax lips pursed. He wrapped his arm around my shoulders and squeezed his grip into my upper arm. To anyone else watching it was a loving gesture between a father and his son. But the discomfort was invisible. His nails managed to stab into my skin, even through my thick ruby jacket that dwarfed my frame.

"I prefer my prey to run. The chase is what makes the hunt worthy," I spoke again, this time keeping my face void of emotion. Bored.

A heavy pat on my back and Master Gathrax let go of me. "Do not worry, my son. If you would prefer them to run, then that is what we shall let them do. But first, may I have a word with my greatest allies? The families of my estate. Trusted and loyal. For this day is for you as well as it is for my family. The Gathrax bloodline has always been the strongest of the four estates. It had been when my great-grandfather Mage Gathrax the Red's power dulled the light of the other three mages. Our blood was most pure. It is no wonder why it is my son who has defied all odds and retrieved his wand when it should not have been possible." Everyone listened in silence as Master Gathrax spoke. His voice carried above the crowd, stilling all movement and sound. Not once did he let go of me.

"May this be a blessing for us all. With the change of tides comes a power shift. One that is going to cause great interest from our brother and sister estates. But there will be more eyes turning our way soon. The North will catch wind of my boy in due time, and when they do our skies will once again be filled with mountain wyrms come to claim him."

A chorus of gasps sounded. Some of the crowd even

looked through the thick foliage of the woods to the sky, expecting to see the very beasts he threatened.

"This time we will be ready. United in a manner of speaking."

Silas bowed to his master and stepped forward into the clearing the group had made for them. "In the coming days, our sister estates will be arriving. Birds have been sent carrying invitations of great importance and urgency. When their carriages carry them across the borders of our Master's domain we shall hold many councils. Meetings that shall determine a new South. Just as our ancestors lived, we want to unite the South once more. Opening borders, demolishing tensions. All for a single purpose."

"Let the reds rule!" someone cried out.

The crowd buzzed at the shout.

"Yes! The great reds."

The crowd shivered with pride. I watched the corners of Master Gathrax's lips lifted upward. His grin curved as he watched on.

"Now, now." He waved his hands to quieten the crowd. "Let us not get ahead of ourselves, my great people. How we all have like minds. It is only natural, as the old mages ruled, so will the new."

"Julian, my heir, will unite us all under one name. A strong, ancient name."

The crowd began to chant. "Gathrax, Gathrax, Gathrax."

"When the estates see one has returned they will have no choice to refuse our request. Then, when the North arrives we will have the numbers to match them. Now tell me, my friends, how does that sound? More to your liking?"

Cries lit up the wood, shaking birds from their nests above and scattering them to the skies. Bows were pumped into the air just as feet stomped on the ground. The entire clearing seemed to vibrate with pleasure.

"Then let us celebrate today with the Hunt whilst tomorrow we prepare our negotiations," Master Gathrax called, "Julian, as this is all in your honor, let it be you who strikes the first down."

I swallowed a lump in my throat, still trying to process everything I had heard.

"Silas, will you do the honors and uncover my son's choice of prey."

I watched. Not allowing myself to breathe as I waited for the innocents to be revealed.

Silas slunk toward the three figures, each as still as stone. I would not allow myself to look away. I followed every subtle move of Silas as he snatched the hoods from the heads of the three.

First, I see the gray of the old maid. The skin around her eyes and head was a puzzle of purple and black. Angry bruises mixed with red, shallow welts. The pain she'd suffered was evident from the crusted blood that clumped her hair in thick strands across her hairline. Her eyes squinted as she finally saw daylight. Then they rested upon me.

Dame.

Copper blossoms across my tongue as I bite down on it. A chill raced across my blood, my bones. Taking hold of my body in its firm, icy grip.

My stare blurred as I looked upon her. Her broken, hunched body. Kind face speckled with blue and black. Nose inflamed with the shadow of crusted blood around it.

Even as the next figure was revealed, I could not look. Not as I tried to read what flashed across her squinting, red-rimmed eyes. Her brows raised as she tried to tell me something.

But then a choke of a sob sounds beside her from the figure in the middle of the line.

My knees buckled as I looked upon my father.

"Steady now," someone sneered, lips close to my ear. Master Gathrax.

Like Dame, the man before me was nothing more than a shell of the father I had last seen.

He winced with each breath. Face pinched in agony. He did not look at me. Not once. Not as I willed him to.

A tear slipped down my face. With my back turned to the crowd they would not see. So, I let them loose. Let them cut streaks down my face and dampen my collar.

Father was covered in his own muck; clothes were ripped and damp. *What have they done to you?* I saw a raw burn, creeping beneath his collar across the skin of his neck. Its deep maroon shade, dotted with yellowed puss. It coated his chin. Even from a distance, I could see it was infected. His skin had paled and there was a sheen of sweat on his forehead. Dark circles framed his eyes, making them hollow and tired.

Look at me. I screamed at him internally. *Look at me.*

But he did not. Instead, he angled his face to watch Silas who reached for the third figure. Father hissed as Silas's hands raised for the hood, revealing the face beneath.

Part of me had already expected the final person to be standing there. Green eyes blinked away her piercing sadness. Her bottom lip puckered and red with her blood.

Wild, brown hair a mess around her heart-shaped face. Some stuck to her forehead, clumps of old, brown blood shadowed in her hairline.

"You understand my need for caution," Master Gathrax whispered to me as I stared at my mother. I barely heard him as I slipped into another world. Through a portal of horror. My soul left my body, assessing the dread before me. "Did I not promise that you would see them again?"

I watched as my father struggled in place, trying to reach for his wife. Mother. His shoulders tensed as he tried to pull from his bindings. Only stopping when Silas brought the butt of his sword into the back of his neck. The crowd behind me muttered in pleasure as Father's knees slammed into the muddied ground.

"I need to ensure you will become my beloved son and behave by my rules. Your magic may not be under my direct control, but you are. I need you to know that I will do anything to ensure you are a compliant pawn."

"You promised not to hurt them," I spit through labored breaths.

"And I have not. Not by my hands."

"I will kill you for this."

He laughed, deep and shuddering. "I have no doubt that is what you wish. But harm a hair on my head and your family will be dealt with."

I turned to him, looking up at Master Gathrax into his dull yet hungry sapphire eyes.

"Now, now, Julian. Like I have just told you, I will not hurt them as long as you behave."

"My name is Maximus," I seethed, bring my face as close to his as I could, voice rising slightly. It was enough for him to hear. The crowd behind us hardly faltered in their conversation as I spoke.

He moved from me with a speed I did not imagine his frail body could muster. His hand reached behind his shoulder and pulled forth a blade. It happened so quickly. He flicked his wrist and threw the blade. A blur of silver twisted toward the waiting prey, followed by a hollow thud.

A trill of birds burst from the trees as I screamed.

The crowd finally silenced.

Dame dropped to the forest bed with the dagger embedded in her chest.

In the deathly quiet, I could hear only the gargled breaths of Dame.

She peered down to the hilt which protruded from her body. Her hands shook as she reached for it. But before she grasped it, she toppled to the ground, face first.

"Take the rest away," Master Gathrax shouted to Silas whose face is stricken with shock. Voice filled with uncontrolled disappointment. "My son is not feeling well this day. We will not proceed any further with the Hunt."

No one makes a sound, including me, as I watched Silas beckon armored men to step forward, re-hood my parents and drag them away. Back in the direction of the estate and its grounds.

"But…" Xander began, his voice timid as he stepped toward me.

The slap echoed across the woods. Xander's round face snapped to the side, his cheek bloomed red.

"Do not question me, Xander. Leave us, all of you," Master Gathrax shouted, addressing the crowd whose anticipated faces had melted into confusion and something else. Disappointment.

I did not care for them. For any of them. Not as my parents were taken from me once again. Dame was left.

Before my very eyes, the color of life from Dame's skin evaporated, the forest bed drinking her life source as it seeped from her chest.

"Your love for them will cost you. You have embarrassed me. Disobeyed my every order and for that, you will pay."

"Do it," I spat, "I do not want to play this game."

"It is not a choice you have, boy."

As I stared at the dead body, I wished for Beatrice to return. The feeling became a burning inferno within. *Take me. Take me away from here. From him.*

Master Gathrax reached a hand for my jacket and pulled at the dampened collar. "This is your final chance to comply. Step out of line and you will next see your parents in their graves. You have a final chance to cooperate by choice, mage. One final chance. I promise you nothing but misery if you do not comply. For as long as I live, I can promise you that. Compliance is key to their survival. So be it on your neck if they do not live through the week."

Compliance is key.

The words were etched into the darkness of my mind. Glowing with fire in the pits of my chest. My heart entrapped in an ache of pain.

There was a package on my bed by the time I returned to my room. Pushed over the threshold by Xander who had escorted me with rough, small hands. His cheek still red with a handprint.

It was left on my pillow.

Beatrice. It had to be from her. A note. A plan.

Once I heard the lock of the bedroom door, I ran to the package. My shaking hands fumbled as I unraveled the coarse ribbon and tugged at the folded paper to reveal the item within.

A finger dropped into my hands. Cold. Slick with blood as muscle and bone jutted out at one end. Frayed skin tickled my palm. I recoiled from the digit, dropping it to the sheets. Red soaked in and spread like fresh, morning frost.

I gagged. Stepped away from the bed in disgust.

And then the note, a flutter of brown paper slipped to the floor like an autumn leaf.

Slowly I reached for it. Tugging at the paper to reveal the words written in ink. Elegant writing. Gathrax's writing.

"Compliance is key," I read aloud.

I dropped the note and looked to the finger. The faded gold band wrapped around it was one I had seen many times before. I had even worn it as a child, making Mother laugh as it slipped from my small, childish finger.

Her ring. Mother's finger.

I DID NOT NEED TO PRESS MY EAR TO THE DOOR TO LISTEN for the gossip that spurred beyond. The first estate had arrived. I could pick up enough that Mistress Calzmir and her family had arrived in the early hours of the morning. The second powerful estate after the Gathrax. The family were given the entire eastern wing of the estate to unpack and rest from their days of travel.

A click of keys sounded beyond the oak door and I stepped as far away from it before it opened.

"Morning," the deep voice of the boy said as he stepped backward into the room. Attention on the silver tray he held as he tried not to drop it. "Hungry?"

His question was flippant. Rushed. With a kick of a foot, he closed the doors behind me. Then faced me.

Simion. The boy from my first night. A boy that should be dead.

Beatrice. They had come for me.

"Take this, will you." Simion handed over the tray to me. My hands were numb as he dropped the weight of it into my hold.

"Have you come to take me?" I questioned, the smell of baked cinnamon goods wafting from the tray I held.

"So you have put two and two together?" he said, moving for the window and opening it ever so slightly.

"Beatrice said she would come back," I said, flatly.

Simion huffed, his eyes racing across me. "She has been, occupied, these past days. Now even more so. That is why I have come for you myself."

"I thought he killed you."

Simion leaned on his hip, jabbing his thumb toward the door behind me. "Did my sister not inform you? I am simply hard to kill."

"She did," I said, placing the tray down on the bed. Not caring as a splatter of hot liquid seeped onto the sheet.

I rubbed at my eyes, cleaning the sleep dust from their corners. It did nothing to calm the puffiness that stiffened the skin around my eyes.

Simion stepped toward the bed. Walking through the room as if it was his own. "Milk?"

"What?" I stammered.

This man, Simion, was frantic. He spoke of one thing for hardly a moment before moving onto the next.

"Do you want milk with your tea?" His brows furrowed as if my question was silly.

Shaking my head, I declined.

"I do not want tea. I want to leave. Beatrice said she would come for me and she hasn't."

Simion rolled his eyes. His sun-warmed, honey eyes. "You have scuppered our plans. Believe me, for our sake, we are trying to get you removed from here safely. But we cannot do anything now. Not yet."

"Why?" I questioned. For the first time since he entered Simion did not look at me, instead skimming around the room. His eyes hardly landed on my mother's finger which had laid discarded on the floor. Not an ounce of horror was exposed across his face.

"You are a mage, you and Beatrice. From the North."

Simion cringed as I asked him, putting a finger to his full lips. "Keep it down, honestly, Max. You truly are a thorn."

Max. He said it. My name.

"What did you call me?"

He stalked toward me, raising both his hands before me. "I am not a mage. But I cannot speak on behalf of my sister."

Not a single mark covered his palm.

"My gifts are not of the divine, Maximus."

He said it again. As Beatrice had done. I had not heard my given name in days, so much so it sounded strange as it slipped from him.

I had many moments to dwell on it since her last visit. How the vines had moved and she had disappeared in moments. Magic.

How many times had I been with Beatrice over the past years, and not once had I seen her hands free of gloves as she worked.

"If you are not here to take me away, then what are you doing?" Frustration and desperation shone from my plea.

"I have been tasked to ensure you are fed today." Simion reached for the tray and picked the bun from the decorative plate. Raising it to his mouth, he took a bite. White teeth cut into the sponge-like bun as honey dripped down his brown skin.

"And to take you from this room for a short walk around the estate. To go anywhere you would like to go. Within reason," he said through a full mouth. Swallowing heavily, he grinned my way. "So I will wait beyond the room until you are washed and dressed. I trust you do not need me to fill the bath for you again."

My neck warmed. A single brow of his raised in jest.

"Silas will come for me," I announced. "He does every morning. If I am not here…"

I thought about Mother's finger, glancing at where it lay. If he came for me and I was not here it would be yet another defiance. For their safety, I could not do that.

Compliance is key.

"Silas will not be calling for you today. He is preoccupied with the visitors. And it was him who gave me the orders to come for you."

"What are you? One of his mice?" I questioned.

"Perhaps." He shrugged his wide shoulders. "Like you, Maximus, I am one of many things. Becoming what is needed for the task at hand."

Simion's departure was abrupt. One moment he was before me with lips covered in glossy sugar. The next he was gone. Leaving me in the room alone once again.

"Finally." I heard Simion mutter beneath his breath as I stepped out from the room into the expansive corridor beyond. Like a statue he stood beside the door, hands held behind his back, chin up high. That was a posture of importance. I would know, I had seen it many a time on the Gathrax family themselves.

"Where are we going?" I questioned, voice clear as crystal. It was not only Simion but other servants standing watch beyond the door. Not even one looked at me. Pushing down my true self, the one Simion had awakened with his call of my name, I became Julian once again. This time finding it easier to slip into the deceased boy's demeanor.

"If you will, mage." he replied, voice void of the character he had only moments before. Now he spoke to the illusion. Not me.

He took off without another word, taking large strides as his long legs allowed. I had stayed far behind him.

Julian's room was in the west wing of the estate. The library was in the east wing. Where I had heard the guests would be. To get to it we had to follow the corridor to its end, passing through another two function rooms before reaching the grand staircase that led to the ground level of the estate.

There were five visible floors. And one more beneath the ground level; a cellar which was full of the scuttling of Gathrax's staff.

Today it seemed that every single person who worked, dwelled, and lived beneath Gathrax's thumb was out to watch me.

This was not a simple outing, but a parade.

For those to look upon the mage. Upon me.

No matter how Simion made me feel, I wanted nothing more than to skip a few steps closer to him and hide behind his back. But that was not a luxury I had anymore.

Retreating into the back of my mind for safety was what got me through the short walk to the library. I thought of my parents and where they were. Of Mother. Only hoping she would not be in pain.

Sickness gripped across my stomach.

I do it for them.

"I shall wait for you outside," Simion said as we reached the doors to the library. Bustling members of the estate moved around us as they cleaned and worked. All because of the recent arrivals.

"No," I refused his offer. "You will come inside with me."

I had further questions for Simion.

I could see the burning desire to refuse me pinch at his face. Even his plump, full lips seemed to tighten as he fought the urge to reply. A reply that he caged.

Nodding, he forced a smile. "Certainly."

As if coming up from the belly of the sea, Simion gasped for breath as we entered the library. Shaking his arms and legs he said, "I am not used to being so... stiff."

"I have questions for you," I said, ignoring his use of words. "And I need answers."

"I am sure you do. Ask away."

Simion moved for a cushioned bench that was built into the rows of bookcases. He sat, legs crossed over each other, and waited for me to speak as I stood above him.

Arms folded over my chest, I began.

"Where will you take me if we leave?"

"We will go North."

"Why?"

Simion leaned back, arms flexing as he rested his hands behind his head. "Because if they come for you, it will not be good for anyone here. We should reach the North before they come looking."

"Because she will kill me?" The Mad Queen.

"*She*," Simion purred, "will do anything necessary to keep you from being used as a pawn. That is not your purpose. Believe it or not, her preferred methods are far from the same as the barbarians you currently live among."

"I will not leave without my parents," I told him.

"I know. That is what is taking us some time. We could have removed you from this place far before this all happened. Before you revealed yourself as the lost mage."

I shook my head at him, tutting as I paced. He simply watched, amused from his perch.

"I did not ask for this. Do not want this." I walked away from him, looking over the shelves for what I longed for. Books. Books about mages. Anything that would give me insight into what I was. What they kept telling me I was.

Hungrily, I began pulling tomes from the shelves. Stacking them one on top of the other.

"Let me help." Simion stood close, inches behind me.

"I am more than capable," I said, an edge of one of the books dug into my chin where it rested. One sudden move and it would fall.

"If I am seen letting you carry it all back to the room then I will not be treated kindly." Simion sounded desperate now as I rushed back toward the doors to leave. He pounced in front of me. His large hand held the door closed. "Wait, Max."

"You keep calling me that."

His brow rose. "Well isn't that your name?"

I let him take the books from me.

"Light reading?" he moans, peering his head to the side to look at the gold-leafed writing across one of the spines.

"I need to learn. I am a mage and hardly know what that means."

Simion's eyes glared over the stack of books at me. "We have a place for learning. In the North. An academy. A haven for you to learn about your linage and train your magic."

"An academy?" I questioned aloud, eyes lost for a moment.

"Indeed."

I felt the stone barriers of this illusion begin to crumble. The ever-present tugging in my gut intensifying at the thought.

"When do we leave?" I asked him again.

"Soon."

Frustration caused me to shout. "Why is everyone keeping me in the dark? You and Beatrice! You say you want to help. But you do not. You are treating me like the rest of this place is. Keeping me in the darkness for whatever reasons you deem necessary."

I wanted to knock the books from his arms. Hit out. Punch the wall behind him. Instead, I pushed at the doors, leaving him in my wake.

He trailed me silently as I half walked and half ran back to my room, the kiss of his stare a constant on the back of my head.

The maids jumped from their seats when they saw me coming, hastily opening the doors to the room. Simion now steps behind.

Once in the room, he spoke, throwing the pile of books carelessly to the bed.

"You are just like them you know," he seethed; handsome face flushed.

"Like who!" I snapped, turning on him where he stood.

"Arrogant. Spoilt. You fit the role well." His arms taut at his side, Simion was dead still. Back straight and gaze pinned on mine.

"I want you to leave," I told him. "Go and do whatever duties you have. But leave me."

"You are my duty," he said, sharp.

My words faltered as what he said settled across me.

"Believe it or not, Maximus, you have been my duty for as long as I can remember."

Then he was gone. Leaving me to my drowning silence.

14

"Book worm," Silas drawled as he entered my room. I looked up. The hues of dusk filling the room. The ache in my legs echoed how long I had been sat on the bed poring over the texts before me. Not focusing on the real world beyond the pages.

I closed the leather bound tome, shutting off the same story I had read over and over. The same retelling of the fall of Mage Gathrax. How he had been valiant and brave in the face of death. Each one a ballad of his strength.

Biased accounts. Not one from the perspective of anyone but a Gathrax.

Silas snuck in, hardly opening the door to allow his wiry frame to enter.

"Wha—what can I do for you?" I asked, keeping my voice steady. His appearance unnerved me.

"Do not ask me that…" he breathed, tongue wetting his colorless lips. "I have come on request to prepare you for supper this evening."

"With whom?"

He regarded me for a moment. "You have a spark of

him you know. Julian. I sense a change in you. You are finally learning to comply."

I hissed, "Compliance is key."

"That it is, mage, that it is," he said through a sly grin.

"Who will I be meeting with?" The thought of food twinged my stomach. The scraps of lunch littered the sheets in crumbs around me.

"Your *father* has requested your presence. A final meal before tomorrow's hosting begins. Our final guest will be arriving tomorrow. It is going to become busy for you. Gone are the times to enjoy a simple book in this room."

I had more heard than seen the commotion as the remaining families from the lead estates had arrived from beyond my open window.

Always open. Left on the latch for Beatrice's return.

"Come, child." He reached for the book in my hand. His cold skin brushed against mine for a moment. Enough for me to pull away.

"Leave the books for the evening. Let us not keep our master waiting."

I arrived at the dining hall before anyone else.

Silas spoke not a word to me the entire way there, only going so far to open the door for me to enter then closed it behind me.

The dining room was modest. A personal dining space for the ruling family of the estate. Not a place for showing off wealth and hosting grand parties as those that no doubt would follow in the coming days.

The room was narrow, barley fitting the dark pine-carved table in its center. When the chairs were filled, those presenting food would hardly have space to breathe let alone walk around the table.

Red velvet curtains hung on two of the four main walls. During dinner, they would be drawn to cover the many frames that were hung. At least only when Mistress Gathrax ate within the room. She couldn't stand the sight of the preserved palms of mages passed. How the skin had dried and curled at the edges, kept only in place by the pins that secured it to the frame. Each showing the same markings that I now had upon my own hand.

The mark on my palm seemed to warm as I regarded the frames around the room. I had to force myself to look away, not needing more reminders of what I was.

A deep pomegranate table runner draped off either side of the table, finished with impressive beading and tassels. Besides the table and chairs, there was only one other piece of furniture. A chest of drawers at the end of the room, placed beneath an arched, diamond glass window. Red candles burned in holders beside picked holly and fresh greenery.

A breeze slipped inside as the door opened. The flames of the pillar candles danced in the gust.

Master Gathrax and his wife entered, hand in hand. Both were dressed in finery. Elegant postures and equally regal costumes they both wore. Mistress Gathrax swaddled in a gown of ruby silk. The gleam of the material matched that of the gem that hung from her thin neck on its large, golden chain.

I stepped into the corner of the room—out of their way.

Without more than a subtle glance to where I stood, he pulled a chair from beneath the table and urged Mistress Gathrax to sit. Fussing over the chair as he pushed her in.

"I am glad to see you down here so promptly," Master

Gathrax said. "Silas had no problems with herding you here I see. Good. Take a seat here please."

He had walked to the opposite end of the table where his wife sat, glaring at me with eyes full of disdain. For me, he did not pull it out. Only waved a hand for the chair he wished for me to take up.

There was noise beyond the door before it opened. Silas stood proud as two unrecognizable figures stood behind him.

"May I introduce," he began, stepping to the side to allow them to walk forward. "Mistress Amilia Calzmir and her son and heir, Camron Calzmir."

With a bow he let the two enter the room. Both Master and Mistress Gathrax stood from their seats in welcome.

It was Xander who was entrusted to teach me of the other three estates that jointly shared rule over the south of Aldian. And his lessons did not go to waste. I recognized them both. Mistress Amilia Calzmir was a tall woman. Bending her knees with a click as she ducked beneath the door frame into the room. Giant's blood surely coursed through her veins.

Her nose was her most prominent feature. Hooked and large, it dwarfed the some-what beautiful elements on her face. Her aged stare was crowned with wrinkles. Even the corners of her painted lips were jagged and pursed.

"Blue suits you well," Master Gathrax drawled where he stood.

"As red suits you," Amilia replied, her trill voice lacking welcome.

She was dressed in her estate's color. A cobalt gown hugged her frame. Like water, it slipped over the hint of the curve at her hip, held by two straps at her narrow shoulders. Her skin peppered with freckles. With a bejew-eled hand, she pushed a loose strand of auburn hair over her shoulder and raised a hand back for the door of the room. "Come, my son. No good just dallying in the shadows. We have much to discuss."

Still standing, I followed her welcoming hand to Camron who sauntered in next.

Each step he took was precise. Militant. Only adding to the air of command that oozed from him.

I barely noticed Silas who finally slipped into the room and pulled a chair opposite Mistress Gathrax for Amilia to sit.

Camron did not drop my gaze, so I ensured I held his. I warmed beneath it. There was fire within him. More so than his mother's eyes. His were a pure inferno. A dance of autumn and summer. He too was tall. Enough that he had to look down at me even from a distance.

"May I?" he said, face still.

I did not respond at first. Not out of rudeness but the inability to notice it was me he addressed.

Not waiting for a response, Camron moved for me. I inhaled, taking in the fresh smell of salt and open air. It flooded my senses with pleasure. It was a chair that he reached for. Pulling it out, his azure jacket flexed at his arms as he did so.

Then he stepped back, gestured a hand, and said, "Please, take a seat, Mage Gathrax."

Master Gathrax coughed from where he still stood, waiting, at the head of the table, urging me to move.

I dipped my head, struggling to hold the heir of the Calzmir estates' gaze. His striking face intimidating.

"Thank you," I murmured, sitting in the chair with my back to him. I looked to the audience of four then. Each who seemed to study us both from where they stood.

Strong arms gripped the back of the chair and pushed, gently. "You are most welcome."

He had leant in close whilst he tucked me beneath the table. Just shy of my ear, over my shoulder.

I gripped the red cloth on the table. Heart picking up in pace.

Never had I been so grateful for Master Gathrax to finally speak.

"May we welcome our sister estate with this meal. A feast to celebrate the coming days of union." Master Gathrax's words raised above the room. And the rest of them sat.

I was aware of the man that pulled a chair beside me and sat down. Not next to his mother who seemed unaware as she muttered quietly to Mistress Gathrax about something.

Silas whispered to his master. Both looked my way. Then a nod of Master Gathrax's head and Silas dispersed, returning moments later with a flurry of servants, each carrying plates of steaming food.

Monkfish circled with a bed of boiled potatoes were placed before us. The smell did nothing to cover up the scent of the man beside me. I could not look at him. But I was certain he glanced at me, the shift of his body moving so slightly.

Then the brush of a foot beneath the table. I gasped, pulling my legs beneath me.

"Apologies," Camron drawled. "I have a habit to wander where it is unseen."

The hair on my neck prickled.

"It is no bother." It was all I could manage to say without my voice breaking with nerves. Then I picked up the knife and fork before me and busied myself with the food. I listened in to the conversation between a Master and Mistress of two, equally powerful, estates. Well, until I came and shifted the scales.

"We were truly sorry to hear of the passing of your dear husband," Master Gathrax said, lifting a fork full of fish to his mouth. "And how equally apologetic we were for not attending the service of his burial. I do hope our gifts sufficed our absence."

Amilia hardly spared him a glance. Xander had told me of the passing of Master Calzmir. It had been almost three years ago. He had passed from a battle with a terrible sickness that ate away at his lungs.

"Do not be sorry, Jonathan." Her sharp, angled brow raised. "For it does not suit you."

Master Gathrax's knife screeched across his plate. His lips pursed white. On Amilia went, eating without acknowledging how her comment had sliced at Master Gathrax.

"I must say, years have been kind to your heir. Camron," Master Gathrax now spoke to him, "You have truly grown into a handsome man. A spitting image of your father, I am sure of it."

At the comment, Amilia looked up. Her cheeks tight as she smiled at her son. "One would think looking upon his face would only be a reminder of what was lost. But how can such beauty ever inspire sadness."

"Only ballads and songs I am sure," Master Gathrax added.

"Indeed." Then Amilia's eyes were on me. The first time since she had entered. "However, I cannot say the same for your heir, Jonathan."

Master Gathrax cringed as she flung his name at him.

"His features are not much like yours or your dear wife's."

There was clear silence for a brief moment. Even Silas side-eyed the woman as he swept around the room, filling the glass with red wine.

"Inquisitive as ever, Amilia. As you know, for you would not have returned my letter otherwise, my son takes more after his great-grandfather. Both in looks and… power."

"Ah," she breathed, eyes alight with interest. "Mage Gathrax the Red. The last to fall after my own great-grandmother all those years ago. And now it is your heir that has defied odds and become what we all thought was lost."

Her gaze searched me. Frantic. Hungry. Looking for what only could be a chip in the illusion. I kept my chin up as she did, forcing a smile in return of hers.

"Handsome nonetheless, do you agree, Camron?"

My smile melted as I waited for his response.

"Very."

Both Master Gathrax and Amilia shared a look. A grin on both their faces.

"Then let us toast to that." Master Gathrax raised a glass, wine swirling. "To us. The Gathrax and Calzmir. Great siblings for years, soon to be united."

Everyone lifted a glass. Even Mistress Gathrax, her hand shaking slightly and her face lacking a smile. But Camron did not. He sat still, both hands resting upon the table.

They did not seem to mind as they took swigs from their glasses and proceeded with their meal.

The conversation that followed was little interest to me. Both leaders of their respective estates discussed taxes. Comparing wealth and other political commentaries that brushed over my head.

I could hardly focus on anything but the shallow breathing of Camron beside me.

It was late evening when the meal came to a close. My body was heavy from the day of studying. I clenched my jaw against each yawn that threatened me.

"…and there will be a display," Amilia said, chair screeching across the stone as she stood from the table. "You promised me a display. I may take your word for it, but the other estates are already talking, Jonathan. Not all can simply believe."

"I do not care much of what they think, but yes. They shall get the demonstration they crave. Before tomorrow's ceremony."

Amilia tipped her head. "Then I shall retire. Rest for the day ahead. Thank you both for this meal."

She reached for Mistress Gathrax's hand and held it in her own. "I look forward to us growing closer."

Mistress Gathrax's face was flushed white. Ghostly. "And I," she spluttered.

"Come, my son, let us rest. Tomorrow will be long for us. You especially."

They both left. The smell of salt and ocean breeze still lingered in Camron's wake. His shoulder had brushed mine as he stood from the chair. There was no need for it —not with the plentiful space between us. But he did. His touch warm for moments after.

15

I BUSIED MYSELF WITH THE PILES OF TOMES I HAD YET TO search through, attempting to dive into these stories to rid myself of the thought of the evening's meal. Camron's intense aura simmered around me as night ruled on. The interaction, although minimal, left its mark. A fresh scar across the skin of my mind.

On I read, yet another retelling of the War of the Wood. Aloud, I followed the words with a finger on the page, fighting the tiredness that racked my body.

The story told of Mage Gathrax the Red's power. How he had conjured the very trees to dance as they reached for the Mad Queen atop her mount. A beast. A dragon that spat ice out across the world as it cut through the skies.

It told of how Mage Calzmir had fallen. One blast of the dragon's breath and she had crystalized before the very eyes of those who watched on. As she fell, body connecting with the muddied battlefield, she had broken apart. A million pieces of iced flesh and blood. Shattering like glass across the battlefield until she was left to melt into the ground.

I looked up at the noise beyond the door. It was too late for the maids beyond to be busying themselves.

Sitting still for a moment in silence, I stretched out my hearing as far as humanly possible for a sign of what it might be.

A click. The turning of a key in the door.

Eyes pinned to the handle, I waited for it to open. I became suddenly aware of the breeze from the open window. Was Beatrice here, finally, to take me away?

I jumped from the bed. The cold slabs a shock as my feet pitter-pattered across the room.

Hesitating, I reached for the handle myself. Turning it and, slowly, pulling it open.

The corridor was soaked in obsidian shadow beyond.

"Hello?" My whispered voice echoed beyond. I braved a step out. *I could run now.* " Simion?"

Dark silence responded. The glow of the candles within my room hardly penetrated the shadow of the hall-way. I squinted, trying to make sense of the shapes that seemed to move.

The seats were empty. The maids had left for the night.

Everything about it told me I should be alone. But my gut buzzed with something more. A knowing feeling that tickled my skin and sent the hairs on the back of my neck on end.

"Beatrice?" I called again, this time for the being that stalked me.

"Julian, I cannot tell if it is the darkness that makes you look different or the long time between my last visit." A deep voice greeted me. I snapped my head toward it and watched a boy—a young man, detach from the wall. He walked into the light of a burning red candle. "And your eyes…"

I stuttered a response, stepping back to my door as Camron stalked forward.

His hair was a summer flame. Not a single strand out of place.

"What are you doing here?" I croaked, voice shaking slightly from the unexpected surprise.

"You seem frightened?" Camron hushed.

He ran a finger over the coarse hairs that shadowed his sculpted face. A light beard that fit perfectly in the hollows of his cheeks. One brow is raised in interest as he studied me up close.

"Surprised at your unexpected visit is all." I swallowed, the lump in my throat bobbing. But I held his stare, unwavering now.

"I must say, I am surprised to find your door locked. It took little for me to obtain the key from the maids, although the custom is for me not to see you the night before."

"Night before what?"

His eyes narrowed, racing across my face.

"Mother was right. You truly look different than before."

Suddenly conscious under his stare, I turned to leave. My hand gripped the door. But he stopped me. His strength was unwavering as he put his foot in my way to hold the door ajar.

"It is late." I forced command in my tone. "I should be in bed, not here. Speaking with someone I do not know."

He grinned at this. Deep, warm eyes alight with something knowing.

"So, you admit that we do not know each other? That you have not seen me before?"

I wanted to hit my head against the very door he held open.

Close to the glow of the many candles that burned in my room, I saw more of him. Unlike the meal, he was no longer dressed in finery and riches. Before me now he looked, disheveled.

The white tunic was unbuttoned, revealing curly hairs across his chest. I first thought his trousers are black, but I soon see I was wrong. They were a dark blue, made from velvet, giving them a darker impression. Blue. Calzmir blue.

"Not once have I known you to be so … quiet. This is the first time you have ever been lost for words with me and I must admit I prefer it."

I let my shocked expression melt from my face, making way for one I had seen on Julian many times. Boredom.

"I didn't expect to see you…" I muttered through a forced yawn. "It is late. You should leave."

"No," he said, some far-off sadness in his gaze which was lost for a moment. "Tell me why they lock you away, Julian?"

"For my safety," I lied.

"And yet your guards are tired, untrained maids? I see that they will do nothing to protect you once the North comes to take you. There are rumors of it, you know."

I tensed my hand, mage-marked palm warming at his comments. "I can look after myself, Camron. I am a mage —I do not need maids as protection."

Camron tilted his head like a puppy, hand raising for his chin and running a large finger across it. "A mage without a wand. Helpless from what I can remember from the stories we have all come to know."

"I—" My gut tugged. Words failed me as I was too slow to conjure another lie.

"Your *father* is adamant your new magic has caused

some dramatic changes in you. That is why he keeps the wand from you."

He leaned forward, bringing with him the fresh scent of sea-salt once again. And now something more. I wrinkled my nose at the scent of spirits that infiltrated me with a sting to the eyes.

"You are drunk," I told him, now noticing the slight detachment in his stare.

"Nothing gets past you, does it."

My cheeks warmed.

"It has been a pleasure." I tried to close the door on him, tugging at the door and taking benefit in his sudden wobble. Camron fumbled, his movements slow and awkward.

"I can see through the illusions of this place, mage. Your master forgets that it was not the dryad's gift to create such falsities. I have experienced enough to see through it."

Nymph, the water spirit. Sisters to the long-lost dryads were said to create physical illusions. Changing appearances and blessing visions that drove men mad.

"Camron," I said, ignoring his hand, pretending I knew his name all along. "If my... father has already warned you of the changes my magic has had on me, I trust that you know to leave me now. I have stayed out long enough."

"Whatever has changed in you... I prefer it. The past two years have been kind to you... *Julian*."

His dark eyes trailed every inch of me as he said the name.

Camron grinned, straight teeth flashing. I blushed. *He is handsome.* Devilishly. In his loose shirt and dark beard, he looked like a pirate. And behaved like one as he swayed where he stood.

"Good night," I said, backing away from him.

"Before you go," Camron said, finally letting go of the door. "Are you going to leave me without telling me your name?"

Ice gripped a hold of me.

I shook my head at him, unable to look into his sharp eyes.

"You know my name for you have used it one too many times already. Now, Good nig—"

"Come on now. Julian *was* an ugly, mean-hearted boy. I know Master Gathrax expects us to believe it, but I have stared into that boy's eyes many times and all I saw was deceit and mischief. Do not get me wrong, I see mischief in you as well, but it's not the kind that is threatening and vile."

I stilled as his finger grazed beneath my chin. His touch was gentle. And warm. Very warm. I did not pull away. Not as a shiver raced from the place of his touch, spreading across my entire body.

"My name is Julian," I lied. For the sake of my parents. This could be a test. He could've been sent here by Master Gathrax to look for a missing piece to my new self.

"They can make you look like him on the outside, but I can see through the shell of this mask." Camron's eyes widened. "I apologize if I have intruded too far."

I stepped back from him, his hand dropping from my chin. "Did you consider that your little appearing act might have startled me? I don't know what you are used to in your estate, but in mine, we don't sneak up on others unannounced."

My comment caught him off guard. "Incredible. You almost have me convinced. For the first time, you sounded like him. Like Julian. But your eyes… they are nothing like his was. They are portals of truth. Even if the rest of you is changed. Shaped into what they want it to be, your eyes tell a different story."

"You are drunk. Please leave me."

I expected him to refuse, but he does not. Instead, Camron bowed slowly, a wobble threatening him to topple over on the spot.

"If you are adamant to keep up this illusion then you will have no problem answering my parting question."

He wanted to catch me out. I conjured Xander's voice in my mind. Ready to race through the pockets of information he had told me about the relationship between the Gathrax and Calzmir estates.

But his question was personal.

"What did I present you with when I left you after my previous visit?"

A smirk lifted his lips.

I stood there in silence. There was no point in lying again. I closed the door in his face and he did not stop me. His low chuckle sounded beyond the room, slowly fading as he walked away.

I unravelled with a breath, a shaking sigh at the interaction that had caused this mask of Julian to crumble in my very grasp.

He knows.

I slumped to the ground, back pressed to the door. My parents on my mind.

Camron would tell Master Gathrax. Would ruin this all.

And it would be them that suffered the price.

I sat like that for a while before crawling into the warmth of the bed. When I closed my eyes, I finally realized something from our encounter.

I had not heard the door lock when Camron left.

He had not locked me away.

16

Camron was right. The next morning I studied my reflection in a mirror. Splotches of brown stood out proud against the false blond color. Part of me wanted to laugh. My bright, forest-green eyes shone with defiance. There was no hiding my true self. I wondered all night and morning if Camron had told Master Gathrax of our meeting in the dark corridor. But there were no bloodied gifts waiting for me. The morning was void of threats. So far at least.

"Maximus."

I spun to see Beatrice, perched on the windowsill once again. Morning light haloed around her as she crouched on the window ledge.

My heart leaped in my throat. "You came back."

"I did and we must leave now," she said with urgency.

"You got my parents?"

Her gaze did not falter from mine, but she kept her lips straight.

"No. But I can explain. We must go."

I held my ground. "I told you I will not leave without

them."

"You have no choice, Max."

"I do!" I slammed my foot, shouting at the girl who watched on. "You have disappeared for days and now come demanding I leave with you? What do you want from me… to jump from the window and run off into the distance?"

Her cheeks blossomed with heat. The face of my friend twisted into a scowl. "I do not have time for this shit, Max." She jumped from the ledge, landing soundlessly upon her feet.

"Is sneaking into rooms another talent you have from the North… mage?"

"Yes." A hint of pride turned the corner of her lip upward. "A skill you would have known if your *parents* had not taken you from us."

She reached me in a few strides of her long legs. Dressed in form-fitting clothes, the dark-green material hugged her frame. Her grip took a hold of my upper arm and squeezed. "Now."

I resisted, skin screaming as I tugged back at her. "Get off me, Bea, let go."

My cheeks burned hot. Anger stormed through my being. As if I had slapped her, Beatrice stumbled back a step. Mouth agape.

Then she moved, throwing the cloak from her side to reveal the strappings that hugged her chest and stomach. A harness of sorts. One that held a once hidden staff upon her back.

With a large sweep of her hand, she held it before me. Her eyes glowed from within. The staff she held was wooden. No different than a walking stick. Narrow and long, with a knot of wood at the top which she held inches before my chest.

"I will not hesitate to take you with force. Do not make me do this." There was a plea in her eyes as she stared me down, the tip of the staff inches from my chest.

I shouted now, not caring about who heard behind the still unlocked door. "You are just like them. Telling me what to do. Threatening me."

An inferno of days of pent-up anger stormed inside of me. Like the beat of a second heart, it pulsed deep within. My palm spasmed in response to its call.

Her breathing deepened as she studied me. Although Beatrice kept still, I felt the outline of her frame shiver with anticipation. I held her stare, noticing her eyes which seemed to glitter with untamed, raw power.

Magic. I could smell it. Awash in the air as it filled the room. It reminded me of autumn mornings when the northern winds cascaded over the wood with hints of damp soil and sweet maple.

"Something has happened." The staff dipped slightly. "Your parents have been taken from here."

My shoulders rose at her remark. "What do you mean taken?"

The staff lowered another inch. Then I noticed the deep, dark circles that shadowed her eyes. The way her skin was lacking in its usual tone. Her posture slumped and tired.

"I have been trailing them. Planning to get them out... for you. But last night they were taken from their holdings and moved."

"Where? Where are they going?"

She shook her head, sharp cut fringe falling over her eyes for a moment. "I do not know. Simion is trailing them south-west from here. Max, he will try to get them back. But for now, we have to get you far from here. Before—"

Beatrice stopped dead. Her eyes shot to the door

behind me. Within a blink, she was moving closer to me. Her finger pressed into my lips.

"Something is happening in the estate. And it involves you. Today. I do not know what they have planned but I can guess."

I wanted to question it more. But voices grew louder as they approached the room.

In a gust of wind, she was gone. Skirting into the bathing room. The dark cloak barely escaping into the unseen before the door was thrown open.

As I looked upon Master Gathrax I felt nothing but hate. It burned in my chest. Gripped a hold of my throat and squeezed, keeping me breathless.

What have you done with my parents? My thoughts were a storm.

"What a day this will be, my son. A wonderful day." He gestured for the window and the world beyond. "Beautiful skies. Perfect for such a day."

I was frozen as he enveloped me in a stiff, cold hug. My hands hung awkwardly beside me. Fists clenched. Then he held me at arm's reach. "Today is only the beginning. A shift in the tide."

The wand was in the holder at his wrist. It peeked out the sleeve of his red lapeled coat. One swipe and it would be mine. I could take it.

"We have much to prepare. You need to be bathed. Dressed and ready."

I tried to steady my voice. "For what?"

He tapped my nose. One swift hit as he called for an army of maids to enter. I almost yelled out as a group of them walked for the bathing chamber. Expecting them to cry out as they found the concealed girl within.

But nothing.

"It will be clear to you soon. But now we must prepare you."

"I want to see *them*."

Master Gathrax rolled his eyes, grip tightening on my shoulders. "After today it will not be me who you must put this request to. They are safe, as I promised you, but no longer under my control. You can ask Camron Calzmir further on this when you see him."

Words failed me.

Camron had them.

I ran through our conversation last night, looking for a sign or a hint that he had this planned all along. But I resurfaced, empty-handed.

"Listen to me, my boy. Today will be historic. A moment which will be sung about for years. I have great plans for you. Strategies that will keep us on top of the South and its resources. With the help of a few, expendable parts along the way. I will need one thing from you today. A favor in return for your parents' guaranteed safety. Show them your power. Show them the mage."

I searched his face, looking for any sign that he lied. But there was no flick of his gaze. No dripping of sweat from his thinned hairline or a shudder in his hands.

He told the truth.

"What do you say, mage, will you do this for me? Display your power to our audience and show them why the Gathrax family will once again be restored to our rightful place?"

"I will," I vowed. "You will all finally see the power of the mage you all seek so desperately."

Master Gathrax eyes glowed, deviously, and he grinned manically. "Make me proud."

I cut a smile back. "I shall."

I did not see Beatrice as the maids fussed over me. But I felt her. Her presence close. Watching. For a moment I wondered if she had heard what Master Gathrax had said about my parents. Perhaps she'd relay the message to her brother.

But they would be hours ahead now.

I had to find Camron. To admit what he already knew about me. It was time to plead for their safety from yet another master.

This time one washed in blue, not red.

Hands fumbled across me, pulling at the shirt they had given me, buttoning up the red jacket that was adorned with intricate ribbons of gold thread. They slicked my hair back from my face. Wrapped me in fine materials and fabrics that screamed wealth and power. The clothes gave me extra height. An aura of the boy they tried so desperately to turn me into.

At some point, Silas had snuck into the room unannounced. His creepy tongue wet his lips as he slouched in the corner of the room and watched as they worked on me.

Only when the atmosphere changed did I notice him. The women and young men darting away from him. Heads always down. But their eyes surely brimmed with fear at the man and his unpredictable hands.

Silas did not stop reaching for me. His trill laugh made me sick as he played his game.

"Keep your hands to yourself, Silas," I warned, speaking to him through my reflection in the gilded mirror.

"Someone has found their voice. And in perfect timing."

I glowered at him, lips lifting above my teeth. "Silas,

you have been a good teacher to me over these days. Truly. Giving me all the information about being a mage, I had needed to know."

"Is that so?" He pushed from the wall, folding his lanky arms over his chest.

"Indeed." I nod my head with a smile. "But I think it is time for me to teach you a lesson in return."

He took a step toward me as I waved off the young girl who fussed over the collars of my jacket.

"Let me remind you, Silas, of your place. You are nothing more than a master of mice. And I am the mage."

The group of maids silenced. I sensed their trepidation as if it thickened the air of the room.

"Do not forget who you talk to… boy," he hissed, yellowed teeth bared. "One word to Master Gathrax and you know whose wrists will bear the punishment."

There. He stepped into my trap.

I strolled toward him. Shoulders rolled back. Although I wanted to cringe away from the rotten smell that seeped between his lips, I did not, summoning everything in myself to hold my authority around those who watched on.

"But they have left here, haven't they?" I whispered.

Silas paled. All the confirmation I needed for the truth.

They were out of their grasp, which meant their leverage over me was gone.

A spark of hope mingled with the pull of the strange power that had built within my stomach over the few past days. Simion would get to them. He had to.

So I would leave. I had it decided in my mind. With Beatrice, I would help retrieve my parents and put miles between me and the Gathrax family.

But not yet. No.

They wanted to see the mage. So they would.

EVERY SET OF EYES TRAILED ME AS I ENTERED THE ANCIENT chamber. Every head had turned my way and followed my movements as I walked up the narrow pathway that split the room in two.

"Stand for the mage."

Only the rustling sound of bodies shifting and wooden pews being pushed across the ground sounded in response.

Whereas the audience watched my every move, I kept my eyes on Master Gathrax where he stood at the head of the chamber, on a raised stone platform.

Silas had left me at the door, urging me to walk ahead alone. "Go to him."

As I moved toward the waiting Master Gathrax I studied the room. A chamber of sorts. From the lined pews and tall ceilings, this was a place of worship. A room in which the memory of the Mage lived on. No wonder I had not seen it before. Until now it had been locked, closed off.

It was a large room, with ceilings so high it was almost impossible to see the roof. Pillars of stone stood guard on either side of the chamber, leveling off into arched beams draped with red cloth. The same red cloth was made into a long section that split the chamber in two. It started at the great doors and pooled off at the bottom of curved steps that lead up to a higher stadium.

On either side of the red-carpet walkway, clusters of the leading estates stood together. Faces and names I had studied with Xander. Uniforms in all the colors. To the left, I saw the bright whites of Master Zendina and his group of followers. Beside them was a sea of depressing gray suits and dresses of the Makan Estate, led by the youthful Mistress Makan. The youngest of the leaders, her beauty untouched.

To the right of the chamber, the Calzmir Estate stood solitary. My gaze found his. Camron. His beauty snatched at my breath. But there was sorrow in his detached gaze. It pulled down at his furrowed brows and kept his lips straight. The woman beside him did not share the same emotion. Silver jewels pulled down at her ears, a choker of gold strapped proudly around her neck stood out against the azure gown she wore. For the glint of a ruby sat there.

Red in a sea of blue. Two colors that, my lessons had taught me, never were put together.

Union. The words rang out in my mind.

Her glaring grin matched that of Master Gathrax who had raised a hand for me.

I took the steps up to the stage where Master Gathrax greeted me. Until he opened his mouth to speak the entire chamber was silent with anticipation.

"Welcome, my son." His voice boomed, echoing across the chamber. Even the flames of candles seemed to flicker as he spoke. He looked up from me and back to the waiting crowd.

"I want to extend my thanks to all of you for jour-neying such a way to visit us. Master Zendina, I understand you have been on the road for days, even missing your own celebrations and feasts just to see us."

I caught the blush of Master Zendina at the back of the crowd. He bowed his head, a sheet of black hair falling over his face. But he never looked away. The whites of his eyes visible through the strands of his hair as he tipped his head. But never dropped his gaze from me.

I knew little of the Zendina estate. What I did know was they were the farthest south. Nestled by the edge of the world. It was the smallest estate out of the four and relied on trade to survive. Unlike the Gathrax Estate they had no money, wealth, and little power. Yet their estate was most populated. Master Zendina was a small, round man. His long beard ended at his bulging waist and was flecked with gray and white.

"…you each have come to see the spectacle of a miracle. The return of the mage. I knew the moment word of his magic reached your borders you would be keen to see it with your own eyes. I do not blame you for housing such intrigue for it is a sight to behold. It has been many years since we last saw such a display."

Someone shouted out from the crowd.

Mistress Makan stepped forward as her people parted for her, dressed in a long, slim gown of alabaster that trailed behind her, gathering dust from the floor. Her straight raven hair flowed down her back, matching the intensity of her eyes. "I must admit I find it hard to believe that each member of this audience remembers the fall of the mages of Aldian. The winds still carry the burning tang when the Heart Oak was destroyed. Yet somehow fate smiled upon your family kindly. How did your son, Julian, come to find a wand? That is the part of the story the messenger bird seemed to miss out."

Out of the corner of my eye, I caught Master Gathrax

moving forward. He tipped his head to Mistress Makan before replying. "The years have been kind to you, Stephine."

"Drop the falsities. I have no time for your compliments," Mistress Makan replied. For someone so young she glowed with intensity.

I fought the smile as Master Gathrax's expression hardened at her comment.

"I would appreciate it if we skipped the conversation and got to the part we are all here for. Seeing the magic ourselves. The Gathrax Estate has always yearned for control over the rest of us. For all we know this is a ruse for you to finally retrieve what you so desire."

Bodies dressed in white and some in gray called out in agreement with Mistress Makan.

"Let me assure you, Stephine, I do not desire to take sole control of the South. That is not, nor will it, be the first action my son takes as mage."

Lie. I tasted it across my tongue.

Mistress Makan moved onto the red carpet which muffled the click of her heels. She walked up, taking two steps up toward the stage, then turned to face the watching crowd. Her straight back to Master Gathrax and I.

"I see the boy you call a mage, I hear the rumors like tweets of birds. But I do not see his wand, nor sense his power." Over her shoulder, she threw her stark-sky blue gaze at me. "Show us, then we will listen."

The crowd whispered in agreement. The tugging in my gut panged at her calling.

"All good things come to those who wait." Master Gathrax voice carried around the room, stilling the conversations. He ran his tongue over his teeth as he extended a hand for Mistress Calzmir who had stayed silent on her side of the chamber. "We first have a special celebration that must occur first."

"What is more important than proving your son is the mage you say he is?" Mistress Makan's voice raised in pitch.

"A handfasting ceremony."

I turned to face Master Gathrax. My lungs failed to take in a breath. Mistress Calzmir stepped forward, hand in Master Gathrax's with a devilish grin across her stunning features. *Impossible*. He was already wed to Mistress Gathrax, this was not possible. I scanned the crowd for her. But she was unseen.

"It has been years since our family has witnessed, let alone taken part in, a handfasting. I have decided it was time that was rectified. Myself and Mistress Calzmir of her estate have news to bring to you all. I am elated to share this day with you all, Mistress and Master alike. Please, Stephine, take a seat with the crowd so this can begin."

"Never has an estate married, joining in such strong bonds." Mistress Makan looked as shocked and angry as the crowd below her. Master Gathrax's smile did not waver. "It is against belief to marry when already handfasted to another."

"Blasphemy," someone shouted.

"Oh, Stephine, do hush. It is not I that shall be taking part in the handfasting. I respect belief as much as the rest of you do. It is my son, Julian, who will be taking part."

My wide eyes scanned over the woman in blue before me.

"No…" The word escaped my control and silenced the room. I no longer saw anyone or heard a word. As I rested my surprised gaze upon Master Gathrax he only smiled.

"It has been agreed that Julian will handfast with the

Calzmir Estate, creating a new, stronger alliance out of the existing two."

My ears rang as if bells themselves hid within them.

Mistress Calzmir spoke up for the first time. "My son, Camron Calzmir, has agreed to take Julian's hand. Forever joining the two estates and creating a new, harmonious one."

Camron. He stood now. All sadness void from his face —making room for a new, strange emotion that tugged at his warm eyes.

"…as I informed you, Mistress Makan, it is not I who will be taking control of the South, but a new house."

The room was alight with moving bodies. Shouting, angered cries as the truth settled across them all.

This was his play. The move on the board for more control. The doors slammed shut amidst the shouting and armed Gathrax guards stood watch. The two remaining families scattered, and it was then I noticed they were all unarmed. Not a single weapon draped from their belts. No. This was a place of worship. They each followed the rules of the chamber and left their weapons beyond its walls. Yet Master Gathrax did not follow his own rules as his guards entered. Herding the crowd by the point of swords as if they were no more than sheep.

Camron moved, untouched, up toward the stage. He walked straight to me among the panic of the chamber and wrapped his arms around my shocked body. I expected him to be rough, but I was wrong. His arms hovered inches from me, not once touching me but making it seem like he had to anyone watching.

"Play along, this is not ideal. Listen to me and I *can* keep you safe."

His whisper warmed me. His voice was not full of command, but something else. Was it sympathy?

He pulled back and greeted his mother, ignoring the crowd as the armed guards silenced them.

"Now now, dear friends. Do not fight and fret. This is a happy occasion. A new chance for the South to reclaim the power we once had. With the return of the mage and the joining of these estates, we will create a new estate, undivided by borders and names," Master Gathrax called to the frightened crowd.

"It sounds wonderful, doesn't it." Mistress Calzmir clapped, her son now stood beside her.

"Silas," Master Gathrax called, and his minion followed. He sulked up the steps. "The cords, if you will…"

From the depths of his oversized pockets, he revealed two roped cords. One was red, the other blue. Handfasting ties.

My body moved against my frozen mind. I began taking steps away from them until Master Gathrax noticed and whispered something to Silas who grabbed me and pulled me up.

"Now, son, be still. Comply."

I stared at Master Gathrax, hoping my hate could burn him where he stood. "I will not do this."

"You have no choice." He pulled me from Silas's warm, sickly grasp and stood me before Camron.

No longer facing the crowd, I could not see their infuriated expressions.

"Shall we begin?" Master Gathrax's voice rained down on us.

I gagged as dread overwhelmed me. Mistress Makan and her followers pulled away from the guards that kept them in place. I heard her call about the commotion to stop this. Her worried gaze locked on mine.

Camron took my frozen hand in his. I looked down,

suddenly grounded by his touch. My hand was small compared to his, nestled within his smooth palm, his fingers knotted to keep hold of me. He did not let go. Not until Master Gathrax stepped forward, blue and red cords in hand, and begun weaving like around my extended arm first. He spun the cords like a spider weaving silk.

The handfasting began.

CAMRON'S STARE WAS UNWAVERING AS MASTER GATHRAX instructed him to take over. His touch was gentle, fingers dusting across my skin like no more than a fleck of snow as he kept wrapping the blue cords around my forearm. But his warmth—even the minimal touch could not discern the fire that spread through me.

Camron's lack of shock told me everything I needed to know. He had known. Perhaps last night when alcohol riddled through him. Even the dinner began to take shape in my mind.

A celebration before a celebration.

Except this was nothing of the sort.

Camron's touch once again brought me back into the moment. He took my arms, lifting them until his hand clasped my forearm and my scarred palm pressed against him. We were linked. United by flesh and cord as Master Gathrax begun weaving them around both of us.

I studied him, my hands feeling the slight difference of his skin. Then I saw what caused my fingers to fumble over his rough touch.

Scars twisted across his arms, leaving no skin untouched. Burn marks—old but still raw. I did not flinch from him. Did not let go of my hold. And he noticed, his forever inquisitive stare only intensified as his eyes widened and brows furrowed.

These marks could mean only one thing. Camron had suffered from the plague of flames. It made sense as I held on tighter. His warmth—a fever that would never break. And the skin marked from the fire that had ravaged inside of him, destroying him from the inside out. However, he stood before me.

Alive. Unlike his father.

Then the scars began to be covered by the cords that Master Gathrax began to weave. Over and over, he spun us into his web. Blue and red overlapping in a knot of tight rope.

I had only heard of handfasting ceremonies through the stories Mum would read from the books in the library. In hushed whispers, she told me once of her handfasting to my father. Two years after I was born into the world. In the belly of the Wood of Galloway they had snuck off and tied the knot.

With only the trees as their witness. Long forgotten spirits of the dryads watching as they joined with each other—forever.

I had fantasized about my handfasting since I had heard of the wonder that followed the ceremony. In those quiet moments before sleep took hold, I had often dreamed of the love I would find. In what shape the man would come to me in. The man I would imagine was fully formed. All besides the features of his face. I suppose, as I look up at Camron, he would have been a perfect fit. He was handsome, so much so it snatched my breath. His eyes were kind, and hands soft.

But this was not my choice.

Camron's fingers drummed across my arm as Master Gathrax talked across the crowd once again. The cords tight around us both.

I looked over those who watched in my shared horror. The pinched face of Mistress Makan and her people. The subdued Zendina Estate who no longer caused a ruckus as the guards rallied around them. Perhaps they had worked out what I had.

It was too late to stop this.

The book Master Gathrax read from was old and worn. The leather bindings almost fell apart in his very hands. The words he spoke did not make sense to me as my mind stormed. I could not grasp the meaning behind his words.

He spoke of harmony and love. Of caring for one another until our bodies would simply cease to exist. A union for a lifetime and more.

By the third page, the entire audience was silent. No more shouting and commotion filled the room. Only the ever watching quiet as they witnessed a moment in history.

A sniffle sounded from where Amilia Calzmir stood behind me. I did not have to turn to know a tear was rolling down her hollowed cheek.

There was nothing in me left to shed. No tear lucky enough to escape down my face.

Although tied together, Camron did not once release his hold on my forearm. His placid face was unreadable.

"...and, before the many witnesses, I pronounce you both fasted together through health and life until death claims you when *she* is ready."

No one clapped. That was what was supposed to happen after a handfasting, was it not? Clapping and tears, smiles and shouts of pure joy. Not here. Not now.

"We will not follow you," Mistress Makan spluttered, face paled. Her body seemed to quake with explosive anger, mirroring the members of her estate. "After all of these years, the snake has finally struck for his bite at control. If you believe my estate will follow along with this disturbed idealism, then let me remind you just how wrong you are. Since the fall of the mages, we have lived and ruled separately, that will not change now."

In my mind, I longed for Mistress Makan's support. A statue of unwavering strength, she had more power in her words than even Master Gathrax. I pleaded silently to her to carry on her fight against him.

Not once did she look my way.

"What a speech." Master Gathrax chortled. "I do love one after a handfasting. Although it is usually left for the family. The guests are to be complicit and watch with a smile."

Mistress Makan glowed with determination. Taking yet another step closer to the dais, she challenged Master Gathrax. "Pray tell, how do you expect to force an entire estate to follow you? My people are loyal to the Makan family. Your family name only fills their mouths with the taste of spoiled dirt."

Master Gathrax raised a hand for Mistress Calzmir. "It will not be my family's name that you and your people will claim loyalty to." Master Gathrax's gaze snapped to Master Zendina who practically cowered in the shadows of the room. "Silence becomes you, Master Zendina."

"Wolves always prey on the weak." Mistress Makan placed her body in the middle of Master Gathrax's line of sight, blocking Master Zendina from view. Much younger than him, she stood her ground.

"Now, Stephine, act like a lady for once." He smirked, snapping the book closed in his hand.

She glowered at him as she titled her head, lips snarling and teeth flashing. "I can show you exactly how a *lady* acts in my estate, Jonathan. Why not come down here and see for yourself."

"Now, Stephine, really, you have embarrassed yourself long enough."

"Amilia, you of all people would have been the last to join with this estate. Your ancestors would be ashamed."

Mistress Calzmir battered Stephine's comment away with a swift hand. "The Makan estate has never had the right to speak about my family. You do not have the esteem to do so."

"Bitch," Stephine hissed, hands flexing at her sides to reveal the sharp nails that awaited.

Amilia's cackle slapped back at the furious Stephine, only angering her further.

"My people will not follow this foolish plan. They will not follow *you*."

"Oh, but they will," Master Gathrax chimed in.

"Indeed." Amilia grinned at him in agreement. "You see, Master Gathrax here came to me yesterday evening with the proposition and I must say I was *very* pleased with his suggestions. Of course, when talking about taking control, I had the same question as you, Stephine. How will we make the other families south of the wood follow *us*? What will stop them from revolting? Yes, your soldiers may not be as trained and well-armed as ours, but combine your population and a coup would be easy to orchestrate. Believe I do not doubt it."

"Get to your point, *crow*."

Amilia ignored the insult slapped at her. "My estate has provided loans to each of you. I am correct in thinking... without my estate, none of you would have one. Each of you..." She began pointing her finger at the cluster of families in the room, her nail sharp. "are in my debt. For years we have given you money to keep your estates afloat. If I stopped those funds, you would just, well, fail to thrive. Your people will overthrow you if they get a taste of weakness from their ruling estate. Then they would come willingly to us."

Master Gathrax beamed during the entire speech. I watched him study every reaction in the room as Mistress Calzmir began calling out the truth.

Still, Camron held on, his touch warm and calming.

"So you see, you will *comply* because if you do not we shall watch from the borders as your estates crumble. Then we will just sweep in and take you out when you are down. You can listen, keep your positions of power whilst reporting to the new ruling house, or you do not. And you can guess how that will end for you."

The chamber was bathed in silence.

"Master Gathrax, Mistress Calzmir." Master Zendina stepped through the crowd, his frail body pushing past the now silenced Stephine. "Let m..me assure you my estate will b…bow to you. We trust in our alliance and would no…not throw it away for pride."

"You are a smart man, Master Zendina."

"Pathetic man, as you all are," Mistress Makan said with conviction.

"You will not be following beneath the Gathrax or Calzmir name." Master Gathrax reached for the cords and tugged, letting them slip from mine and Camron's arms. Even after we no longer were tied together Camron kept a hold of me.

"For it will be a new estate. Stronger. That will rise from our ashes and rule anew."

Camron trailed his fingers down my forearm and laced them around my waiting fingers. He squeezed and blinked.

He wanted to say something, his lips shivered, parted. My husband, by law and truth.

Camron spoke to me aloud. But his words were meant for the room.

"Oakan." The freckles around his lips flexed. "That is our name of choice."

"Oakan, Estate Oakan will become the new capital in the South. We will begin tearing down the borders, spreading the family color across the land from shore to wood, town to city. Everyone south of the wood will know of our house and welcome a new era of the mage," Master Gathrax explained. "Now let my son, *Julian* Oakan, show you the power you so dearly wish to see."

I did not recognize the name at first. Both parts a lie. I was not Julian, and only by law was I Oakan.

Master Gathrax leaned into my ear and whispered, "Show them your power, make your *parents* proud."

"Step back from him." Camron's sharp tone split the room.

Master Gathrax rocked back slightly, turning slowly to Camron who towered above him. "Watch how you speak to me."

"Remind me, Jonathan, how is one supposed to address their master?" Like a puppy, Camron titled his head slightly. His expression one of calm. "Is it not I that is now master, as you have proclaimed it before these good people?"

Reluctantly, Master Gathrax turned to him, his face as red as his shirt. Even Mistress Calzmir's expression was one of bewilderment.

This was not part of the act.

"My partner's wand," Camron commanded, hand outstretched. He stood tall, almost an inch larger than Master Gathrax.

"Fu—"

"Now!" A deranged laugh burst beyond my lips as Camron struck forward, grasping hold of Master Gathrax's arm and exposing the wand holder beneath his long sleeve. From shock or confusion, I was unsure.

Master Gathrax tried to pull back, but his attempt was futile. Camron was stronger both in body and mind.

With one hand Camron pulled my wand from Master Gathrax. Shivers coursed down the back of my neck, that ever-present tugging stabbing within.

The crowd erupted in breathless gasps at the sight of it. It had been many years since they last saw one.

"You—"

One large shove and Master Gathrax was on his knees, fumbling to stand as Camron loomed over him.

"Guards take this man. He threatens your new leader," Camron called, his voice steady. Now holding the wand for all to see, as if it kept the crowd enthralled in commanding manner. Instantly, almost rehearsed, the two Gathrax guards in red stood forward and seized their original leader, holding Master Gathrax's arms behind him and dragging him to stand.

He thrashed in their hold. Face wild with panic as his people turned on him with ease.

Then the wand was extended to me. An offering from the man I had been forced to unite with.

Finally, it sang within me. *Maximus*.

19

Master Gathrax's knees cracked as they collided with the ground. His face was flushed with panic, the guards not breaking a sweat as they held the feeble man down.

"Let go of me." Spit foamed at the corners of his white lips.

Their only response was an elbow to his jaw.

At some point, Amilia Calzmir tumbled into the arms of other guards. These with the ribbon of blue above their hearts. Her cry shrieked across the chamber at the betrayal of her son.

"Camron, enough of his!" his mother hissed, the slip of her dress falling over her sharp shoulder. "You stupid boy."

Camron had turned his back to them both, his focus on me entirely.

"Take it, it is yours."

Still, he held the wand for me. I had not moved an inch at the change of events. How it had all happened so suddenly.

Camron took my hand, holding my fingers around the hilt of the wand.

A breath of power shattered through me. Energy unlike any I had experienced in days sang through my veins. My bones shivered at the touch of wood to my scarred palm. Gone was the tugging in my gut as the wand was reunited with me.

Camron held on, his hand wrapped around mine. "I promised you could trust me."

"Why…" I managed, my blood alive and buzzing with raw energy.

The corners of his lips lifted, his smile reaching his warm gaze. "No one should ever be kept from who they are. Who you truly are… Maximus."

My name. It rang out between us.

And the tension melted. The illusion of Julian slipped away between my very fingers.

"I cannot say I am wonderfully surprised with this show," Mistress Makan called out. Only a beat later did Camron drop my gaze and let go of my hand. "…but what do you say about all of this?"

He cleared his throat and addressed the crowd. "As the leader of the Oaken Estate, my first command will eradicate possible threats from those within it. Unlike Jonathan Gathrax and my dear mother, I do not have hidden agendas. I have watched, as you have, the unfair treatment of our people. You will not be forced by my hand to follow. I will allow you to join *us* willingly."

My entire focus is transfixed on my wand now. I memorized the twisted design, the slight red stain on the wood. The way it fit in my hand perfectly.

"Mage Maximus Oaken… forced to become the false son of the Gathrax Estate. For the benefit of the ruling family. A lie that has been spread to us all. One that my mother thought to use for her own gain."

My name. He said it again. And the crowd listened. I could see it on the tips of their tongues as Camron, the stranger, revealed my truth.

"Strip this illusion you have been forced to uphold and do what you have so long desired. No longer will the man beneath you hold control over you. Return to the boy you once were." Camron spoke to my very soul.

My *real* name was whispered across the room.

With every person who said it, more of myself returned. Mother was right, there was power *in* a name.

Days of hate for Master Gathrax released in a single breath. I did not need to think for my body moved without me, hand lifting until the tip of the wand was inches from the man's face.

He became cross-eyed, transfixed by the weapon in my hand, body trembling violently as a trickle of blood seeped from his nose.

You know what I desire.

I held the wand firm and steady. Not a single shake of my hand. For once I was calm.

"You hurt them," I spoke to the pathetic excuse of a man before me. "Punished them and not me."

He snarled, frantic spit along his lips as he spoke. "I should have done more."

I smiled, shoulders shrugging his words off. "Perhaps you should have. But now it is too late."

When I would look back at this moment, I would see the realization cloud over Master Gathrax's eyes. No, not Master anymore.

Then I called on the pool of magic. The simmering ocean of power that had built over the days I had been separated from the wand. One simple thought, an acknowledgment to the magic, and it was at my command.

I gripped a hold of it in my mind and pulled.

The room shook. Bricks and stone broke, sending clouds of dust to settle across those who watched.

"Send my love to Julian," I whispered above the noise of the chamber as it cracked. Even before my intention caused the death I sought, I heard the scratch of wood as another death mark was added to the base of the wand.

The wild infiltrates the chamber. Roots and vines snaked through the cracks they had created while heeding my urgent call. The crowd shrieked, jumping from the moving, living earth that raced toward the man before me.

But my intention is not for them.

They reached the man beneath the tip of my wand. Coiled around his wiry frame. Constricted the very breath from his body.

His eyes bulged as the earth folded over him. Skin turned red as he fought to scream, giving an opening for my power to reach inside of him.

A finger of a root made use of his cry, filling his mouth and splitting his lips at the seams.

I reached down with the earth, farther and farther until my reach filled his body, searching for his wretched heart.

Then it was over. The final breath of the man was forced from his body.

My magic recoiled back into its hold within me, retreating into the cage it had forged in the pits of my stomach.

He is dead. His body was unable to fall to the slabbed ground as the snake of roots and vines held him entrapped. His bulging, lifeless eyes stared endlessly at me.

A hand rested upon my shoulder. Camron's gentle

voice an anchor to retrieve my focus. "It is over now. You can be free."

His hand found mine and we turned to the motionless figures. Each with horror and awe sliced across their watching faces.

It was Stephine Makan who bowed first, her voice full of authority as she called across the quaking chamber.

"It is *our* honor to follow you. Long live the return of the mage."

II

THE TRAITOROUS CORDS

METAL COLLIDED WITH WOOD AS THE GUARDS HACKED AWAY at the roots that bound the dead master. The steady beat thundered through my bones. Bang. Bang. Bang. Over and over. Blinking heavily from my seat, I could imagine his deathly skin imprinted with thorns and marks from where my power had a hold of him.

I was alone. Sitting in the room that Camron had led me to at the rear of the chamber.

I still felt his touch lingering on my palm even after he had sat me here and dismissed himself to deal with the drama beyond the door. His deep voice sounded above all other noise as he spoke to the crowd.

I drowned in exhaustion, sat slumped in the chair, struggling to focus on anything else. Only his voice. And the wand still gripped in my hand. I turned the wood over in my palm, studying the two notches that had carved themselves into it. Death marks. One for Julian and the other for his father.

The coiling of magic was more apparent now. A single thought and I knew I could reach into the reserve and call upon it. Holding onto the wand, my mind was clear as morning oceans.

My eyes then moved from the wand, past the mage mark on my palm, and to the new markings that had snaked around my wrist. Black lines that connected completely. Stained over my skin, matching the bracelet of black that would also loop around the man beyond this room.

Camron. A gift from the handfasting.

My heart sank. The tattooing cold to the touch. Permanent, no matter how hard I rubbed at it. A band of obsidian, thick and without frills.

I sat like this for a millennium. Staring endlessly at the truth that was gripped in my scarred palm, and the markings that connected me to a stranger.

Until death do you part.

"Maximus." I looked up at the sound of my name. Camron stood in the doorway, large hand gripped around the frame for support. The same black markings were visible as his long shirt tugged back from his wrist. "It is done."

His face was flushed. Even in the lightless room, the red of his cheeks caused his freckles to stand out. In the dark, his orange flame hair was out of place. No longer smoothed back from his face, strands hanged over his forehead.

There was silence behind him. A glance over his shoulder and I could see the chambers now empty of the crowd. Only the destruction of my magic was left in their wake.

His feet rustled over the dusted floor of the room. Then he was on his knees before me. "Your family will be on their way back here the moment my message reaches my people back *home*."

I did not have to ask about them. He must have sensed my question on the tip of my tongue.

"I need them with me." I choked on the words, hands beginning to shake.

When I saw them would they be in the same state as the last time. Thinner? Weaker?

"I understand." Camron reached a hand for mine, hesitating slightly when our skin touched. "And they will in no more than two days."

"Are they… safe?"

Camron nodded slightly, not once dropping my stare. "Maximus, I assure you they are and will be fine. I will not hide from you the state they both were in when Jonathan first gave them to *Amilia*. Your mother needed to be healed. Her hand was in a bad state. Your father was not the strong man I am sure he once was. I promise you they are being seen to."

I pulled my hand from him, noticing how his hand lingered in the air for a moment before he too moved away.

"Why are you doing this?" The chair clattered to the ground as I stood. My body vibrated with distrust. "Two days ago I had no idea who you were and now this. I have learned a lot about trust and your words will simply not do. No, I want my parents here. I want them now."

"Maximus, I think you need a moment to calm down."

The magic was close to my touch now. It danced within my blood as I paced the empty room. "You have no idea what you *think* I need."

"You are right, I do not. But I am trying to do the best I can."

Whereas I raged across the room like a storm, Camron was steady and calm. Not once raising his voice or sharpening his demeanor.

I pointed the wand at him, his expression barely changing as I glared down the wood at him. "I do not trust you."

"I am not asking you to."

"Then what do you want from me?" I lowered the wand. "Everyone has wanted something since this. You can be no different."

Camron was before me, gentle hands holding onto my shoulders. Did he feel the quake of my body beneath his touch?

"Trust is earned, Maximus. Unlike those who have used you I have no intention to control you and you will see that."

He did not answer my question. Instead skirting around it like a dancer across a frozen lake in winter.

"You knew," I whispered, unable to hold his stare this close. "Last night when you saw me, you knew what Master Gathrax had planned today."

Camron paused before responding. His eyes flicked to the floor as he thought over his words. "I did."

"You want me to trust you, yet you have let this happen." I raised my wrist before him. The inked mark visible to us both.

"Maximus, I have told you that I do not want you to trust me. That is earned and we have only just met. Jonathan informed us of his proposition. Telling me and my mother of his son and the magic that had returned. My mother is a selfish woman—always wanting more. And then Jonathan offered it to her. A way of ruling as one. A uniting between his heir and hers. But when I saw you at the meal, I knew he had lied to us. My mother could not see it, but I did."

I studied his face as he spoke, looking for a chip in his mask to reveal his motive. Everyone had one—he had just not revealed his yet. Master Gathrax wanted me to gain power. Camron would want something.

"I had to see you afterward. To confirm what I knew to be true."

"How did you know I was not the true heir of the Gathrax Estate?"

"Truthfully?" He smiled softly, freckles that lined his lips flexing. "My estate has had eyes and ears within this one and others for as long as the end of the War of the Wood. It was Jonathan's fault; he did not pay his staff a fair wage which gave them the incentive to keep silent on matters. I heard of Julian's murder from his own consultant."

"Silas?"

He strolled across the limited space between us. "The one and only. King of Mice. He had been feeding me information for weeks."

"Not your mother?"

Camron pushed the strand of hair from his eyes. "Silas is a sly man, but not stupid. Since the death of my father my mother has been distracted from her focus on the estates. She gave me the responsibility to take in information on our sister estates with the intention of telling her what she needed to know. I just chose what to tell her and what to keep quiet."

"That is what you want. To take over as ruler of your estate."

His deep chuckle washed over me. "My father wished me one thing before he passed. On his death bed, he was able to see his life and realize the way Aldian has been ruled for generations has been wrong. Unjust. He simply wanted me to do it better."

"And now you can complete his wish." I stepped away from him. "And to use me to do it."

"No, Maximus, you are wrong."

I gripped the wand tighter. "Am I?"

"I promise you—"

"You knew the truth and still have let them unite me with you. I had no choice. And now we are linked forever —an unbreakable tie."

Camron glanced down at his wrist. He was silent now. Void of excuses. His silence only urged my anger to boil hotter.

"You think of me as a stupid boy," I shouted, the air vibrating alongside my intensifying emotion. "A hand-fasting is a life-long commitment. It cannot be broken. You, as Master Gathrax planned, have sealed my fate. I am yours, your property. Do you really think that I believe you will not use me as he tried to do? Do you?"

Camron heard the rumble of earth as it clawed its way up to me from the ground far beneath the floor of this room.

"Three years ago I almost died." Camron rolled the sleeve of his shirt up, exposing our handfasting marks and the mottled scars that covered his arm. "Whilst I laid on my bed, struggling for breath and feeling fire eat me from the inside out I prayed to the dryads. To anything that would listen that if given another chance at life I would do it right. I would make a change as my father had promised before the same plague took his life from me."

Camron unravelled his truth like golden silk before me, baring all.

"Like you, Maximus, I only want to do what my guardian asked of me."

As he spoke, I released the grip of the magic. The clambering earth beneath our feet stilled once again.

"How did you get it?" I whispered, wanting nothing

more than to reach out and touch those marks as I had when the cords had been wrapped around our arms.

"I have seen more of this world than I would have liked. Since a young boy, I had wanted to explore the seas and the lands beyond. It had taken years for my father to provide me with the funds needed. And when he did, I thanked him by bringing back his sickness from my travels. You have taken two lives, Maximus, the notches on your wand speak that truth. These are my reminder of a life I took."

"I am sorry…" A cold sadness clung around my gut.

Camron bowed his head and closed his eyes. The silence that hung between us was treacherous. It stretched on. I urged Camron to speak, to fill the awkward quiet that surrounded us.

"It has been a long day. And I fear that those that follow will only be harder. Change is afoot so you will need rest. Will you join me in the morning for breakfast? A fresh start as we face the day ahead."

"I think it best." I stand before him, knowing I should leave but being unable to find the energy to lift a step.

He reached for my hand, lifting the marked wrist to his lips and holding it there. "Until tomorrow, Maximus."

I WAS FREE TO GO AS I PLEASED. MY DOOR NEVER LOCKED. A guard never trailing behind for any reason other than added protection if requested. Not that I needed it. I felt assurance in the magic reserves within me. Although I knew little of the power—until the promised mage scrolls arrived with my parents, I trusted in it.

Camron had, in most, left me alone since the handfasting. Only sending short, handwritten messages every evening updating me on the events across Aldian.

Already news had spread of our union. Reflected in the lack of red around the manor. That was the first of the tasks completed—removing the Gathrax red around the estate. Carpets ripped from the ground, giving way to ancient wooden floors. Banners had been torn down from walls and curtains replaced once the material had been dyed.

As I walked the estate, freely, I witnessed the change daily.

It was last night that Camron informed me of my parents and their arrival. He had delivered his evening briefings himself. It was clear how tired he had been from the shadows that dusted beneath his gaze. How he trudged in and updated me between yawns.

He had not stayed long. Although it would seem he wanted to as he hesitated for the door handle and peered over his shoulder before walking away.

Tomorrow. They would reach the estate and I would be reunited. I struggled to sleep after that.

So I opted to walk the estate. Both inside and out—thankful for the fresh air.

This morning was crisp. The skies void of a cloud. But the breeze was sharp and caused my breath to fog with each exhale. I folded my arms over my chest, aware of the leather harness that was strapped around my forearm. The wand nestled in place perfectly.

The holder had been pried from the corpse of Jonathan Gathrax. I had requested it before his body was buried for his wife and two remaining children but they had been taken from here. Camron ordered for them to be prisoners—but not in the sense I had been.

They would live comfortably on, in what had been, the Calzmir Estate. Now, I suppose, it was one large extension of our own.

"So, you are growing used to your newfound comforta-bility." A voice rang out ahead as two figures stepped out from behind a manicured conifer.

Beatrice and her brother looked at me coldly. Simion stayed back a step from his sister, his once soft stare now intense as his thick, dark brows furrowed toward me.

I stopped walking, taking in the two before me. "I have been wondering when you would show up, Bea."

The last time I had seen her was the morning of the handfasting.

"It would have been sooner, but as you can imagine, we have been busy putting out fires."

Beatrice signaled to her brother, but he just stood still. Not risking a blink as he looked at me.

"You should be careful," I warned them. "You both do not exactly blend in well around here. One might start asking questions."

Beatrice recoiled from me. "There is a difference in you, Max."

I raised a wrist at her, flashing the black cord inked around my skin. "Have you not heard? I am a married man now."

"Didn't we say we have been putting out fires?" Simion finally spoke.

"You do not know what that has done." Beatrice pointed a finger to my wrist.

"Don't I? Because from my knowledge it means I have forever linked to someone I do not know. Someone who I know shares control over the south of Aldian. And there is no way for me to break it."

Simion stepped next to his sister. Seeing them together showed their differences to one another as well as their similarities. Although both their skin was rich in color, Simion's was darker. Beatrice had more height than her brother, but he was wider with muscle.

Both of them wore forest green clothing. Matching trousers and jacket that hugged their taut frames. Beatrice, like the morning she had come for me, wore her cloak.

Simion was without.

I did not need to see it to know the staff was held across her back. As if sensing my interest, Beatrice called out.

"The amplifier has been returned to you. I heard you caused some havoc after your ceremony. Shame, as your friend I would have thought I would share such a happy day."

She pushed at me. Urging me to bite back.

I took a breath. "You are not my friend. The girl I had known before this was a friend. You… I do not know who you are anymore."

Beatrice snarled at me. "The feeling is mutual. All I have tried to do is help and you have been nothing but a problem."

I knew she was right. But still, I felt anger toward her.

"Steady, Bea." Simion put his large hand on her shoulder. "He is confused."

"Do not speak for me," I snapped.

Simion looked up slowly with a blank expression. Almost bored.

"We have not come to argue with you, Max," Simion said, hand still holding his sister steady. "There is no time for it."

"We believe the North has sent others to collect you. Meaning we have failed to return you peacefully. When they arrive, they will not be as kind as us. I am your friend, Max, you may not think it. But I am. And as your friend, I am telling you we need to leave."

"Now," Simion added.

"I have told you; I go nowhere without my parents and they are on their way back to me as we speak. Not because you retrieved them for me. But because my new fast-mate was true to his word."

I waited for them to tell me otherwise. To confirm that Camron was a liar like the rest of them. But they did not.

"I tried to—"

"Do not bother, Simion. He has made his mind up." There was a faint sadness in Beatrice's wide, russet eyes.

"We tried. It takes a stronger person to know when to give up."

Simion looked me up from my boots to my reddened face. His stare was heavy. I almost felt my skin itch as he studied me. "I will not make you do anything, Max, but I need to hear it from you. Come with us or stay."

I paused, studying Simion's outstretched hand.

"I go nowhere without my family. I have not been through this, to get close to seeing them again, only to simply leave. Ask me when they have arrived—I may have a different answer."

Birds rustled from trees as the shrill laugh of Beatrice shocked the world. "Fool. Come on, Simion, I have had enough of this."

Beatrice tugged at her brother's arm, turning with a swish of her cloak, toward the wood.

Simion held back a moment longer. "You have a lot to learn, Max. I, we, would have been willing to teach you. I only hope we still get the chance."

Then he was gone, chasing after his sister, and leaving me to the cold of the morning.

CAMRON'S STOMACH WAS AS HARD AS STONE. HIS SHIRT DID little to hide ridges and hollows of his muscles. Which made it impossible not to think about them. I was only glad that his back was to me.

With my hands wrapped around his waist, I had to hold onto something as the mare he had chosen rode with intensity throughout the town.

His invitation for me to join him for breakfast had arrived when I returned to my chamber after leaving Beatrice and Simion. Not being in the mood for small talk, I had kindly declined. Using the need to visit the town as an excuse. Although it did not keep him away. Camron had turned up shortly after, dressed ready for riding.

"I would very much like to join you," he had said, leaning against the door frame as he tugged at the sleeves of his riding jacket. "If you would have me that is."

With him standing before me I did not decline.

Now, suddenly conscious as the warmth of his body pressed to mine, I wished I had refused.

The horse trotted down the long drive of the estate, passing the boundary wall in a blur. Only when we were comfortably out of view from the many watching windows did Camron urge the horse to slow to a trot.

"I hope you do not mind that I accompany you," Camron spoke over his shoulder. "I thought it a safer option to visit the town with you. What with being such an important commodity to the new ruling estate."

"Is that what you see me as?" I tried to force some humor into my tone. "A commodity."

"Of course. You are the only living mage of the South. Keeping you out of harm's way is extremely important."

"And that is the only reason?"

"Well, it is a good excuse to spend some time with my husband."

I released my hold on him. "Please don't call me that."

"I jest, Maximus."

"What are you wanting to do in town?" he asked me. But it was the one question I did not want to answer.

"You are not going to be one of those overwhelming, needy partners, are you?" I fired back at him. "Because if you are, that can be nipped in the bud right now."

Camron's low chuckle warmed me. "I admit I did not expect you to have such a dry sense of humor. Careful, because it may be my favorite trait already."

"Believe me, I am not joking."

Camron shrugged. "Consider my interest in your daily activity eradicated."

The morning had passed to early afternoon and with it, the sun had melted the remains of the frost. Winter had truly settled now. It would be a matter of days before swollen clouds brought with them bouts of snow.

"Tell me something interesting about you, Maximus," Camron asked, focusing on the road ahead.

"There is nothing interesting for you to know."

"Oh come on," he drawled. "I understand this situation is not ideal. For you and me either. However, I think we could both agree that we should get to know each other. It would be a beneficial use of our time."

The horse jolted over a ditch, sending me bumping into Camron's strong back. Without more than a thought, I hooked my arms back around him. The threat of falling from the saddle became more of a promise as the road worsened closer to town.

His hand held onto mine as they were clasped around him. His stomach jolting as he laughed.

"What is your favorite food?"

I paused at his question. "You have got to be kidding."

"Not at all—we have to start somewhere. I will go first. If you put a honey-glazed gammon in front of me then you have won your way to my heart."

I found my lips curving into a smile. "That is too sweet for me."

"Sweet enough, are you?"

If he turned to face me he would have seen cheeks pinched in red. "Never had the chance to have many sugary foods. I have grown used to bland tastes—our options were limited growing up."

"As a member of Gathrax's staff?"

An image of my home sprung to mind. How it had been sat empty for a while. It was hard to justify just how much time had passed since the wood and Julian.

"They did the best they could, my parents, to give me what they could manage. After everything… I have caused them nothing but suffering thus far."

"Not for long." Camron patted my hands as I held on. "They will be back with you soon enough."

Not able to dwell on it for a moment longer, I changed the subject with another question. "Cats or dogs?"

"Maximus, now that truly is a hard question."

We spoke for the entire, short journey. Question after question we learned more about each other than I had with anyone since Beatrice. How Camron preferred the hotter months of summer to winter and how he had three dogs back at his home estate.

"Thank the dryad for that," I said. "My allergies are terrible with cats."

"Lucky I am without then otherwise you would never be able to visit."

"So you have plans to return to your estate?"

Camron paused. I did not know what I expected him to say in return.

"I am," he said. "Like you have expressed this union was not planned. This, in a strange way, is your home. Although not in the way you have been used to. And mine is back at my family estate. Once the South has settled into its new ownership I thought it best that I return. Give you the space you may need."

It was impossible to ignore the spear of cold that cut through me. "Is my company that bad?"

"Of course it is not. After everything you have been through, I thought you would prefer some time with your family. To claim this new life you have found yourself in without me shadowing behind. Did you not say you did not want a needy partner?"

I hesitated, unsure of how to respond.

We had reached the town in silence, Camron waiting for my response but I was unable to give one.

Beneath the bright day, the town looked different than I remembered it. That and the faces of those we passed beamed at us as the horse moved down the middle of the street. Happiness. It vibrated in the very air. Civilians waved, some even shouted our way. But not angered shouts. They were calls of celebration.

"Everyone is … happy," I said aloud, more to myself.

"Why would they not be? Their oppressive leader has been dealt with. They are more thankful than anything."

I followed their faces, waiting, expecting to see someone who hated me. But instead, it was my name whispered on their lips.

"They all know, don't they?"

"Indeed, they do. I thought it best that our people are not kept in the dark of past events. It had not taken even a full day before word reached all occupants of this estate and beyond."

"Perhaps this was not a good idea," I admitted, the weight of those who looked upon us heavy.

"Maximus, this may be our first disagreement as a couple. I think this was a wonderful idea. Let them see you for what you are. Silas had told me of the lack of presence the Gathrax family had in their town. Only the family color being the reminder for its people of their authority. Let them see you."

"Us, you mean?"

"If that is your preferred way of seeing it then yes, let them see us."

Camron was right. Much like the estate we had left behind, there was not a sign of red across the town the deeper we got into it. No longer did the ruby banners hang over the street. Now empty wooden postings stood awkwardly in their place. I scanned the crowd, looking for red ribbons pinned to their chests. But I saw nothing.

"And will we be replacing the red with something else? A new color to establish our estate?"

Camron looked over his shoulder, amber eyes squint-ing. "I like your use of our, Maximus."

I rolled my eyes, using it as an excuse not to stare into his. "This ruling thing is very new to me. I have no idea what should or should not happen. If I am honest, not in a million years did I think I would be in this situation."

"Nor did I. Three weeks ago I was planning my next trip overseas. Now I am sat on a horse, walking through a town that is not my own with a beautiful boy clinging onto me."

His words settled over me. Sending a shiver of pleasure across my skin. I was thankful, in that moment, for the thick jacket I wore, concealing my reaction beneath.

"I think I can walk from here," I told him.

"Are you sure?" he asked, pulling on the reins. The horse neighed in response, his head shaking the curtain of dark, black hair. "Steady… steady now."

Camron's voice lulled the mount to calm.

"I know this town better than you could imagine." I released my hold from him, pushing off the saddle and jumping down. My legs jarred at the impact.

The hushed whispers of those around us stopped. Their attention fully on me as I now stood amongst them.

"May I ask in, a not annoying or suffocating way at all, where you may be going?"

I could not tell him. Not that I did not want to, but it was the idea of offending him that summoned my lie. "To see an *old* friend."

Camron took my silent hint and did not question further.

"Then I too will run an errand. It would be my plea-sure to take you back home when you are ready?"

I looked up to him and nodded. "If you can find me among all this."

He spared the crowd around us a glance.

"I will always find you, Maximus."

With a knock of his boot to the horse's side and a clicking sound, he was off. Leaving me to watch him trot farther into the street.

23

I STOOD BEFORE THE ESTABLISHMENT, JUSTIFYING IF MY next move was necessary. The home sat within the shopping district of the town. A stone's throw from Beatrice's workshop... although I knew now it was only an added ingredient to her illusion.

The building leaned ever so slightly. An old crack that laced up the face of the brick wall had been filled awkwardly. Windows were in awful condition. Rotten wood and the occasional wooden board that had been put up to cover broken glass.

It was a miracle the building still stood as it did. Frail, a single winter storm would surely tear it down.

I was aware of those who watched me as I stood before the town's local home for the aged. A crowd had gathered as I walked toward my destination. Never getting too close but staying far enough away that I still heard their excited whispers.

It was that thought alone that made me finally take the steps up to the large, oak door and push it open.

Rust coated the doorknob, coming off in my hand as I pulled away.

A thief would never make it inside this building without being known. The loud screech of the old door gave away my presence immediately.

Once upon a time, the gallery I entered would have been grand. Tall ceilings and a sweeping staircase took up most of the space before me. But now it seemed that only cobwebs and their patrons dwelled within.

"Hello…" I called out, almost gagging on the stale air that infiltrated my mouth. The residence of the wand strapped around my forearm kept me grounded as I walked farther into the building.

This establishment was filled with those who couldn't remember. For in some, old age clawed through the cabinets within a mind, ripping out the memories from new to old, leaving those afflicted with a warped sense of reality. It was here that I would hopefully find answers to the markings around my wrist.

I took the stairs, stepping around ripped carpets and broken wood of the curved banister. Almost every step creaked as I made my way up to the next floor.

The corridor before me was long and narrow. Wheel marks had scratched themselves into the paneled flooring from the many years of the occupants being moved from one room to another by those who cared for them.

On each side of the corridor were doors. Closed. The walls leaned awkwardly, long, web-like cracks evident on almost every surface.

I heard noises from behind the closed doors. Muttering voices. Screeching of metal as old wheels rolled back and forth.

It would be within one of these rooms that I would find answers.

I hoped.

Before I reached for the first door, a woman called out.

"What can I—" The woman stopped at the end of the corridor and stared down at me. Even from a distance, I could see the widening of her eyes and the blush of red that crept up her neck. "Mage Oaken, I did not expect your arrival."

I bowed my head to her as she did to me. I could not place a finger on why she seemed so familiar. Her doughy, aged frame and features tugged at my memory. "Apologies, I should have sent word ahead of my arrival."

Confusion grappled across her aged, tired face. She carried a tray in her hands. The glass jug clouded with overuse. Her unruly hair had come away from the bun atop her head. Sheets of black hair with gray framed her pale face. The only color seemed to be her bright stare that studied me.

Taking a deep breath to reinstate my confidence, I moved through the corridor to greet her.

"Forgive me if this comes across wrong, but what are you doing here?" she asked, placing the tray down and straightening her dirtied apron.

"I have come to see one of your patrons of this fine establishment…"

"This is anything but fine," the lady said, tucking her hair behind her ear and attempting to smooth out her appearance. "It has been many years since this place was anything close to fine."

I did not disagree.

A low groan sounded from the room she had left. Someone called for her. "It has been a long night and it is going to be an even longer day. I will need to move on."

I sensed her need to rush.

Stepping toward her, I reached for the tray before she had a chance to pick it back up. "Let me help you."

"No, no," she huffed through a smile. "There is no need for that, Mage Oaken. Do not worry yourself. I am perfectly fine. Busy is all, but fine."

"It seems to me that you are the only one here working. Please, I have nothing better to do. I can help."

She paused, eyes narrowing as she searched for something in my face. "It is not your place to help. Please… let me."

Her hands were steady as she took the tray back from me. I let her.

"I have much to do. I really should get on with it." On cue, another call sounded from behind yet another closed door. The lady blew out a sigh, the hair bouncing from her face.

Not wanting to keep her any longer, I told her of the person I came to visit. Someone who broke a handfasting and survived. I could see her brows raise with interest at my request, but her lips stayed pursed.

"I trust this stays between us?"

She nodded, her chin gesturing to the space around us. "Even if I wish to, there would be no one to tell. Please, Mage Oaken, follow me."

On her heel, she spun and skipped with quick feet up the corridor. I picked up my pace just to keep up with her.

The farther we walked into the building, the worse its state became. It was clear that the Gathrax family paid no mind to this place during their reign.

The wallpaper had peeled, exposing patches of dark mold that had taken root. Wooden buckets caught drips of water that fell from the ceiling. We navigated around them, the lady not sparing more than a thought toward it as I did.

The woman looked at me for a moment, noticing the disgust that masked my face. "It has been many years since the Gathrax family cut funding for this home. Once Mistress Calzmir's mother passed, they did not need to keep the money coming. Apologies if the state of the place is not up to your... taste."

"I did not mean to offend," I told her, skipping a step to catch up.

"Believe me, Mage Oaken, the time for offence has long passed. We simply do the best we can with what we have got."

There was a lack of furniture. Some doors had even been removed from rooms to show the frail bodies of occupants lying on beds with nothing else but empty wheelchairs waiting beside them.

"How many staff work here?" I asked as we took a flight of stairs to the next level.

"Depends," she said, "on many factors. Having people work here means we need a wage to pay them and... there is no spare budget for that. I rely on volunteers and the charity of those living within the town."

"It is just you then?"

"Yes." Her response was cold. "Just me. This building has been in my family for generations. Yet it will be with me that it stops running."

"Why?" I questioned, unsure if I pried too far.

"For I have no one of my own to take over."

Plans to help soared across my mind. "I can help."

"Why would you do that?" She laughed, a sharp bark as she came to a stop before a single door at the end of yet another corridor.

"I—"

"Mage Oaken, you must understand. The Gathrax family cared nothing for this place. To them it was no more than a waste of time, housing lost causes. The illness our occupants suffer from never touched the Gathrax family as it has for so many other people that you pass every day. What makes you so different?"

"I am not like them…" I muttered, more for me than her.

She paused, studying me up and down. "That is yet to be determined. I do hope you are right."

I knew who she reminded me of. Dame. Her blunt attitude and motherly tone. My heart tugged at the thought of her. They could have been sisters.

"The lady you seek stays in that room… I will not ask exactly what you need with her but please, respect her. Do not pry or upset her."

I followed her finger to the closed door ahead of us. "Thank you… I am sorry. I have not once asked your name."

"Kallie. I will wait outside for you but please do not be long. I have much to attend to today and already lack time."

I smiled at her, making a silent promise. Now I had the chance to make changes to this estate, to fix the shadows and overlooked issues that the Gathrax family ignored.

I would speak with Camron later. A warm buzz spread from my heart and tingled across every inch of my body.

Perhaps being in control would not be as bad as I first thought.

The door clicked shut behind me. Then there was only silence.

In a chair, facing away from me, sat a hunched body. Only her shoulders rose and fell slowly.

I took a cautious step into the room, but still, the body did not react to my presence.

"Good morning…" I called quietly. "Forgive my intrusion. I only wish to ask you something."

She looked to the wall. A single picture hung at an angle before her. Of a man, a painting that had faded with time.

I knelt before her, staring into her lost gaze. On her lap, she rested her frail, bent hands, exposing both of her thin wrists. One plain. The other covered in a mark. But unlike the handfasting band at my wrist, hers was broken. The inked mark not connecting.

I took a breath and steadied my own shaking hands.

My story spilled from my lips. Out it came, from start to finish. There was something about having a silent witness to listen that kept the story of my truth flowing.

"…and now I am handfasted, joined with someone, for the rest of my life, who is still a stranger. No matter if he is handsome and kind, I still know nothing about him. This is not how I wanted my life to be."

I cried, tears cutting down my cheeks as I spoke to the woman who showed no sign that she knew I was even there.

"They used to whisper stories about you across the estate. Telling of the woman who broke her handfasting for a man she truly loved. I wanted to see how you did it… how *I* can do it."

Still silent, the woman looked only at the picture of the man that hung on the wall behind me.

A hand pressed down on my shoulder. "Come now, you need a warm drink, Mage Oaken."

I looked up to Kallie, not the woman in the chair. She

still had not moved, solidifying the horror I already knew. Breaking a handfasting left you in a lost state. Going against the sacred fasting would snap your soul, leaving you to wander the plains of the unseen lands, searching for that lost piece of you.

"I didn't mean to listen in, believe me." She helped me from the floor, her touch gentle as she guided me from the woman.

"Have you ever just felt the need to cry?" I asked her, laughing through a snort.

"More than I would like to admit," she said, reaching a finger and clearing the tear from my cheek. "You have a gentle soul. I can see that now."

"I should not have come and taken up your time." I felt defeated. "It was a silly hunch to follow."

"People will try anything when they are in desperate situations. We are all the same, all of us."

There was noise far beyond the corridor we stood in. My ears tickled to it. Kallie seemed not to notice the cry.

"The woman you seek the answer from has not made a sound since she came into this home years ago. When she was brought here by her fast-mate he told us about her betrayal to him. It has been a long time since he has returned to see her. But she does not mind. She is clueless to this world now."

"Do you know how she did it?" I asked Kallie.

She shook her head. "And I would not like to know. You can see what it has done to her. Turned her into a shell of a person. Mage Oaken, do not go looking for ways to break your fasting. We will need you to be fully aware when the time comes."

Another scream. This time Kallie looked up from me. "It would seem I am being summ—"

A noise split the world. So loud that it shook the walls

of the building. We had no time to find the cause as an explosion of force rocked across the building.

My body hit the floor. Dust rained down upon me. It took a moment to regain composure as a roar shattered my hearing.

Kallie was laid away from me, hands clapped over her ears. Her mouth was open, her face pinched in terror. Was she screaming? I couldn't hear anything but the ringing that imprisoned my mind.

"Are you alright?" I shouted, trying to scramble across to her. My question sounded as if I was speaking beneath a body of water.

Frozen water.

My breath fogged out of my mouth. My skin tickled as the temperature dropped.

The crackle of ice chorused around us, spreading across the walls like crystals.

We both watched as winter devoured the building. Spreading ice from the very room we had just left.

Kallie pushed herself up from the floor and ran for the door. She hissed in pain when she reached out for the brass knob. Even I could see the burn that was left on her palm when she pulled away.

I was next to her in moments. My wand in hand without more than a thought.

The door was thrown open, exposing the horror within. As if winter had taken the room prisoner, all was ice and snow. The intensity of the freezing air slammed into my face and pinched my cheeks red.

We could hear screaming now. Calls from outside the frosted window. But that was not all. A flapping, pounding of large wings as if a flock of woodland kestrels flew outside.

But no kestrel had claws so large as the ones that pierced the walls without effort.

No kestrel had the force to rip the entire wall from view right before my very eyes.

No. This was no bird.

"Dragon!" Kallie screamed.

24

THE WALL CRUMBLED AWAY, EXPOSING THE BEAST OF horror. Stone and brick fell into the street beyond. A rush of frigid air ate away at the room.

The dragon's snout protruded through the hole. The remaining wall of the room cracked loudly beneath the weight of its claws, talons as long as spears stabbing through plaster and brick.

I was frozen in horror. Slowly its hulking jaws separated, exposing lines of pointed, serrated teeth the size of blades. A tongue, pink and forked slithered out in search of its next meal. The body of the woman sat in her chair, unmoving, covered in dust and rubble. The painting nowhere to be seen.

Kallie screamed with ferocious might, anticipating the creature's next move.

All I could do was watch, frozen to the spot and as the monstrous face tilted, jaw opened wider, it snapped the woman from her chair.

All noise seemed to fail in the moments that followed. All but the loud drip of blood across the floor. Drip. Drip.

Blood and saliva drawled from the mouth of the dragon, hissing as it disappeared from view.

The entire world seemed to shake as the dragon pushed off from its perch on the building. I stumbled beneath the force. Monstrous wings flapped and the dragon was gone. But not before I saw the shape mounted on its spiked, obsidian back.

Someone rode it.

The North had arrived.

Kallie tugged on my arm, shouting blending with the screams of terror from the street far below. I pulled away from her. Not caring to see as she ran off into the shaking building.

I waded through the destruction. The chair that lay in pieces across the floor, covered in red blood. It had begun to frost over from the icy air left in the beast's wake.

Stepping over gore and rubble, I moved for the opening in the wall. Hoping for the dragon to have left.

Leaning against the broken brick, I looked up into the sky, catching a glimpse of the creature that still lingered above. Far above, diving between clouds, I watched the shape of the dragon with horror. A creature of the mountains. Of air and ice.

From this distance, I could not see its features, all beside it being a passing illusion of black claws and spikes. But I heard it. Its cry sent burning anxiety across every inch of my body. It filled the sky, like a raging storm each cry rocked the world.

The streets beyond the care home were filled with its screaming occupants. Many ran. Many watched, hands pointing to the creature that dominated above them.

I wanted to shout at them from my place up above. Tell them to run and hide.

Then I looked for him. For Camron. Searched the

bustling streets of fearful bodies for his amber hair, his strong demeanor.

He was nowhere to be seen.

From what I could see, no other building had been targeted. Only the one I was within. Nor did I see signs of death or destruction.

"Mage!" someone beneath me screamed, pointing up to where I stood. The winds caught my hair, picking it up in dancing tufts, and quivered my jacket. One hand held onto a crumbling brick, the other gripped the wand.

"Help us!"

"Please, mage, spare us!"

The one who noticed me caused many more to point and cry. Until the call of the dragon rained out again and they dispersed like frightened geese.

Something warm ran across the back of my hand. I did not need to look to know it was blood. Blood of the woman I had come to visit. Blood of the beast's supper.

Beatrice and Simion had warned the North would come. They promised. And now another life had been lost because of me.

This one didn't leave a death notch on the wand.

I watched the blood coil around my wrist and carry on its descent to the floor where it puddled. The magic pooled in my stomach, twisting as anger overtook my mind and body. Like the raging waters of the ocean, its presence thrashed within me.

Release me. It sang in a symphony that raced shivers up my arms. *Release me.*

With livid speed I left the building and exploded onto the street, hand raised to block the sun out of my eyes. I searched for the dragon. *It will come back for me.* I knew it. I sensed it.

I pushed through the crowd that had materialized

around me, apologizing to each person I touched. The need to help was powerful. But so was the fear that had embedded into my gut. With each blink, I saw the layered blades of the dragon's teeth. Would I meet them next?

I ran across the street ahead of me toward an alleyway. I didn't look back to the care home and the destruction I had brought to its door, but I vowed I would fix it. Legs and arms pumping, I kept up pace, unsure of where exactly I was headed.

Then the shadow of the dragon passed overhead. Instinct took over and I ducked as more cries of terror reacted to the diving beast.

The intense cold nipped at my arms as I hit the ground and covered my head. Frost, pure and white, spilled from the flying beast's jaw like icy lava. It kissed buildings, smashed windows, and altered the very air around it

Up, I told myself. *Run.*

Leaning homes towered above from either side, blocking the sky the farther I got down the alley. I risked a glance and saw no dragon. But I could hear it terrorizing some unseen location a few streets across. I kept running toward it.

The screams of the town would not cease. With each beat of my heart, they built and built. Blending in with the roars of the beast that claimed the sky for its own.

I could not stop myself from running toward it. Had it killed more while I hid among the shadows of the alley?

Coward, I scolded. *Run.*

The wand's smooth hilt was a steady force in my hand. I reached for the power; its familiar guidance poised for me. Little I knew of the power, but I trusted that it would help when needed.

And run I did, faster and faster. I held my breath, forcing as much power into my limbs as possible.

I reached the opening of the following street and stopped, skidding across the now frozen path. The beast was before me. Still as a cat on the prowl. Still unseen, I pressed my back to the wall of the building that cornered the path and watched.

My breathing was harsh, but I had to quieten it for the dragon had its back to me. Its focus on something unseen before it. I could not see around its hulking frame or the long tail that thrashed behind it.

Jagged lines had been etched into the ground where the creature had landed in the open street. Not a body or soul could be seen besides myself and this creature. Did civilians watch from windows or through holes in their closed doors?

The dragon was unlike anything I could ever imagine. Seeing it up close, without the broken remains of a wall to cover its body, I took in every inch of it.

It prowled on its hind legs. The sharp talons on the tip of its wings dragged itself forward. The sound of its stomach scraping across the cobbled street sent my skin shivering.

Its body looked like a sculpture of aged bark. Rough and coarse, yet it picked up the sunlight as if the large scales were made from glass or crystal. Black as night, but the light twinkled across patches of its scaled armor. The tail that slithered behind was as thick as a trunk and moved like a garden snake. Side to side it swayed, the spiked tip looking no different than a mace.

But it was the body on the dragon's back that obtained my attention.

A Northern warrior.

I could see the Northern soldier, decked from helmet to boots in polished, silver armor. The breastplate reflected the white ice that clung to the buildings.

I held my wand to my chest for comfort. As my foot moved to step forward the beast roared out in pain. I clapped my hands over my ears to block out the noise.

An axe was embedded in the dragon's lower left side. Shocked, I searched for the culprit, only to find a man reaching for the handle with a face of sculpted bravery.

Time seemed to slow. The Northern warrior shouted and pointed their sword at the attacker. The dragon reacted, its long neck swishing round to face the man who spilled black blood from the open wound.

The axe was no more than a thorn in its side.

The man did not cry out or scream for help as the snapping jaws shot forward.

My magic exploded within me. This time its power felt different. Sharp and hot. Not the same as I had used when I had called on the earth to kill Master Gathrax. This feeling was the same as the night in the wood.

Lightning crackled across my skin, lifting the hairs on my body to standing.

The sky cracked above; dark clouds danced into view, blocking the sun.

I raised the wand before the jaws devoured the brave man. A white, jagged glow crawled across my skin and up through the wand, and a bolt of light shot for the beast.

The power slammed into the side of the dragon's snout.

The man took his chance and ran as the beast turned to me with a roar. Smoke smoldered from its scaled skin.

On its hind legs, the beast reared up. The warrior was knocked from its back, sent clattering into the street.

Ice spread from its jaws as it cried out in pain. It spun rapidly, tail smashing into anything close to it. It threw carts of fruit and veg across the road. One smash left a dent the size of a door in the side of someone's home.

My magic had hurt him. But it had also alerted both the beast and its rider to my presence.

"Traitor mage," the soldier shouted, voice raw and stern. He pushed himself from the ground, helmet askew and sword discarded far off in the street. "You were given the chance to join us. You resisted. Lower your *amplifier* and come now or face the ever-lasting darkness that waits for you."

Death.

I squared my stance, and I kept my wand pointed; stare unwavering. "As I told your fellow Northern allies, I will *not* come with you."

"They are no allies of mine," the warrior shouted, his voice young but spiked with power. "You leave me no choice."

He stalked for the sword, sweeping it from the ground. His beast still thrashed across the street in agony.

The warrior mirrored my stance, the tip of his weapon pointed in my direction. The metal blade sat perfectly in the hilt of wood; the sword was not of common creation.

"You will be known as a waste of power and potential, the lost mage who was felled for betraying his own kind." The dragon had shifted, purring ominously behind the warrior. Its scales blackened by my scorched bolt of light, no sign of lasting blood.

My wand felt suddenly heavy, brimming with a power which only begged to be released.

This is it.

"We are nothing alike," I said, bending my knees in anticipation. I had no chance to win this, I knew that deep down. But for the sake of those who hid and watched, I would go down trying. "Leave before you're—"

The soldier sprang forward before I finished speaking. I acted with equal speed. A sudden crack of lightning split the darkening sky. I raised my wand for it and called for its assistance.

Before the metal of the sword reached my waiting neck a bolt of lightning exploded onto the street between us. A shield of white, boiling light that crackled like the chorus of a musician's melody.

It sliced across the gap between us, reaching the warrior in a blink.

Then it was gone. Waved away like it was no more than a cloud of mist. Around the sword the remnants of lightning crackled, dancing across the metal. The warrior's laugh shook my soul.

"Dragon kissed, you truly are a waste."

Then another crack split the sky as the warrior raised his sword and summoned the same power I had, taking it from my grasp and stealing it for himself.

I LEARNED THE MOST VALUABLE LESSON ABOUT THE strange power inside of me. It had *knowing* of its own. A diluted sense of knowing what to do. It worked on instinct, not command. I was no more than a silent witness, watching from a dark cave in my mind as my body moved, dancing to the beat of the wand and its control.

It owned me. Perhaps that was what it meant to be a mage. Being owned. Something I longed to be free of. But among this power, I had never felt so free.

Between the hands of the warrior, a ball of white energy grew. The bolts of lightning laced around his fingers and wrists, frantically dancing as he conjured the power. With a cry he thrust it toward me.

The wand moved my hand, slashing my arm upward. It split his attack in two, slamming the power into the wall of the shop behind me. Glass and brick exploded, shrapnel hitting into the back of me, followed by the smell of burning as the lightning turned to flame.

Sword raised, the warrior took my moment of distraction as his signal to move. He ran for me, blade aimed for my stomach. The power within me surged again, calling on the earth this time. The ground beneath us shook. I fell, knees screaming as they collided with the cobbled street. But the warrior also lost his footing—an angered cry raging out as he collided with the floor.

The dragon mirrored his cry, jaws opening and frigid winds materializing between pointed teeth. I scrambled to get up before the icy breath of the beast rushed over me.

But the warrior was crawling before me, in my line of sight. Between me and the dragon. As if the beast had some mundane recognition it swallowed its magic. Wings flapped wildly in angst instead.

It would not hurt the warrior.

Up from the ground, I held the wand out in warning as the warrior clambered up. In his armor he was awkward. He ripped the helmet from his head, exposing the young face below.

He was younger than I. His face was not covered with stubble, or lines of age. Ocean blue eyes narrowed on me. With our storm still clashing above, winds and booms of thunder splitting the world, his mass of long, dark hair flew around him.

The air fizzed with the raging storm. My magic against his.

"I do not want to fight you," I shouted above the winds.

The boy smiled. "Of course you don't."

He lifted his sword, both hands now holding the wooden handle at its base. I should have moved for him as he closed his eyes. But the buzzing of magic slammed into me, locking me in place.

Roots burst from beneath my feet, wrapping around my ankles and feet. Their vise-grip squeezed across my flesh, threatening to snap my bones.

I cried out, falling back as I struggled to get away before they fully encased me. My ankle screamed, twisted in place as I collided with the ground.

Sickness washed over me. The pain in my ankle almost too much to bear.

A shadow passed overhead. The nick of a blade pressed against my neck as I writhed on the ground.

"You will be known across our history as a waste of potential," the warrior spat, teeth exposed as he grinned down at me.

The warm kiss of blood bloomed beneath the warrior's sword. I did not struggle, did not take my eyes off his. He should have ended it there. Not allowed me to lift the wand without him noticing and press it into his stomach.

Before his blade could spill any more of my blood, I forced the swirl of magic within straight through my body and out of the wand.

A great gust of crackled wind snatched the warrior away. The force of it pushed me back, and I cracked my head across the ground.

My vision spun, reality slipping through my grasp.

I saw Mother. Her body was unharmed, her face sad.

She raised a hand for me. Urging me to take hers. Regret wet her cheeks as tears spilled down her face.

My son, I am sorry.

I vaguely felt the roots slipping as they crumbled from around my feet. Noticed the lack of their pressing weight across my twisted ankle.

My eyes were closed but the world beyond seemed darker. Prying my eyes open, a rancid smell slammed into me, keeping me to the ground.

The dragon prowled above me, in place of its rider. Jaws open, globs of spit falling to the ground around me.

Deep in its throat, I spied the conjuring of blue light,

cold as mountain ice. It grew in the pit of its belly, ready to wash over me. One breath to end the rest of mine.

Death was upon me.

My magic spurred again, weaker this time. I felt the reserves within me emptying. I gripped onto what power I had left, forcing it through my wand and toward the dragon. A hot, white bolt crashed within the creature's mouth, colliding with its own ball of magic in an explosion of heat and ice.

"*Glamora!*" screamed the warrior from his hidden perch. The buildings shook as the dragon fell to the ground, withering across the street like a butterfly beneath a pin.

I got up, putting the weight on my one good ankle, and watched as the dragon's tail thrashed madly, slamming through the unlucky buildings around it.

The warrior stood between us. Body glowing with magic and anger. The ground echoed his emotion. It trembled, stones lifting off the street. The cloud of earth spun around the warrior and his sword. A vortex of magic.

His shoulders rose and fell rapidly. More dirt, stones, and broken brick mixed with the storm that blurred around him.

Breathless, I watched. Waiting for the known attack that would come. The magic within me was a calm river. The storm in the sky no longer mine.

I was empty.

Silently, the warrior thrust his sword forward and the storm of earth listened. I raised my arm to cover my face a moment too late. Exposed skin tore as the power ripped over me.

Blinded, I did not see the fist before it collided with me. Then another. One after the other the warrior pummeled my body. Each one knocked me back. Blood filled my mouth. It spilled down my nose. It washed over my eyes.

Pain blossomed ferociously.

Once again I gave in to the ground, body crashing against the cobbled street. Not even my arms came to my aid to soften the blow.

Something flashed in my peripheral. I had a second to move but not fast enough. Something sharp cut at my cheek; red overwhelmed my vision. Through blood, I peered up at the warrior who stood above me in time to see his blade.

The wand, my shield, raised my arm once again. *Thud.* Metal and wood connected.

"Southern bastard!" the soldier shouted, pulling his sword back. For a moment I was lost for words, taking in the perfect wand. "She was a fool to ever want you to return." Flecks of his spit rained down on me as he hissed.

"Stand and greet your end." He pointed the tip of his sword at my jugular.

I could not move. I had nothing left in me.

"I never wanted this…" I croaked; the lump in my throat tickled across the end of the blade.

"Do not waste those words with me. Only your Sire is to blame. Her selfish actions have led you down this path. Shame, the spineless bitch is not here to see her greatest failure…"

My power thrashed like a starved snake, ready to strike.

"She deserves the same fate as you—exile is not good enough."

A crack of lightning sliced the sky above the warrior.

"Perhaps I will end her life as I will with you. Take both your bodies back to my queen as a gift."

The hairs on my arms stood on end as bolts of lightning filled my veins. I tasted the warmth across my tongue as it spread from my body to my mind.

Like the beating of drums, the intense power built in pace until its crescendo was so close I felt as if my skin would shatter. It seeped from the ground into my bones. Filling the empty vessel within me.

The power needed an outlet.

So I became one.

With my spare hand, I wrapped it around the sword's blade. Not caring as the sharp edge cut deep into my palm. I gripped tighter onto the wand in the other hand.

My body vibrated with the need for release. The storm within me raged, threatening to burn me from the inside out.

Pure, white-hot light spread from my hands and engulfed the blade. Before the light sparked, I saw the final look of surprise across the warrior's face. His mouth parted and his eyes bulged.

The power raced up the sword, through the wooden hilt, and into the body of the boy.

Backward he stumbled, smoke seeping from his open mouth, his nose. Even his blue eyes cried with smoke as he fell.

The faint notch of wood filled my ears, a new death mark cutting across the hilt of my wand.

The power was in me, then it was not. Gone in a single moment.

Blinking, I saw double.

Two skies. Two, open jaws of a dragon.

"Enough!" a familiar voice screamed.

Beatrice.

The beast was above me once again. This time I had nothing to stop it from coming down upon me.

A forked tongue slipped from the dragon's mouth and

tasted my broken skin. My arm went numb as the rough texture of its tongue searched me, licking up the blood.

"*Glamora*, stop this," Beatrice shouted, hidden from me. "It is done."

I tried to open my mouth but couldn't.

With each blink, I felt myself slipping away. The lids of my eyes grew heavier.

This was the end.

Time was lost.

I opened my eyes and no longer saw the dragon.

With the next blink, I heard the chorus of hooves across the street and the shout of others.

Another blink and I was lost to the darkness.

Someone's hand lifted my head from the ground. Eyes cracking open, I saw Beatrice. Her mouth was moving but her words did not register. Her face pinched with worry.

She ran a hand down the side of my numb face. When she pulled it back her skin was slick with blood.

I blinked again, this time lost to the darkness for longer.

Camron now held me. Beatrice no longer in sight.

"Oh, Maximus." Camron's hand slipped behind my neck. "You brave fool."

I groaned beneath his touch as he held me to his chest. Beyond Camron, I could see what was happening on the street.

Beatrice was in chains, strapped to the back of a horse. The dragon was held beneath a net of iron, countless men and women pinning it down.

"Sorry! I am so sorry. You are safe now, you are with me. Safe…" Just his touch was enough to distract me from the pain. "I am going to get you home and fix this. I should have never left you… I am sorry."

My throat scratched violently as I replied. "They came for me as they said they would…"

"And they shall again, but I will face them by your side."

Lips pressed to my forehead. Warm and gentle. The kiss shivered across me, dulling the pain that had latched onto every inch of me.

I gave in to the sensation, closing my eyes, not opening them again.

26

I woke to a touch. A hand ran across my head, smoothing my hair with its gentle, circular motion.

It spurred me from the dark web I had been entrapped within. I could not feel my body at first as my mind awoke. Everything was quiet beyond my closed eyes. No commotion. No storm or rumbling of earth.

"He finally wakes," a voice said beside me.

I cracked my eyes open, the overwhelming light forcing me to clamp them closed immediately. My neck was stiff, the discomfort lacing down my spine as I tried to lift my head.

"Ah, ah, ah! Lie back down before you undo my work."

Even if I wanted to refuse, I could not. My body was no more than a deer on ice. Awkward and slow.

I opened one eye, forehead tensing as I adjusted to the bright light.

"I have been starting to worry about you." Simion stood above me, haloed in light, his brown skin glowing.

"Camron?" I stuttered, mouth dry. Simion looked down, mouth tugging with obvious disappointment.

"Dealing with your estate. There has been a lot to sort."

Memories of the North's attack came flooding back all at once. Flashes of ice, dripping blood, the dragon. "You did this. You—"

"*You* were warned, Max. We told you that the queen requests your return and going by the arrival of that mage suggests she has grown impatient. Trust me, neither one of us wanted it to happen this way. We tried everything to spare you from that."

My arms weak and odd, I pushed on the bedding until I was sitting. I hissed at the stabbing agony that shot up from my ankle.

"Steady, Max." Simion tried to reach for me, but I swatted him away.

"You… you do not get to tell me what to do."

He stood back as my harsh words slammed into him. All I wanted was a drink. To wash away the knives that covered the inside of my throat.

"I just want to help."

"Is it not too late for that?" The hairs on the back of my neck lifted in defense. "I want you to leave me."

Simion paused, hands fumbling before him. "I can't."

"Why not," I croaked.

"Your fast-mate has asked me to tend to you. Until you are better, I am not to leave your side."

"Camron…"

Simion busied himself, taking a mug of liquid from the bedside table and lifting it before me. "You can ask him yourself when he comes to visit. It will be soon… he has practically slept beside you nightly."

"Why are you helping me?" A flash of the Northern warrior sped through my memory.

"Why shouldn't I, Max?"

I could not give him an answer. I knew little of what the North wanted me for. Except now it was death.

Simion had not once taken his eyes off me. Not as he guided the mug to my mouth and lifted it. His thumb and finger held my chin up as he slowly let the welcoming water flush through me.

"How long has it been?" I asked. The sloshing of power within me had refilled. Not wholly, but enough that I knew some time had passed since the attack. Although the power was dulled now. A barrier separating me from it.

The wand.

I pulled away from him, looking around for it.

"What is wrong?" Simion stood back, spilling water across the sheets.

"My wand." I panicked. My leg screamed as I shifted my weight to get out of the bed. I had to find it.

"If you do not calm yourself down, you are going to be bed-bound for longer than necessary, Max." Simion was inches from me now, his hands on my shoulders as he urged me to lie back down.

His full lips parted, allowing the smells of forest pine to wash over me.

"I will get it for you, but only if you promise to stop threatening to jump out of bed."

I looked up at him, unblinking. His sharp cheekbones close enough to me that they would cut skin.

"OK."

"OK," he sighed, nodding as he trusted my words. "Good. Now, wait."

I watched him from the corner of my eye as he moved for the hearth. On the ledge above it, he lifted my wand from its concealed resting place.

Seeing it roused the power, thrashing against the barrier within me.

Only when my fingers laced around the hilt of wood did the barrier crumble. And the rush of breath coursed over me.

"Bea would tell me about the addictive nature of an amplifier. I had not seen it so… desperate before."

I ignored his insult. "You call my wand an amplifier. It is not the first time I have heard it said."

Simion's full lips rose into a smile. "In the North, we do not refer to a mage's amplifier as a wand. Unless that is the form in which they wish to use it."

"The warrior, he had a wooden hilt in his sword."

His smile faded before me. Lines creased across his forehead as his brows furrowed. "He did. That was the form in which he chose to manipulate his amplifier."

"And Bea…" The vision of her being with me on the street stilled my words. "Beatrice, she was taken."

It should not have worried me for all she had lied about. But it did. Her hands bound in chains was all I could think of.

"Yes, but your fast-mate has assured me she is safe. As long as you heal, she will be fine."

"He knows… about you both."

"If I had not told him everything, your ankle would still be shattered into countless fragments. Your body would be coated in bruises. If I had not divulged all my secrets to Master Oaken, no one would have been able to help you besides time itself."

"How?" I breathed, noticing the lack of pain throughout my body. Yes, I ached and my ankle screamed with each movement. But I did not feel the fresh cuts across my skin, my face. My hands were unmarked as I raised them before me.

"Something you will soon come to learn is that a mage is not all quaking earth and bolts of lightning. There is much more to the capabilities of a child of the wood. I, like Beatrice, just so happen to have tapped into a power which you have benefited from. Although I am not the same as you and my sister, I still benefit from my ancestral line. There are people like me in the North. Healers."

I looked up at him, into his intense unblinking stare. "Thank you for helping me."

"Could you try that with a smile? Might make it seem more… believable."

Simion's deep chuckle tickled me as he towered above me.

"Now you are up, and my job is deemed finished, I am under strict instructions that if you wake, I must retrieve your companion immediately. You have missed almost two days and a lot has happened. It is only fair that Camron is the one to tell you."

My heart lifted into my throat. It was not what Simion said but the way he said it that lured my anxiety out of its cave. "Wait!"

Simion's hand hovered inches above the brass knob of the door.

"My parents… I want to see them."

If I had lost two days, they would be here. The thought of seeing them both finally became a reality.

I wondered if they too had visited me during my days of rest.

Simion dropped my stare, looking to his feet in silence.

"I will retrieve Camron. He can update you on it all."

My heart dropped like a rock through water, plummeting through my chest and threatening to burst clean out of me. "What has happened, Simion?"

He reached for the door.

"It is not my place, Max. I will be back soon. I am sorry."

I paced the room, nails in my mouth, ignoring the ache in my ankle; that pain did nothing to cover up the new agony in my chest.

"I am so sorry, Maximus." Camron reached out to me again. "I take full responsibility."

Angry, hot tears dripped down my cheeks. "They could be dead now! I saw what the dragon did to the woman in the care home. Just like that, she was gone. What…"

I swallowed a gag that crept up my throat at the thought.

"This is just another play. A move the North had orchestrated on the board which gets you a step closer to their land. I believe, wholeheartedly, that your parents will not be harmed. They are merely bait."

They had been taken. It was the first thing Camron had said as he ran into the room, Simion close behind. The North had stolen my parents from Camron's safehold, only a matter of hours before they should have arrived at the estate.

"Don't call them that!" I snapped back at him.

Camron lowered his gaze to the floor and crossed his arms. "Forgive me, I did not mean—"

"Quiet, please." The more my head throbbed the harder it was to breathe. I knelt, hugging my knees to my chest.

There was a shuffle of footsteps and then the warmth of a close body. Peering through my lashes, I saw Camron who was before me, his forehead close to mine.

"Whatever you want to do, I promise to aid you."

I replied, "I must get them back."

"I know you..."

"You are not going to stop me?"

Camron pulled a face. "Never. My task is not to make life difficult for you. I understand how important your parents are to you. I have played a part in their disappearance. It was from my estate they traveled from. This means the North knew everything that has been happening here. If you feel that you must go, then go. I will not stop you."

That would be my move on the board game the North had begun. I would go to my parents, follow them North and get them back. I had to.

"I hate them. The North," I hissed through a clenched jaw. Simion flinched from where he stood in the shadow of the room. He had been silent since bringing Camron here.

Camron's warm hands cupped my cheeks. "They do not deserve anything else from you."

"If I ignore this they will come back, won't they?"

"I do not doubt it for a moment." Camron lifted my face to his. He was so warm. I wanted nothing more than to melt into his touch. "Maximus, we are lucky that the lives lost during the attack was in the single digits. Next time *they* come I have no doubt they will come with a heavy force. It has been two days and all of those who dwell close to us already wish to flee from our estate."

I shook my head. "I will not let that happen."

"Tell me what you need of me," Camron whispered; his breath fresh as snow.

"Just do not let go of me yet," I told him.

Simion cleared his throat. "You are right, more will search for you, Max. It will only be a matter of time."

"I know what I need to do," I spat at him, unable to look at his beautiful face without the overwhelming urge to jump from Camron and punch it.

"Maximus, do not let this overcome you." Camron pulled my attention back to him. "I must admit it is a brave move having two fugitives hiding among the estate. But I understand that without them both we would not be having this conversation right now. Simion and Beatrice want to help. They are friends."

His trust for them was misplaced.

"They are no friends of mine."

I did not need to look to Simion to know he flinched.

"If you are serious about going North you are going to need friends."

"How long is the South safe?" I turned to Simion, finally letting go of the warmth of Camron. "If I go, what is to say they come back in a matter of days, weeks? To come and finish the job they started. Camron will be staying which means he is still a thorn in their side. What is to say they will not come and harm him."

"Camron is no threat without you around. He is merely a man with a title grander than his truth. Whereas you are a child of the wood. You have the abilities to live up to that name." Simion stepped into the light of the window. He towered inches above Camron and me. A warm hand slipped into mine as we both regarded Simion.

I knew what was needed. And I knew what I wanted even more than that.

My parents.

"Then it seems you have got what you wished," I said to Simion. "When do we leave?"

27

THE COLD AIR SLAPPED INTO ME AS THE GRAND DOORS TO the estate opened. I hugged my arms around my chest, all aches from the fight had left me. Only a faint twinge across my ankle remained as I left

The clothes on my back were stiff and itchy. No matter how I tugged at my sleeves it would not offer me a reprieve from the discomfort. Although I was thankful for the layers as the chill of the winter washed over me.

Camron was my furnace, his warmth a blessing to my side. He must have noticed the shake of my hands as he hooked his arm in mine and cupped my hand in both of his.

"The sun shines down on us," Camron said, leading me down the steps of the estate. "I take that as a good sign."

"Are you suggesting it is celebrating my leave?" I replied, nibbling my lower lip to maintain my anxious thoughts.

Out the corner of my eye, I noticed his lips slip into a grin.

"Ah, I see how it could sound like that. However, it would be foolish to celebrate your departure. I wonder if the same sun shines beyond the north of the wood."

"Maybe the sun does not see the North fit enough to shine for them," I said. And I meant it. Since yesterday morning the truth of going North had settled in. Once the initial anger of knowing they had taken my parents had calmed, I felt nervous. A lamb going to the slaughter. What waited for me there? Answers to what I was; what I could become. Then the thought of my parents among the rough hands of the queen soon ceased my moments of thrilling wonder.

"You can change your mind at any moment, and I will support you."

"There is no room for me to keep chopping and changing my decisions. I have to get them back."

Camron's thumb ran calming circles across the back of my hand as we stood in silent understanding. My parents and the safety of all the civilians, whose lives could be threatened, made it impossible to stay behind. No longer would I leave them as a waiting meal for the dragons.

"Those siblings are strange to me," Camron said, guiding me around the slabbed path toward the expansive gardens to the back of the estate. Even this early, many of the staff were working. Pruning bushes, deadheading flowers that had been claimed by the winter chill.

"I thought you said they were friends," I said, echoing his own words.

"But I did not say if I trust them. That is two entirely different matters. The Gathrax and Calzmir estates were friends but we know how that went." His thumb brushed against the fasting mark that circled my wrist. "The boy, Simion is it? Seems adamant of using the dragon as your means of travel. The beast should not be trusted."

The dragon, Glamora as Beatrice had called it, both frightened and thrilled me. If I didn't have my hands clasped together anyone could have notice them shake with anticipation to see it again.

"Time will tell," I replied, not wanting to do anything to scupper our plans of seeing the creature.

"You are quieter today. Mother used to tell me a quiet person makes for a loud mind." Camron's face morphed into one of concern. "I hope you know you can talk to me. It is the least I can do for you."

"I have a lot to occupy me."

We stopped walking under Camron's control. He turned to face me, pulling on my cold hands now. His warm touch sent a shiver across me.

"You are always so warm," I told him, melting into his touch.

"It is not always a blessing, Maximus. Come the summer months I can hardly venture outside. It may seem wonderful now but I assure you it is not. A lasting scar from the plague."

I held onto him tighter, showing him I was not afraid of his touch. "Then we both have a lot to occupy our minds."

"We do indeed," his deep voice drawled.

A blush crept across my cheeks. His strong stare entrapped me to the spot. I could hardly hold his gaze, shifting between the safety of looking at my feet and to him.

"This may seem forward, something I am supposedly notorious for, but I admit that an unsettling feeling has overcome me. Letting you simply leave is… well it just feels wrong."

My breath pinched in my throat. The blush overcame my neck with its obvious and embarrassing red glare.

"Have I overstepped?" he whispered, making me feel like it was only him and I at that moment.

"I will not be gone for long," I said, trying to convince himself as well as I. "Get my parents, show I am no threat to the North, and then I will return."

"Then what?"

"Then..." Words failed me. Then I had what I always wanted? A life away from the oppressive thumb of control. I hated to admit it, but when I looked at Camron, I saw that as a possible future. His heart felt like it was in the right place, wanting to make things better for those living in the South. And I would be by his side as it happened.

"I suppose when you come back it will be a conversation we will have."

"I am sure we will."

He released a gentle sigh. "I hope so."

The dragon, Glamora, was chained to the wall. Hulking constraints wrapped around its beastly neck and thick hind legs. The constricting chains pinned its wings down, giving no room for movement. Not that it had any in this cramped cavern.

All around it, giant metal pins had been nailed into the ground and walls. Pinned to the ground, the dragon had no room to move. Nor was it trying.

I stood in the mouth of the dungeon; a deep sense of discomfort imprisoned my gut as I watched on.

"Has it been kept like this since the attack?"

"Yes." Camron's reply was as cold as the ice the dragon coated the town in. "This creature is dangerous, it does not deserve comfort."

I agreed with him. The dragon was dangerous. But I could not shake the discomfort at seeing it kept like this. "I did not know this place existed."

The dungeon was a man-made cave of sorts. Dug beneath ground level, from beyond it looked no more like a mound of grass and moss. But when inside it was dank and dark, smelled of cold soil, and clicked and creaked with unseen insects and creatures.

"Not once has it tried to break free. It has been calm since it was brought here. Too calm if you ask me."

Curled tight into its large body, it looked no more like a polished ball of obsidian. Its back rose and fell with each breath which caused the dust on the forgotten ground to dance.

"Has *Glamora* been fed?" I asked.

I sensed Camron stiffen as I used the dragon's name.

"It will not eat. That or we do not know what it is they digest. I might be brash, but I am no monster. I have always wanted to see a dragon so I will not mistreat it for no reason."

For the first time since I had met Camron, I sensed a lie in his words. He said he had always wanted to see a dragon, but when faced with it he looked nothing more than disgusted.

"This is coming from the person who ordered it to be chained to a wall in a dank place?" I tested.

"Hmm. I think we both know what would happen if this beast was let out near others. I will not risk more lives being forfeit to the appetite of the beast."

"Then why have you kept it alive? Why not let *it* die like its rider?" I asked. Saying it aloud felt as wrong as it sounded. But it was a fact. The new death notch on the base of my wand told me as much. There were three marks now. One for Julian, another for his father. And the final for the Northern soldier.

"Collateral I suppose. And I am glad we have kept it… alive. You are looking at your ticket beyond the wood," Camron said.

"Have *they* decided when we leave?" I had not seen nor spoken with either Beatrice or Simion. They had been kept away. Camron's suggestion. He did not want news that more Northern mages were among the South. It would only cause greater issues.

"Tomorrow, no later."

I peered back to the resting dragon. "You said you have been on an adventure before. Were you ever scared before leaving?"

I felt insecure asking. Like a child admitting something silly aloud.

"Scared would be a meek word to use to describe how it was that I felt. But it is what makes the journey. The unknown can be a frightening place. But something I had to remind myself as our ship set sail was that it is the unknown that will make you stronger from here…" He placed his hand on my chest. "And here."

Alone in the belly of the dungeon, with the sleeping dragon in its quilt of chains, Camron brushed the curls from my forehead and placed a kiss upon it.

A shiver spread from the base of my head down to my toes. My hands relaxed and my shoulders lowered. Camron pulled back slowly, his eyes picking up the faint light of the fire-lit torches, and grinned.

"Promise me one thing."

I could not blink for fear I would miss a moment of his gaze. "What is it?"

"Rush home. I have begun to enjoy your company."

The corner of my lip tugged skyward. "I cannot promise that."

"Then I can promise you this... I will be wishing for your swift return. Perhaps I will watch the skies in anticipation."

I sighed, heart pounding in my chest at our closeness. "You might get a neck ache."

"It would be worth it."

I spotted the note the moment I stumbled back into my lodgings. It sat upon the blanket of my bed.

'Time for your first history lesson. S.'

Simion. He had left this for me.

I pondered for a while whether to open it. It would cause a distraction from the thoughts my meeting with Camron had left me. And for a moment I wanted nothing more than to revel in them. I changed and sat on the chair before the roaring hearth. Bringing my legs up to my chest, I pulled out the letter within and dove into the neat lines of Simion's writing.

Once upon a time, a man and a dryad fell in love. When the moon took its place among the sky and the sun had bid farewell for another day, the man would run into the wood to greet his partner. Night after night he would return, sharing tales of his day and listening to the songs the dryad had to share. Trust blossomed like fresh, spring flowers between them. As a gift, the dryad provided her love with a piece of her to take with him during the long days they spent apart. In his hand, it looked no more than a mundane piece of tree. Imbued with the magic of the dryad, the man came to know of it as the first amplifier.

Miracles occurred in the South. Harvests flourished, crops grew healthy and full. People from all over the South came to see the man and his spectacle. Yet not all showed him such respect and awe. A group, small but mighty, held jealousy in their hearts. Burning, hot, evil jealousy.

One night, when the moon hid beneath the clouds, unable to watch the coming horror, the jealous four followed the man into the wood to witness the origin of his power. Seeing him with the dryad as the couple caused the trees to dance and the wood to sing with magic the four ambushed the lovers.

Blood was spilled.

I released a breath that I had not known I held.

This story felt familiar yet different. Like I had heard it before.

On I read, unable to stop.

As death came to claim the man the dryad contested. Using her magic, before the eyes of the jealous four, she gave up her life and encased herself and her love within a tree. Only then did the moon break free to witness the birth of the Heart of the Wood.

"Heart Oak…" I muttered aloud.

The jealous four cut their palms and bled for the tree. In a twist of cruel fate, they claimed it for their own. Taking from its branches the very power they longed for.

But as they left the wood with magic in their control, they knew little of the salvation that the dryad had carried for nine months.

"No," I breathed, turning the piece of parchment for more writing. But that was it. The end of the story.

I jumped from the seat as the fire dwindled to a low ember and dashed to the window. My body moved of its own accord. Flinging open the window, I called out for Beatrice or Simion. The answers I needed lay with them.

But they did not return my call.

It took a long while to fall asleep, but when I did my

dreams were riddled with bleeding trees and burning magic laying waste to the wood. The jealous four, with blurred faces, watched on from the shadows as I navigated the dreamscape. Although I could not see their features, I felt like I knew them. Had known them.

By morning I would claim the answers I longed for.

2 8

THE TENSION WAS THICK IN THE AIR AROUND ME. IT COULD have been sliced clean through with a blunt butter knife.

"Perfect day for a journey," Camron mused. "The weather could not be better."

"Are you seriously talking about the weather now?" I said, skipping a step to keep up with him. His mood had been undoubtedly optimistic since he woke me that morning. Whereas I had a headache that constricted around my very skull from the second I came to. The story I had read played on my mind, even during sleep I didn't escape the vivid dreams that overwhelmed me.

"What else shall we talk about? I am open to suggestions."

I had toyed with the idea of telling him about the story of the dryad and the human. But something kept me from spilling it out.

"Tell me I am doing the right thing."

Camron slowed his pace until he walked by my side. "What makes you say that?"

"Nerves," I said, although I was not entirely sure why I

questioned my decision. Of course, it was the right thing to do. I was keeping the innocents from harm. I was going to retrieve my parents. This *was* the right decision.

"Nerves are a silly emotion. One I have felt many a time before. Embrace them, do not let them run wild in your mind."

"How poetic." I forced a smile and nudged his shoulder with mine.

"Well." He turned, walking backward to face me. "What can I say? I am full to the brim with words of wisdom."

"Whatever am I going to do without them?" I rolled my eyes, surprised by the burst of a laugh that slipped past my lips. My forehead tingled. The place where he had kissed still lingering with the heat of his touch.

"Funny, Maximus, I was wondering the very same myself."

For the rest of the walk, we were quiet. A cloud of something dark came down on us both. I could not deny the feeling a moment longer. We passed many members of staff at the estate who offered their good wishes for the journey. That warmed my soul to hear.

Each step closer to the open courtyard at the front of the estate, the more the tugging in my gut intensified. I almost tripped when Camron reached out to stop me.

"Forgive me, Maximus…" He could not hold my gaze. "I fear if I do not do this I may just regret it over the time you are gone."

A lump formed in my throat. "Do what?" I whispered.

His hands, warm and soft, lifted and cupped both my cheeks. Like ice over the flame, I felt myself melt into his touch. Only then did his confidence return, and his deep eyes met mine.

"May I?"

His question was for me and only me. As if nothing around us mattered at that moment.

I did not use words to answer him. Up onto my tiptoes, I closed the small gap between us.

When his lips pressed into mine the twisting in my stomach relaxed.

His kiss was soft. Distracting. The shape of his mouth the perfect fit with mine. I felt myself rising more on my toes just to get closer to him. His strong arms wrapped around me, keeping me to him. At that moment I was overwhelmed with his scent of lavender which did little to hide the undercurrent of sea-salt that still clung to him.

Time was impossible to understand. The moment could have gone on for eternity and I would not have known. Even when he pulled back for breath, I barely allowed it, pressing myself back into him.

I felt his lips form into a smile beneath my kiss. His chuckle washed over me as his taste mixed with my own.

He pulled back and sighed through a smile. "You have just made it impossible for me to watch you leave."

"The feeling is mutual."

Camron smiled, his lips wet. "I have something for—"

"Uhmm." A throat cleared behind us. Beatrice. I turned on my heel, embarrassment overcoming me.

Beatrice stood with her legs crossed as she inspected one of her nails, a complete air of disapproval around her. My body stiffened. I straightened my jacket and flattened my hair as she peered over her hand at me. All I could hear behind me was Camron's deep chuckle.

"Are you ready *now*?" Beatrice asked, gaze narrowed on Camron rather than me.

My attention flicked back and forth between them.

"Problem, mage?" Camron kept his smile up, although something threatening coated his words.

"Not at all. Would just rather prefer that we get this started before the day is lost to us."

"Yet it would seem that we are still waiting for your brother to arrive." Camron looked around then shrugged.

"Where is your brother?" I intercepted before the tension between Camron and Beatrice bubbled over. My stomach jolted at the thought of Simion watching.

"He would have been here sooner if our means of travel was treated with a lick more of respect." She stabbed out with her comment.

The back of my neck prickled as the sun beat down on us, only adding to my discomfort.

I had folded the note Simion had left me and put it into the breast pocket of my jacket. For a thin piece of parchment, it felt suddenly heavy.

"And you are certain the beast will cooperate?" Camron asked, ignoring Beatrice's jibe.

"There is only one way to find out," she said as a noise filled the sky above.

The shadow passed over ahead, blocking out the sun for a moment. I looked up to see the dragon, wings spread wide, as it sliced through the clouds. A force of air pushed down, even from its great height, and swept the hair from my face.

It came back around again, this time lower. A small shriek escaped me as Camron and I ducked out of the way. It was Beatrice's turn to laugh at us.

The dragon changed direction back into the skies and twisted in midair. For a moment I caught the figure on its back. Simion.

"Did I not ask for it to be brought by foot?" Camron said aloud, annoyance coating his tone.

"You expect *her* to walk after she has been chained for days?" Beatrice muttered, gaze pinned to the sky. "You truly know little of the North. Glamora is a god of the sky, her kind should never be caged."

Beatrice was right. This creature belonged in the sky. Its roar did not bring on fear, but a feeling of elation. As if I understood the pure pleasure it experienced as it flew once again.

"Stay back," Beatrice warned as it finally finished its dance and came to land. As its monstrous clawed feet touched down the ground quaked.

Glamora's wings flapped bouts of air across us as she stood back on her hind legs. My hair, now faded back to its chestnut brown, danced within the powerful torrents. I had to steady my stance to stop myself from falling back. Blinking back the tears, I fought the urge to laugh, not with Camron close behind me. This display did not amuse him.

She was even bigger than I remembered her being. When Glamora was kept within the dungeon beneath the estate she seemed smaller. Curled in a protective ball. But now, surrounded by freedom, she was colossal and proud.

"Beautiful isn't it?" Beatrice whispered over her shoulder at me.

"She is," I mumbled, unable to take my eyes away from her.

Glamora began to sway strangely, a movement that a drunkard would partake in after a night of ale. Her body moved from side to side as she lowered her underbelly to the ground—spreading her wings out across the grassy bed.

Simion slid off Glamora's back. Her extended leathered wing allowing for him to elegantly slip and land on the ground. His neutral face only highlighted how effortless the move was for him.

"Show off," Camron whispered, loud enough for me to

hear. I watched his throat bob as he swallowed his pride and extended a hand for Simion.

It hung before him. Simion gave it a look and ignored it.

A flare of heat shimmered off Camron for a moment.

"Shall we go?" Simion spoke only to his sister. His voice was deep and rough. It made the hairs on my arms stand up. Finally, it was time. Glamora purred, parting her long snout to flash her needle-like teeth in agreement.

"A word?" Camron said to me, putting his hand on my back.

Simion hardly looked at me as he busied himself with Beatrice.

Once out of earshot Camron spoke. "Are you ready?"

"I think so," I told him. But inside I screamed yes.

"Be wary. Be smart."

I peered over my shoulder at the siblings in deep conversation. "I am sure it will be fine—"

"Not just those two, but everyone dwelling North. They will tell you what you want to hear, lie if they need. Please, remember this and take everything they say with a pinch of salt."

"I am going for one thing and one thing only," I said, squeezing his hand. "Once I know my parents are safe and I revoke whatever power this mage-hood gives me then I will be coming home."

"Home?" Camron smirked.

"Yes. Home."

For a moment Camron rummaged in the inside pocket of his jacket and retrieved a leather-bound book. It was small in size, not the same dimensions as the many others in the estate's library. "I want you to take this."

The book held onto the warmth of Camron's chest as

he handed it to me. The pages were yellowed and crumpled within the binding.

"What is it?" I muttered, studying the gift. A feather was used as a bookmark, the dull and colorless tip of it poking out the top of the book.

"My journal. You may find that reading it will make you learn more about me. Take it as a way of us getting to know each other better but from a distance."

I held the journal to my chest. "If I had known we were giving gifts I would have prepared one of my own."

Camron smiled, closing his eyes with a sigh. "Your promise of a return is the only gift that I needed, Maximus."

I shivered at the use of my name.

"I will look after it," I said, slipping it into the inside pocket of my jacket. It added extra weight, but the feeling was welcome. Its warm presence was a constant reminder of the man before me.

I closed the space between us and lifted onto my toes. Camron leaned in and allowed me to place a kiss upon his cheek, his face warm beneath my lips.

"Thank you," I breathed.

His mouth was inches from my ear as he replied. "That was a tease."

"A taste for what may wait for you upon my return." I pulled away. Camron put a hand to the cheek I had kissed.

"Max, come. The North has waited long enough!" Beatrice shouted at me, ruining the moment.

I left Camron standing at a distance from the siblings and the dragon.

"Are you certain the beast will carry all three of you?" Camron looked at Glamora with eyes of burning distrust.

"Certain." That was all Simion said in response.

"I wish you a safe journey." Camron waved a hand. "We all do."

Behind him, we all watched the faces of the estate and the many who hid beyond. Watching.

He was right. In the distance, the curtains moved in each window of the estate, covering those who had seconds before had been spying from the safety of the brick and mortar. All they knew of dragons was the destruction that came in their wake. From the stories we had all been told, to the destruction Glamora had left the town in. She had solidified herself in the horror of those watching.

Beatrice moved first, clambering up the side of Glamora with ease. Up this close, I could see all the small spikes of bone that curled down Glamora's wings. It was those that Beatrice grabbed a hold of as she climbed up. She scrambled herself up onto the dragon's back until both her feet were on either side of its body.

"You next," Simion said behind me so close his breath tickled the back of my neck.

"I, I—"

"Try not to be scared." He leaned in close to my ear. "She will smell it."

Camron got between Simion and me, his large hand resting on the small of my back. "Let me help."

"I'm fine," I replied. And I was. It was not fear that I felt for the beast. More wonder and worry that I would harm her as I climbed onto her.

I moved forward, stepping around the wing and leaving Camron's touch.

"It is the scales you need to watch out for. They will slice a finger off with more ease than steel."

Simion's warning did not help.

I cautiously wrapped my hand across a cold horn on

her wing and pulled myself up with as much strength as I could muster.

As I bent down to begin my crawl, the dragon shifted with anticipation. I knew that was what it felt as if it was my own emotion. My hands ran across its smooth wing as I pulled myself up. Not once did Simion offer to help. Only when I got up its back did Beatrice offer a hand.

"Is there no saddle?" I asked, feeling the rough surface of its scaled skin rub through my cotton trousers.

"Since when did you look upon the dragon and see a horse?" Simion joked as he jumped up behind me. His hands held firm upon my lower back.

"I did not mean it like that." My tone became defensive.

"Trust me, Max, when we are in the skies, you will not be worrying about your numb behind." Simion patted my back.

"Got it," I said, ignoring his condescending nature.

Camron stood at a distance. Our gazes collided and I sighed. His lips parted, lips that I had kissed, and he smiled. I wanted to raise a hand and wave, but I feared I would lose my grip and slip straight off.

"I have been waiting for this for a long time," Beatrice spoke her thoughts aloud.

I wanted to reply but my stomach shifted, making me feel ill.

"The North will smile to see your return, sister," Simion said from behind me. "You have paid your time."

"And then some."

Glamora moved suddenly, pushing off from the ground and standing. A shiver ran down her scales and she released a sound that sang with anticipation.

"Hold on," Simion whispered behind me. "Tight."

My stomach turned in circles and I pinched my eyes

closed. The vision of Camron was imprinted in the back of my mind like a fire burning in a dark room.

And into the sky, Glamora flew. Only a few pounds of her grand wings and it was enough for us to swing high into the expanse of blue.

I felt the cord then. An invisible chain between my wrist and the man left far below. A connection. Closing my eyes, I imagined the chain of silver that linked us. It comforted me as the beast rose higher in the sky.

He would be with me.

Simion shouted above the roaring winds. "Open your eyes, Max, you will not want to miss this."

I opened my eyes, looking across at the view beyond. It snatched my breath away. A sea of wood and cloud. The estate no more than a dollhouse far below.

My lips, still warm from Camron's kiss, parted. I peered over the side of Glamora and watched the estate grow smaller and smaller.

This is it, I thought, looking far ahead of me toward the North. Intent raged through me, my pool of magic awakening against the emotion. I would finish this chapter of my story and return to start a new one.

With Camron.

III

THE RETURN OF THE LOST

29

I WANTED TO SCREAM, TO SHOUT INTO THE ABYSS AROUND us as we sliced through the clouds. I could have stayed airborne for the rest of my life. That high, among clouds and flocks of birds, I felt free. Birds did not show such feelings toward the growling beast we rode upon. Flocks of them joined in on our journey, barely keeping up with the speed.

Pulling my cloak around me to fight off the cold temperatures, I focused on the view to keep me occupied. There was no room for talking this far from the ground as the winds screamed terribly in my stinging ears. All day we had flown, and all that I had seen was the seemingly never-ending sea of the wood. Mountainous oak and cedar trees blocked most of the view of the wood's underworld. Only now and then would the sparkle of a body of water catch the fading sunlight.

The lullaby of the color-changing sky muted my mind. I fought a yawn as it lulled me into drowsiness. With Beatrice's hard frame before me and Simion behind I did not feel prepared to give in to the heavy lids of my eyes.

Focusing on the sea of green below, I urged myself to stay alert.

We flew like this until my behind ached and my legs tingled.

Once the blue sky melted into the dark pinks of dusk, Beatrice leaned forward. The movement distracted me from my thoughts. With her face close to Glamora's forehead she seemed to be lying down. But she soon straightened again seconds before the course of the dragon's flight changed.

Down the beast dove. My stomach jolted, sickness a tidal wave that threatened to explode from my mouth. The lulling cry of wind turned into a high screech as we shot for the ground below.

Glamora's wings folded into her obsidian body as she nose-dived into a clearing of the forest. The wall of thick green foliage came up so fast; I expected to crash right into the trees.

I clamped my eyes shut, teeth biting into my lip as I tried not to cry out. At the last moment, I heard the beast's wings snap out, slowing our descent as winds caught in her leathery limbs.

Prying my eyes open, I peered ahead. The clearing she flew toward was large enough to fit the dragon, but that was it. Trees lined on all sides, so dark that it was hard to see far into the forest. Anyone or anything could have waited among the shadows of the dense wood. But there was a sense of serenity about this place. Untouched and safe.

I only allowed myself a breath once Glamora's claws dug into the bed of the wood. Anchoring us to the unmoving, blessed ground.

It was Simion who spoke first, sliding on his backside

down Glamora's wing and onto the ground. "This will do nicely for tonight."

I could not even think to reply as I swallowed down the sickness that sprung upon me.

"She could have gone till sundown," Beatrice said from her perch on Glamora's neck. "It would have shaved off time if we kept going."

"I know she could, but she deserves a good meal. And so do we."

Beatrice rolled her eyes. "Nothing has changed in the years, have they?"

Simion patted his stomach and winked.

I ran my hand across Glamora's scales and thanked her silently. The sloshing illness finally settled.

"She said you are welcome," Beatrice mentioned, adding, "Although you should scream less. Your lack of trust could insult a dragon. Just something to think about in the future."

The dragon seemed to purr beneath my touch, echoing what Beatrice had said. "The dragon told you that?"

"Of course *she* did. I have often longed to hear one of the dragons speak. Your southern creatures are not as… how do I put it? Well versed in the art of conversation between a human. There is nothing better than the crystal chime of an intelligent beast."

Glamora snorted heavily, causing bouts of dust and dirt from the ground to swirl into the air.

"I did not know."

"And why would you." Beatrice's tone sharpened.

"I do not know what I have done to offend you—" I started, feeling the creep of red spread up my neck.

Simion interrupted, his hand reaching for me. "Maximus. Come, let us leave my sister with Glamora. There is much we need to discuss whilst we gather wood for tonight's fire."

I paused for a moment, looking into the back of Beatrice's head with intent, waiting for her to spew some more angry words my way.

I was ready. Ready to tell her exactly what I thought of her. How I had reason to treat her how she had treated me.

But Simion tapped his fingers to my thigh, distracting me. He widened his eyes and nodded his head, urging me to follow him.

I took the trip down cautiously. Simion's long fingers gripped mine and coaxed me gently to climb from Glamora's side.

As soon as my feet touched down on the ground the slight spinning leveled off and my head calmed.

"I have questions," I muttered to Simion, hand reaching for the note still folded in the chest pocket of my jacket.

"A lot of them, I am sure," Simion replied. "Luckily for you I am the bearer of answers."

Simion began walking into the dark shadows of the surrounding trees, leaving Beatrice upon the dragon. Still, she did not look my way. Swallowing my pride, I followed after her brother.

We navigated the dark space of the wood. Over half a day away from Camron and the estate, this wood was thicker. Untouched. As I moved around monstrous trunks of trees whose roots devoured the very ground, I could not help but feel we had been the only people to walk through in countless years.

"Bea is as stubborn as I last remembered."

I latched onto Simion's voice, skipping a step to catch up. "I know what she is like. At least I thought I did. She is treating me like a stranger when she has been the closest person to me for years."

Beneath the anger at the way she was acting toward me was true sadness, occupying the pit in my stomach.

"Beatrice is dealing with a lot. Everything she has been preparing for since she was exiled is coming ahead. I think she is just coming to terms with it in her own way."

"Exiled?" I asked. "From the North?"

"My one and only sister sent packing from her home for something my parents did. It was a way of punishing our mother more than it was for Beatrice. But yes, exiled from the North. But not for long."

"Because of me?"

Simion stood in a small clearing. The canopy of trees were thinner here, allowing the fading light of day to give us some idea of what we stood amongst.

"You were her duty. To find the lost mage and return him. It was a task given to her to reclaim her place in the North."

"When did this happen…" I racked my brain, trying to remember how long she had been in my life.

"Since she was young enough to forget herself. Likely why it took so long for her to recognize you for what you were. Some would even argue too late. With your eyes, it is close to impossible not to see the truth."

Simion was inches before me, staring down at me with his large, dark eyes.

"Green like the forest. Like your mothers."

I shook my head, unable to look at him a moment longer. I started pacing the clearing instead. "Beatrice was exiled from the North for something your parents did! That is truly cruel. What could they have done that was so bad that Beatrice had to be punished in their place?"

Simion paused. "My mother helped yours to take you far from the North."

His words did not settle across me. Not for a moment, until they slowly pieced together.

"Why?"

"That I do not know."

"It is my fault then."

"In a way," Simion replied. "Yes. I have not seen my sister for over ten years because of you. But I do not hate you for it. You are as innocent in this story as my sister is. Both of you are being punished for our parents' own, selfish actions."

"That is why they took them, isn't it? My parents."

Simion took a moment to reply. His lips parted as he studied his response internally. "I do not know why they have your parents, Max. It was never the plan. That part is still a mystery to me."

"If they hurt them…" I growled, my magic spurring in my stomach. "They will never get what they want from me."

"You will soon learn, Max, that the North is not what you believe them to be. We do not simply hurt and cause pain for the desired outcome. We are *very* different than the South. You will soon come to learn this."

A noise sounded in the trees around us, the crack of a branch beneath a foot. I could not still the gasp that escaped me.

"There is nothing to fear here. We are comfortably alone."

"In the South, we hear of ghosts and spirits that lurk in the wood. You would be a fool not to be scared," I replied.

"I am glad to remind you that we are no longer in the South. The wood does not belong to either your home or mine. And I assure you, nothing lives within this wood anymore. Only animals and… trees. You can thank your people for causing such a vacant place."

"The story you left me," I said. "That is what you mean. Dryads. They left because of what they did to the dryad and her human companion?"

"I am glad you spent some time reading," Simion muttered, rummaging around the forest bed as he inspected the discarded wood laying across it.

"It is true then?"

"No… it is yet another made-up story! Of course, it is true. Please tell me you have heard of that tale before? Have you ever questioned how your mages came to be in the South?"

My answer was simple. "No. We were told the mages gained their magic through their bloodline."

"And you simply believed it?"

I did not want to argue with him, tell him that there was never room to simply disbelieve the ruling estates.

"Tomorrow you will see the place in which the traitorous, jealous four stalked the man and the dryad. You will see the burned remains of the Heart of Galloway which stands as a reminder to both the North and South about the origins of this story."

"Do you mean the Heart Oak?"

Simion grunted. "No, Max, I do not mean the Heart Oak. Galloway was the name of the man who fell in love with the dryad. Thus claiming it for her name as well. We remember it by Galloway out of respect for the two who sacrificed much in the sake of love."

"There is so much to learn." I did not distrust what Simion said.

"Indeed there is."

I did not know what to ask next. It was impossible to

grasp onto a thought as my mind rushed with a tidal wave of questions for Simion.

Simion lazily dropped the stack of twigs and branches he had begun to collect. "We have some time to spare. I suggest we fill it by starting with your first lesson—one that is arguably the most important and defining feature of being a mage."

The wand warmed on my forearm. "Magic."

30

"Woah there." Simion laughed, raising his hands in defeat. "Don't get ahead of yourself. We are not going to duel."

I lowered my wand. "Are you not a mage?"

His healing abilities said otherwise.

"Not in the same manner you are, Max," he drawled, hand on hip. "I am what is known as a gleamer in the North. A mage with passive abilities. I heal, other gleamers have minor telepathic abilities. If you crack a bolt my way I am powerless to stop it."

"A gleamer?"

"And you are a parrot by the sounds of it." He tugged on the loose collar of his shirt to exposed a cord around his neck. A pendant of wood hung between his broad chest, nestled perfectly between each mound of muscle.

Averting my eyes quickly, I hid my sudden embar-rassment.

"This is my amplifier. Carved by my hand when I was a boy. Without it, I cannot access my inherent abilities. Just like you would not be able to call on the earth without your… *wand*."

"And here I thought you wanted me to show you what I can do." Confidence riddled my words.

"Why would I want such a thing when you do not even understand your capability? It is like me asking a child to run before they can walk."

My cheeks warmed and my skin itched beneath his insult.

"It seems there is a lot more to being a mage than I first thought."

Simion grinned, flexing his hands before him. "It has been tasked upon me to test you and find out whereabouts you may fit within the academy's system. Gleamers are one of three main groups that every child of the wood fits into. Abilities that are vital to both the defense and offense of our kind. Positions equally important in the queen's eyes."

"You are going to need to slow down with your explanations as I am struggling to keep up"

With exaggerated hand movements, Simion responded. "An academy is a big tall building. A schooling system for us to learn about our abilities and train."

"Do not belittle me." I flicked the wand up again in warning.

Simion only smiled further, lips threatening to split his cheeks. "I jest, Max."

"Did you go to the academy?" I wanted to know more. Mother had taught me to read and write herself. The Gathrax family never wanted their subjects to be well educated as that came with the threat of knowledge.

"We both did. Me and Bea. Although my stint with education was longer than my sister."

Because she was exiled.

Interrupting my guilt, Simion continued. "Now I do

not think the tests are necessarily that important as you have displayed your powers… without a problem. It is clear you are not a simple gleamer like me. But you could be one of two options: a ryder or an elder. And I have a hunch of which one you are."

I shied away from his narrowing gaze. "And what is your assumption?"

"Ryder," he said plainly. "Mages that are used in offense rather than defense. You have displayed your ability of the earth and commanded it as your own. That is the main ability of a mage. However, you have displayed a second gift. Dragon kissed—giving you the ability of the winds. Some can even call upon lightning, the true weapon of the skies."

The voice of the murdered mage filled my mind. "He had said that to me."

"Who?" Simion pushed further.

I spun the wand in my hand until the death notches were visible to Simion. "The warrior I killed in town."

Simion's face pained for a moment. His smile slipped into nothingness, even his eyes lost their sheen. "Dragon kissed is a gift all children of the wood are given upon birth. It is a ritual we all go through—although it only affects some. It is not clear as to how or why. But when children are taken to the mountains, the father of all dragons would blow his life force upon them."

I put my fingers to my temple, pushing at it in hopes it would still the throbbing. "I should be sitting down for this flood of new information."

"I am easing you into it, Max. There is much to learn, I can assure you—this is hardly scraping the surface of what waits for you beyond this wood."

It thrilled me and unnerved me at the same time.

"I cannot understand why Mother kept me from this. And Father."

"He likely did not know," Simion said "Your father is not from the North. Only your mother left with you alone."

I stilled. My lungs became as heavy as the leaden weight of my heart.

Simion noticed his mistake, rushing to me with outstretched hands. "You did not know?"

I snatched my arms away from him, turning my back so he did not see the tear that leaked from my eye. "No." It was all I could manage. Any other words and my voice would crack beneath the dam of emotions within me.

"I think I have said enough." Simion rested a hand on my shoulder.

"No, Simion." I turned to him. "You are the first person to say the right amount of truth to me. You, a stranger. Whereas those I have known for a long time have done nothing but lie to me."

Anger was a familiar companion of mine now. It became easier for it to slip into the place where sadness had been.

"I am sorry, Max, I have a big mouth."

Not able to hold the tears back a moment longer, I left Simion in the clearing. My pace picked up as I navigated the dark wood back to Beatrice. Thankful that only the darkness could see my cry. That the thick wood swallowed the sound of my sobbing.

As I lost myself to the emotion, I realized what it truly was.

Betrayal.

THE WARMTH FROM THE FIRE BARELY REACHED ME. ONLY teased me in moments of comfort before dissipating in a cold breeze. I brought my knees to my chest and held on for dear life—hoping the little heat left in my body would not leave. I could not fathom having to sleep as the cold of night engulfed our makeshift camp.

Simion did not seem to have a problem falling into sleep. He was snoring only moments after finishing the roasted rabbit that Beatrice had caught for us, leaned back across the forest bed with his hands supporting his head. His relaxed demeanor told me that he had done this before.

I had not said anything to Simion since he returned to the camp with firewood. Out the corner of my eye, I could see him look at me in brief moments, but I did everything I could to avoid his stare. I did not want to talk about what he had revealed. Not to him or anyone. Not that I had a problem worrying Beatrice would spark up a conversation. She had busied herself with the rabbit, skinning it, preparing it, then roasting it over the fire that Simion had erected.

Perhaps I should have asked if they wanted help. Instead, I kept to myself.

Beatrice chewed on the rabbit's bones, sitting on the other side of the campfire. The flames glowed across her dark skin. Her staff was laid across her crossed lap as she devoured the little meat left on the bones. Glamora was behind her, almost invisible in the dark as her obsidian body was curled in a ball. The rattling of her sleeping breath blending perfectly with Simion who snored feet away from her.

I studied the markings around my wrist. The dark band of ink that connected me to Camron all those miles away. In a way I missed him. Especially as the cold surrounded me. His body warmth, his assuring voice. His kiss still lingered across my mouth—a phantom feeling that tingled as I thought of him. He had not once kept something from me. Not like my parents.

It surprised me that another tear escaped from my eye. I had thought it impossible that I had any left to shed. With a rough hand, I brushed it from my face.

"Just because you love your parents does not mean you have to like them."

I looked up to Beatrice across the flames of the campfire as she spoke. Gaze still fixed on the clean bone in her hand.

"Simion told you?"

"He didn't have to," Beatrice replied, throwing the bone into the fire. "He means well, my brother. In the years that I have not been with him, his bashful sincerity has never faltered. He had a tendency to speak before thinking about the consequences."

I looked to the snoring boy. His long limbs stretched

out when he recognized his name in the dreamscape he was drowning within.

"They lied to me. All my life my mother kept the truth locked up, and for what?"

"I have come to learn that it is best not to dwell on the actions of others. Even if it affects the course of your own life. Trust me, Max, I have been angry for a long time. So much so that in the past years I gave up on my task to find the lost mage. I found it easier living in ignorance. It was easier to cope with what my mother did. Forgetting about her and everything that I was forced to leave behind. And with time, the more I forgot the North."

"Until now…"

Beatrice's eye widened, looking at me over the fire. "I do not hate you, Max. I hate what you *represent* but not you."

I swallowed the lump that had embedded itself in my throat.

"I wish it was not you, you know. You were one of the few that I had got close to. Perhaps I knew deep down that there was something different about you. Or familiar I should say."

"Are you not happy to finally be going home?" I could see an internal struggle as Beatrice lost herself inside the blazing campfire.

"Home…" Beatrice barked a laugh. "I am not sure where I claim as home now. I have always dreamt of returning. But now I am not sure it is what I want. What do you want, Max?"

"I am not sure either," I admitted. "Answers… from my parents. I want to hear the truth. And this…" I pulled the wand from the holder and held it up. "I had hated magic for as long as I can remember. Mother would blame it for the way of the South. But now I feel that giving it away will be impossible."

"She will never let you return to the South with it." Beatrice's voice dipped. Her tone sent a shiver across the back of my neck.

"Who?"

"The queen. The one you know as the Mad Queen. Her entire existence has been to ensure that power was removed from the South and for it to never return. If you are hoping to return home it will be under *her* rules. You will be different."

The pool of magic sloshed deep within me. The barrier between it and my control dissipated as I held onto the wand. Feeling its familiar touch was as much as a comfort as the flames before me. Just the thought of being without it caused the power to thrash.

I was unable to think of it a moment longer—instead opting to change the course of the conversation.

"I never noticed your mage mark. Nor did I see your staff before."

Beatrice stilled for a moment, lifting the staff before her and running her hands across its smooth wood. "Simion returned my amplifier to me when he reached the South. A gift from the queen to assist in helping me retrieve you. I had been without it for a long time; it stills feels like a stranger to me. My magic has been harder to call up when required."

I remembered the discomfort caused when Master Gathrax had kept the wand from me. I could only imagine the pain that Beatrice had gone through while she was kept from her staff for years.

"That must have been hard," I replied. "Removed from a place at such a young age for something you had no part to play in."

"We are similar, Max. Both taken from our homes at a young age when we had no choice in the matter. I remember when it happened, you know. Not in a matter of words and actions but in a feeling. I was no more than three when my mother was taken from our home and put before trial. I still remember the feeling of wanting to see her. In hindsight, I was too young to truly understand what was happening but I knew the queen had taken my mother and she had never returned. It was another three years later when I was just six years of age. I was called to the high court and presented before her majesty. Told of my task in the morning and removed from the North by late afternoon. I was originally escorted to the Calzmir Estate and was taken in by an orphanage until I was old enough to leave by myself. I looked for a couple of years—for signs or news of something with magic. I knew the person would have been only a year or so younger than me. I clung on to the feeling of home for those years, passing from estate to estate, looking. Then I settled in the Gathrax Estate. Took up a job with the local smithy as he would never question me wearing gloves day in and day out. I quickly settled into a new routine—keeping busy so that I soon pushed the thought of my task to the far reaches of my mind. I was tired, very tired of having to search for you."

Beatrice spilled her heart out before me. Tears sliced down her beautiful, grief-stricken face. I could not cry for her. Could not pity what she had been through at the fault of my family.

"I am sorry, Bea," I murmured, choking on my own emotion. "For what you have been through because of me. Because of my family."

I stood, legs aching from the hard ground I had sat on for a while. Navigating around the fire, I moved for my friend, kneeling beside her and wrapped my arms around her strong frame. I held her like that for a moment—forcing as much love for her from my body as I could conjure. Then her arms snaked up and found me.

And we held each other, tears soaking our shirts until the campfire dwindled into smaller flames and charred wood.

Sleep failed to greet me. No matter how I tried to will it into existence. I found my frustration rising with each passing moment.

I rolled over, reaching for the jacket I had put behind my head as a pillow. My fingers found it, the cold leather of the journal Camron had given me.

My stomach jolted. I sat up slowly, not wanting to wake the others. I tried hard to keep my movements minimal as I dragged myself closer to the dwindling fire to get a better look at the gift he had given me.

A shiver coursed down my spine as my touch explored the journal. I ran my fingers gently across its face, sensing the phantom marks left by Camron's touch.

The thought alone warmed me greater than the fire I sat before.

I cracked the journal open. The firelight danced across the yellowed pages. The feather had been used as a bookmark so I took extra caution not to lose it in the dark.

The first few pages were empty.

Then I read his name.

Camron Calzmir.

. . .

I traced my finger over the curved calligraphy. His writing neat enough to read, but it seemed he allowed his emotions to dance while jotting down his thoughts.

A few more turns and I found the beginning of his story. The fire before me cracked loudly in my shared anticipation. I felt as though I was on the brink of discovering a man I hardly knew, ready to dive in and learn what I could about him in a way that felt more... personal.

His very thoughts had been laid out before me.

And I devoured them.

Day One

I will never forget today. Not for as long as I live. I have stolen this moment to write down the happenings but in truth, I wish I was up on deck with them all now. It does not feel right to be sat down here, in my chamber of plush fabrics and wealth, when I should be sharing an ale with my crewmates.

Camron, remember this moment.

Mother thought I would chuck up my insides the moment the ship set sail, but she was wrong. The smell of salt and warm wood, I hope that stays with me for as long as I remember.

If I could bottle up the scent and send it back to my mother I would. Hell, I would keep it in a vial around my neck and smell it whenever I needed reminding.

Even writing this I know how it may read. But this day is important to me. I have been entrusted to explore the lands beyond as I have petitioned for years.

It feels like my life has only just begun.

There may be more time to journal tomorrow but I must join the brave souls above deck.

Tonight we drink, tomorrow we journey.

. . .

My face ached from smiling. I could almost feel Camron's enthusiasm for his exploration as though it seeped from the very pages and into my being. Even his handwriting had grown messier toward the end of his first entry. Rushed to do as he said. *Tonight we drink, tomorrow we journey.* My eyes strained trying to keep the words from floating as I read his story in the fading light of the campfire. But it did not stop me. On and on I read, reading of him tackling storms with his crewmates, describing his first weeks upon the sea as he searched for slips of land.

It thrilled me. For I felt we shared the same emotion in a way. Our stories were linked intrinsically. For I was on a journey of my own.

As I lied back down, the journal stuffed back into my jacket pocket, I could not help but feel that this was Camron's way of keeping me looking forward.

You inspire me, Camron Calzmir.

Already questions for him rattled through my brain, questions I'd have to keep a hold of for when I returned home.

Beatrice told us not to pack camp when we woke in the morning. Even if I wanted to I couldn't, not with my body stiff and aching from lying on the woodland bed all night. Simion had agreed with his sister, promising the wildland would soon devour the cold campfire. With the kingdom in the North still a two day ride away, we clambered onto Glamora's back and began our journey.

It was Beatrice who offered a hand for me this morning. Her face lifted into a smile, brows soft and forehead lacking the lines that had found themselves chiseled across it. The tension between us had washed away like the tears we had both shed last night.

Although the day was bright, more clouds painted the sky today. It made seeing the expansive wood below almost impossible. Glamora kept above the clouds, her wings steady and stretched beside her as she flew.

I was becoming accustomed to the chill this high up. How it stung at my cheeks and had my eyes streaming. I had not felt this awake in weeks atop the dragon.

"Here," Simion shouted, although his voice was barely

audible as the winds screamed. He sat behind me, his hands outstretched on either side of me. He held swaths of material—the browns of his cloak which he wrapped around my quaking body.

His hard arms squeezed around me, capturing me in his cloak until it fought some of the chilled breeze off. I did not know how long it took for me to forget that he held onto me. But it must have been when my pride gave into the fact that I did not want to freeze to death.

Glamora dipped violently. Before I slammed into Beatrice's back, I clenched onto my core. However, it was Simion's arms that held me in place.

"Steady now…." he murmured into my ear. "I've got you."

I kept my gaze forward, thankful he could not see my cheeks redden. Opting to forget that the boy held me in place, I allowed my mind to wonder about the possibilities that lay ahead.

I had imagined what lay beyond the vast wood many a time and had only the hate and propaganda of the South to conjure images of what I'd find North. A Mad Queen, riddled with age. Barren lands filled with normal people living *normal* existences beneath the tyrant of a woman. A masked army. A horde of dragons. All these images used to spread disdain throughout me.

Everything Simion and Beatrice had told me negated what I was forced to believe. Their home sounded like a place of wonder. Humans and dragons living among each other. An academy where magic was praised and harnessed.

But there was still one factor that chilled my insides.

Why had Mother taken me? What had made her run?

That thought stayed with me the entire day. And only

intensified as the sun began to lower over the world and bless the sky with dark blues of the incoming evening.

Beatrice moved, peering over her shoulder, the tip of her nose bright pink. "We are close."

Simion, still holding onto me, shouted back. "Lower us, sister."

Beatrice turned back to face the expanse ahead, lowering herself to speak to Glamora. I readied myself for another dramatic move from the dragon, but this time it was gentle. My stomach spun as Glamora lowered us beneath the line of clouds, enough for the woodland beneath to be in view once again.

"Can you see it?" Simion called above the wind.

Simion relaxed an arm around me and pointed to a dark shadow that sliced across the wood below.

I rubbed away the tears that streamed from my eyes and focused on the strange mark that scarred the wood.

A large clearing was charred and black. Void of life. A graveyard of wood and ash. As if a star had fallen from the sky and landed across the forest, leaving nothing in its wake.

The Eye of Galloway.

The same place the dryad and her lover were forever entombed in Heart Oak. The very place the first mages from the four ruling estates came to reclaim their wands. The very reason the War of the Wood began.

My heart ached in my chest, the vision below coaxing a deep sorrow to devour me.

It was the strange feeling that came with looking upon such destruction. It settled in one's stomach like a stone and made a home amongst the aching of a heart. I found myself pressing a hand on my chest to still the overwhelming urge to cry.

The destruction was unforgivable. Even this far up I

could not ignore the tang of smoke that tickled at my nose. As if the fire was new. Fresh. But I knew it was not. Close to a hundred years had passed since the North burned the Heart Oak.

But looking down upon it, I was certain some fire still burned below.

I craned my neck just to keep looking at the destruction for as long as I could manage as Glamora lifted back into the cover of the clouds.

Simion no longer held onto me. Beatrice was a statue as she directed Glamora on.

The scene had not only affected me but the two siblings that I was sandwiched between.

The rest of the day passed slowly, filled with nothing but horrible thoughts. Just seeing the heart of the wood had truly solidified the story I had read on Simion's note as fact. I imagined the emotions of the lovers, and the pain the betrayal must have caused them. Then I thought of Camron and felt the strange, intense absence. His warmth would be welcome here. His hold around me was needed.

It pained me to think of the distance that separated us.

I only hoped our story did not end in flames.

Beatrice reached a hand for me, helping me from Glamora's back.

"Thank you... for showing me," I said, slipping from Glamora's back, my legs like jelly as I landed beside Beatrice.

"No need to thank me." Beatrice patted my shoulder. "If it were my choice we would have navigated around *that* cemetery. Simion was the one who likes painful reminders it seems so you can thank him."

I looked to her brother who was stretching his long limbs dramatically. "For us in the North, the Eye of Galloway emits nothing but sadness. It would have been stupid for us to not show you. It is important to our very existence."

"Children of the wood," I echoed what he had previously told me.

"You are a fast learner, Maximus," Simion said, "You never cease to impress me."

I hugged onto his cloak, looking to his sister.

"And you never cease to stop being insufferable," Beatrice said to him. "Simion, do what you do best and fetch some more wood for kindling."

Raising a hand to his forehead, he saluted. "Your wish is my command."

And in a few backward steps, Simion slipped into the darkness of the surrounding wood.

The clearing we had landed in was smaller than yesterday's. Two trees lay torn from their roots as collateral when Glamora had landed here. Her hulking body snapped a third as she had spun like a dog looking for a comfortable place to rest.

"Help me with this," Beatrice said, throwing a small leather satchel at me.

I hardly caught it in time as the heavy contents winded me. "Are you certain we are good now?"

Beatrice shared a hearty laugh. "We certainly are Max-a-million."

She had not called me that in a long while. It warmed my insides, brushing away the cobwebs of chill from the days' flight.

Discarding the bag by my feet, I helped Beatrice clear debris from the ground, making space for a new campfire.

"Why did you not want to see the Eye of Galloway?" I asked her.

She paused for a moment, fussing over the pinecones and sticks that she collected in her hands. "Why would anyone want the reminder of such misery?"

I shrugged. "If it is so hard for the North to see then why did they burn it in the first place?"

"Max," Beatrice hissed through gritted teeth. "You have been brought up to believe so many falsities. Can you tell me why exactly the queen would have given orders to burn the very place her parents were kept? A shrine to her origin?"

In my mind, I began placing the pieces of the puzzle together.

"The fire, the one that started the first war. I understand her tactics, to sever the Heart Oak from ever being used in the South again. But... that was her parent's tomb?"

"Max, the queen did not burn the Eye of Galloway."

"What?" Confusion thrummed through me.

"You said it yourself, why would she do that? It was the burning of the Heart Oak that provoked our queen to finally act and send her army into the South. She did it because the South burned the wood."

I stared at Beatrice. "That is not true."

"It is fact," she replied. "There is a lot for you to learn."

"So tell me." I stomped my foot in protest. "I am willing to listen and see the story from your point of view. But you need to tell me."

"When you threw your amplifier into the fire the night of the festival... did it burn?"

"No." I felt the cold wood across my forearm, remembering the kiss of fire across my arm as I reached into the bonfire to retrieve the wand.

Beatrice reached for her amplifier, pulling the staff from its holder on her back and placing it before her. "You need to understand that no ordinary flame can burn Heart Oak. It is the product of a god, Maximus, a dryad. Wytchfire was the source of the fire. When the queen and her army invaded the South it was to find the source of the wytchfire. It was believed the Southern mages and their families had stores of it. Ready to use to clear the entirety of the wood separating the South and North. When the origins of it were not found, she left. The South is not the enemy and never was. It is why they have not been invaded since."

"She did not return for the South because the mages had been killed."

"Magic is not the enemy in this story, Max," Beatrice said, leaning on her staff. "It is merely the victim of a still unknown threat."

"I don't understand. Why would the South want to destroy the wood? Without the Heart Oak, they'd be powerless."

"It is believed they were tricked. Manipulated by another for their twisted gain. They were likely promised that the Heart Oak would be spared, the North would be destroyed, and the families would have the ability to spread across the land, claiming it for their own."

I sat down with a thump. My gaze was lost to a single spot on the ground. "Who? Who is this *other* you speak of?"

"Wytchfire can only be created by a phoenix, natural enemies to the dragon for centuries. Long before our kind came into existence the two species warred for power."

Dryads ruled over the earth, dragons reigned over the

sky. The phoenix was a bird of fire and flame, a powerful creature that only existed in stories.

"They were destroyed years ago," I said, adding in the little information I knew of the gods of fire.

"I would say that they were more 'driven away' rather than destroyed. Exiled much like myself to another land. Unlike the other creatures of life, the phoenix is the only being with the ability to live on. Immortality that was lusted after by the dragons, dryads, and nymphs."

Glamora purred behind us.

"I am no historian, Max. I should not be telling you all about the history of this land for it is not my expertise. Perhaps we can obtain some scriptures when we reach our destination, and you can learn from a new point of view."

I looked at my friend as she stood over me. "Why do I have a sense that I am about to uncover some truths that I would prefer stayed hidden?"

Crouching down before me, Beatrice extended a hand and smiled. "Believe me, Max, after years in the South I was beginning to forget all of this. We can uncover it all together."

I reached for it. Her hand was bigger than mine, engulfing it; her touch was soft.

"To blowing the lid off the lies and finally getting answers."

I muttered back to her, "Here, here."

3 3

My body could not move. No matter how I thrashed at the bindings of vine and wood, I was entrapped. In the web of the earth that constricted like a snake, squeezing across my body. The tension stabbed agony through me. I felt that I would pop as the earth wound tighter. Straining my eyes, I could barely see as my body disappeared among the thick ropes of flora; every inch of me devoured by the living, wild foliage.

My mouth was split in a scream, but no sound came out. There was no noise in this dark abyss. The silence was deafening.

All I could do was wait for the creeping fingers of vines to reach my face, for their exploring touch to snap through my teeth and drown me internally. Just like I had to Master Gathrax.

This was my penance. A just punishment for a murderer.

I cried out for my parents. But they did not come to my aid. My silent pleas devoured by the vines that wrapped hungrily around my throat and squeezed.

Max.

Someone called for me. A face, white as snow, peered through the dark. Sharp cheekbones edged by the shadows, amber hair spilling down over ears as the face lingered inches from mine.

Camron. He had come. He opened his mouth, lips moving.

Max.

There was a delay as he spoke my name. But his voice was different. Muddy and weak as if he cried it from the bottom of the ocean.

Max.

Why was he smiling at me? The thought was clear as I looked up through bulging eyes as the last of my breath was taken from me.

"Max!"

I bolted up, my spine aching and head spinning. Blinking away the harsh nightmare, I looked frantically around the wood for Camron. My hands ran across my body, expecting the vines to still be wrapped around me.

But all I felt was my quaking chest through shaking hands.

Simion was there, kneeling beside me with his arms frozen before him. In the dark light of early dawn, his face was pinched with both tiredness and concern. Dark shadows rimmed his eyes and his hair stuck up in places it usually would not.

"You were having a nightmare," he whispered, his voice calm and low. "You are fine."

I still felt that I would slip back into the hellscape if I blinked. I strained to keep my eyes open until they blurred with tears.

"It was… horrible," I muttered, covering my face with

my hands. The phantom touch of the earth still lingered across my body.

"You have a lot on your mind, Max. Dreams are your mind's way of helping you deal with your worries."

I let out a large sigh, enough to spook Glamora who stirred from slumber on the other side of the clearing. "I would appreciate it if my *mind* did not feel the need to help."

Simion laughed through a yawn. "It is still early. You should try and get some more rest."

"Did I wake you?" I asked.

"You did indeed." He leaned back on his arms, large hands splayed against the ground. "But I'm a light sleeper, I heard you muttering and simply wanted to check on you."

I felt the creep of a blush threaten to taint my cheeks red. "Thank you… for waking me up."

"Do you want to talk about it?" he asked, one dark brow raised. "It helps to slay the nightmare by exposing it during waking hours."

I opened my mouth to spill what I had seen. But stopped myself short. "No, I think I just need to shake it off."

"Fair enough. But if you change your mind, I will be here…" He slumped backward, back thumping into the ground. "You should try and get some more sleep. We have a long day ahead of us."

The thought of closing my eyes again scared me enough to decline. Instead, the rumble of my stomach provided me with a perfect excuse. I pushed myself from the forest bed, legs like jelly, and stood above Simion. "I think I will try and find us something to eat for breakfast. Last night's supper…" I rubbed my hand across my stomach. "Barely touched the sides."

Simion pushed on his thighs to stand but I waved him off. "Alone if you do not mind."

"Of course." Simion could not hide the disappointment in his face even if he wanted to. Instead, he flopped back onto the ground and put his head in his hands; the muscles on his forearms flexed wildly as he did so. "Suit yourself. But fetch us something hearty. We'll need it."

I turned my back on him, catching a glimpse of Beatrice who still snored from her spot on the ground.

There was a part of me that hoped Simion would offer his assistance again as I walked for the outline of trees. Besides having no idea on how to hunt for fowl or other catchable meats—I also did not want to enter the wood alone.

But I forced one step after the other until I was out of sight.

I came back with a handful of mysterious red berries that Beatrice had deemed too unsafe to eat. Although she thanked me for my effort nonetheless. With empty stomachs, we prepared to leave camp. The promise of a decent meal when we reached the North was all I could think about as I walked the campsite in a daze of hunger.

I contemplated taking the wand from the holder on my arm and conjuring an apple tree. That was what the mages of the South used to do with their power. But the thought of calling upon magic only reminded me of the dream. So I left it, the cold touch of wood still pressed to my skin.

Beatrice swore beneath her breath as she fussed over Glamora. The dragon was noticeably restless.

"What is wrong with you?" Beatrice shouted louder. "Will you calm down, Glamora!"

The dragon pushed off the ground, rising onto her hind legs and kicking out like a horse. Beatrice tumbled backward just in time, hardly missing the large claw that reached for her.

"Steady now, girl…" Simion raced forward, hands raised in surrender.

I offered a hand for Beatrice and she took it.

"I don't know what is going on with her, but her mind is a race of panic," Beatrice said, pressing a hand to her forehead. "I can't make out a single thought."

Unlike Beatrice, I could not read the creature's thoughts. But I could sense the emotion that rolled off the beast in icy waves. "She is scared."

Something had spooked the dragon, that much was clear. Simion was still trying to calm the beast but failed miserably.

Her roar shook the clearing, urging an unnatural cold wind to ravage across us. Simion fell back from the serrated teeth that flashed before him.

The ground shook as Glamora pounded her limbs across it. Her tail thrashed around as she spun, slamming into trees. One was smashed straight through, angling to fall in our direction.

My breath was knocked out of me as Beatrice pushed me out of the way. We both rolled across the ground before we were crushed beneath the weight of falling debris.

The world turned upside down. I watched from my place on the ground as Glamora beat her wings furiously. Wind battered down across us. Then she was up in the air, her dark shape bolting into the distance.

Beatrice was up and screaming after Glamora. "Get back here, you hulking fool!"

Panting, we watched for the dragon to turn back for us —but she did not.

The clearing was quiet. Too quiet. Simion was still lying on the ground ahead of us. Beatrice too busy shouting at Glamora to notice.

Had he fallen and hurt himself in the panic?

I pushed myself up and moved for him. "Bea, I think Simion is hurt."

She snapped her attention to her brother, reaching him before I did. Still, he had not moved.

"Stupid beast," Beatrice said, hands snaking beneath her brother's head. "She didn't mean it, Simion, you know that."

He didn't reply. His lips, frozen shut, shivered. His eyes bulged as if he tried to speak through them.

Beatrice did not speak aloud again. Instead, she wrapped her hand around Simion's closed fist and shut her eyes for a moment. As if she held her breath and dived underwater, she was silent. Then, bursting to life once again, she sprang up and twisted around the waiting dark of the wood.

"What?" I fumbled, panicked by her response.

"Take out your wand," she commanded, pulling her staff from her back. "We are under attack."

My tongue thickened in my mouth. A cold sheen of sweat spread across my forehead and neck.

Beatrice crouched above her brother, eyes squinting into the shadowed line of trees that imprisoned us.

"Is he OK?" I asked, the wand gripped firmly in my hand as I searched for the hidden threat.

Beatrice peered over her shoulder at me, eyes narrowed and full of silent warning. "He will not be unless we reach the North and soon."

The air buzzed as a sharp projectile shot from the dark of the surrounding trees. It whizzed violently through the air, missing Beatrice's shoulder by a hair and embedding itself into the ground.

Beatrice ducked in time for another spike to zoom over her head. She slammed the butt of her staff into the bed of the wood. It vibrated beneath the thud. The earth spat out mounds of mud and dirt until a wall of it lifted before us.

Shadowed beneath its height, I looked to my friend. Her head was bowed, eyes closed as she forced her magic through her amplifier and into the earth.

"Who is it?" I asked amongst the snapping of other sharp projectiles that now embedded into the wall shielding us.

"Not who…" Beatrice seethed. "Worcupines."

With a forceful shout Beatrice pushed out her staff and the wall of dirt rolled away from us. It raced across the ground, guided by the magic that oozed out of Beatrice's body.

Now, without the protection of the wall, I could see the scene once again. Bright yellow eyes shone in the hidden depth of the wood.

The wall crashed into the trees and Beatrice sagged. Out the corner of my eye, I saw as she leaned on the staff for support. Just as a creature sauntered out of the darkness and into the light of the clearing.

34

At first glance, they looked no different from a wolf. The creatures had matted coats of stone-gray fur, sharp, jagged teeth, and long limbs holding their muscular frames. The one in front was the largest of those that slunk out of the wood. It was as tall as Beatrice and I. Whereas the others that followed its lead prowled low, bellies scraping across the ground as they readied to pounce. Only the §of dark saliva that dripped from their snarling jaws was left in their wake.

But there was one difference to wolves that made these creatures stand out.

A mane of sharp spikes framed their thick necks. Black and brown needles that flexed and quivered with each step toward us.

The alpha's coat was speckled with patches of white. His head was almost the size of my torso. One snap of those dripping jaws and it would be the end.

Beatrice snarled, "Keep still, Max. Any slight movements and we are done for."

"Done for!" I hissed back out the corner of my mouth. "We are about to be their breakfast."

I counted five of them as my mage-marked palm dampened.

"If we are lucky they will leave us alone. It is not us they want."

"Then who?" It sure seemed that they were interested in our group. Their hunger burned through the many yellows eyes that were pinned to us.

"Glamora."

One of the worcupine's buzzed with frantic energy. Unlike the others that moved slowly, this one was an excitable, hungry pup. It snapped its scarred jaw back and forth, tongue lapping across its stained teeth.

I sensed its movement before it happened. It howled a rough noise that sounded as if someone scraped a rusted iron sword down a tree. Three sharp yaps and it pounced, breaking away from the pack and racing toward us.

Before Beatrice could lift her staff, I called on my magic, reaching into the pits of reserves deep within. With the wand in my hand, there was no barrier stopping me from commanding it.

I used my movements to guide my intention, flicking the wand skyward as roots of all sizes burst from the ground. A single thought and the magic obeyed, entrapping the beast in a web of roots as it leaped mid-air.

Its body snapped as it cascaded back to the ground.

Beatrice and the rest of the pack watched on as the worcupine was dragged beneath the ground; the woodland bed itself turned to soft sand. No matter how much it yelped or pawed at the ground to get away, it could not. The creature was mine to play with.

It took moments until its snapping jaw disappeared

beneath the earth entirely. Leaving hardly a trace of what had been in its wake.

"Well… that's done it," Beatrice said, standing straight as the alpha howled.

I did not have a moment to gather my reserves before the remaining four burst forward. "*Shit.*"

Unlike my panicked voice, Beatrice's command was sharp and calm. "Kill them."

I watched for a frozen moment as she pounced from the ground, twisting within the air and missing the snapping jaw of the alpha. She flipped over the beast, slamming the wood of her staff across its jaw. The beast lost its footing and skidded into a heap on the ground.

It cried out, shaking the very trees with its croaking voice. More black gore spilled, but the beast did not stay down

Its focus was solely on Beatrice.

Which left the other three racing for me.

I wanted to run. But Simion laid helplessly beneath me. His eyes were unblinking and riddled with terror as he remained completely frozen.

"The needles cause…" Beatrice shouted as she twisted the staff in her hand, fending off yet another attempt from the worcupine, "paralysis. Don't let one touch you."

Once glance back down to Simion and I saw it. The remains of a needle peeking out from his back.

I gave into a thrilling instinct. With a whip of my wrist, the trees above the pack shuddered under my control. I felt the very weight of them in my arm as if the wand swelled in my hand. Forcing my arm down, I willed the branches to follow.

And they did.

A large crack echoed around the clearing as branches snapped from the trees and fell. Upon impact, the sheer size of them caused the ground to shake. The beasts did not have a moment to cry out as the heavy wood cascaded down over them. One died beneath the weight. Crushed. Two remained.

They split from one another, flanking on either side of me.

Like shadows on the wind, they moved with great power. It happened without a moment to dwell on my next action. Both pounced for me. I threw myself to the ground, body covering Simion. It knocked the wind out of me. My ribs ached as I rolled off his body.

I only hoped I had not hurt him.

I expected to feel the weight of the worcupine on me. But they had missed. Barely.

"Get up!" Beatrice shouted from a distance, breathless as she fought the beastly alpha.

Hot breath invaded my nose as a worcupine stalked forward. I scrambled backward across the ground to get away. Fear burned hotter within me as I heard the noise of another behind me. I did not need to look back to know it was there.

I was trapped between them both.

Intense emotion overwhelmed me as the eyes of the creature peered to Simion who laid beside me now. A tongue, long and white, lapped out for him. This close I could see spikes that were slathered across it.

"Do not touch him!" I shouted at the beast, jerking the wand forward with vigor.

The air crackled with lightning, conjured from the tip of my wand. I thrust it up, burying my amplifier into the belly of the beast as it jumped for Simion. It passed, effortlessly, through muscle and skin. The yelp of the beast's pain was a song to my ears.

As I had with Julian and Master Gathrax, I filled my

body with the same sensation. An emotion that was riddled with the want for safety and protection. But this time that feeling was not for me, but the boy beside me.

A streak of white, hot lightning shot out the back of the worcupine and sliced into the sky. The air crackled with its heat and the copper tang of blood. I felt the warm blood drip down my arm and coat my chest. The beast's lifeless body became heavy as the life left it. I cried out as I pushed it from me, my wand left embedded within its stomach.

I expected to see another death notch on the wand, but this time the wood was left unmarked.

There was no time to retrieve the wand. Not as the final beast ran for me. Its cry a mixture between a whimper and a growl.

It jumped. I ducked and rolled, putting more distance between myself and my wand.

The reserves of magic still sloshed within me. A storm of unreachable power, blocked off by a familiar wall that had built itself around it.

The air whizzed and two more spikes embedded into the ground in front me. The worcupine shook, its mane twisting and releasing the spikes in awkward, random volleys. I moved my foot only a moment before a spike would have cut straight through the leather of my boot and the muscle of my foot.

I called for Beatrice, powerless to stop the beast that moved for me. His nose sniffed at the air as it tasted my fear. Backward I stumbled as the worcupine advanced, its snapping jaws ready to devour me.

A rush of cold wind crackled over me. The ground rippled as if it was a tidal wave in response to the sudden bout of air. Beatrice commanded it. In the distance, she had raised her staff with a cry. I could almost see the power radiating off it.

The worcupine lost its footing, legs spreading out on either side as it went down. I took the moment to run for my wand, leaving the struggling creature to gain its composure.

I had to put my foot on the dead body of the worcupine to be able to dislodge my wand from its gut. The wet sound that followed should have made me sick. But I felt nothing but relief and pride. For the moment my skin came into contact with my wand the wall within me fell and I grasped for the magic.

I reached out for the earth and clambered my hold on what I could connect with. Dried needles of pine that littered the ground shifted and lifted into the air. Thousands of small needles hovered in the space between me and the creature; it brought with it the smell of winter festivals.

I urged my magic into the very air around me until not a single pine needle was left on the ground. Satisfied, I flung the wand forward and willed the needles to follow.

The worcupine could only wheeze as it was stabbed over and over, the pine needles embedding themselves into every inch of skin they could find. Countless cuts and puncture wounds caused it to bleed out furiously, leaving a puddle of dark blood for it to fall into.

Even after it fell its body seemed to shiver.

My head spun as my energy gave up on me. I stumbled forward, unable to stay upright as the sudden lack of magic was void within me.

I had exhausted my reserves, leaving only tendrils of magic within me.

My head was heavy and my neck ached as I watched Beatrice who still fought the larger creature. Sweat caused her forehead to gleam, her hair stuck to her neck in wet chunks.

I could see her losing energy just as I had. Her movements were slowing, becoming frantic and aimless.

As if the worcupine knew, it taunted her. Spiked quills shot for Beatrice, missing her and littering the ground around her feet. If she fell she would surely land on one, leaving her in the same state as her brother. She was wasting more energy dodging the constant barrage of attacks.

I pushed myself to run for them, but tripped over my own feet and tumbled to the ground. I wanted to cry out for her. To urge her to carry on but distracting her would end this sooner.

A deafening roar lit the sky above.

Glamora.

She dove toward the ground, wings folded into her hulking body as she speared for the worcupine.

It was enough of a distraction that Beatrice needed. With both hands on her staff, she slammed it into the ground. I felt through my power that command. A pillar of earth shot up beneath the worcupine and sent it airborne. It yelped, body twisting furiously as it lost itself to the air.

Glamora threw her wings out at the last moment, ceasing her plunge. She took the worcupine within her jaws in one fell swoop. Her teeth sunk into the creature's soft underbelly as if it was butter.

Dark blood of the creature rained down on us as Glamora took it higher into the sky. I shielded my eyes from the torrent of warm gore. It coated the world around us.

"Are you hurt?" Beatrice was by my side.

I shook my head. "Just… empty."

Her voice was slow and her skin paled. "We have not

eaten a proper meal in days and it has caused our magic to slacken quickly."

My head spun as I took her hand to stand.

Then a loud bang sounded behind us. I gasped, gripping onto Beatrice who lifted her staff out before her. I could not ignore the sway of her body as she did so.

The alpha worcupine was no longer in the jaws of Glamora, but in a heap on the ground.

I studied the mess of muscle and spikes that was a mound before us. Glamora cried out above us with glee; I sensed it as clear as day.

She had killed the creature that had caused her such fear.

"We need to get out of here before more arrive," Beatrice muttered, pulling me away from the mangled body of the creature.

Glamora landed among the clearing once again, jaw dripping with worcupine blood.

"I have never imagined... such a creature," I said, helping Beatrice with Simion.

"Long forgotten beasts," Beatrice said through gritted teeth as we carried her brother to Glamora. "Sworn enemies to the dragons, and protectors of the dryads. Unlike the latter, the worcupine have been left within the wood only to grow feral."

We hurled Simion, stomach first, over the neck of Glamora. The needle from the worcupine now clear as day. It was embedded deep into his shoulder blade.

I reached for it, wanting to pull it from him.

The back of my hand stung as Beatrice slapped it. "If you take that out the poison will be released. It is only keeping him paralyzed for now, but it will kill him if tampered with."

"Tell me what I need to do." Desperation laced my voice.

Beatrice clambered up onto Glamora's back, her brother resting before her.

"Get on and quickly. We need to reach our destination and soon."

I followed suit, arms and legs aching as I pulled my heavy body onto the dragon's back.

"Will he be OK?" I willed her to steady my worry for Simion. But her response only tugged at my gut.

"I don't know, Max. I don't know."

3 5

WINDS SCREAMED PAST MY EARS AS GLAMORA CLIMBED THE sky; the screech was almost unbearable. She flew harder than before. We passed the dense barrier of clouds, barely missing the flocks of birds that scattered as the dragon flew into their path. Without Simion behind me to steady me where I sat, I felt vulnerable. One harsh jolt and I feared I would end up like the worcupine we had left on the ground far below.

The ache within me was terrible. My reserves exhausted and my stomach spasmed with the need for food. If Beatrice felt as weak and detached as I, it was close to impossible to believe we would reach our destination.

It was down to Glamora now.

Long after the climb into the sky steadied and Glamora flew straight and narrow to the North, I could not stop thinking about Simion.

Would he make it? Over Beatrice's shoulder, I could still see the worcupine spike protruding from his shoulder. What if the winds tore it clean out and let the poison run havoc in his body?

I chilled at the thought. Freezing between my internal turmoil and that of the terrifying winds that we sliced through.

Time slipped between my fingers. It seemed that every blink left me missing much of the journey. I would close my eyes and open them again to see a darkening sky. Another blink and Beatrice had laid out across her brother. Her head bowed down, one hand still firmly holding Simion in place. The other gripping hold of Glamora's hulking horn to anchor herself.

My eyes closed again and when I finally conjured the strength to open them the world was bathed in darkness. Stars littered the sky above and the gargantuan moon hung proudly. Its pearlescent light danced across the deep, obsidian scales beneath my hands. Glamora's body looked like the waters of a dark lake.

There was a nudge in my chest. Through slow, groggy eyes I looked to Beatrice who had turned to face me. Her dark skin had turned ashen. Her brows heavy and her forehead lined with creases. Her mouth moved but the roaring winds snatched her words away. There was a haze in her eyes as she gave up on speaking and lifted a hand to something in the distance.

Above the clouds, it was impossible to see the ground below. But that was not what Beatrice wanted me to see.

A spire, towering and as white as fresh chalk, the tip of which protruded through the clouds and seemed to glow beneath the moon's light.

Beatrice sagged back across her brother, her breathing slow.

I put my hand on her back and felt the steady beat of her heart as Glamora flew toward the tower.

We had made it to the North.

The closer we flew the easier it was to make out a

group of figures who stood across a waiting podium. It protruded from the towering spire, a large enough space for ten fully grown dragons to sleep upon.

The powerful, frantic beats of Glamora's wings calmed and we glided through the nightly wind to our destination. Still the clouds beneath us cloaked what lay far below us, but I was certain I saw the glow of red firelight.

This was not how I had begun to imagine our arrival would be. Not with the hidden world beneath the clouds—the North still left to my imagination.

I hardly paid mind to it as each time I craned my neck to look down I almost lost my ability to breathe.

Five. I counted the waiting bodies as Glamora prepared to land. Readying myself, I gripped my free arm around Beatrice as the dragon landed on her back legs, wings spread wide as if she was a pheasant showing the colors of her feathers.

The entire world seemed to shake as she finally dropped down onto her front legs and folded her black wings in.

Everything had calmed. No longer did the winds scream around us. There was no noise besides the raspy breath of Simion who was now held in Beatrice's lap.

My body stiffened as the figures surrounded the dragon. Each cloaked in dark gray, with hoods to hide their faces in shadow. All except one. They wore red. Gathrax red. Blood red.

I tried to swallow but my throat was dry.

"Maximus," the red-cloaked figure called. Her voice was feminine and powerful. The hairs on my arms stood on end as I recognized a warning behind the way she called my name. "The lost mage has been returned."

Beatrice shouted above the cloaked figure. "Sim—Simion needs a healer."

Not a single one of the figures seemed to hear Beatrice who was left panting over her brother.

"Come, Maximus." The red-cloaked figure raised a hand. "We have awaited your return for many years. I did not believe we would see the day that you would be returned."

"Help him!" Beatrice cried out, her breathing frantic. "He is going to die."

Glamora snarled, adding to Beatrice's urgency. A bout of frozen wind slipped out of the dragon's jaws, threatening to blow the hood from her face.

"Please…" I added, speaking to the lady in red. Although her face was still shadowed beneath the material, I tried to stare where her eyes should be. "You have waited a long time, I am sure you can wait a moment longer. Help Simion first."

The lady paused. Then raised a hand.

One of the figures in gray moved forward and reached for Simion. Beatrice threatened the mage as their hands found him and pulled him from Glamora's back.

Simion was carried in the arms of the cloaked figure through an arched doorway ahead of us, the tower's entrance. Both Beatrice and I released a sigh of relief as he disappeared from view.

I did not know what waited for him in the tower. But it was better than staying on the back of the dragon.

"Maximus," the lady in red called. "By the queen's orders, you are to be placed under arrest for your crimes."

Beatrice almost jumped from Glamora's back. "What!?"

"Quiet, Beatrice," the woman snapped. "Or you too will face further consequences."

My magic sloshed within me. Weakened, but still there. Beatrice reached for her staff but stopped as the remaining figures around us lifted their amplifiers in our direction. Staffs like Beatrice's and a sword with a wooden hilt, much like that of the mage that I had murdered.

"You are to be put on trial for your crime," she proceeded. "I would recommend you come peacefully. You both are in no position to resist."

A guttural sound rumbled deep in Glamora's chest. It had one of the figures taking a step back.

Was this the welcome Beatrice had waited for? Returning me here only to be taken prisoner? But they did not want her. Only me.

"What will it be, Maximus Oaken?" she spoke again, her hands clasped before her, void of an amplifier. She did not need one. Not with a voice spiked with command.

I looked to Beatrice who buzzed with nervous energy, waiting for her to tell me what I should do. But she was stiff and silent. I felt that she did everything at that moment not to look at me.

I gave up, shifting to climb from Glamora's back to join those who waited. Before I began my descent, Beatrice struck out, gripping her hand around my upper arm. "You will be fine."

I could have laughed in her face as the sinking realization settled over me. I had left a place where I'd just gained my freedom from a tyrant. Now I was going into the hands of another.

"You knew this would happen," I accused, shaking off her grip. My jaw popped as I gritted my teeth and started climbing down, never taking my eyes off her.

Beatrice shook her head, tears clinging to her lashes. "I promise, Max. I didn't."

Suddenly hands were on me. I gasped, sending a shock through Glamora who threatened to throw Beatrice off her back.

"For the murder of a child of the wood and the crimes of conspiring against the North, Maximus Oaken you are under arrest and will await trial to determine how you will be dealt with."

Fingers reached beneath the sleeve of my dirtied jacket, removing the wand from the holder on my forearm. Then my hands were yanked behind my back. The cold kiss of iron clasped across my wrists, tethering my hands together.

I shook violently. Both from exhaustion and fear.

Almost tripping over my feet, the three figures cloaked in gray pulled me away from Beatrice and Glamora. They walked me in the same direction as Simion had been taken.

Before I entered beneath the firelight of the arched doorway, I craned my neck back to see Beatrice a final time.

The woman in red had pulled back her hood. From this distance, all I could see was a river of white hair that spilled down to the small of her back. As if sensing my stare, she peered over her shoulder only slightly.

As I was taken into the darkness of the tower, the last thing I saw was the smirk that lifted the woman's lips. Her face was familiar. But it was hard to grasp why as I was dragged away.

It was a smile that I had seen before. But not on the face of the same person, but someone younger.

Beatrice.

3 6

Over the two days that passed, I had grown accustomed to the schedule of being a prisoner to the North. I had long given up on the hope that this misery would end. When morning arrived a masked figure would come in carrying a wooden bowl of gruel. At first, I had left it untouched. The mixture thick and cold—the lumps within enough to make me spill my guts on the floor of my cell. But the pangs of hunger won in the end and I always ate it.

No one would return for hours. And when they did it was yet another guard who also wore a mask. The evening meal had been the same both nights. A slice of crusted bread, the dough within hard with age. And a lump of yellowed cheese. I wasted no time in eating that offering— refilling my reserves and stilling the hunger for just a while longer.

Neither visiting guards spoke to me. Not that they could with the sheet of metal that formed the mask over their faces. Masks I had read about when the army of the North invaded the South. Each was a depiction of a face—

made from dark metal that swallowed all light. Only slits for the eyes allowed for the color of the wearer's iris to shine through.

The morning guard's mask frightened me the most. A face had been etched into the metal—one of terror. A mouth split in a scream, lines across the forehead to high-light the terror of the expression frozen in metal.

It had filled my moments of sleep—or the few that I managed whilst curled up on the floor of the cell.

I had not long woken on the cold floor. Cheek pressed against a slab of what felt like ice, wet from the dribble that leaked from the corner of my open mouth. Every muscle ached. My bones creaked as I pushed myself from my resting place.

The space was mostly dark, lit only by a single red flame that sat proudly in a bowl a few feet ahead of me. I had hardly slept. The evening was still upon me.

It was a soundless place. Empty. The shadowed world beyond the metal bars was invisible. Only ever lit when the evening guard arrived with my supper. Now, in the dark, if I peered long enough, I was certain that ghouls watched on.

The only noise was the click of my bones as I lifted myself to sit.

I reached a hand into my jacket, my fingers found the journal, and pulled it free. Only during the evening when I knew there were hours until my next visit did I read it. It was slow as I had to focus on the pages in such minimal light. But I had grown used to following Camron's journey from Calzmir Estate to lands across the sea. It was a relief, reading of his fate as I waited for my own to be revealed.

Even in such a dismal place, the journal brought me warmth. I simply held it to my chest and closed my eyes, breathing in the thick, dusty air around me.

Footsteps echoed in the distance. Impossible, it was hours until morning. I stilled, listening to them grow closer.

Not wanting the journal to be discovered, I slipped it back into my jacket pocket and curled into a fetal position on the floor. Panic surged through me. Was this it? I waited, the footsteps growing louder; these were not just the usual set of one.

They were coming for me.

There was the deep clink of metal, but I kept my head down, forcing the illusion that I was asleep.

"Wait for us outside." I barely made out the voice as a door to this cell was opened.

I squeezed my eyes shut as the light of a flame haloed around the cell.

"Maximus…"

My heart slowed for a moment.

"It is me."

Another clink of metal against metal and the screen of the cell being opened was a song to my ears.

"Simion?" I rolled over, squinting against the light of the flame. My voice was hoarse. I had not used it since my arrival.

"The one and only." Hands found my back, gently urging me to stand up. "Are you hurt? Have they mistreated you?"

I wanted to pull away, but the touch of someone familiar was welcome. "I am a prisoner—they are treating me just as I believe they would."

Simion's eyes scanned over me. Orbs of dark hazel flicking across every inch of me—searching. "I am sorry, Max, we both are. This was not the welcome either of us had in mind."

"It would seem that the North is not as trustworthy as you had made me believe."

Simion shook his head. "They are... at least they were."

"But they healed you." I could not help but feel relief course through me at the boy who kneeled beside me.

The corner of his lip lifted. "Do not worry about me."

I did. I looked to the ground, unable to hold his stare. "What do *you* want with me, Simion?"

"To help you."

There was a pause. A beat of silence between us as I struggled to find the words.

"Have you not helped enough?" Annoyance curdled with me. "All of this is because you wanted me to come with you."

"You did murder a mage, Max..."

My back prickled. "In self-defense! And it would not have happened if they did not feel the need to come and ruin my hometown. Would he have been punished for the death that was caused upon his arrival?"

The face of the old woman in the home flashed across my mind. Her blood still warm in my memory.

Simion let go of me, hands raised in defeat. "Arguing is not going to help the situation. That is not what I came for."

"Then what did you come for?" I turned my back on him. "Because if you do not mind I need my rest for whatever waits for me tomorrow."

"To take you with me." Simion's voice was soft. "The moment Bea told me of what happened I requested an audience with the queen's council who have agreed that you no longer need to be kept here."

"As prisoner?" I asked, arms folded over my chest.

"You are still in custody, Max, but it will be under my watchful eye rather than locked up here. Unless you would prefer to stay... that is your choice."

The worn soles of my boots squeaked as I snapped around to face him. "Do not patronize me, Simion."

"Then do not be stubborn."

I buried my face in my hand, muffling my apology. "I am tired. Tired from the lack of sleep and the lack of knowing what is going on."

A hand rested upon my shoulder. Simion had closed the gap between us. "I should be the one apologizing to you, Max. I promise I came as soon as I could. We are doing as much as we can——"

"Why?" I whispered, the anger slipping away like the rush of water over the edge of a cliff. There was nothing to stop it and bring it back now.

There was something about being this close to Simion that caused me to shudder and lose all confidence. His height above me and intense, dark stare set my nerves on edge.

"Can we talk about this… somewhere else?" he asked.

"Something has happened…" I could see it in his eyes. The way his gaze could not hold mine as I asked, looking everywhere but at me. I did not need a gleamers telepathic ability to know it.

I reached out and grabbed Simion's arm as he began to turn away from me. He was cold but firm. My hand hardly circled his forearm.

Simion stopped resisting. He looked over his shoulder at me, the wide-eyed sympathy was still evident in his dark eyes. This time I did not shy away from his stare. Not when I could almost see the waiting truth of what he had to say shine within them.

"I promised to return your parents as I know what it is like to be without. But I failed you."

"What do you mea——"

Had the queen killed them for what they had done?

Did we get here too late? Questions spun around my mind, dizzying me.

My knees slammed into the hard floor of the cell before I registered I had fallen. Simion had not confirmed my fear, but I sensed it. The tension laid heavy upon me.

Simion was before me. Both of us bathed in darkness as the candle was dropped for him to help me. The only sound the was flameless candle as it rolled across the floor of the cell.

"Where are my parents?" I managed to croak, breaking the silence between us.

"They never came to the North, Max, never."

I could not believe him.

"You are lying!" I muttered into the dark. "They are here. They must be here…"

"We have no reason to lie, Max, I wish I could tell you otherwise. During my audience with the queen's council, their fate was brought into question. They confirmed that your mother and father were never brought to the North. In truth, it was only the single mage and Glamora who was sent to retrieve you."

I began to shiver, teeth chattering. Squeezing my eyes closed, I hoped to fight the pounding headache that rattled my entire being. "Then where are they?"

"From what our great seers suggest, they are still south of the wood. They never left."

"I don't understand…"

Simion cupped my face in his hands. His firm touch welcome as I could not stop shaking.

"He lied to you. To us all. They were not intercepted by the North on the journey back to your estate. They never left *his* estate."

"But you…"

Simion had confirmed they were not there. Had seen their caravan destroyed.

Reading my thoughts, he replied. "It must have been a ploy, to make it seem that another Northern soldier had intercepted their journey. But it was made to look that way."

Ripping my face out of his grip, I stepped away from him and shook my head. "No. This was your plan all along. To turn me against the South. That is what you are trying to do…"

My shouting ceased once again as Simion's hands found my cheeks and held them. I could not see his face but felt him move close to me. "Breathe, Max, just breathe."

My sanity was slipping. Why would Camron keep them and lie? He would not, no. I couldn't believe that.

"If it helps, it is believed they are still alive." Simion moved his hands from my face and slipped them beneath my arms. With one great lift, he got me to stand. Although I had to lean on him to stop myself from falling to the ground again.

"What makes you believe that?" I managed. I did not know what I believed anymore. I was surrounded by so many lies and false truths.

"Because if it was Camron's deception, he needs them as leverage."

The journal felt cold as it pressed to my chest—for the first time since he gave it to me I wanted to rip it out of the pocket and throw it into the fire. Destroy it. Scratch the fasting band from my wrist and denounce him.

But deep down I recognized the stabbing pain in my chest. How my heart seemed to split ever so slightly.

"He lied to me…" I whispered to myself more than Simion.

"You need proper rest. Then you can face what I have told you. Beatrice and I vow to help you make sense of what has happened. That has not changed. If you truly trust Camron then your parents are safe."

What Simion said last should have calmed my nerves. Only moments prior I held Camron's journal to my chest with nothing but positive feelings for him. But now... Something was wrong, I knew that much.

Silently I scolded myself for allowing myself to trust Camron. For *ever* trusting anyone with what mattered to me the most.

He had tricked me to come to the North. That much was clear.

But why?

37

"WATCH YOUR STEP." SIMION'S WARNING CAME AT THE perfect moment. I steadied my footing, careful not to miss the sudden drop in the stairs before me. It was hard to focus on much as a wall of noise slammed into me the moment the doors were thrown open, revealing the outside world.

I squinted against the bright sun, reaching for Simion as the fear of falling overtook me. "It is so loud," I complained, ears ringing from the sudden wall of noise.

"Notoriously," Simion muttered, his hand gripping onto my arm. "Wythcombe is a big city. You will get used to the noise soon enough. Now go slow. It is a long way to fall and an embarrassing moment in history if you do."

My eyes focused on the view beyond. To the waterfall of white, stone steps that washed down before us. The street below was a rush of horses and carriages. A river of traffic followed up and down the wide cobble road. People ran between the moving transport, dodging other groups of people that had huddled around in mid-conversation.

The city teemed with life, everyone enjoying the bright day and the cloudless sky.

"There are so many people…" I whispered. More to myself than Simion. I had known, as we all had in the South, that others lived beyond the wood. But now, seeing it with my own eyes left me speechless.

It was as if all the bodies in all the estates of the South had joined in one place.

"Welcome to Wythcombe, Maximus."

On the perch at the top of the steps, for as far as I could see, was life. Grand buildings with shop signs hanging above doors nestled between smaller ones with full seating areas outside. My mouth watered at the smell of baked goods and the plethora of other scents that wafted from the eateries.

Simion began the descent, tugging at me to follow. I skipped a step to catch up.

All down the rolling steps, groups of people sat around. Some looked our way as we passed them, others ignored us. Which surprised me as a flank of masked guards trailed close behind us. Although I noticed other guards stood across the steps—their presence seemingly a normal occurrence in Wythcombe.

"Where are we going?" I mumbled to Simion. He kept his face forward, his usual smile void from his lips.

"To a quiet place. Somewhere to hold out until your trial."

My heart dropped like a stone at the mention of it. As if sensing my unease, Simion squeezed my hand and that stone seemed to soften around the edges ever so slightly. "Beatrice is going to meet us there. It is a cabin outside of Wythcombe which was owned by my family for generations. I can promise it will be a place where we can all plan our next steps."

"Our?" I questioned.

"Yes, Max, we are in this together. Ah, our carriage awaits. Let's get out of here before *they* find another reason to keep you."

We flew down the final steps toward a static coach which Simion gestured toward. Others sped past it, narrowly missing the four horses that waited with pride at the front. They were still and unbothered by the traffic around them. Only their tails flicked as they kept away flies.

There was one noticeable difference between the one we moved toward. It screamed wealth. Its wheels were painted in gold and accents of red, purple, and green. Colors so vibrant it almost hurt my eyes as much as the sudden light.

The decorated guards fanned out around Simion and me as we took each step down toward the coach. Signaling to the many around us that the masked guards were not an ordinary display—but something more.

I snapped to look toward a sudden burst of ruckus from our side.

Looking around I saw multiple groups of young adults sitting upon the steps with open books across laps and quills in hands. They must have all been around my age. I noticed similarities between the glaring watchers. Each wore a cloak of ivory with an emblem sewn onto their breast pockets. It was hard to make out what the image depicted whilst moving so quickly.

"Traitor!" someone shouted from the steps behind me. I snapped my head back to look but Simion urged me forward.

"Ignore it."

"Traitor Mage!" Another joined in, this time from before me. A group we had yet to pass.

The edges of that stone in my gut hardened once again —growing in size to that of a boulder.

"Focus on me," Simion murmured, his voice acting as an anchor.

The masked guards tightened around us as the groups began to run toward us. It seemed that all eyes were now on me. Carriages slowed, windows wide open so the patrons within could see the fuss.

The sound of a shattering plate from an eatery not far from us cut through the noise.

Everyone watched on as the younger groups of cloaked people pointed and jeered in our direction.

"They hate me…" I panted, shying away from the many who glared down pointed fingers. It seemed that each shout conjured others' courage to join in. All around me I was surrounded by screaming, hateful words.

"They hate what they believe you are." Simion's hold tightened, but not uncomfortably. "When this all passes I am certain you will prove them all wrong. Remember your feelings toward the North and its people. It is not much different here where the South is concerned."

"You killed him!"

The call split the world entirely. Simion threw the door to the coach open but not in time for me to see who shouted it.

A huddle of three watched on as one of the masked guards held them back. In the middle of the group was a girl. Hair as white as snow fell across both her narrow shoulders in two, thick braids.

Her equally icy eyes were rimmed with red, tears leaving marks down her cheeks.

"Murderer." She did not shout it, but I watched the

way her lips moved. She, like the other two beside her, wore a cloak of gray. The same emblem stitched above their hearts. Her one was barely visible as she wrapped her arms around herself. Her chest moved in rapid, shallow breaths as her body was overtaken by sobs.

I could not take my eyes off her.

"Max," Simion hushed. "Max, come on."

I shook my head, ripping my eyes from the girl entrapped in grief. Then to Simion who was hanging out the door of the coach.

Inside I collapsed on a plush cushion upon the back bench. Simion yanked the door closed, drowning the shouts beyond into no more than muffled sounds.

I felt like I had run for hours. My breathing hard to calm. I pressed a hand to my chest, hoping it would steady the crashing of my heart within. Simion was sat across from me, fussing with the deep brown curtain in which he pulled over the window. The light still shone through the thin material, but it did the job.

No longer could I see the girl crying beyond.

"Did you see her?" I asked, the ache in my chest reaching a crescendo.

Simion rubbed his own eyes with the base of his palm. "Do not dwell on it, Max."

"She knew him," I said. "The mage I… I killed. That is why she was so distraught." Saying it aloud only urged my heart to slam heavier in my chest. If it did not calm soon, I felt it would rip clean through my ribs and land on the floor of the coach between us.

"Her name is Leska."

I looked at Simion when he spoke, eyes trained on me. He leaned forward and rapped his knuckles on the wooden wall behind me. Three times.

"You know her?"

We both jolted as the carriage began to move.

Simion flopped back into his seat, sighing. "Leska is a student in the academy and has been a peer of mine for many years. And the boy she cries over is indeed the one you... well, killed."

My entire body grew heavy in my seat. "I am sorry."

"You will have your time to say that to her."

"I am a monster," I muttered to myself, chin to my chest.

"We are all monsters. Even Leska. Given the choice you were put in we all would act in ways that deem us as the villain in someone's eyes—even if we believe what we are doing is just. Do not dwell on it now. Try and breathe, we will soon be away from all of this."

I gave it a moment before the nervous energy overcame me. Wobbling as I tried to stand in the moving coach, I had to tilt my neck to avoiding hitting my head on the low ceiling. I moved for the curtain, and with a gentle hand, shifted it to the side to spy the world beyond.

We had put some distance between Leska and us, so I could not see her among the crowd that blurred up and down the steps. But it was the building that we had exited that I could still see, even from this distance. The enormous spire disappeared into the clouds. Erected from stone as white as snow, it glistened like a monstrous shard of crystal. Its outer walls were smooth and round.

And there, catching the sunlight were words etched perfectly into its facade. The calligraphy was legible even from far away.

Saylam Academy of Magery

38

Simion sat silently before me the entire journey. There was much to say, but words failed even me.

Traitor Mage. I added the name to my list of titles. I contemplated them during the quiet, my eyes focused on the window which Simion had opened halfway through our trip. Julian Gathrax, the false son. Maximus Oaken, the lost mage. And now this: Traitor Mage. But the question I asked myself was what name would I give myself next?

Wythcombe blurred beyond the window of the coach. The sounds of life dwindled the farther we moved. I hated the silence. It was devouring—allowing my mind to run rampant with my anxieties.

I thought of my parents. Then of Camron—his journal heavy in my pocket. Why did he lie to me? My thumb fidgeted across the fasting mark around my wrist. No matter how I fussed over it the black mark was still there.

Simion watched me until I caught his stare and he looked away. His lips pursed as he closed his eyes and leaned his head back. He did not open them again until the coach finally came to a standstill.

There was shuffling beyond the carriage and then the door was opened. Simion spluttered awake to the sound.

Relief softened my limbs; I thought he had pretended to sleep this entire time, his way of not wanting to engage in conversation with me.

The masked guard who held the door open spoke—his deep voice muffled by the metal across his face. "Your sister has already arrived."

Simion nodded, fighting a yawn. "Very good. I trust we do not need to send word for you to return for our collection?"

It was impossible to ignore the command that sounded from Simion. Shoulders rolled back and chest held out, there was an air about him.

"I will personally see that someone is sent to return you."

"Thank you, Gaius," Simion said, slipping from the coach and offering a hand to me. "Shall we?"

The scent of salt and sea slammed into me as I joined Simion beyond the coach; the familiar smell caused my heart to stutter, and I pushed thoughts of Camron from my mind. A fresh wind cocooned us, lifting my greasy curls from my forehead and coating my skin. All around me was blue. From the clear sky to the vast ocean that danced far beneath us.

We stood atop a cliff, overlooking the expanse of crashing waves for as far as I could see.

Simion talked to the guards in hushed tones as I lost myself to the view. Taking a few steps forward, my stomach jolted and my knees almost buckled.

Beneath me was a sheer drop of white chalk that ended where the cliff met the sea. Jarred teeth of rocks cut through the water as the waves crashed upon one another.

A roar filled the sky above. I looked up as another chorused in response.

I watched two dragons fly overhead and off into the far distance. They danced, diving and twisting amongst each other's long limbs. One was a lighter color than the other. Into the sea they dove, wings folded close to their spear-like bodies. Only to explode once again from the rough surface of the sea.

I felt my cheeks turn red as the cold wind enveloped me. Raising a hand to them, I felt how clammy my skin was.

I needed to wash the days of travel and imprisonment from my skin.

I buried the twang of disgust and turned away from the view to see Simion standing alone watching me. No coach. No guards.

Just Simion.

"I thought you would appreciate something more… familiar," Simion called, winds lifting the lapels of his deep navy jacket. He lifted a finger and pointed to the left of us. Following his hand, I spotted a small cottage-like building nestled among flowerbeds of roses and creeping vines that covered the white walls and black wooden beams.

"Where are we?" I asked. In the distance, I could still see the tall spike of the academy, but it was a long way off to be diluted in color and almost blurry.

"Far enough away from the city for you to relax but close enough for the council to remain content. Technically you are still a prisoner to the queen, but one with a dash more comfort than others are permitted."

I joined Simion on the beginning of a stone path that led to the cottage. "And Beatrice, she did this?"

"Indeed she did."

"How?" I wanted answers as to why Simion and Beatrice had the treatment they did. For someone who was exiled and a boy who lived in the shadow of his mother's mistake, they were both treated like… royalty.

Before Simion could answer, the door opened to the cottage and out stepped Bea. Seeing her lit a fire in my belly. It was like seeing a trusted friend and a stranger all at once.

"They are not here…" I called to her, voice breaking under the weight of the truth.

"I know," she said, her brows furrowed.

I walked to her, leaving Simion at the head of the path. No matter how her secret life had caused a rift between us, she was still the closest thing to home this north of the wood. She opened her arms and I ran into them.

"Everything has gone wrong," I cried, tears soaking into the shoulder of her loose shirt. The intense smell of lavender from the large bushes on either side of the door made my nose run. "Why would he lie to me?"

"I never trusted him," Beatrice added.

"Because you are cynical, Bea. There was no way of us seeing this was going to happen," Simion replied.

I buried my face in her shoulder. "I am a fool. A stupid fool who trusted someone so easily when I never knew him."

Simion squeezed his large hand into my shoulder. "We don't know his motives, Max, but I promise we will help you figure this out. Together."

"Yes, enough of the moping, Max." Beatrice pushed my head from her and looked at me deeply. "I have some food readied for you. That will help you control your emotions. But first I think you should wash." Her nose crinkled and Simion laughed. "Before you put yourself and me off lunch."

I rubbed my leaking nose on my already dirtied jacket. "Is it that bad?"

"Why else would we take you so far from Wythcombe? Not only your protection but that of the noses of those who live in the city. Now come on."

And just like that, Beatrice shattered the stone within me into a million fragments. With my friends, we would face the gravity of our situation together.

39

The following days at the cottage passed in a blur of conversation, food, and sleep. Simion had a habit of disappearing daily—coming and going in the same decorated carriage that had brought us here. No one asked where he went. Nor did I care. My mind had other matters to dwell on.

Even Camron's journal had been left untouched. I had almost thrown it into the fire during my first night along with my sodden, dirtied clothes. There was something about his unfinished story that kept me intrigued, but not enough to flip through the pages.

Not yet at least.

"You can leave me, you know," I said to Beatrice who fussed over the stove. It was a routine of ours. Beatrice cooked up stews and soups—anything that was worth making from the supplies that Simion came back from Wythcombe with.

"And why would I want to do that?"

I shrugged, flexing my mage-marked palm. It had ached more as time went on without my wand. Simion had explained I would not be allowed it back until the trial. If it went in my favor, although he never said that much. I had grown accustomed to his optimistic outlook. Unlike Beatrice and I who weighed heavily on seeing only the negative possibilities.

"I just do not want you thinking you have to be tethered to me night and day. You have been kept from the North for years and from what I have seen you have not experienced much of it since being back."

"Nor do I want to. Trust me, if I did not fancy spending my days chopping up potatoes and cooking you boys your evening meals then I would leave." She threw a potato at me in jest, barely missing my head as I dodged the projectile. "Stop worrying about what we are doing or not doing, Max."

I could have changed the subject back to our most common line of conversation—the trial. But I could not stomach it.

Beatrice and Simion did not have answers. That or they did not want to worry me.

They had explained on numerous occasions that it would likely be a private affair. An audience between me, the queen, and her council. What was to be said was still a mystery to them as it was to me. So I opted for another route.

With Simion having only just left for his daily trip, the thought was fresh in my mind.

"Why is it that you and Simion are treated like royalty?"

Beatrice stiffened, her arms stilling mid-chop.

"What do you mean?" she replied, shaking her head and carrying on as if I had not noticed her pause.

"Where do I start…" I murmured. "This place. An entire cottage to ourselves. One conversation from you and

I was taken out from imprisonment. People on trial for murder are not usually treated with such comfort. How does that work? Oh, and the carriage. I've been around power enough in the South to know that the workmanship it takes to create it is not wasted on just... well, people like me."

Beatrice dropped the knife onto the block of wood before her and turned to face me. "It is not what you know, but who. Or in more accurate words, it is who you are related to."

"Related to?" I questioned.

She nodded, brown hair falling before her eyes. "My aunt—my late mother's sister, has a very high standing in Wythcombe. Her influence was enough to order your early release."

Beatrice had not talked about her family—not like this.

"I did not know you had an aunt."

"And why would you?" she snapped, then relaxed her face. "Sorry."

"What was it like?" I asked, dragging a chair from the round, worn table into the middle of the dining area. "Seeing her again."

"You tell me," she scoffed, sitting down so fast the chair beneath her groaned. "You were there."

The woman on the podium. The one that greeted us as we arrived. The very one that ordered me into prison in the first place.

"Yes, exactly. That was how I felt."

I quickly dissolved the shock from my face, much to Beatrice's amusement.

"She is not as bad as you would think, though. Unlike my mother, I believe her intentions are in the right place."

I poked at the barrier of secrets she kept around her

family, urging Beatrice to reveal more. "Do you miss her, your mum?"

"Don't remember her enough to miss her. I did, miss her, a long time ago. When I was old enough to notice that everyone else around me in the South had a parent and I was without."

"And what of your father?" I asked.

Beatrice looked up through her lashes, her hand stroking the back of her neck. "I think that is a question for another day, Max."

I raised my hands in defeat. "Consider the conversation changed."

Knocking her palms into the table, she stood, turning back to the task at hand. "Good job, all that sad tripe bores me." Beatrice faked a yawn over her shoulder and carried on chopping up the vegetables littering the board. "Simion should be back soon."

"Early for him, isn't it?" I replied. "Normally he does not come back until later."

"With the trial tomorrow he said he did not fancy staying away all day. Just in case you had any more questions which we both know you will."

"Can you blame me?" I said, nibbling at the nail on my thumb.

"That is a bad habit, Max." Beatrice tipped the knife to my thumb. I lowered it, awkwardly. "And no, I can't blame you. But if Simion says you have nothing to worry about then you need to take his word."

"Last time I took a man's word they ended up lying to me about my parents."

Camron's devilishly handsome face was imprinted in the shadows of my mind.

"I think we should give him the benefit of the doubt."

I could not believe my ears. "What?"

"Well, we don't know what is going on. For all we know, they could have been taken by anyone in the North or the South."

"Bea, that's not helping." My breathing became shallow at the thought of another party involving themselves in this internal war.

"Worrying won't help. Let us work through each day at a time. Once your audience with the queen's council is over tomorrow then we can focus on getting your parents back to you."

It was Simion's first port of call as Beatrice had told me a day ago. He had not revealed it to me himself, but he was already bargaining for the council to order a scouting party to fly South to get them. But Beatrice had explained the request had been denied on multiple occasions. My mother was not welcome North. Unlike Beatrice who was exiled with the promise of returning, my mother would never be welcomed back.

Not after what she did.

Perhaps that is why Simion had not told me of his attempts. He did not want to disappoint me.

The dust settled down over me like snow as the thatched roof of the cottage shook. It always did when the dragons would slice through the sky above. This time I hardly flinched, instead looking out the window, watching the beasts as they danced above the cliffs around us.

There were more of them today. Dragons of different shapes and colors. Some bigger than others as they spun through the cloudless sky. Catching the wild sea breeze beneath their wings. They would roar, bringing with them bouts of ice as their breath spread across the sky.

I hoped to see Glamora among them, but not once did the obsidian creature show herself.

"You could claim your own, you know." Beatrice

watched as I studied the dragons from beyond the window. "As a Ryder, it is what happens. It is part of the academia in Wythcombe. You would also be more favored because of your dragon kissed affinity. Some of the best Ryder's in our short history were dragon kissed."

I continued watching the beasts of ice and power— imagining their cold breath enveloping me as a baby as Simion had described.

"And what about you?" The idea of having a dragon to call my own thrilled me.

Beatrice joined me, leaning her elbows on the windowsill. "I hope I get the chance. However, my test, like yours, has not been completed."

I had seen Beatrice use her power over earth, enough to know she was not a gleamer like her brother. "You are a Ryder like me then?"

She shook her head. "Oh no, Max, you think of me that plainly? I am not a Ryder or a gleamer. I am a perfect mix of them both."

"Both?"

"Trust Simion to miss out on that part of the lesson. I am an elder mage. Taking after my aunt herself. An elder has both the offensive powers of a Ryder and the passive powers of a gleamer."

"Do you heal…" I flexed my fingers. "Like Simion?"

"No—mine is much cooler than that."

I did not have to urge Beatrice to carry on for she spilled it all out before me. "I can project emotions. At least I am not the best at it yet with the lack of training and years from being kept from my amplifier. It is currently like holding melted butter between my fingers. But it is there nonetheless."

"So you are telling me, that all this time I have been

feeling like this, you could have taken it away?" I joked, but it was edged with honesty.

"Magic is not simple, Max. You cannot just take something away without exchanging it for something else. As you know, when you use your powers it takes a drain on your supplies. A gleamer's ability is much the same. For me, I can trade your emotion for my own. That is the catch with my power. And Simion for example: when he heals others it takes a toll on him personally. It can take him days to recover fully."

I remembered how tired he had looked when I awoke after the attack on the town. He had given up his energy to heal me.

"For someone who has been away from the North for a long time, you surely know a lot," I added.

"What can I say?" She smirked, but not enough to conceal the storm clouds that passed over her gaze. "I have an affinity for remembering."

I nudged into her shoulder. "I would not have expected any less of a response from you, Bea."

"Come on. Let us get this soup on so Simion has something to fill his belly the moment he gets back. As you probably can tell, he has been used to such comforts since I was exiled. We do not want to start treating him any differently, do we?"

Through a chuckle, I glanced back to the dragons for a brief moment, witnessing just how free they were as they skimmed down into the unseen pits of the ocean, breaking back through the icy water with roars of glee.

Just imagining having one of my own sparked a fire in the pits of my soul.

That was if I lived through tomorrow.

40

"If I am boring you, you can retire for the night. I won't be offended."

I was thankful for the hand that covered my yawn as it hid the blush that crept across my cheeks. Simion watched me over the lip of the tankard which hovered carefully before his mouth. I had come to know that he was always watching.

"It has been a long day," I replied, brushing off his comment. That and the ale that we shared had made me feel exhausted. I edged on the side of caution when Simion had offered me another refill. Although it dulled the worry for the day to follow, it was still within me. Just not the roaring tidal wave it had been before the alcohol had settled into my bloodstream.

"It has been a long few weeks. Today has been nothing but a blip in comparison."

I could not disagree. Beatrice had left us both to sleep as the sky beyond the cottage had turned to the dark blues of dusk. Now we sat still before the burning fire—Simion stoking it now and then—as night had settled proudly on the world outside.

"Are you sure you do not want a top-up?" Simion shook the bottle of ale before me, the almost clear liquid sloshing within its entrapments.

I waved him off. "I should keep a clear head for tomorrow."

"Suit yourself." He poured it into his tankard, spilling liquid carelessly over his breeches.

"Careful…" I laughed through a burp. "You are going to look like you've wet yourself."

He rubbed at the patch of wetness across his lap and chuckled. "Then I will just have to take them off."

Simion began tugging at the belt, his hands fumbling over the buttons of his breeches.

I threw the down feather pillow at him. He made an *oof* sound, throwing his head back as if he was run through by an arrow. "Is there any need for such an attack?"

"No one wants to see you in your undergarments, Simion."

He pouted. "No one?"

Heat crept up the back of my neck and the band around my wrist seemed to tingle. I brought the glass to my mouth and downed the last dregs. Once my innards warmed as the ale spread through them, I stood, bidding my leave. "I should get some rest."

"I didn't mean to make you want to leave so soon." Simion stood abruptly too. His brows furrowed, his eyes skimming all over me. "If I said something…"

I waved him off. "You have not done anything, Simion."

He hadn't in truth. It was my thoughts that prickled through me with a mix of discomfort and warmth. Simion was handsome—like Camron; it was hard for me to hold my stare with his. But I could not give in to the jolt of my stomach when we were together. Nor the way my mind wandered as my eyes did.

"I think I should have a clear head for tomorrow and already I know I am going to wake with a sore head."

"Here…" He stepped forward, closing the gap between us. He stood before the fire, his broad body haloed by the red light from the flames. "I can help with that. May I?"

His hands hovered over my chest as he asked for permission. Intrigued, I parted my mouth but could not speak. Instead, I nodded for him to carry on.

I closed my eyes as his hands splayed across my chest. His touch was gentle but assertive. I lowered my chin, admiring how his hands made me look so small in comparison.

Simion loosed a long breath from his nose, the sound like a quiet breeze of nightly air that brought a chill alongside it. Then the feeling began. It started in my chest and spread outwards throughout my body. Unlike Camron's touch, this was cold. But it did not displease me. I closed my eyes against the rush of magic that Simion sent through me. His phantom hands reached far into my soul, clearing the cobwebs that the ale had strung up throughout me.

I was uncertain how long we stood there. His hands on me. My mind open to his power that explored me. When he finally removed his touch, I sagged a little.

"There you go," he whispered, looking down upon me. "That will help with the sore head."

I put a finger to my temple, aware of the lack of grogginess within me. It was like I had never touched a drop of the honey-sweet ale that Simion had brought back with him from Wythcombe.

"How do you feel?"

"Awake," I said, lowering my hand to my side where I flexed it. "Like I have just come back from a swim in a cold lake and my entire being is alive. Thank you for doing that for me."

"Don't thank me yet." He still stood there, inches away from me.

"Simion, listen. I have a lot to thank you for so please let me. It would make me feel better knowing I got this out."

One of his dark brows rose. "Go on…"

"Bea told me that you have been trying to influence the council to send a party for my parents."

His mouth parted into an O shape as my words settled over him. "I have failed in my attempts, so your thanks is misplaced."

"No, it is not. You can be as stubborn as your sister, you know."

"We are blood-related, Max, what do you expect?"

"Can you not just take my thanks and be done with it?"

Simion scrunched his eyes and forced a smile. "I, Simion, gratefully receive Maximus's misplaced thanks as I adore the attention and it is why I do it all for the recogniti—"

I rose on my toes and placed a kiss on his cheek. Simion stumbled over his words and became silent.

"There you go," I said, pulling away; all I could smell was fresh pine, as if his scent clung to me. "You may not accept my words in thanks so I guess you are the type to prefer actions."

Simion raised a hand to his cheek and held it there. "Consider it received."

"Well, that is good then." I turned my back to him, ready to take leave to my room that was on the other side of the cottage's living quarters. But a hand reached out for my wrist and stopped me.

"Wait… Max. I want to give you something."

I looked over my shoulder to Simion, all hints of playful attitude void from his face as his gentle hold released me. Simion fussed beneath the aged chair he had recently vacated. From behind it, he pulled a parcel wrapped in brown paper.

"What is it?" I took it from him, the weight sudden in my arms. Although it was heavy, the parcel had a soft feel about it, hiding something crafted from material inside its wrappings.

"Tomorrow you are going to have many eyes on you and I thought it best that you had something to wear. A statement you could say. A way of showing the North that you can blend in but be different. A gift since you have not complained once about wearing my clothes for the past few days."

"You did not have to do this for me," I muttered.

There was nothing to complain about, that was why. Simion was both taller and broader than me, which meant his garments hung across my wiry frame. I had opted to tuck the oversized trousers into thick woolen socks at the ankles to stop myself from tripping on the material. Same with the tunic I had worn. The sleeves of the cream material had been rolled up to my elbows to keep them from covering my hands, making them useless.

"I know I didn't, but I wanted to get something for you as a present. It is almost Noyel and I thought you might like this. I thought of you when I saw it."

I ran my hands over the parchment, holding myself back from tearing into it. "I have never received one before…"

"What?"

"A present for Noyel." The thought made my eyes prick with tears. I scolded myself on how pathetic I would have looked to him as droplets splashed into the paper of the parcel, staining it darker.

Simion grinned, his eyes squinting. "Well, I am honored to be your first."

We had never had the spare coin to provide gifts for each other at Noyel. Mother was usually working during the festivities, making sure Master Gathrax's twin daughters were busy playing with their new toys and gifts, leaving me and Father to roast nuts and dates over our fire.

"I feel as though I need to give you something now… that is the custom, right?" I smiled through the tears.

Simion just tapped a long finger to his cheek and breathed, "You already have."

I stood there for a moment, watching him as he looked upon me. It was Simion's following words that urged me to finally build the courage to move.

"Goodnight then, Max. I hope you rest well."

I tipped my head, hugging the parcel to my chest. "Night, Simion."

And with that I turned, leaving him standing before the fire. His gaze prickled into the back of my neck long after I closed the door to my room, shutting him outside it.

I THREW THE SCRUNCHED UP PARCHMENT INTO THE dwindling hearth in my room and studied the cloak that had been folded within.

It was made from a thick material—the inner layer soft to the touch where the outside was wiry and rough. I held it to the fire, getting a better look at the colors adorning the cloak. The clasp was made from twisting rose-gold in the shape of a wing. A dragon's wing. It was pinned together with a swath of red material that ended in black, as if the cloak had been worn and trailed through mounds of soot, the two colors a perfect contrast.

The cloak was beautiful. My skin shivered as I ran a hand down the length of the material and held it close to me.

And there, just a faint whisper, was the scent of pine. Simion's scent—clinging to the cloak as I held it.

Not long after, I had laid the gift down with care and swaddled myself in the thick blankets across the bed, sleep did not follow. It was cold, this far up on the cliffs. The whistle of winds seeped in through cracks in the old bricks and spaces where the windows did not fully fit the crooked walls.

I tossed and turned, unable to find a place to relax. Then my eyes landed on it. Camron's journal held my attention for a long moment.

Giving up on the soft bed, I took the blanket and a single feather-stuffed pillow and moved to sit closer to the fire—journal in hand.

I contemplated finally throwing it into the fire. Allowing the flames to devour the story of the liar. A liar I had trusted.

Guilt wrapped around my stomach. A vise-like grip that dug nails into my gut.

Unraveling the leather twine, I ran my fingers across the worn face and took a deep breath. *Would this help me trust in Camron again?* The colorless feather rested between the pages of Camron's story that I had reached days ago, waiting for me to pick up where I had left off

Day 62

Another five gone. Just like that. Dead. Only the night before I had shared the last dribbles of ale from our final barrel. We laughed and danced, sang and cried. Reminiscing about home. Home. Still so far away. And now I wake to the empty gap their non-existent lives have left.

It had been a hard time these past days, with others coming down with the plague but I admit that nothing has hit me quite like this. Today is bad. Will tomorrow be even worse?

Already I felt a lump in my throat as I swallowed after the beginning of Camron's entry for day sixty-two. So little words and yet I felt like I was there with him.

· · ·

I did not want to tell my friends of the feelings that have begun to grow inside of me. I did not want to scare them. There was only a few left now. I needed them and their strength to get us home.

My arm will be impossible to hide by tomorrow, maybe even sooner. Just writing this aches. Do not think that matters now. Not that my close friends are dead. Food for the beasts in the sea. I cannot help but believe I put them in their watery graves. Did they catch it from me as I poured them tankard after tankard?

No.

It started as an itch at the base of my neck. I could hide that with the collar of my shirt. Now the marks are spreading to my arms… I cannot hide it any longer. I write this in hopes that someone can understand this strange sickness we have called the burning plague. I call it by another word.

Firebird. I feel the wings of heat curling in the deep pits of my belly. As if the creature is waiting to awaken and devour me from the inside out.

Maybe the heat is making me crazy. Senseless.

Whatever is happening… if this is the end…

I breathe heavily as I come to the abrupt end of Camron's entry. As I went on, his words were frantic. They made little sense. I knew how Camron's story ended—with him returning to his family estate. I put the pieces together and knew that his father had caught it from him upon his return.

But Camron had survived, and the others had not.

On I read. The days no longer numbered. Sometimes Camron would not write on many pages, making me think he had stopped scribing his story. But then I could turn a few blank pages and find more rushed, almost illegible scribbles.

.   .   .

I dream of the bird. Sometimes I wake to more feathers around me.

No one checks on me. Do they think I am dead in my room? Perhaps they are all dead above deck.

Days have gone by, I am not sure how many. I have lost count.

I have not heard a single soul for at least three.

I try to stay awake just to stop myself from staring into the burning eyes of the bird. In the dark of my mind and behind the lids of my eyes it waits for me.

Its feathers ripple, true burning fire. Some are deep blood red, others sunny ambers and golden yellows.

I hate them.

No, I should not focus on the bad. My arm hurts less, and my mind is not as foggy.

Am I getting better? Beating this sickness?

Or much like a storm, is this the calm before the true danger and pain arrives?

Pinched between my thumb and finger, I studied the feather used as a bookmark. It was not red or yellow—but muddy and brown. Colorless. But it invoked an image of a bird on fire.

The name of the bird dusting across my lips silently.

Questions I wasn't sure the journal would answer.

My body is coated in sweat and grime. But I shiver nonetheless.

Someone must be alive for I woke to a candle. The hot wax had dripped down upon my bed, burning the side of my neck where I lay.

The scar would look no different from the rest that spread up the back of my arms.

Feathers, they prick me from all over the bed. One by one I collect them. Just moving hurts.

But I have to do it.

The bird showed me.

I burned the feather in the small flame from the candle. Like dry kindling, they exploded and… gone. They are all gone.

It is magic. I am magic. Not like my great grandmother… no my power is new. Stronger.

Magic.

I am magic.

The bird is magic.

My skin cooled as I read over Camron's words twice. A bad taste coated the back of my throat each time I swallowed. Magic. How insane had the burning plague made Camron?

They open when they touch fire. Uncurling, spitting like colorful fireflies. Then gone. I write this to remember. The bird told me I was not going to die but change. So I must remember.

~~*Burn. Burn. Burn. Burn.*~~

I burn them all until the bird dances in the flame of the candle. I see it. It sees me.

Burn. Burn. Burn.

Magic.

I could not read anymore. Camron's distress oozed from the pages—invoking a terrible and guttural feeling. Ditching the journal on the floor, I moved for the fire. Feather in hand. I felt the need to do this. To prove to myself that what Camron had experienced was nothing more than an illusion brought on by the high fever of the plague.

307

This beautiful bookmark, but now a symbol of the pain Camron had been through.

Without another thought, I tossed the feather into the fire.

The fire took a few moments to catch across the feather. Then, slowly, it burned. Curling in on itself as it became fuel for the hearth.

I watched it—unblinking—as I thought of the boy I had left behind. Like Beatrice had said, perhaps I should give him the benefit of the doubt. He had lost his father—that pain would be impossible for anyone to get over. The thought of him keeping my parents from me was hard to grasp.

He knew what it was like to lose someone he loved.

Sitting back down, I leaned my head back on the soft armchair and closed my eyes. Focusing on my breathing, I pushed the worries deep down, forcing them into a cage that I had constructed so perfectly since the night of the wood when my wand got its first death notch. The gentle roar of the fire helped dull my mind.

But as the grips of sleep finally took me into their embrace, I was certain I heard a noise.

A call of a bird that sounded close enough to be inside the room with me.

I opened my eyes, scanning the room for the creature but it was empty.

Only the crackling of fire before me answered my intrigue.

4 2

No one came for us the next morning. Simion paced the living room while Beatrice fussed over making yet another soup. Her chopping was frantic, movements fueled by her silent anxiety.

I just sat there between them, stifling a yawn from the pathetic sleep I had last night.

"They should have been here a while ago," Simion huffed.

"As you keep reminding us."

Simion snapped his head to Beatrice. "Comments like that are not helping the mood, Bea."

"Nor is wearing holes into the floorboards, brother. Just sit down, they will come when they come. I swear you are putting me on edge."

"On edge?" he bit back at his sister.

"Perhaps lay off the ale next time, brother. It may help you with controlling your emotions."

Simion looked as exhausted as I felt. Shadows circled his brown eyes. As he shuffled across the floor his shoulders were bowed and back hunched ever so slightly.

"Did you even sleep?"

"Yes, I slept." His voice was sharp. Simion shook his head as if to rid himself of his annoyance. "I am going to get some fresh air," he announced before leaving for the front door of the cottage.

"Now we can breathe, Max," Beatrice said as the door banged closed.

We had barely a moment to take an inhale when the door slammed open again. I turned to see as Simion stood, chest heaving, in the doorway. His face had paled and his eyes widened.

"Something is wrong."

His words stabbed my chest like spears of ice. In a moment I was at the door, Beatrice beside me as we joined him outside.

Then the smell hit us. Smoke. The odor so rancid, it stung the back of my throat with my first inhale of the air beyond the cottage. Beatrice had clapped a hand over her mouth as we all witnessed a plume of dark smoke slithering into the sky in the far-off distance. Right where Wythcombe was nestled.

The sky rumbled with thunder as a dark shape separated from the plume of smoke. A dragon.

I raised a hand to my brow to see it but even from a distance, I recognized the shadow of wings and claws that cut through the discolored sky.

Glamora.

We were all silent as we studied the horizon, waiting for the dragon to reach us.

The moment Glamora touched down on the ground, Beatrice had her hand rested upon the scaled hide of the beast; she had raced forward, legs pumping across the grassland until she reached Glamora.

"She has been instructed to get us. Something has

happened within the city," Beatrice called to us, sparing me a fleeting glance. I could see the panic of ignorance oozing from her frantic arm movements and tense shoulders.

Simion was already clambering onto the dragon's back. "Did she divulge what exactly?"

Beatrice took her brother's hand and jumped upfront. "Fires are all over the city. Started in the early hours of the morning. That is all I can work out from her; Glamora's mind is a race of panic."

I stood there, arms wrapped around myself to fend off the winds.

"Max, what are you waiting for?" Beatrice called down at me.

"Go without me…" I wanted to tell them I was useless to help, but they likely knew that.

Simion extended a hand for me. "Whatever is happening may be serious. We should stay together. I would feel better keeping you close to me and not left alone."

"The trial?" I asked.

Beatrice pointed in the direction of the city. "If the council has not been burned down then perhaps we can go and find out what is happening with the trial. Now get *on*."

I clambered up Glamora's back until I had to take Simion's hand so he could pull me up. He guided my hands and wrapped my shaking arms around his waist. "Hold on tight."

Glamora pounded across the cliff face, wings spread as she readied to catch the winds beneath them. With the powerful force of her legs, she pounced into the skies. The force snatched my breath away. Into the skies, we flew, right in the path of the growing clouds of smoke that swirled above Wythcombe.

The ground fell away beneath us as we rose into the

roaring winds of the sky; down below was nothing but ocean and cliff. We joined the clouds, climbing higher and higher. Once we were above them, the chill of sky nipping at my cheeks and nose, I could see the spike of the Saylam Academy ahead. We flew for it.

At least that was my guess. We got close enough in no time at all, Glamora flying at speeds I had not witnessed before. Her wings and diamond-like body sliced clean through the blue.

There was so many dragons. Hordes of them passed us as we flew over Wythcombe at a great height. I stifled a cry as they burst from the belly of clouds beneath us, slicing through the plumes of white, so close to us that Glamora jolted from side to side.

With a giant cry of warning, Glamora changed course. More a warning for the dragons around her than the three of us who gripped tighter to prevent falling off.

My stomach jolted as Glamora took a sudden dip, diving beneath the clouds. Ensuring we were out of the other dragons' path. The towering spire of Saylem Academy was before us. The shard of white stone dusted with ash as the billowing clouds of smoke now raged around us.

The city was a blur beneath us. Streets full of people who watched the skies as the dragons sped above them. I could see the beasts as they flew toward burning buildings—pouring their icy breath across the flames to still them.

From such a height I finally took in the grandeur of the city. For as far as my eye could see were buildings and streets. A hub of life far greater than I could have possibly imagined. A twisting river winded its way completely throughout. Glamora's shadow passed over terracotta roofs, towering white buildings, and small, black and white homes that reminded me of the cottage we had only just left behind.

Buildings were ablaze. Dots of angry red flames ate away at them, spreading from one to another before our very eyes.

As if sensing the spread, I watched another dragon as they flew toward the fire and blew ice across it. As they stopped one burning yet another would begin.

Tears streamed down my cheeks as we flew on, brought on by the harsh tang in the air and the speed at which we flew. I hardly had a moment to focus on more than one thing at a time. Looking over my shoulder, I could see the academy which we had passed. It looked like it sat proudly beyond the city's edge. Dark spots of buildings surrounded its base much like what I remembered from when Simion guided me out yesterday.

Glamora dipped lower. I first thought she was going to join in the effort of putting out the flames. But we continued flying toward a strange building ahead.

Like the ruins of castles I had read in the books in the Gathrax library, this building was wide and tall, made from moss-covered bricks. But through the broken ceiling was a large tree. Full and green, large birds flew in and out of the shaded belly of the foliage. Then I noticed the roots. Large and demanding, they had devoured entire walls and weaved in and out of the broken steps that led up to the entry of the castle.

Upon the steps stood many hooded figures. Mages. Some looked up at us as we soared overhead. Others stayed looking into the distance. Waiting. Protecting.

Statues of tense posture, each facing across the empty streets before the castle. Some held staffs, each different than the next. Others had their hands raised, poised and ready with polished swords and hulking shields in their spare arms.

An explosion of noise and heat sounded from behind us. Glamora careened away from the blast. I felt the muscles across Simion's stomach tense as I gripped on. Beatrice had lowered herself to Glamora's neck, both her knuckles white as she clung to the black horns across it.

The sudden flare of heat had nipped at my skin. Rubble rained down beneath us as the roof of a building exploded clean off the frame, sending shards of burning wood across the street.

Woven in with the blast and roaring flames was a shrill squawk of a bird.

43

A LINE OF CLOAKED FIGURES SNAKED AROUND THE ENTIRETY of the strange castle, mere inches left between them. And not a single one of the masked mages flinched as Glamora hovered in the skies above them, shadowing them with her hulking frame as she positioned herself to land.

My mind was lost to me in the chaos of the city. All around, for as far as I could see, more pillars of smoke and fire conjured to life. I could taste the harsh ash at the back of my throat with each inhale. Simion threw himself from Glamora's back, his eyes squinting through the thick, smoke-filled air. Only once Glamora pounded her wings and careened back into the skies did we have a moment a rest from the heavy air. The wind created beneath her powerful limbs brought a much needed breeze of cool ice with it.

"What is happening?" Beatrice said through a cough, her mouth nuzzled into the crook of her arm.

"I don't know." Simion shook his head, gaze lost to the destruction beyond the ring of masked mages. His face was split in disbelief. "We need to find Aunt and get answers."

"And help…" Beatrice added.

We were at the front of the castle, beneath the shade of the giant oak that had split through the rubble of the broken roof. Pillars covered in moss dwarfed us as we stood beneath them. It would be a short climb up the steps before us to reach the entrance of the castle.

"No one is at the doors," I said, pointing to the top of the steps.

"If we are under attack—" Simion began.

"Which it would seem that we are," Beatrice interrupted.

Simion rolled his eyes. "Then no one has enough power to pass *them*."

I followed his pointed finger to the backs of the countless mages that stood in their formation around the castle.

"We did," I muttered, watching as other masked figures joined the ranks. With haste, they filled the gaps until I noticed fewer.

"They are about to shield the castle. We need to get inside now."

Fear prickled down my spine at Simion's urgency. A fear that only intensified as Beatrice added, "Boys, hurry! Up the steps."

We ran. Missing steps as we flew up the stone stairs toward the unguarded entrance of the castle. Over and around the roots we navigated; I narrowly missed tripping when my boot caught on the end of one.

The oak that had split through the castle had truly spread its reach far and wide. It shadowed the steps the farther we climbed.

Then the roar of winds began. My power seemed to hum as they picked up.

The siblings turned to watch from the top step, both their faces flushed red. From our great height, we watched as the mages moved in tandem. Power thrummed through the air as it thickened around us.

It had sounded as if every dragon that flew over Wythcombe was headed our way. Their cries of war and anger a warning. But then the sky darkened above. Clouds swirled into one another as the smoke-filled sky darkened into dusk.

A crack of thunder and the hairs on my arms stood on end.

Silver light pooled around the tips of staffs, open palms, and the occasional wooden, hilted sword that I noticed in the crowd. Like newly lit candles, the light sparked small at first until it grew into a spinning vortex. Up into the sky, it lifted, tugging on the very winds, catching the bolts of lightning from the sky and encompassing them into their shield of wind.

My neck ached as I followed the light, reaching up and spreading above us like a dome.

The sound of the city beyond had become muffled as the shimmering bubble of power had completed its task. The surface of it sparked as bolts of white lightning raced across it.

My mouth had dropped open in awe. Unlike the acts of magic I had called upon, this was something different. So beautiful yet terrifying.

Smoke curled up against the barrier of power from the outside, but not once reached through.

A hand was on my shoulder. "That is the power of the dragon kissed, Max. That is what you would have been called to do if you had grown up here."

I looked over my shoulder and at this close distance saw the smudges of ash that were peppered across Simion's cheeks.

"I can almost feel it." I pressed a hand to my stomach,

putting force above the reserves of my power that longed to join those of the mages beneath us. Up against the wall that kept it in, the power thrashed and reached out with its clawing, phantom hands.

Without the amplifier, I could not give it the release it wanted.

"Maximus!" Beatrice scowled from the shadow of the archway behind us. "Simion! Stop gaping and get inside now. The shield will not hold for long."

Would it not? I wanted to question as I felt the shared power so intensely. It felt... immortal. Fueled by what must have been hundreds of dragon kissed mages.

"NOW!"

My eyes longed to make out the details of the castle's interior, but everything was shrouded in shadow and darkness. It was clear that the flames that had once burned proudly in the many iron-wrought lanterns had not long been extinguished. Ribbons of gray smoke still slithered from their charred wicks.

Sound did not seem to exist here. Only the heavy slam of our boots echoed across the barren hallways as we ran forward, Simion leading the way. In this dark place, it was impossible to imagine the chaos beyond it.

This was not the home I had expected for a queen. Where was the luxury and comfort? The wealth and power that would have dripped from the walls if someone like Master Gathrax dwelled here?

All I could see were empty corridors destroyed by the hungry limbs of the oak tree that had grown through it.

The midnight tunnel seemed to last forever until a faint emerald glow spilled from beneath large, closed doors ahead. It emitted enough light for me to make out the outline of the siblings' legs as they slowed to a stop before it.

Breathless, I joined them, hands resting on my knees in hopes I could calm the beat of my heart.

"Here?" Beatrice whispered, but her voice echoed across the walls, making it sound as if three of her spoke at once.

"They would have retreated into the catacombs." Simion nodded, reaching a closed fist for the door.

Beatrice hesitated, reaching for her brother before he could knock. "Are you certain we should... all go down there?"

I could not help but catch her stare as her gaze flicked to where I stood.

"We go together. He is our charge and if we are called to help, we must do it as one."

Beatrice slipped between him and the door. "And what will they say when they see me?"

My heart jolted at the quiet voice that spilled from Beatrice's tight lips. Her eyes were wide, blinking as they glistened with water. "What will they say about me?"

I felt as if I should look away.

Simion placed his hands on her shoulders and pulled her into his chest. They were both equal in towering height that they dodged heads before they crashed into one another. "You are welcomed home now, Bea. Keep your chin up and show them all what they have missed out on all these years. They will be proud, as am I, of the woman you have become."

"I don't need their acceptance, you know," she said, clearing a whimper from her throat.

"And nor will they be giving it to you. Believe in your worth, Beatrice. You are not the product of a mother's mistake. You are the means to fixing it after all these years. Alright?"

She pulled away from him, a smile tugging gently at the corners of her lips. "Together then."

"Sister, never again will we do this alone. From now on it will always be together."

Beatrice paced wildly, cloak disheveled around her shoulders. The glow made her skin take on a deep green shade, reflecting off her eyes. She looked ethereal, powerful but worried.

"Do it then," she told her brother, flicking a hand to the door. "Summon them."

Simion wasted no time and moved for the door. With three raps, he banged. Each hit sounded like the rumble of thunder as it echoed down the barren corridor.

With bated breath, I waited for something to happen. Beatrice did not stop pacing until a creak from the large door sounded and it began to open.

"Mage Raylie awaits for you within," a hooded woman said as she revealed herself between the opening.

"Don't want to keep dear aunty waiting," Beatrice said, barging her way inside. The small woman hardly had a moment to get out of her way.

Raylie. Beatrice and Simion's family name.

Simion urged me forward and whispered an apology to the old woman. I kept my face forward as I passed her, but felt her eyes on me. They stung into the back of my neck like the prickle of winter holly.

Although I could not see her face beneath the shadows of her coal-gray cloak, I heard the age in her voice. It was almost rough, weathered.

"Will you take us to them?" Simion called to the hunched woman.

"Certainly, Mage Raylie—please, this way," the old woman croaked.

"This place…" I breathed, "is unbelievable."

This view before me was straight from the yellowed pages of a fictional tale.

I craned my neck, eyes searching every inch of the grand room we found ourselves in. It was no more a room than a forest. As if the Gods had picked up a portion of the wood and placed it in the middle of this castle.

At the crown of the large, endless room was the base of a tree. Monstrous and ancient, it was unfathomable in size. Up the dark it climbed, far above where the tree had smashed its way through the ceiling of the room.

The song of birds greeted us. The tree housed birds of all colors. Everywhere I looked I saw more. Wood pigeons to wide-winged birds whose plumage contained a plethora of bright colors. Other smaller rodent creatures ran across branches, hopping from one to the other. Each was high-lighted by the same glow which emitted from the very leaves of the tree. It was the only light needed as the dense foliage of the oak tree blocked out any possible life far above.

"What… is this… place?" I murmured.

"This is the very life source of *our* queen," Simion replied.

"A glorified throne room…" Beatrice chortled to much of the old woman's disgruntlement.

"A sacred place where life meets with earth." The older woman shuffled around to face me. I could see her aged features beneath her hood. I had never seen someone so old before. It seemed that the woman herself was moments from passing onto the next life as her features were hollow and her skin wrinkled beyond imagination. "The home to our protector. A place where her power, the first child of the dryad and her lover, lives on. For us all."

"Do you know what is happening out there?" Simion questioned as the old woman began to walk, slowly, toward the tree in the distance.

"Not good," she mumbled. "Not good at all. It has been years, but she knew a time would come when they would attack."

"They?" Beatrice skipped in front of the old woman, walking backward until she got her answer.

We all waited in silence for the crone to divulge the answer. But instead, she began to hum, joining in with the song of the birds that flew through the air above us.

"Whatever is attacking the city has spurred enough fear to separate the queen from her *source*. Putting her in the catacombs for safety is always the last option. The threat must be serious," Simion said.

"The academy taught you all that?" Beatrice fell back into line as we followed the old woman.

"And Aunt helped."

"I'm beginning to think you have been treated as the golden child all these years. Let us hope your special treatment is going to aid us during the time to come," Beatrice cooed.

Simion kept quiet, face forward and gaze focused as we followed the ancient woman through the throne room.

I followed at the back of the group, taking in the incredible beauty of the roots that rose and fell in their silent wave across the outskirts of the room. A worn carpet muffled our footsteps as it trailed beneath us.

Was this the place where I would have stood trial? My only witnesses the council and the oak tree ahead?

And there, nestled in the rough bark was what seemed

to be a chair. A cranny in the wood for a small body to sit within.

A throne for a queen.

Would that have been where she would have sat as she told me my fate? As I begged for her help to have my parents returned to me?

I tore my eyes away, unable to look as I imagined the mysterious woman that now hid far below the castle. *How powerful was she truly if she hid from fire and flame?*

Pillars of smaller trees began to line each side of the walkway up to the giant oak. No one seemed to pay much mind to them as I did.

Soldiers of wood that stood proud. Knots of roots and branches gave the trees the shape of twisted, human bodies.

I blinked once. Twice. Faces, I was sure of it. Etched across the bark seemed to be sleeping faces. Buried deep in the dark browns and yellows of the smaller trees.

I shook my head and skipped to catch up to the group as I had lagged behind.

Impossible. My mind was playing tricks on me. An unwanted gift from the rush of anxiety and chaos that raged within me.

Then there was movement. I stopped dead as I caught the shift out the corner of my eye.

But I studied the tree in question and saw nothing out of place. Just a trick of the mind.

Yet deep down I was certain I had seen something.

"One at a time. That is it. No pushing but be quick. Mage Raylie waits below."

The steps curved around sharply, the walls suffocatingly close. There was hardly room to put either hand upon each of the walls as we trailed down the stairs. The entrance had been hidden around the back of the large tree. A shadowed archway that would have stayed invisible unless the woman had not pointed it out.

I had to trust in my other senses to guide me with the lack of light. Soon we were immersed in complete darkness as the glow of the tree disappeared out of view.

Down we clambered until a musty and damp smell itched at my nose. The intense scent was so strong that I couldn't imagine ever clearing it from my senses.

Low voices sounded ahead as the familiar flickering orange glow of fire conjured into existence.

Simion, who was ahead of me, picked up the pace and turned the last corner of the stairwell.

"You made it," a voice announced. "And I was beginning to think the dragon was not enough of a hint that we needed you—I needed you."

Mage Raylie. She was here.

"What in this world and the next is happening up there?" Simion greeted.

"Hell," Mage Raylie replied, long white hair cascading over the shoulders of her cloak. In one hand she held a staff, larger than any I had seen before. She seemed to lean into it, one foot raised slightly above the ground. "We are waiting for a report, but the cause of the fires seems to move rapidly. We have yet to see what beast is creating them, although we have our suspicions."

"Beast?"

"Niece." Mage Raylie's eyes winced at the corners, lines wrinkling across her rich brown skin, only highlighted by the flame. "I am glad you came."

"Why wouldn't I have?" Beatrice snapped, arms folded across her chest.

Mage Raylie hardly flinched from the hate that poured off Beatrice. She closed the space between them. Being so close I could see how similar they both looked.

"I know you have a lot of feelings toward me, and believe me when I say I share them. That hate you feel toward me is only a fraction of what I have felt toward myself for allowing *them* to do what they did to you."

"You have no idea how I feel," Beatrice seethed, stepping away from her aunt. "You do not know me. Don't think for a moment you can compare how you now feel to what I have *felt*. You would never understand."

Mage Raylie bowed her head, shame pinched across her face.

Simion wrapped an arm around his sister and I watched as her shoulders relaxed a fraction. "Tell us what is going on. Who is attacking the city?"

"Not who… but what. We believe that it is a phoenix, although the flame is not Wytchfire. But no other creature has the ability to cause fires in such rapid succession."

My blood cooled, almost freezing within my very veins. Clenching my hands into fists, I only hoped no one noticed the sudden shaking that overcame me. *Phoenix.*

Camron's journal flashed in the depth of my mind as I squeezed my eyes closed.

"They have not been recorded in years, are you certain?" Simion asked, voice a low growl.

"No, we are not certain. But whatever it is has moved its course for the castle in a clear line. It will reach us shortly and soon reveal itself."

"But the shield…" I spoke up, all eyes turned to me.

No, they are just stories.

I thought of the journal, resting on the bedside cabinet in the cottage. What stories awaited further into it? More delusion and warped horror of Camron's sick mind? The illness he was riddled with threatened to overwhelm my thoughts.

"Let us hope it holds." Mage Raylie looked directly at me for the first time, her upper lip raised in a snarl.

"Max will help," Simion added, stepping between us, Beatrice joining without a moment of hesitation.

"*She* will be the judge of that." Gone was their aunt's sad and meek demeanor. "Come and face the queen, Traitor Mage, and find out what waits for you."

I swallowed my dread as her threat settled over me. Raising my chin, I looked to her across the dark room, not once dropping her hateful gaze.

"What is all this waiting about then?" I tried to stop my voice from shaking as I spoke to Mage Raylie. I had faced much worse than her. That thought alone helped me rein in my fear. "I am ready to face *your* queen."

44

THE OLD QUEEN STOOD PROUD, AS STRAIGHT AS THE HUNCH which protruded from her back allowed. I feared if she moved I would hear her old bones snap like twigs.

Nonetheless, she radiated power. Not the kind that came with strength and statute. But with the gift of age.

Like a crescent moon, mages fanned out behind the woman. Unlike the many I had seen thus far, these mages were unmasked and of similar ages to Mage Raylie and my parents.

These were not students at the academy.

The council, the thought thrummed throughout me.

At least half the height of the mages around her, the queen was dwarfed. Even more so by the towering stone statues and rock formations that hugged the edges of the catacomb.

An ancient being entrapped in the body of a child. Although the body was riddled with age. This woman made the one we left in the throne room seem youthful.

I was certain the many lines on her gaunt face could

tell the very stories of her long life. She watched me as I watched her, lips pursed white.

Simion and Beatrice bowed the moment they stood in her presence. Mage Raylie took it a step further and planted a kiss on the woman's hand which hovered out before her in anticipation. I spared them a glance, not wanting to look away for long in case the old woman simply vanished with age.

The queen. She watched me with bright, grassland colored eyes. Silver hair, like the webs of spiders, sat atop her head and trailed far down, stopping inches from the dusty floor.

It was the crown of winter thorns and leaves that kept the knot of hair in place. Frosted and white, it seemed she had plucked the crown from the belly of a forest in midwinter. The only color was the stark red of berries that ran in a cluster down the side of her gaunt face.

The simple gown of emerald and black shifted over the uneven floor as she took a careful step forward. It reminded me of Mistress Gathrax's nightdresses she would wear. No shape and no embroidery. Simple and elegant.

"Maximus…" she croaked, her voice harsh and thick. The catacomb was deathly silent beside her voice. "Come closer, child of the wood, let me see you."

Slowly she raised a hand for me, willing me to step forward and take it.

"Go on…" Simion whispered out the corner of his mouth. A steady rock beside me.

I forced myself to step forward, fearful that my joints had seized up beneath her watchful glare.

One step at a time. The closer I got to the woman the more intense the smell became. It was not an unpleasant smell. If I would have closed my eyes, I would liken it to the open forest during a heavy downpour of rain. Fresh and crisp, a multitude of earth tones woven among spring flowers. This woman, the queen. She *was* the forest.

I bowed my head and lifted my hand and took hers. Like touching the shell of an egg, I feared I would hurt her frail hands. I kept my movements slow and careful.

What should I say to her? My cheeks warmed beneath her stare. *Would a simple hello suffice?*

"I have heard much about you," I said, voice low.

Her fingers wrapped around mine with a strength I thought impossible for someone of her age. With a tug, my arm was held before her.

"I can say much the same as you, Maximus Wodlin. Son to a deserter."

As she spoke, her bright eyes studied my wrist. "I sense the fasting lines are fresh and strong. They move among your blood and soul. The spell is yet to be unbroken. Yet that is what you desire, is it not? To break from the boy at the end of this tether?"

"Camron," I said. "I do. But it is impossible."

"Nothing is impossible," she drawled. The queen closed her eyes, lids heavy as they sagged slightly. "I sense your power as well. Deep within you, it has spread its roots. But it calls for release. Without the proper guidance, you will be dangerous. Unpredictable. Oh, what are we going to do..."

"I did not ask for this," I said, words echoing across the room. "If I could give it back, this magic, I would."

"And return to your old life? You would give up this gift to become... normal?"

"To be with my parents again, I would."

"Ah, your parents. I hear that they have become lost somewhere along the way. My council have informed me that they believe your *fast-mate* has kept them from you.

That is what they do, the mundane, they lie and cheat. Look what they did to my parents."

There was magic in the old woman's touch. Pure, powerful magic. My own called to it, like for like. Her touch urged it to thrash within me just as the masked mages that protected the castle had as they shared their power.

"I have read your story," I told her, imagining the letter Simion had given me that spoke of the dryad and her lover, encompassed in the tree for their protection against the mages that betrayed them.

"Pray tell what you thought of it." She dropped my hand, letting it fall to my side. Her touch left a chill where she had held me. "Did my story touch your soul? I imagine it conjured a great pity for me."

I held her gaze as she tested me. "Yes, it did. I felt that you would know how I may now feel. Being separated from my parents is a punishment that I feel is undeserved."

"What punishment do you believe just for you, Maximus?" Her eyes widened as she questioned me. "Tell me what it is that you feel would be the right course of action for me to take."

Beneath the weight of her questioning, I buckled. "I did not mean to kill the mage you sent for me. Nor did I mean to murder the son of my master… I understand you and your council have a habit of punishing children for the actions of their parents, however, I do feel that your methods are unjust."

Beatrice took an inhale of breath behind me. One glance and I could see how both siblings had stiffened.

"Hush now, child." The queen waved a hand in dismissal. "It is important in life to learn from mistakes. I know of how the South view me and how, in turn, you have been raised to see me in their same tainted light. The

Mad Queen." She chuckled, her chest heaving with each intake. "I must admit it is a name that I honor greatly. That name alone has kept the South in line. They did not deserve the power they stole from my parents—yet they still wanted to war over the destruction of my parent's tomb. It was a foolish thought, that they could confront me. Blame me. So I took the power from them and left the South in the normal state it deserved. Until you. Granted, you have spilled blood, and this is not the path on which I want my children to follow. Unless required. Although your actions scream insidious, I know your intentions are pure. Everything you have experienced, your story up until this very moment, has been *my* own doing."

"Enough," Mage Raylie spluttered.

The queen turned toward Mage Raylie with the speed of a viper.

"Quiet now, dear, I do not want to hear it."

Mage Raylie backed away, hissing her next comment, "He is a murderous boy, tainted by the South. We cannot trust him."

"My dear, compose yourself." There was something stern and threatening about the queen's sudden change in tone. Her voice, rough and old, boomed across the catacombs. "Your very amplifier wears more marks than Maximus's. You are in no position to judge this boy. He is a child. You must let go of the torment of your past and accept that he is forgiven. Has he not returned your bloodline to you?"

Forgiven. The word alone threatened my knees to give out. But Simion was there, his hands caressing my elbows to steady me as I swayed.

"That child killed my sister." Mage Raylie pointed a finger at me, spit flying from her mouth.

"I killed your sister," the Queen said and the room

silenced once again. Only the heavy breathing of Mage Raylie filled the space. "It was I who gave the orders. Not this boy. Your anger for him is misplaced, my dear girl. He is merely a figment that represents what I had to do. When you take my mantle, you will one day understand."

Mage Raylie was the next in succession. I looked to Simion for answers but he shook his head.

Now was not the time.

The queen raised a gnarled hand for Mage Raylie's face and cupped her cheek. Like a child, she leaned into the queen's touch.

"What of his trial?" one of the council members behind the two women spoke.

"It is over. For greater concerns cloud my mind now. Let it be known that Maximus is forgiven for the murder of his fellow brother of the wood."

Simion firmed his hold on me as my legs swayed again.

"But under one condition." The queen looked back to me once again.

"Tell me what you need of me," I replied, looking down upon her.

"You are to learn in my academy, under the watchful eyes of your peers and academics. If you want to control your power, your urges, you must understand it. There is much for you to learn about your origins. Maximus, you are a child of the wood. You must understand what this means."

I nod, unable to refuse her. But two faces come into the forefront of my mind.

"My parents…" I murmured.

"Where do you believe they are?" Her frail finger tapped on my chest, directly above my heart.

"I am scared to say it."

The queen took a breath and looked around the room

at her followers. I could still hear the shallow breathing of an angered Mage Raylie and the rumble of strange sounds from the castle above us.

"They are not welcome in my lands. But I will ensure they are out of harm's way."

My hands shook violently. "Another had promised me the same. Now see where it has left me."

"As you have learned, I can forgive. But in many stories, I cannot forget. Your mother stole you from me. She is as much to blame for the path you have gone down, as I am for letting you slip from my grasp."

"But you..."

"Your parents are south of the wood. Where they will stay."

"Please—I need to see them," I begged, pulling myself from Simion. Tears pricked in my eyes. "You have to help me. I will not stay if you do not help me."

I sensed the queen contemplating my request. The silence dragged on for an eternity. *This was the punishment she felt was just.* I knew what her answer would be for I heard *no* echo around my mind. But then her true answer shattered my worry into a million pieces.

"Retrieve them."

Two words sliced across the room. I sucked in a breath and stilled.

"No!" Mage Raylie shouted.

"I am queen, it is my choice. It is decided, retrieve his parents."

"This is a mistake. You did not give my sister the same fate. The deserter deserves the same outcome."

"Let me remind you, that without your sister and her meddling we would never have had a deserter in the first place. Now, enough. I am tired of this conversation," The queen announced.

Mage Raylie swept into the shadows of the room, lost to her anger. No one called out for her. Not Simion or Beatrice who I was certain smiled at the anger of their aunt.

"Maximus, you will help us neutralize the threat above. Once you have proven yourself, your parents will be brought to you."

"I will do what I can—"

The queen's face pinched in pain. Her eyes widened, whites growing red as her mouth split open. A frail, meek, and quiet sob slipped past the links of spit.

Mages behind her shot forward, grabbing her body before it tilted to the ground. I stumbled steps back, a hand clapped over my mouth as everyone moved into action. Her cries were unnatural. The shrieks cut straight through me.

Simion was beside her in moments, hand hovering above the skin of the queen. "She is burning up."

A glow emanated between his hands and the heaving chest of the queen as she was splayed across the council members that held her. Simion's brow creased and his lips thinned. "I can steady her breathing and dissolve the pain. It is like… she is being burned from within."

I was certain I could smell smoke. It filled the dark room, infiltrating my nose.

Beatrice lifted her chin to the air and sniffed. She smelled it too.

A monstrous groan sounded from the ground far above us. I looked up toward the origin and watched as dust fell from the stone ceiling. And there, curling around the rocks of the catacombs was smoke.

The smell was not from the queen.

"The tree is burning." Simion choked.

WE FOUGHT OUR WAY UP THE NARROW, WINDING STAIRS from the catacombs toward the flickering glow of fire above. It was near impossible not to trip as the bodies pressed in on me from in front and behind. The closer we climbed, the warmer the air became. It boiled with the heat that raged above.

I had pressed my hand across my mouth, hacking coughs paining my chest as the smoke that lathered the air around me invaded every sense. Beatrice had pulled her staff from her back, thrusting it forward with a gust of conjured wind in hopes to create a tunnel through the smoke. But her attempts only gave us a moment of respite from it.

"Stay close to me," Simion warned from behind me. His breath was steady as he kept pace. I almost turned to him but the threat of tripping would cause the group of us to all tumble back down. Keeping my stare on Beatrice's back, I carried on running.

The plumes of smoke stung at my eyes. The smell clung to the back of my throat and burned with each inhale. No matter how many times Beatrice thrust her staff forward, smoke kept worming its way back over us.

The moment I rounded the last step and looked upon the throne room all I saw was destruction. No longer did birds and creatures fill the air or clamber across the branches of the great oak tree.

Only snakes of black and gray smoke slithered around the once full branches of the great oak. But it was not that which burned.

Mage Raylie was on her knees, bent over a heap of smoldering flesh. The corpse was of the old woman that had let us into the room. Mage Raylie turned to us, cheeks scorched red from her tears.

One word spilled from between her taut lips. "Wytchfire."

We fanned out—each of us running farther into the throne room which was devoured in flames. Sweat prickled instantly across my brow as the wall of heat slammed into us.

The line of smaller trees were engulfed entirely in flames. A dark fire I had never seen before. Limbs of wood thrashed as the twisting red and black flames consumed them. They were moving. Dancing bodies of bark—but it was the sound emanating from the rows of burning wood that turned my blood to ice.

Shrieks. They cut across the room, echoing off the stone walls that began to char from the hungry flames. The noise was awful.

The trees that framed the room's carpeted walkway no longer stood still and protecting. Alive, they danced in agony as the unnatural fire ate away at them. Branches flailed and trunks quivered and shook. Bodies of branch, wood, and leaf cried and screamed, creaked, and bellowed.

"The dryads!"

"Put them out!"

Volleys of shouts choroused along with the cries of the trees—but I did not take my eyes off them. Not as the truth settled over me.

Dryads. The very creatures that I had known so much about—yet not recognized as I had passed them. Beings of myth which now burned before my very eyes. I watched on at the mythical creatures as they burned to death and ash.

Dryads. Here.

I wanted to scream for them. To cry *with* them as their shouts of pure agony shattered my soul.

The queen's council ran for them, only to be battered away as the obsidian flames reached for them. They moved with no reason—as if they had a mind of their own.

"Max, do not go near them," Simion warned, his hand gripping my arm. "I cannot heal you from Wytchfire."

"What of the shield?" I snapped back, looking toward the doors that we had entered. They were still closed—no sign of forced entry or otherwise. I felt some link to the power beyond the throne room, but the connection was weaker.

"It is still raised. Barely," Beatrice replied, standing on the other side of me. Sweat glistened across her skin too. "There is a fire outside this room—keeping us from leaving and keeping help from coming in. It is just us."

I could see the flickering of black fire beneath the closed doors. Beatrice was right.

"Stay back," Mage Raylie shouted out, snatching my attention. "I said stay back, you fool."

Another of the council members moved for the burning dryads. Arms outstretched, he summoned an unnatural wind to his fingertips—his amplifier not in sight. A slip of a leather cord hung around his neck. I could only imagine his amplifier hung over his chest as Simion's did. A pendant of wood.

The mage's dark hair was forced back as the power he created shot forward across the burning deities. Instead of putting out the strange flames it only fueled them more.

He sobbed, legs shaking as he forced more power into his attempt. But he failed.

The obsidian flames caught the corner of his cloak. It took no time for the entire swath of material to be engulfed in the hungry fire.

Another council member ran for him to help, but Mage Raylie thrust out her staff to stop the attempt.

"We cannot help him," she murmured as the agonizing screams of the mage joined that of the dryads as they now burned together.

His knees smacked into the ground with a crack, his shouts melding perfectly with the roaring of the fire that drowned him. No one moved forward to aid him under the command of Mage Raylie.

"What can we do?" I said. "We must be able to help."

Simion didn't drop his stare from the destruction as he replied. "Wytchfire is not stopped until the source has been destroyed."

"Then we destroy the source!" I declared, gripping onto that hope.

"To do that…" Beatrice murmured. "We must find the phoenix that has set such a blaze."

Phoenix. As she said it my body spiked with fear.

I broke from Simion's grasp and moved for Mage Raylie who was calming her fellow council members. "Let me help. I need my wand."

The reserves of power were burning as hot as the chaos around me. The magic thrashed like waves in a stormy sea. But it was useless without my amplifier. And I knew she had it. I felt its presence as I had when Master Gathrax had kept it from me.

"You are untrained," she spat. "What can you do to help? You are nothing in the face of this."

"I can try." I kept my voice firm. That and I wanted its security. If we were under attack, I needed it to protect myself. My instincts needed no lesson on how to work my power.

"Give it to him," Beatrice snarled, facing off her aunt.

"I will not. He cannot be trusted."

"You are not to be the judge of that," Simion added and Mage Raylie's face pinched in surprise. He laid a hand on my shoulder, his touch the foundation I needed to keep my chin raised and stare unwavering on Mage Raylie.

"Please…" Simion said.

Mage Raylie took a moment to respond, her hesitation clear as she reached for a fold in her cloak. Even in such times of dread, it was painfully obvious that Simion was her favorite. Much to Beatrice's scoffing.

"I suggest you remove your hand from my fast-mate…" a voice called out, encouraging the blaze of black and red flame to burn higher and hotter. "Before it is nothing more than melted flesh and charred bone."

I turned so fast that my neck threatened to break.

Sat on a throne carved in the body of the tree, a figure bathed in flame stared down upon us all. The features were distorted among the fire but the voice was recognizable. I did not need to see his face to know who it was.

I stepped forward, my mind spinning wildly. "Camron?"

"How I have missed you." The figure stood, flames diluting into a dull glow. Now I could see him. His amber hair and sharp, defined face. Freckles still covered the bridge of his nose and he looked… normal. All but his left eye which burned with a glow of a sparking inferno. The radiance of red surrounded his iris. "Tell me you have missed me too?"

Camron's voice, although the same, had a hint of difference to it. It was deeper and harsher than before. As if he spoke with two voices, not one.

"What has happened to you?" I asked, my voice barely more than a whisper. I could hear Mage Raylie fussing over Simion who called my name. I ignored him, focused solely on the boy ahead of me. Questions flooded my mind, whirling in a vortex of confusion.

"A rebirth," Camron called out. "Did you not read the story I left you? I imagine you have been too preoccupied to read my tale…"

His stare flicked to Simion behind me and my stomach sank heavily, the fire within it flaring for a moment.

"I read it." I kept my reply short, stalking closer to him. "This is all your doing, isn't it?"

He would not hurt me. Not with our lives tethered together, the symbol proud around my wrist.

"Maximus, you read enough of it to call me here," Camron said. "It was a gamble, I admit. But here you are, and here I am. I hoped your intrigue in my tale would cause you to summon me through the flame."

His smile sent a slice of unease down my spine.

"What is he talking about?" Simion shouted from behind me.

"The feather."

Camron nodded. "Phoenixes are tricky creatures. Birds of limitless life and potential. They scatter their feathers before their life cycle ends. It is those very feathers that are used as a tether for when they are reborn. In fire. You called me here the moment you discarded the feather into the flame. I am so proud of you."

Anger boiled inside of me, drowning out the dwindling screams of the dryads.

"My parents. You lied to me." My fists balled at my side. I thought the room trembled violently, but it was my own body that reacted to the devouring emotion within me.

A storm was building.

"I had to lie to you, Maximus," Camron replied, unbothered. "And I was not the only one to do so. Believe me, it pained me to do so." He pressed his large hand to his chest. Sparks of orange flame flickered beneath his touch. "I vow to return them to you, once I am finished. It is my duty. It is what I *survived* to do. My fate. And once it is done, we can return home. Together."

"The plague, what did it do to you?" I looked at him, face pinched in hatred.

"It made me stronger. It gifted me with power far greater than that of the dryads. I survived when many others had not. I was the one *they* waited for." Camron spoke quietly as if this was only for me.

"Who… what waited for you?"

Camron laughed, sparks of fire jumping across his skin. "You know the answer to that, Maximus. Think, think about what you have read. My story. It was not all the words of a boy in the thralls of delusion and illness."

I couldn't take my eyes from his own. Camron raised from the throne, leaving a charred imprint upon the wood behind. Frozen in place, I could not move an inch as he closed the space between us.

"Shh, shh, I will not hurt you. I could never hurt you."

I whimpered, my jaw clenched as his fingers reached for me, expecting the burn of fire. I was wrong. The flames shied away from his hand, exposing his scared skin. Then he touched me.

It took everything in me not to let loose the tear in my eye. My mind told me to relax into his familiar touch, but my heart screamed otherwise.

"I want you to tell me what you are," I demanded, teeth bared. It was not a question and he knew it. It was a command.

"Just as you are the product of the very creatures that burn within this room, I am the same. My masters have grown jealous over time, seeing through the fire how the woman *they* call queen has created her very own kind. Warriors with abilities that should never have been given…"

"Children of the wood," I whispered.

"Mages have grown stronger in the North, with each passing year there are more of them. It is unnatural, upsetting the balance of what was."

I shake my head, forcing Camron's hand to drop from my cheek. "And your masters…"

I knew the answer. Pinching my eyes closed, I saw the feather in my fingers before I threw it into the fire. The image was imprinted into the very depths of my mind.

"Say it…" Camron urged.

"Phoenix."

"Even now the bird still lingers within me, lending me his strength. Its power. We are two but joined as one."

I looked into the fire that circled his left iris as if I stared directly at the creature that now possessed him.

As if the very word lifted a weight from Camron's shoulders, he sighed. It was not a natural breath he took. It caused the flames in the throne room to thrum. Behind me, somewhere unseen, those who watched on shouted.

I glanced over my shoulder but only saw a wall of flame keeping them from me. The heat kissed at the back of my damp neck.

"Do not hurt them," I begged. "Camron, whatever you want from this… please it is not worth it. You are ill. It was the plague—it did this to you. I read your journal. You do not need to do this."

"Oh, but I do." Camron shook his head, flakes of flame dusting down to the floor. One fell upon my hand like snow, leaving a burning kiss upon my skin. "I do not have a choice. It is what must happen—it is my task. The end of the mages is here. Stay by my side and be welcomed into a new world. One not divided by magic and mundane."

Sweat coated my skin, causing the curls of my hair to stick to my forehead. The warmth of the fire was increasing once again, the fire devouring the tree that framed Camron and the entire room behind me. The queen's life source.

I imagined her in the belly of the catacombs, her life coming to an end as the tree finally burned into nothing but ash.

Someone called my name. A crystal chime of a bell in the dark of this nightmare.

Camron's eyes look behind me, his chin lowered and eyes narrowed. "I see he has grown fond of my fast-mate."

I pulled away from him and snarled, "I am not yours, Camron." Not in the way he thought.

"You have let him inside of your head." His arms reached out for me, hot hands tight as his nails dug into my skin through my shirt. "Do you know the punishment of betraying a fasting?"

Without my amplifier, I was helpless in Camron's grasp. Or that was how I wanted him to think.

I leaned in close to him, my nose inches from his own. "Why don't you remind me?"

His lips curled as he opened them to reply. But with a

heave, I lifted my knee and thrust it between his legs.

Camron wheezed, his eyes bulging as he doubled over. I stumbled back from him, taking the moment of surprise to create much needed distance between us.

The barrier of flame that had raised between me and those beyond it flickered. Enough for me to run through it, cloak held in my arms to protect myself.

It happened so fast that I fell to the slabbed floor beyond. Simion was there.

"I've got you…" His hands fussed over me. "Did he hurt you?"

I shook him off, looking up at Simion through my lashes. "I am sorry. I did not mean to bring him here."

Simion took his thumb and cleared the tear that slipped from the corner of my eye. "You couldn't have known."

The shout that followed conjured fear to prickle every hair across my arms and neck to stand. Camron breathed violently, his shoulders rising and falling as he looked over us.

"You disappoint me," he seethed, gaze pinned to where I was crouched in Simion's hold.

"And you disgust me."

Camron calmed his breathing and stood tall. "You've left me no choice. Finish this…"

He no longer looked to me when he spoke. His eyes were fixed on something beyond my shoulder.

I turned in time to see the butt of a staff aim for my face.

My vision doubled as the wood slammed into my skull. I tried to grip onto reality as it slipped from me. Into Simion's waiting arms I fell, with one face imprinted across my spinning mind.

Beatrice.

"BEATRICE," I MUTTERED, THE SPLITTING PAIN SPREADING across my skull as I looked up at my friend. "Bea, not you."

She glared down at me. The glow of the fire that slowly crept up the tree caused her skin to gleam.

Mage Raylie raced forward, staff held like a spear in both hands as she thrust it for Beatrice. Her battle cry was all I heard as a bolt of hot, white light burst into life. Only to be distinguished in a puff of smoke as it slammed into a wall of flame that burst from the ground and shot skyward.

From the rippling shield of fire I watched as Mage Raylie was thrown back, her feet torn from the floor at the sudden force. When she landed, in a heap, she did not move. The council members rushed to surround her, their amplifiers held ready.

"You were not supposed to get in the way, Max. I had hoped you would see my side more than theirs." She held a hand out, arm extended down for me to take. "Help us."

Simion stood up, knocking his sister's hand out the way. "What are you playing at!?"

"I am doing what I have wanted to do since the

moment *they* exiled me," she sneered. "Don't think you can stop me now. I will not let that happen."

Camron laughed, fire building higher, controlled by his manipulation. "And nor will I."

I pushed myself from the floor, arms weak and shaking as I forced myself to stand. "Why...?"

"Why do you think, Max. Look how they treated me. Kept me from the truth for years for a crime I did not commit. This is how they are. How they look to rule. Don't trust them, Max—aid me in my revenge and we can rule together. You are nothing but a pawn in this war."

"There is no war," Simion scolded. "Don't be stupid, Bea. What has gotten into you?"

"A promise..." Camron said, stalking toward us. His footprints left curling flames across the slabbed floor he paced. "And one that will be seen through."

I watched, frozen to the spot, as Camron took Beatrice by the hand.

"When... when did you betray us?" Simion's deep voice cracked as we watched his sister join Camron's side.

"Betray you?" Beatrice chuckled, her face screwed up in disagreement. "I am merely doing what was done to me. You would be a stupid fool to not see my side, Simion. Camron saw my true desire and gave me the means to do it."

"Power—uncontrolled by the pathetic sticks and branches that your kind cling so dearly to," Camron said, a grin cut across his face. "Both mine and Beatrice's desires are entwined. I see it as fate. Just as you, Max, should join. Let us do what needs to be done."

I stepped forward, chin raised. "And what would that be, Camron?"

"Put an end to the mages, once and for all. It was what those blessed to be a host for these magnificent creatures failed to do when they burned the Heart Oak. All it did was throw the South into disarray but left the North to carry on creating the mutated beings they call mages."

"Help me understand," I said, aware of how close Simion now stood. Everything was too warm. I wanted to rip the cloak off and pull my tunic with it as the material now clung to the curve of my back.

"Don't encourage *it*," Simion warned.

I looked over my shoulder at him, moving my mouth in a whisper I hoped only he could hear. "He has my parents."

That was all I needed to say. Camron was dangerous, and he still had them.

"Maximus, there is plenty of time to tell you everything. But we must first complete the task that has been set upon me."

"…and then you will change me?" Beatrice said, wide-eyed. "Give me what you have?"

His fingers found Beatrice's jaw and ran across it. She closed her eyes under his touch and loosed a breath. "You will soon join me as a host as promised. But first, you know what you need to do."

Beatrice's attention snapped to the council that hovered beyond the wall of fire Camron had conjured. Mage Raylie was conscious, being helped up by those around her.

"I do."

Simion stepped before her, his hands raised as he pleaded. "Don't do this, Bea. Don't listen to him."

Beatrice hardly looked his way as she swung the staff with great force, knocking it into his chest. Simion doubled over, eyes bulging. His mouth split open as he tried to gather breath.

She did not need to use her power on him. As a gleamer, he was nearly helpless.

As was I. Helpless to stop Beatrice as she walked through the curtain of flame, split by the controlling hands of Camron. As quickly as the fire parted allowing her through, it soon rushed back and closed the gap.

"You have a choice as well, Maximus."

I could not take my eyes off the huddled mages that readied themselves for Beatrice. She prowled toward them —a cat ready for her prey.

"Do I?"

"Of course," Camron answered. "I am not like those who seek to control you. That I never lied about. Only bent the truth in a manner of speaking. Know that it was always my intention to tell you. It is why I gave you my journal. For you to learn about me…"

"And trick me into calling you here."

He bowed his head, eyes closing for a moment. "You can put it like that, yes. But it needed to be done. By burning that feather you opened a portal from home to here."

"That is a lot of trust you put into me." I said through gritted teeth.

"I thought the same. Your dear friend Beatrice knew the location of the feather. In time she would have done what needed to be done to open the portal."

I tasted bile at the thought of Beatrice's planned betrayal.

"Portal?"

Camron grinned. "The magic that I possess—that soon many others will once the plague of flames determines who is a strong enough host for the mighty creatures—has unbridled limits."

His hand moved in a circular motion. The air before him sizzled as heat was conjured from nothing. It spun wildly, a vortex of color that spat a wave of hot air over me. I squinted against it, raising a hand in hopes to bat away the discomfort.

"I did not want to use you, Max. But there is far greater magic that protects this place—a power even I do not have access to. Without you burning that feather, the tie to the bird that sleeps within me now, I would not have been able to do this. Let me thank you."

As the vortex grew, an image as clear as seeing through water appeared. My parents stood hand in hand as they watched us.

My knees buckled. I almost did not register the pain even though it felt as if the bones had shattered upon impact with the floor.

They waited beyond the vision. Mother's face wet with tears.

"Enter." Camron's voice boomed.

It should have been impossible. The illusion of my parents moved upon command, stepping through the rippling air until they were reality.

"Mother?" I questioned, speaking quietly in case my words shattered this vision into a million pieces. But her voice was strong and clear.

"We are here."

I pressed my forehead into the ground, unable to look a moment longer. How could he do this—trick me with such power?

"You are not real!" I cried, tears mixing with the damp sweat that covered my face. "You are not here."

Then a hand rested on my shoulder. I looked up, expecting Simion to be there to console me from this trickery. But it was not.

Mother's emerald stare was inches from me. Not an ounce of grime or dirt on her face.

"I've got you, my boy." She pulled me into her chest and held me there. "I am sorry for this. I am so sorry."

I felt the beat of her heart as my face pressed into her. With each thump, it grounded me once again. *This is real, she really is here.*

Pulling away, I looked to my father who remained at a distance. No longer did the portal of fire spin behind him. He was hesitant, fear evident across his face. He looked to the wall of fire, then to me and Mother as we stayed crouched on the floor.

Mother extended an arm in invitation for him. He shook his head in refusal.

Simion moved for Camron—a lump of charred wood held in his hands. Camron was too focused on us to notice but I knew that was wrong. Whereas Simion would not see the signs, I noticed the slight flick of Camron's stare. How his fists balled at his sides and his posture stiffened.

I watched, stunned, as Simion swung the branch at Camron. With ease, Camron moved, knocking the weapon from Simion's grasp and lifted him by the throat.

Simion was far taller than Camron but his feet still dangled beneath him as he was raised from the floor.

"You think me stupid!" Camron bellowed, his grip on Simion's throat tightening.

I pounced out of my mother's embrace, and into the madness before me. With as much strength as I could muster, I threw myself into Camron's side.

My shoulder screamed as if it had connected with a rock. But the force was enough to send him off balance. Down we fell, the three of us tumbling to the ground. An entanglement of limbs and bodies.

An audible crack sounded, but I was uncertain if it belonged to me or the others.

I opened my eyes to see the great branches of the tree above. Everything was doubled. Then a face, with one glowing eye, looked down upon me. A trickle of blood seeped from his nostril.

"After what I have done for you! This is how you repay me?"

Spit rained down on me. Before I had a chance to respond, the air was stolen from me as hands wrapped around my throat.

"You could have loved me…" he seethed through gritted teeth. "But I suppose you are much the same as your fellow mages, even though you had not been spoiled by their ideals."

I slammed my palms into his body, not caring about the fire that spread across him. Camron did not flinch as I raked my nails down his arms and neck. No matter how or where I hit, he did not let go.

"I suppose the only thing left is to break this fasting. Just as you so wished. Did you truly think I would not know why you visited that desolate place? Looking for answers how to rid yourself of me." Shadows crept along the edges of my consciousness. "I will be the one to give you want you want. Let death become of you, Maximus."

For as long as I could muster, I would not turn away from him. I fought at the exhaustion that welcomed me to give in. It was a calm ocean, ready to envelop me in its hold. To protect me from this pain and horror.

It was a siren call to my soul. Peace. And I wanted nothing more than to give in to it. But for the sake of my parents who watched on from their unseen perch, I stayed awake. I fought to keep myself above the waves.

Camron was frantic—lips curling as he held me down on the floor. Doing everything I could to still hold his gaze. As my want to breathe slipped away, so did my boundaries.

I wrapped my weakening fingers around the sides of Camron's face. His skin boiled beneath my touch. The pain of the heat as it seared my palms only joined the riddling agony that encased my body and mind.

My thumbs found his eyes. Camron snarled and flicked his head, trying to remove me from him. But his hands were too busy as they squeezed my throat.

A strangled noise escaped my lips—and with it the final breath that I had so dearly held onto.

As darkness overwhelmed me, I forced myself to act a final time.

My nails found his soft eyes and I pushed, digging them in until the warmth of gore slipped down across my hands.

Camron shrieked a moment before releasing me. The sudden lack of pressure across my throat banished the shadows that called for me.

I coughed, my chest heaving as I tried to fill my lungs with breath. But each inhale only brought in the smoke-filled air. With each breath it felt as though knives sliced at my throat.

On my hands, I scrambled back—pulling my body toward the base of the tree behind me. I watched Camron as he writhed on the ground, hands pressed to his face, red oozing out beneath his fingers.

The wall of fire that separated us from the war of magic beyond dwindled. Allowing the muffled sounds to reach me.

Beatrice held her own, but her footing weakened as Camron's cries washed over the throne room. All it took was her missed footing and distracted stare for Mage Raylie and the council to overwhelm her.

With the thwack of the staff into the back of her legs, Beatrice was down. Countless amplifiers held to her in warning and threat.

I looked for Simion and instead found my parents. Mother hovered over him as he lay sprawled across the steps, a pool of red spreading beneath his head. I wanted to call for them but my lungs could not hold onto the breath I longed for. Not enough to make a sound.

There was a gold glow emanating from mother's hand as it hovered carefully over Simion's chest. Magic. Similar to that of his power. But it now came from my mother.

Her hand was pressed to a root from the very same tree

that I had clambered toward whilst the other worked on the unconscious boy beneath her.

She looked at me—her face pinched in hesitation. I could see her desire to come to me. But Simion needed her more.

I will help him. Her voice echoed across my mind.
Mother?

It is the tree, Maximus, much like the first Heart Oak, it can provide those who touch it access to their magic.

Her eyes narrowed across the space to me—forehead wrinkled in concentration. I looked up, my hand pressed to my calming chest, at the great tree that shadowed the room. In the thick branches above, flames licked up its bark and curled leaves.

Heart Oak. Mother was a gleamer like Simion. With her hand pressed to the root it allowed her access to a power she had separated herself from all those years ago.

It is not over, Maximus. Be ready.

As her warning rushed through me, I glanced back to the writhing man that thrashed across the floor. Camron's skin shivered with light, exposed through cracks that formed across his skin. He was broken glass, held together by the very creature that possessed him.

An aura of heat circled him, burning at the very air that dared to brush past his skin. His pain seemed to cease immediately. One moment he was like a beetle on its back. The next he was deathly still.

Flames sprouted from his back. Wings of fire forced his rigid body to stand. And once again the many fires in the room intensified.

He watched me from the short distance—his eyes covered in gore. Tears of blood already dried on his face.

No longer did Camron have control of his own body. His feet lifted inches from the floor as the large wings of fire moved to keep him aloft, and he began to charge at me.

As he had looked when he had first shown himself, his skin melted away to expose fire. His outline shimmered as the creature took over him.

Mother's shout filled both the room and my mind.

"NO!"

Father growled in threat as he ran for Camron. I aided Mother's plea and called for him too. But he did not listen.

My heart stilled in my chest as Mother cried—the glow in her hands fading as she relaxed her grip on the tree's root.

Camron waved a hand in dismissal as Father was mere inches from reaching him. One moment he was there, and the next he was nothing but an explosion of ash. The wave of hot obsidian flame that separated from Camron's hand had washed over Father, devouring his body entirely.

Wytchfire.

Only the snowfall of his ashy remains were left as they slowly fell to the ground.

I felt as though hands were gripped back around my throat and heart all at once. This could not be real. I refused to believe it.

Perhaps Camron had succeeded in killing me. That what I was experiencing was just a fever dream of hell. A punishment for my crimes. I waited, eyes pinned to the dusting of ash that danced gently across the floor. Waiting for this all to go back to normal. To wake back in the small, one-bedroom dwelling at the back of the Gathrax Estate. To go back to the life that I had before this. Before the wand, before the North.

I willed it. Closing my eyes as mother's sobs slammed into every bone in my body. I wished for it to be over.

But when I opened my eyes, I still saw the horror. Father was still dead. And Camron was now closer to me.

"You would have been happy." Two voices spoke from his mouth. "I would have let you live without control. Without this pain."

Tears carved down my face, mixing with the snot that seeped from my nose. "I—I hate you."

"I see now that there is only one way of making you cooperate. *We* cannot have you in our way."

A ball of wytchfire unfurled in his open palm like a rose in summer. Petals of dark fire exposed a heart of power that hovered in the air. "You are strong-willed, Maximus. It would be a waste for you not to be a host. Perhaps you will be a powerful asset of the war to come. A hybrid of both deities."

The flame in his hand changed shape into a bird of black fire. Small and meek, it was no more than a chick. Its beak and body were made from fire and shivering shadows.

"Keep away from me," I sobbed, clambering backward even closer to the great tree. My power thrashed within me, longing to be released. To protect. It was instinctual as the man bathed in flames stalked me. A demon of fire and power never seen before.

"It will be painful, I cannot deny that. But it is an honor. You will soon see."

The wings thrashed on his back, moving him forward. With each beat, it sent a wave of warmth over me. It sickened me, his closeness. A closeness that I had not long ago wanted.

"Camron…" I pleaded for the man I hoped still lived deep down. The one I had read about as he started his journey across the seas. The caring man had split his food and supplies with those he traveled alongside. The man who helped heal the sick as the plague first took hold of the company of his ship. "You do not need to do this. Please... if you hear me. Stop."

He chuckled, the sound was an echo of a man and bird. A cold drip of sweat raced down my neck and beneath the dampened collar of my shirt. As it dribbled down my spine, I shuddered.

"I admire your attempts to call for him." The deeper voice took over him now. It was not Camron anymore. He had given into the phoenix. "You will soon see why he gave himself so freely to us. Our servant."

A voice cried out in the distance of the room. "You promised I would be the first!"

Beatrice cried out for Camron as she was held down, pinned beneath the arms of the mages who held her captive.

Camron showed no signs of hearing as Beatrice's shouts grew frantic and urgent. Without needing to take my eyes of the creature that moved toward me, I knew the girl that had been my friend fought to free herself from the mages, her face streaked with tears, her mouth split in a pathetic cry.

"A waste." It was all Camron said, hardly glancing over his shoulder to look at Beatrice.

"Maximus." Camron held his hand out before me; the small creature of flame and shadow in his hand crying out in angst. "Will you join me?"

Touch the tree. Mother's voice filled my mind. It was the calm chime of a bell that helped steady my breathing as I looked into the eyes of the small bird. *Let go.*

As I had those weeks ago, I reached back and found the familiar touch of earth. Instead of my wand, found discarded in the wood and forgotten, I now felt the full power of the Heart Oak beneath the tips of my fingers.

The creature which possessed Camron had a moment to register what was to come.

For your father.

The wall within me crumbled and my magic was released. Like a hungry horde of dragons, the power flew through my body. I cried out as the feeling overwhelmed me.

Far above the broken ceiling of the castle, I felt the thunder rumble across the sky. It shivered over my bones. I closed my eyes for a brief moment as the bolt of bright lighting awoke every vessel and vein of blood within me.

My arm shook violently as I raised it. Palm inches from the chest of the demon.

The bolt of lightning cracked through the room, slicing from the sky above and through my body. I channeled it, through my blood, bones, and skin until the mage mark across my hand thrummed.

Light flooded the room.

A sharp exhale and it was released.

4 8

CAMRON SLUMPED TO THE GROUND. HIS BODY FOLDED IN on itself before me, the flames across his skin dying out in a single breath. As though he was a candle and a single, pathetic gust of wind blew the proud flame out.

But the wind was not pathetic. It was powerful and electric and it still crackled across the air between us.

And beneath my hand which I kept firmly placed upon the Heart Oak, I felt the notch of wood, a death mark etched across the tree.

Hands reached for me, a face coming into view as I could not stop staring at the body that lay across the ground before me.

"Are you OK?" Mother's panicked voice rushed over me. I looked at her, seeing the grief that drained the color from her skin. Although her hands began to glow with the golden light of her ability as she reached for the Heart Oak.

"Is it done?" I murmured, glancing over the room to the fires that dwindled. No unnatural flames of obsidian were left, only the weakened tones of orange and ruby.

359

"It is."

Her sadness pulled at my own. I pried my hand from the Heart Oak and unleashed the tears, burying my head into her shoulder. Mother held me like that for a long while. Her hand ran circles over my back as I struggled to catch my breath.

And all she did was repeat the same words. "I am so sorry. This is my doing. I am sorry."

A shadow fell over us. I looked up to Mage Raylie whose stare was locked on the body beside us.

"Beatrice?" I said, finding a lack of struggle across the throne room.

"She has been detained," she replied quietly. Mage Raylie was leant over her staff as if it supported her body weight. There was a shadow of blood across her leg that had spread over her trousers. "You have prevented a large-scale destruction, Maximus. However, I fear this is not over. And as for you…" She looked to Mother. "You need to come with me."

I reached back for the Heart Oak and growled. "If you touch her."

"Maximus, it is fine." Mother pried herself away from me, her eyes unblinking as she urged me to calm. She stood tall and faced the woman. "Raylie, it has been many years since I have last seen you."

"You should not be here," Raylie warned, wincing as she took a step forward.

"You are right, I should not."

"The council will have to…"

Mother put a hand on Mage Raylie's shoulder. "Please… let me stay with my son. Just for a moment longer. I beg of you."

"My sister did not get the luxury to beg for time."

Mage Raylie's voice croaked at the mention of her sister. "Tell me why I should allow you what you ask for."

Mother looked over her shoulder. Mage Raylie's stare followed, settling on the pile of ashes that still danced across the slabbed floor beneath an unseen breeze. Fingers gripped into my stomach and I fort the urge to gag.

"Just a moment and I promise to come with you," Mother murmured softly.

Mage Raylie blinked slowly and nodded ever so slightly that it could have been missed.

"See to your nephew." Mother said, lifting a hand for Simion. I looked over to him and could see his chest rise and fall. The puddle of blood had stopped spreading beneath his head. "I have done what I can. He will need more healing."

Mage Raylie left us with a final reluctant glance.

"He is dead…" I muttered. Unsure if I spoke of father or Camron.

"A life must always come to an end. Whether we deem it premature or the right time." A single tear slipped down her cheek. "Your father loved you. He, as I, would give our lives for you."

I wanted to question her, but this was not the time. I had known what Simion had told me about him not being my real father. Not by blood. But the topic was too painful to bring up now.

"I have only just got you back. I do not want them to take you away."

Mother lowered her stare to my hands in which she held between us. "Look."

Her thumb ran across my wrist. The black ink mark had faded to a lighter gray, disappearing before my eyes.

"I had always wanted to be there when you fasted to

another," Mother said, "I suppose I will still get to see that."

The mark melted before our eyes. Broken from the death of Camron. *The murder.*

"How?"

I readied myself for my mind to shatter. Just as the old woman's had, leaving her in that state within the care home far in the town south of the wood. My entire body stiffened in preparation.

"It is not spoken about, the way to break handfasting, for the fear it would cause those to act out in desperation. There is only one way to break a hand-fasting without losing your mind by acting against it…"

"If one is killed by the other."

"Love makes people act in ways that would normally be trapped in the limitations of desperation."

Seeing the mark fade should have brought me happiness. But it was what was lost along the journey that kept that emotion at bay. Mother showed me her markings across her wrist. Unbroken and jet black. "It is why mine still stays strong. *He* will be with me forever, maybe not in the way I would wish." She pressed a hand above my heart. "Just as he will be with you."

We held each other for a while longer—sharing in the silence that soon bathed the throne room. With the promise of Mage Raylie's return, we both took the moment to collect father's ashes.

Mother had plucked a large leaf that had been untouched from the fire that had threatened the Heart Oak. In it, she piled the ashes and wrapped it up with a thread from the jacket she wore.

"Will you keep this with you?" she asked. "Look after them until I return?"

Her hands were warm as she handed me the package. She closed my fingers around it and held me firm.

"You think the queen and her council will permit it?" I asked, chest empty at the thought.

Mother smiled, caressing my cheek with her fingers. "My son saved the North. I feel that will hold some weight in the decision they come to. Do not fret, Maximus, I will be fine."

I pocketed the package and hugged Mother as the sound of footsteps beyond the throne room echoed.

"I will not be separated from you again. I do not want that," I told her.

"What do you want, Maximus?" she asked.

I paused, silent for a moment as I thought over her question. Mother held my arms as Mage Raylie hobbled into the throne room once again, shadowed by a handful of the council.

"A simple life," I breathed, "With you."

Mother sighed, her smile faltering before my eyes. "It was the very same as what I desired for us, my son. I left the North with you hidden, wanting the very same. But you must know that the grass is not always greener on the other side. I searched for it and failed. Now, look at where we are."

"But—"

"Come with us," Mage Raylie interrupted. "I trust you will come without force."

Mother nodded and stepped away from me. "Believe me, Maximus. My greatest regret was leaving."

"Then why did you?" Mage Raylie snapped, asking the question before I could.

"Because I fell in love. And I wanted Max to have a chance of life without the watchful eyes of those around.

Instead, I took him into the hands of a place riddled with greed. And that was my gravest mistake."

"As it should be," Mage Raylie added coldly. "Now come with us."

"Do not worry for me, Maximus," Mother said as she was escorted from the room. "I do not fear what is to come. Neither should you."

49

I WAS SEEN TO BY A GLEAMER DRESSED IN A ROBE OF WHITE cloth. She moved effortlessly around Wythcombe's infirmary—the hem of her skirt hiding her feet, giving the impression that she floated around the room.

Much like her outfit, this entire place shone bright white. Light streamed through the glass window and haloed the bed making the room almost impossible to focus on. I had to squint to make much sense of this place.

"The bruises may take a few days to fade," her light voice announced as she wrote notes on the parchment unrolled in her other hand. "But I have checked you over and am satisfied that you can leave."

I pulled back at the loose gown that was given to me upon arrival, hoisting it over my shoulder.

"Are they bad?" I said, reaching a finger to my neck.

The gleamer did not look up long enough for me to see her true emotion. "They are not a threat to your health so I'm comfortable signing you off. If you need to wash yourself down I can send for a basin to be filled."

I smiled at her kind face. "Thank you, that would be nice."

She bowed her head and took leave. The click of the door sounded and I was alone.

The smell of fire still clung to my skin. I cringed away from the scent as I sat back in the bed, my back propped up by the mound of pillows behind me. Opting to distract myself from thoughts of Mother, of Father, I shifted to my knees and looked out the window at the end of the bed.

For as far as I could see, clouds of dark smoke still curled in the air from the many wreckages that were dotted around Wythcombe. Dragons still filled the air, scanning the city for signs of fresh sparks of fire. The streets were full of people. Some cloaked, others covered in ash and grime from the destruction, and gleamers mixed among the crowds dressed in white.

I craned my neck, looking directly at the street beneath the infirmary to see a line that snaked far away from the building. It was full of people hacking and crying. Pain. I could feel it even from my great height as they waited to be let into the building.

Noise from beyond my room made me aware that the infirmary was busy. Although I could not have imagined it was full of patients already. *Victims* of what had occurred in the city today.

"May I come in?"

I jumped at the voice, not having heard the door crack open. The gown slipped over my shoulder once again, making me fuss to pull it back in place as a familiar man poked his head around the door.

"Simion," I breathed, pushing myself from the bed and ran to him. My bare feet padded over the cold floor. "You are OK!"

"All thanks to your mother," he replied, closing the

door behind him. He was not dressed in the same gown as me, for he had already been washed and changed. The last I had seen of him he was laid across the floor in a puddle of his blood. "The gleamers in this building are some of the most renowned in the North. Even they have expressed their admiration for the work your mother did to help me."

He turned and showed me the back of his head. Nestled beneath his dark hair was a line of puckered skin.

I reached for the scar and ran a gentle finger down it. "Can they help remove it?"

Simion released a breath beneath my touch. I pulled away, suddenly aware of his closeness. "The scar stays, not that I mind. I feel that it will give me a heroic aura so it will be worn with pride. Your mother has been separated from her power for a long time—the healers here are surprised that it was only a scar left and not serious damage."

"Your aunt… they have taken her from me."

Simion's stare raced from my face to my feet and back again. "I know. I have already received a report from *Raylie* on the matters that I missed during my… unconscious moments." He reached for me, taking my hands in his. "Your mother has done a great thing. She saved my life, Max, and that will not go unseen by the council nor the queen."

"The queen lives?" I had questioned it, having left her in the catacombs whilst the chaos had reigned on in the throne room.

"She lives, just. Although she is weakened without the dryads. The Heart Oak will only do so much in restoring her power and energy. But that tree too will not survive long without the creatures that fueled it. My aunt already believes that a premature transition of power may begin with the queen not being able to rule in such a state."

"But if your aunt rules…"

"Your mother will be safe, Max." Simion squeezed my hands. "I promise you."

Part of me resisted trusting Simion. Trust scorned me. I gave in so easily to Camron like a fool. And Beatrice. I had trusted her beyond words.

I was beginning to disbelieve in it.

"Did you ever believe she could have done it…" I muttered, looking to my bare feet. It was unnecessary to say Beatrice's name. Simion knew who I spoke of as his body stiffened at the question.

"No."

"Me either."

Silence hummed between us for a long moment. Only broken by Simion as he cleared his throat.

"Beatrice is being kept prisoner in the belly of the academy. There will be plenty of time for questioning when I am ready to face her. But for now, I am comfortable knowing that I do not need to see her. At least not yet."

Sadness clung to Simion's stare. It made his eyes look heavy and pulled down at the corners of his lips.

"When you are ready…" I said. "I will come with you. If you want me to, that is."

Simion's lips twitched into a smile for a moment. "I would like that very much, Max."

I looked to the closed door behind Simion. "So… what happens next?"

Beyond this room, I knew nothing of what was to follow. What waited for me.

"Perhaps this can shed some light for you." Simion released my hands and fished around in the pocket of his dark, cobalt jacket. Between his slender fingers, he retrieved a folded piece of parchment that had been closed with a red wax seal. "With the briefing from my aunt, this too arrived for you. I have been asked to hand-deliver it to you, which I took as my excuse to come and see you."

I fought the blush by taking the letter from him and pulling carefully at the seal. I unfolded the parchment, straightening out the creases to read the short note that had been scribed in black ink.

Maximus Wodlin,

We, the Council of the Queen, welcome you to join Saylem Academy of Magery to begin your studies and training as a Child of the Wood. A place has been secured for you to begin your studies at the academy after the winter festivities. This is an invitation, one in which you may decline—however please note that your response must reach us before the new year.

Sincerely,

Mage Raylie, Voice of the Council

I lowered the invitation to see Simion's knowing grin. "What do you say, Maximus? Are you ready to obtain answers?"

Words were lost to me as I stared at him. My fingers gripped tighter on the paper, threatening it to rip. "They are confident I will stay. But it depends on what decisions they make about my mother."

Tension riled within me. Their confidence in my ability to comply with their invitation only irked my very being.

"Take your time to think on it, Maximus."

"When do the winter festivities begin?" I questioned, having lost all sense of time since the journey from the South. "How long do I have to reply?"

"A few weeks," Simion said. "And the decision is yours to make either way."

"Is it?" I could not help but feel this was a test. "I do not believe they will simply let me walk home."

"Max, I do not think walking the expanse of the wood will be the smartest of ideas. But I do understand how you may feel. Until the decision has been made, I will help you with whatever you need." He placed a hand over his chest. "It would be an honor of mine to help the mage who saved the North."

A chill raced down my spine. I ignored his statement, rushing to change the subject. "And until then... where do I go?"

"You are welcome to stay at the cottage. With me. Or alone, whatever you feel most comfortable with..." Simion bowed his head, but he looked up through his long lashes.

I studied Simion. He raised his chin and stared straight into me, waiting.

"I suppose the company would be nice."

A bubble of a laugh escaped him. "That was what I was hoping you would say."

News of Mother's pardoning should have been positive, but it felt like a double-edged sword. Only days after the attack at the castle, the council had agreed to allow her to go freely. However, she was not permitted in Wythcombe. Instead she would be sent to a small dwelling on the outskirts of the wood where she would be allowed to live. I petitioned with Simion to beg the council for her to stay with me, in the cottage. But even he could not change the outcome.

Mother was to live alone. But close. And that was what I had to hold onto.

Simion had wanted to come with me to see her, but I had asked to do it by myself. I had hardly slept the night before, knowing that at dawn the carriage would come for me as requested.

If I had known Wythcombe and its surroundings better, I may have walked there. No matter the distance. I was desperate to see her.

But I waited the long night and got ready the moment the skies beyond the cottage lightened.

I studied the view beyond the carriage as it took me to her, watching as we moved away from the cliff faces and toward the wall of towering wood that was miles away from the cottage or… from what I could see… any other signs of civilization.

The moment the carriage stopped I did not wait for the door to be opened for me.

"Shall we wait for you?" the driver said, pulling on the reins to calm the two black steeds that fussed at the front.

I shook my head, calling back over my shoulder as I ran toward the small building ahead of me. "If you wish, but I do not know how long I will be."

The driver just nodded, and I turned from him. Then I heard the slight squelch of wheels over mud as he left. He would be back for me later, I knew it.

"Mother?" I had to reach for the door to stop it slamming open as I pushed with great force.

A voice echoed in return. "Maximus."

Much like the cottage, this dwelling was made up of many rooms. But the one I had entered was worn and old. It was clear it had been vacant for a long while. Cobwebs lined the corners of the room. Dust layered almost every surface I could see.

It was a cramped, worn place. The colors of the walls dulled from the lack of light from the bordered-up windows.

"It will do just fine," Mother said, rounding the corner of yet another dark room. She had a hand on the door frame, holding her weight. "Do not worry about me."

The moment my eyes laid upon her my entire body turned to lead. "What is wrong?"

She winced as a cough overtook her. I took a step, arms outstretched, but she begged me to stay away during the intervals of her coughing fit.

"Don't, Max... don't come closer... please..."

I paused, my body trembling. "I need to call for a healer."

"It is no use."

She fumbled over to the dusty chair that sat proudly amid the room. Her body flopped down upon it, sending clouds of dust into the air in a great puff. "There is no gleamer that can heal me."

"Why...?" I moved closer, dropping to my knees before her. I wanted to reach for her hands but she yanked them away. Not soon enough for me to feel the heat that radiated from her skin.

I studied her, unable to catch my breath. Praying that this was some simple flu or sickness. Then I saw them. Angry marks crept up her neck, enough that they slipped past the collar of her tunic. Her skin was wet with sweat, which caused the loose, wild hairs to stick to her skin. Burns. Boils of angry, puckered flesh that dripped with yellow liquid.

I rocked back, falling on my hands as I fell away from her.

Mother put her face in her shaking hands. "Maximus..."

"No," I muttered, tears blurring my vision as I studied my sickly mother. "Tell me it is not what I think it is."

She winced, her grassland eyes ringed with deep shadows. "I will get better."

But I knew that was only one of two options. From what I had read in the journal and seen in the throne room... this sickness was not one of mercy.

"The plague of flames has come for me." A single tear slipped down her cheek, hissing as it made contact with her boiling skin.

All I could hear for a few moments was the rush of my blood in my ears.

Mother coughed into a closed fist. The sound harsh and painful.

"Simion…" I stuttered. "He can help you."

Mother shook her head. "If they find out… they will kill me before the plague claims my life."

"Unless." I could not speak further.

Mother nodded in understanding, pressing a finger into her temple. "Even now I hear the bird calling, Maximus. It wants me to give in."

"And do you?" Fear kept me in one place. It made my limbs heavy and awkward as I just watched on at my mother who shook violently in the chair.

Her eyes found mine and we held each other's stare as she nodded once in confirmation.

ABOUT THE AUTHOR

Ben Alderson is a collaborator in the NYT Bestselling anthology *Because You Love To Hate Me*.

He grew up in Berkshire, England. Not only does he write he also runs a successful micro-publishing house called Oftomes. He enjoys reading, traveling, greek food, music, and anything fantastical.

Visit his website www.benalderson.com to get FREE gifts!

Manufactured by Amazon.ca
Bolton, ON

20355356R00222